SHADOW OF DOUBT

Books by Terri Blackstock

Newpointe 911
Private Justice
Shadow of Doubt
Trial by Fire
Word of Honor

Sun Coast Chronicles
Evidence of Mercy
Justifiable Means
Ulterior Motives
Presumption of Guilt

Second Chances
Never Again Good-bye
When Dreams Cross
Blind Trust
Broken Wings

With Beverly LaHaye
Seasons Under Heaven
Showers in Season
Times and Seasons

Novellas
Seaside

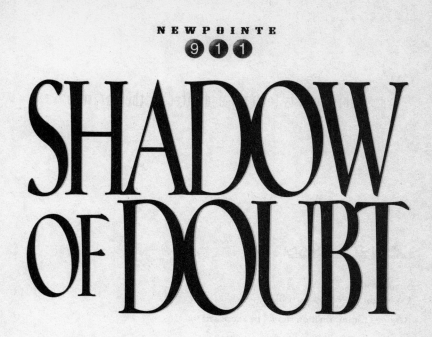

NEWPOINTE
9 1 1

SHADOW OF DOUBT

TERRI BLACKSTOCK

ZONDERVAN™

GRAND RAPIDS, MICHIGAN 49530

This book is lovingly dedicated to the Nazarene

ZONDERVAN™

Shadow of Doubt
Copyright © 1998 by Terri Blackstock

Requests for information should be addressed to:

Zondervan, *Grand Rapids, Michigan 49530*

Library of Congress Cataloging-in-Publication Data

Blackstock, Terri, 1957–
    Shadow of doubt / Terri Blackstock.
       p.   cm. — (Newpointe 911)
    ISBN: 0-310-21758-X
    I. Series: Blackstock, Terri, 1957–   Newpointe 911.
PS3552.L3485S48   1998
813'.54—dc21   98–19195

Published in association with the literary agency of Alive Communications, Inc., 7680 Goddard Street, Suite 200, Colorado Springs, CO 80920

Interior Design by Jody DeNeef

Printed in the United States of America

---

02 03 04 05 06 /❖ DC/ 20 19 18 17 16 15 14 13

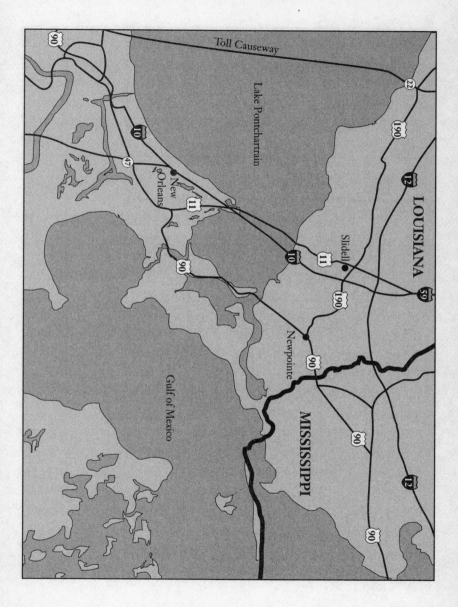

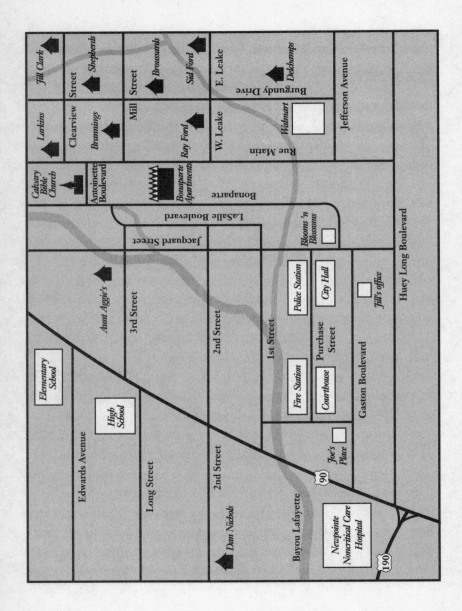

Chapter One

● ● ●

The thing about upset stomachs was that, eventually, they got better, but Stan Shepherd's stomach was proving that theory wrong. He hadn't slept a wink all night. First he'd had stomach cramps, and then it had turned to nausea, so he'd spent half the night in the bathroom standing over the toilet, but that brought no relief. His T-shirt and boxer shorts were soaked with sweat, but he was too weak to change clothes. A cold shower might help—except that the prospect of walking those few feet to the bathroom again was more than he could bear. He was tired, and his head ached. Still, there had to be something he could do. He grabbed the corner post on the bed for support and tried to pull up. His heart raced, and his breathing accelerated as if he'd just climbed ten flights of stairs. Wearily, he fell back onto the bed with a bounce.

Celia woke up and squinted at him in the darkness. "Stan, what's wrong, honey?"

"I'm sick." The words came with great effort between short raspy breaths.

He knew his retching in the bathroom had already awakened her twice, and both times she had scurried around getting cold compresses and glasses of water. Each time he had convinced her he felt better, and she had managed to go back to sleep. Now it was evident that he had lied.

She crawled across the bed and slipped her bare feet to the floor. The lamp came on, and she bent over him, touching his head, looking into his eyes, feeling for his pulse. "You're worse.

Stan, this isn't just a little nausea. I'm taking you to the emergency room!" She tried to pull him up, but he resisted.

"No, I'll be okay. I must've eaten something . . ."

"What?" she asked urgently. "I ate everything you ate tonight, and I'm not sick."

"There must've been something. Just . . . find me some Pepto Bismol. Baking soda. Something. And more water. My throat's on fire. Help me get in the shower first."

She slipped her arm under his and tried to help him pull up, but she was only five-three, and his six-foot, two-inch frame was too big for her. He managed to sit, but then dizziness assaulted him again. She struggled to pull him into a standing position. Instead, he collapsed onto the floor, worrying even as he fell that he would pull her down with him.

"Stan, I'm calling 911!" She was crying now. He hated making her cry. He tried to tell her just to help him back into bed, that he didn't want her to get all nervous and upset. Tomorrow was her birthday, and he'd made so many plans. She needed her rest.

He heard her talking to the dispatcher, Newpointe's busybody who would have the word of his illness all over town before the sun even came up. He wished Celia would just go for the Pepto. If she'd just get him some Pepto . . .

"Stan, can you hear me? Stan? Stan?"

He couldn't seem to respond, nor could he breathe, and the pain in his throat and gut felt like a knife probing around, but he was too weak to double up with the pain. She was pulling on him, trying to revive him, trying to make him sit up, and he kept wishing for the pink stuff . . .

He wanted to throw up again, but it wouldn't come, and he prayed for a breath, just a breath that could go all the way into his lungs, and for the room to stop spinning, and for something to stop the nausea.

And then he stopped praying as he felt her pulling him up. He fell forward again, this time into a deep hole, where it was dark and he couldn't find the end, and there was nothing to reach out for that would stop his fall, and he didn't know where the darkness would take him . . .

• • •

Mark Branning's fire truck was the first one on the scene. Though Celia's panicked call had been for a rescue unit, all of the emergency services of Newpointe responded to the call. That was policy, so even when there wasn't a fire, the fire truck headed out. Because they'd been two blocks over at a call for Mrs. Higgins, a lonely old lady who managed to set a grease fire at least once a month, they'd arrived at Stan's house before anyone else.

As he ran up Stan's driveway and banged on the locked door, Mark wondered what could have happened to the town's only detective to make his wife call with such urgency. Stan was in perfect health, or so it seemed. He wasn't much over thirty, and he lacked the "spare tire" that seemed to be a by-product of a happy marriage. Wasn't Stan too young for a heart attack?

He could hear Celia inside screaming, and he glanced back at the firemen behind him, George Broussard, his shift captain, and Dan Nichols, his best friend. George jabbed the doorbell and shouted, "Celia, open up! Fire department!"

In seconds she was flinging the door open, and she fell into Mark's arms. "Mark, help him! He's dying! Hurry! Please hurry!"

They bolted in as the sirens of the rescue unit and police squad cars grew closer.

"Celia, what happened?"

"I don't know!" She was sobbing too hard to get the words out clearly. "Do CPR, Mark! George, do something! Somebody has to help him!"

They got to the bedroom and saw Stan lying on the floor on his back.

George and Dan stooped beside him, but Mark stayed with Celia, knowing either of them could administer CPR if it was needed. "Celia, tell us what happened so we can help him."

She nodded. "I woke up and he was sick, and I tried to get him to the bathroom, but he was too weak, and he just passed out ..."

The paramedics raced in with a gurney, and Issie Mattreaux dropped to Stan's side and began checking his vital signs. "What symptoms was he having before he passed out, Celia?" she asked as Steve Winder, her partner, began recording Stan's vitals.

"He mentioned stomach cramps, and he was breathing real fast and he was dizzy ... He thought it was something he ate."

"How long since he ate?"

"Um ... what time is it?"

"Twelve-thirty."

"Six hours, then. Nothing since dinner, but we ate the same things. But he didn't eat much because he wasn't feeling very well before dinner. Said his stomach had been upset all afternoon. Please, can't you help him breathe?"

Sid Ford, dressed in his police uniform, came running in, and stopped cold when he saw his friend lying unconscious on the floor. Two other cops, R.J. Albright and Chad Avery, filed in, and Mark wondered how long it would be before every cop in town was here. Even the off-duty ones. The emergency personnel in Newpointe were a close-knit group, and they all worried when one of their own was in trouble.

"What's goin' on?" Sid demanded loudly, as if Stan's collapse had offended him personally.

"Sid," Issie barked out quickly. "Go get samples of whatever you can find that he may have eaten tonight. Celia, is he on any medication?"

"No. None."

"Any allergies?"

"No."

"Has he been drinking tonight? Wine, beer, anything?"

"No, he doesn't drink!"

"The truth, Celia," Issie demanded. "I know some of these guys are your church friends, but it won't leave this room. We have to know what he ingested."

"I *am* telling the truth! Stan doesn't drink!"

"Has he vomited at all?"

"Yes. Several times."

"Chad, go get some samples from the bathroom."

Chad hesitated. "Samples of *what?*"

"Anything you can find," she said. "I'll get graphic if you want. We need something we can examine for whatever's made him sick. Hurry!"

Chad dashed into the bathroom. Mark set his arm around Celia's shoulder, offering her feeble reassurance.

"I'm gonna be sick," she said.

He dropped his arm as her hand came to her mouth. Her face had drained of its color, and she shot out for the bathroom.

"Not in the same bathroom, Celia!" Issie shouted. "You'll contaminate the samples. Guys, help her. She must have the same thing he has."

Mark followed her through the small house, and she barely made it to the tiny bathroom off the kitchen. He stood at the door, embarrassed and slightly repulsed, as she retched into the commode. She grabbed the hand towel next to the sink and turned the water on.

"You've got it, too," Mark said.

"What *is* it?" she cried.

"My guess is food poisoning, but it could be some kind of virus."

She splashed water on her face and washed her mouth out, then hurried back into the bedroom. They were feeding a tube down his throat, but he still wasn't conscious.

"When is he gonna come to?" Celia asked.

"I don't know." They put an oxygen mask over his face.

"Why do you have the oxygen mask on him? Is he breathing at all?"

"There's evidence of cyanosis," Issie said as she worked rapidly to stabilize him.

"Cyanosis," Celia repeated, taking a step back. Mark watched her pale face change. "Blue skin. I hadn't noticed in this light." It was as if the word had triggered something frightening, something that horrified her. Mark started to ask her what it was, but the paramedics' rapid-fire exchange overrode him.

"Set up an IV of LR, TKO rate," Issie told Steve. "He's dehydrated."

"Blood pressure's dropping," Steve said. "I'll set up the IV in transport. We don't have time to waste."

They lifted him onto the gurney. Quickly, Issie checked his blood pressure again. "Dropping fast!" she said. "Call for the medi-copter to Slidell and I'll set up the IV. There isn't time to drive."

"Guys, whatever this is, Celia must have it, too," Mark yelled over the voices. "She just threw up in the other bathroom."

"Go get a sample, Mark, and make sure you mark it."

"But shouldn't that be taken by an evidence technician, instead of a fireman?"

"They're not investigating a crime, Mark," she said impatiently. "We just have to get to the bottom of this. The other guys are busy, so you do it. Celia, how are you feeling?"

"Fine, now," she said almost absently as she stared down at Stan. "Nothing like Stan was."

"Well, if his condition is any indication, you'll be getting worse. You might want to get dressed."

But Celia stood still as that look on her face grew more pronounced, that look that said something was cooking in her mind, something triggered by the word *cyanosis*. Finally, she flung open a drawer and pulled out some clothes. As she disappeared into the bathroom, Steve radioed for the medi-copter and Mark ran from the room to get the sample.

Issie shouted, "Have you got those samples, guys?"

"A bag of all the prescription bottles I could find," R.J. yelled across the house. "And the samples from the bathroom. Sid's still workin' on the food in the fridge."

"Even at the hospital they won't know what to do if they don't know what's made him sick," Issie said as they wheeled Stan toward the front door.

Celia was running out behind them. "Issie, you said he's showing signs of cyanosis. That's . . . that's a symptom of poisoning. I've heard of it in connection with . . . with arsenic poisoning. Tell them to test him for that."

"Arsenic?" asked Sid Ford, who had just come back into the room with a grocery sack full of jars and bottles. "That's Hollywood stuff. Why would you think that?"

"Because . . . I've seen these symptoms before. Real similar. I didn't think of it until you mentioned the cyanosis."

"I'll tell them to test him for it at the hospital," Issie said.

"Copter's on its way," someone shouted from the front door. "They're landing in the street."

Issie rolled the gurney out as Steve ran beside it, holding the IV bottle up.

A boisterous wind whipped up as the helicopter landed, and lights in other houses blinked on as neighbors began to spill out of their homes. They got Stan into the helicopter and gave orders to the medics on board, then Issie turned back to Celia. "Celia, I'll take you in the rescue unit," she yelled over the noise. "There isn't room in the copter."

"No, I have to go with him!" she shouted, trying to climb in. "Please! Please, I can't leave him." Steve and Mark wrestled her back. "What if he dies on the way?" she screamed. "You've got to let me go!"

But even as she struggled to get past them, the helicopter pulled back into the night sky, its wind whipping her hair wildly into her face. She doubled over with misery and wailed, but the sound was lost in the wake of the helicopter.

"Come on, Celia," Issie shouted over the noise. "We'll get you to Slidell as fast as we can."

As she got into the ambulance, Mark saw her staring up at the helicopter lights as they faded from sight.

Chapter Two

● ● ●

The shrill ring of the telephone pulled Allie Branning from a deep sleep, and she slit open her eyes and waited for Mark to answer it. It took two rings for her to realize that Mark wasn't there—he was on duty tonight. Wearily, she rolled over to his side of the bed and groped for the telephone on his bed table. Her free hand automatically went to her eight-month pregnant belly as she brought the phone to her ear.

"Hello?"

"Allie, it's me. I'm sorry I woke you, but something's happened."

She reached for the lamp and turned it on, squinting against the light. Slowly, she sat up. "Mark, what is it?"

"It's Stan Shepherd. He's come down with some kind of illness, and he's in a coma. They're helicoptering him to Slidell."

"A coma? I just saw him yesterday. He was fine."

"It happened during the night. The thing is, Celia's showing a few symptoms, like she may have whatever it is, too, and they're taking her in the ambulance. She's really strung out, Allie. I'd go there myself if I wasn't on duty . . ."

"I'm getting dressed right now," Allie said, sliding out of bed and pulling the phone cord into the closet with her. "Mark, what kind of illness is this?"

"I think it must be food poisoning," he said. "We're not sure. I'm gonna call Aggie Gaston next. She'll want to be there with her niece. She may want to ride with you."

Allie pulled on a pair of maternity jeans, then stopped and held the phone with both hands. "Mark, is Stan going to be all right?"

"I don't know, Allie. Pray on the way, okay? I'll be doing it from this end."

"I love you," she said, suddenly stricken at how fragile life could be.

"I love you, too. Call me from the hospital when you know anything. And be careful."

Mark punched off the cell phone he kept with him in case Allie, in her delicate condition, needed to reach him, and called information for Aggie Gaston's phone number. When there wasn't a listing for Aggie herself, he asked for Dugas Gaston, her husband who had died over twenty years earlier. As he'd suspected, it was still listed under his name. Aggie, the eighty-one-year-old Cajun spitfire who played "Aunt Bea" to the firemen by bringing them at least two meals a day, was one of the town's staple citizens.

"Who you callin' now?" George asked him as he drove the fire truck back to the station.

"Aunt Aggie," Mark said. Though Celia was the only one in town truly related to Aggie Gaston, everyone in town referred to her as Aunt Aggie, for she seemed like family to them all. "I hate to wake her up, old as she is."

"You just afraid she'll be too tired to bring you some good eats tomorrow."

Mark grinned. "And you don't care a whit about that, I guess."

"Hey, I can cook 'em up myself."

"Right. That's why you show up at mealtime even when you're off duty."

The big Cajun laughed.

Mark dialed the number and listened as it rang once, twice, three times. Despite Aunt Aggie's vast wealth due to an inheritance that she'd invested in Microsoft before anyone knew who Bill Gates was, it was just like her to keep only one phone in the house. He pictured her getting up and pulling her robe on, as if anyone on the phone could see her, then turning on the light and making her way downstairs to the telephone in the hallway. As if he'd imagined it all just right, she answered on the fifth ring.

"Hello?"

"Aunt Aggie, this is Mark Branning," he told the Cajun woman. "I'm terribly sorry to wake you, but I thought you'd want to know that Stan and Celia are being transported to the Slidell Hospital. They've come down with some kind of illness, and Stan is in a coma."

"Oh, me, no!" she shouted. "Mark, how my Celia is?"

"Not that bad yet," he said. "Look, I don't know that much, but I thought you'd want to go over there. I'm on duty, but if you call Allie, she can drive you."

"I call her right now."

The phone clicked, and he slipped it back in his pocket.

Dan came into the garage, a barbell in his hand. "Hey, Mark, do you know what Celia was talking about? Saying she'd seen arsenic poisoning before?"

"No. I don't have a clue. She hasn't been in Newpointe but a few years, and she doesn't talk much about her life before she came here. She must have had some experience with it then."

"Yeah, I guess. Just seemed weird. Did you call Aunt Aggie?"

"Yeah," he said. "She and Allie are on their way over there."

He only hoped that it wouldn't be too late.

Chapter Three

●   ●   ●

Not for the first time, Issie cursed the fact that Newpointe didn't have more than a noncritical care hospital and that they had to drive over twenty minutes to Slidell for any serious medical problems. But that, she supposed, was better than driving the forty miles to New Orleans. She hoped that Stan had awakened by now, that he was feeling better.

"How are you feeling?" she asked Celia, checking her blood pressure again as Steve drove.

"Fine," Celia said. "I really don't think I'm sick. It was probably just nerves."

"But this could be how it started with Stan." She listened for a moment, then pulled the tips of her stethoscope out of her ears. "Your vitals are good. Blood pressure's fine. Stan was soaked with sweat, but you're not. Any stomach cramps?"

"No, none."

"Good."

"Issie," Celia said, touching her shoulder and making her look at her. "Is Stan going to be all right?"

"I hope so."

"Even if it's arsenic?"

That question again. Issie stared into her face, trying to read her eyes. "I'm real doubtful that it's arsenic, Celia. But even if it is, they can save someone who's been poisoned with arsenic, depending on how much he ingested and how long it's been in his system."

"It could have been in his system for hours and hours," Celia said. "Arsenic doesn't work immediately."

Issie shook the chill that came over her. "Celia, how do you know about arsenic? Was that in a book you read?"

"No. Nothing like that." Looking distressed, she raked her fingers through her fair hair and looked away. "I just knew someone . . . He had . . . real similar symptoms, and he died."

Issie kept her eyes locked on Celia's. "But lots of things cause stomach cramps, nausea, diarrhea . . ."

Celia wiped her tears away with a shaking hand. "Lots of things don't cause respiratory problems, burning throat, coma . . . and cyanosis."

Issie wondered if Celia's trembling had more to do with her own symptoms than Stan's. "Celia, I want you to lie down. We're almost there, and I'll wheel you in."

"No!" she said, as if that was ridiculous. "Issie, I'm not sick. I want to be with Stan."

"But you might be *getting* sick. We need to run a few tests."

"*After* I've seen Stan."

"No, Celia. Now! I don't want to wait until you've gone into coma, too."

The ambulance stopped. Steve got out of the rescue unit and opened the back doors. Celia didn't wait for the gurney. Instead, she jumped out and headed inside.

"Celia!"

"I'll give them whatever they want, Issie!" she called back. "But first I'm going to see my husband!"

Chapter Four

● ● ●

Allie and Aunt Aggie rushed into the emergency room and looked around for Celia. She wasn't there, so Allie went to the front desk and asked about Stan.

"He's being examined," the uninterested receptionist told them. "Just take a seat and we'll let you know something soon."

Aunt Aggie wasn't easily dismissed, so she pushed Allie aside and leaned over the desk, her eyes only inches from the receptionist's. "Take me to him," she ordered. "I wanna see him."

"I'm sorry, ma'am. That's impossible."

"Then where my niece is? Celia, his wife. You don't take me to her, you gon' be all over this floor."

The receptionist got to her feet and seemed to struggle with whether or not to take this elderly spitfire seriously. Allie would have been amused if the situation weren't so grave.

"Mrs. Shepherd is in an examining room," the receptionist said. "I guess you can go on back."

Aunt Aggie didn't wait for directions. She headed through the double swinging doors with missile-like speed, and Allie followed on her heels.

Celia was having blood drawn in an examining room, but other than looking pallid, she seemed okay. "T-Celia! There you is!" Celia looked up at her aunt and eagerly accepted her desperate embrace. The *T* prefix—Cajun for little—was one she used only on those she loved the most.

Allie touched her chest and breathed a sigh of relief. "Thank God you're all right."

But she wasn't, not really. Allie could see the terror in her red eyes as she looked up at them. "He's dying."

"Is that what the doctor said?" Allie asked.

"No," Celia said. "They haven't told me anything."

"Then you don't know that he's dying. The question right now is, how are you?"

Celia rolled her eyes as if that was incidental. "I'm fine except for a little nausea that comes and goes. But Stan can't breathe, and he's in a coma." Aunt Aggie's bony hand reached out to grip hers as the nurse finished drawing her blood, and Celia turned her troubled eyes to the old woman. "Aunt Aggie, what if he dies?"

The old woman pulled her niece against her as if she were a child and stroked her pale blonde hair. "He won't," she said.

"God wouldn't do that to me twice, would he?"

"If there was a God, I know he wouldn't," Aunt Aggie evaded.

Allie's heart melted with compassion as she remembered that Celia had lost a husband before. "Celia, I forgot you lost your first husband. I know that makes you more afraid that you'll have to suffer that again. But he's in good hands."

"Nathan was in good hands, and he died."

Allie didn't know how to answer that. She assumed Nathan had been her first husband, but since she didn't know how he'd died or why, she was at a loss for words. How could she comfort Celia? She didn't know. At this point, she could only pray.

Chapter Five

● ● ●

Sid Ford found Celia, Allie, and Aggie in the waiting room when he arrived at the hospital. He was just trying to get an update on Stan when a doctor dressed in scrubs came through the double doors and found them.

"Mrs. Shepherd?" he asked, and Celia sprang to her feet.

"How is he?"

"Still critical. But I wanted to let you know that we have been able to confirm that your husband's been poisoned with arsenic."

"*Arsenic?*" Aunt Aggie's reaction resounded in the big waiting room, and the handful of others waiting to be treated turned to look. "You tellin' me *this* is arsenic? *Celia!*"

Stunned, Sid watched Celia sink back into her chair and cover her face with both hands.

"What about Celia?" Allie asked the doctor. "Was she poisoned?"

Sid looked up at the doctor, waiting for the crucial answer.

"No, she wasn't. We didn't find any traces of arsenic in her blood or urine. Just in his."

"Then look again," Aunt Aggie insisted. "She been throwin' up. Don't take a genius."

"We're running some other tests on her, but the lab isn't very well staffed at night, and they're concentrating on Stan right now."

"Yes," Celia blurted. "That's what they should do. You can save him, now that you know, can't you? There's got to be an antidote ..."

"We're giving him dimercaprol to bind the arsenic, and we're treating him for dehydration, shock—"

"Shock?" Sid cut in.

The doctor looked back at Sid over his shoulder, seeing him for the first time.

"His body's been traumatized," the doctor explained. "We're also treating him for fluid on the lungs, and we're watching his kidneys because arsenic will sometimes cause kidney failure. It's too early to tell. We may have to put him on dialysis before it's over. There's also a danger of liver damage, but we're monitoring that, as well."

"Doctor, is he going to die?"

Sid held his breath, waiting for the verdict on everyone's mind.

"We're doing everything we can, Mrs. Shepherd."

It wasn't the answer Sid had hoped for, and his heart plummeted. The idea that his friend could die was too much to bear. He choked back the emotion in his throat as the doctor left them. Arsenic. Stan had been poisoned. As the truth sank into his heart, he understood that the case had just changed from personal illness to attempted homicide.

Someone had tried to murder Stan Shepherd.

He turned his eyes back to Celia and watched her lean back against the wall. Aggie seemed to be in shock since hearing that it was arsenic, and now she stared at Celia with eyes that said there was more to this than Sid knew.

A million questions rushed into his mind, but one seemed to flash urgently in neon colors, demanding an instant answer. How had Celia known? Sid stooped in front of Celia. His voice trembled. "Celia, I need to ask you a few questions. And I need you to be honest with me."

There was a certain resignation in her expression, an expectation that disturbed him.

"Celia, how did you know he was poisoned with arsenic?"

"I *didn't* know." She wiped her tears and squeezed her eyes shut. "Not for sure. But I've seen this before. All the symptoms . . ."

"That's what you said." He tried to keep his voice gentle, realizing it wouldn't pay to put her on the defensive. But his heart was pounding, and his breath was rapid. "When, Celia? When have you seen someone else poisoned with arsenic?"

Celia's mouth twisted as she tried to hold back her tears. She averted her eyes, unable to look at him.

Allie was sitting on one side of her, stroking Celia's hair, waiting for a response that made some sense, but even she seemed to be struck by Celia's struggle. Aunt Aggie, on the other side of Celia, looked as miserable, as expectant, as her niece.

"Tell him, *sha.*" Her voice broke on the Cajun endearment that bore little resemblance to its French root, *chere.* "He gon' find out anyway."

Celia covered her face with both hands and sat frozen for a moment. Sid waited, holding his breath, trying to imagine what it was she had to tell him. It took more physical effort to wait, motionless, than it would have to throw her across the room. The force of his will prevailed.

Slowly, she slid her hands down her face, swallowed back her tears, and looked Sid in the eye. "I was married before," she said. Her lips quivered as she got the words out. "My first husband died . . . of arsenic poisoning."

Sid's face went slack as he stared at her, and Allie caught her breath. For a moment, he couldn't speak, but somehow he managed to find his voice. "Who poisoned your first husband?" he asked finally.

She closed her eyes again, and Aunt Aggie's face got tighter. Allie seemed to wait for a pat answer that Sid suspected would not come. "I don't know."

"You don't know?" he prodded. "They never arrested nobody? They never had a suspect?"

"No," Aunt Aggie interjected. "Now, leave her alone. She upset. Can't you see?"

Sid forgot his resolution to speak gently. Through his teeth, he said, "Aunt Aggie, there's been a murder attempt on a Newpointe police officer. I wanna know who did it, and I wanna know as soon as possible. Now if this is connected to the first murder, I need to know everything. I either have to ask her here, or at the station. Which do you want, Celia?"

"I'm callin' a lawyer," Aunt Aggie said, getting to her feet. "I'm callin' Jill Clark."

Sid looked up at her, frowning. "Why would she need a lawyer?"

"Because I see where this is goin', and she—"

Celia grabbed Aggie's hand to stop her. "Aunt Aggie, I can handle this!" She turned her big, pale blue eyes back to Sid. "There was one suspect," she said as her face reddened. "And one arrest."

"And was there a conviction?" Sid asked.

"No. The suspect didn't do it. It was all a mistake. There was never a conviction."

"Mistakes don't repeat theirselves like this, Celia." Sid's tone was growing louder. "Who was it? Maybe they're at it again."

"Apparently they are!" she cried, getting to her feet and moving away from him. Crossing her arms across her stomach, she sucked in another sob. "But not the person who was tried for it. Maybe the person who really did it, but since the police stopped looking and never found the real killer, we never knew . . ."

Sid was losing his patience. He stood up and faced her. "Celia, who was tried for killing your husband?"

She turned away from him. There was a moment of silence as he stared at her back, fighting the urge to shake her until the truth spilled out. "Celia, I'm askin' you a question. I need an answer!"

She spun back around. "Me, okay?" she yelled. "I was the suspect! But I . . . didn't . . . do it . . ."

Sid felt as if he'd been poled in the stomach.

"*What?*" Incredulous, Allie got to her feet. "*You* were?"

Aunt Aggie put her arms around Celia and sat her back down. "She didn't do nothin', Sid," she said. "Stan knew, 'fore he married her. Celia was a victim, and they pinned her with the crime. The killer was never caught, and now it happened again."

Sid stood frozen, letting the words sink in.

"Celia," Allie said in a disbelieving whisper. "Why didn't you tell me? When Mark was in the hospital, you told me about your first husband, that he'd been sick and died, but you never said—"

"Why would I want people to know that I was arrested for my husband's murder?" Celia asked through her teeth. "When I came to Newpointe, I half expected everyone to know. The news coverage in Jackson seemed so overwhelming that I thought everyone in the world knew. But no one knew in Newpointe, and it was so good to get away from all that. Stan was the only person I told, besides Aunt Aggie, and he loved me anyway." Allie looked away, focusing on a spot on the wall. Sid kept his eyes fixed on Celia. "Allie, look at me. Sid?"

They both met her eyes.

"You know I couldn't do something like that," she said. "I love Stan. And I loved Nathan. I thought I'd never get over it. And then I was thrown in jail . . ." Her face grew more crimson with each word, and she began to sob, but she managed to spill all the words out on a rush. ". . . and they wouldn't let me out on bond, so I was in jail for months and months . . . and my parents believed the lies and turned their backs on me . . . and the press wrote scathing articles about me . . . and I wanted to die more than anything in the world."

"But she didn't *die*," Aunt Aggie said angrily, lifting her chin high. "They let her off, and she come here to live with me.

You know her, Allie, and you know what kind of person she is. You do, too, Sid. You know, don't you?"

Sid was shaking his head, expressionless, almost paralyzed by what she'd told him. His eyes were stinging, whether from grief over his poisoned friend's plight, or mourning over what he was learning about Celia, he wasn't sure. Was this news grounds for an arrest? If Celia wasn't his friend, would he have already read her her rights?

"Just listen," she pleaded, as if she could read the thoughts reeling through his mind. "I just want to be with Stan. I just want to make sure he's okay . . . Whatever you have to do, do it later, okay? You can wait. I'll tell you everything that happened, even get you a transcript of the depositions and the trial, whatever you want. Just let me stay here with Stan. I need to be here with him."

Sid suddenly felt very old, like one of those Van Gogh portraits of wizened age and weariness. Maybe he'd been at this job way too long. He wished he could talk to Stan and ask what he would have done if the shoe had been on the other foot. The thought of arresting Celia seemed almost as painful as the knowledge that Stan could die. If he woke up, the arrest itself might kill him.

He tried to run the facts through his mind. Arrests were made on the basis of current evidence, not past history. He didn't know yet what the evidence was, since they hadn't considered the Shepherds' house a crime scene.

Still, she needed to be questioned, not in a hospital waiting room, but at the police station where accurate records could be kept of what she said—where other law enforcement personnel who were thinking clearly could interrogate her.

"Celia, I need to take you back to Newpointe. We're gonna need to question you further."

"No!" she cried. "No, Sid, please. I have to know if he's all right! Please! You know I didn't do this!"

"Celia, let's do this easy," he said, trying to keep his voice low, despite the fact that others in the waiting room watched attentively for the gossip to take back home, and the nurse stood at the receptionist's desk, staring as if she watched some historical event unfold: *Where were you the day Celia Shepherd was hauled in?* Celia closed her hand over her mouth, half hiding, half muffling her sobs, and he hoped she wouldn't make this harder for him.

Finally, she got to her feet. Wiping her eyes with a trembling hand, she turned back to Allie. "Call his parents," she said. "They need to be here. Somebody might have to give consent for treatment." Her voice broke on a sob. "Tell them I'll be back as soon as they're finished with me. And . . . if he wakes up . . . tell him I love him." Aunt Aggie wrapped her arms around her, and huddled together, they headed outside.

As the car pulled off, Celia wailed in the backseat like a mother being separated from her young. He looked out the window and saw Allie standing at the emergency room door, staring at them, shocked, as they drove away.

Chapter Six

● ● ●

Allie watched through a blur of tears as the police car drove out of sight. The blue lights on Sid's squad car had a haze around them, lending to the feeling that this was a dream and nothing more. But it was real, and Allie didn't know what to do.

For a moment, she thought of getting into the car and following them to the police station, but then she remembered Celia's plea for her to call Stan's parents.

She tried to think in sequence, tried to make some sense of all the whirling facts, and finally decided to go to the pay phone.

She needed to call Stan's parents. She knew them from church. Stan's father, a retired detective, was a deacon, and his mother was the organist. They lived on Bonaparte in that beautiful little house covered with jasmine and kudzu, and they had that dachshund that barked when cars drove by.

Why couldn't she think of their names? Mr. and Mrs. Shepherd. Burt and Hortense? No, but close. Bart ... and Hester ... Hannah ... Yes, Hannah!

She called for information and asked for the number, only vaguely realizing that she hadn't needed their first names, for they were the only other Shepherds in Newpointe. She wiped the tears from her face as the phone rang, and after a moment, Bart answered.

"Hello?"

"Mr. Shepherd? This is Allie Branning. I'm sorry to wake you, but I'm afraid I have some bad news. Has anyone called you yet?"

"About what? What is it, Allie?"

"It's Stan. He's taken sick and is at the hospital in Slidell. He's not doing very well."

"Sick?" His voice was more urgent now. "Sick how?"

"He's in a coma, Mr. Shepherd. I think you'd better come."

"Where's Celia?" he asked.

"She's . . . she's busy . . . all the turmoil, you know. I thought I should call." She closed her eyes and told herself that it would do no good to tell them about poison and murder and interrogations . . . not yet.

"We'll be right there, Allie," he said quickly.

She hung up the phone and pressed her forehead against the wall. Desperately, she tried to think of the next logical step. What could she do for Celia?

Jill, she thought. She could call Jill, their good friend and the best lawyer in town. Jill would know what to do for Celia. Punching in her long-distance code, she called Jill. Jill, who frequently got calls in the middle of the night from drunk drivers who needed a lawyer, picked up on the second ring.

"Jill Clark."

"Jill, this is Allie. If you're lying in bed, you might want to sit up, turn on the light, and shake the cobwebs out of your head so you can hear what I'm saying."

Jill hesitated a moment. "Allie, what is it? Are you crying?"

Allie took a deep breath and wished for a tissue so she could blow her nose. "Where do I start? Jill, tonight Stan Shepherd was poisoned with arsenic. He's in a coma."

"That's not funny, Allie. Is this one of those jokes where you shock me with some horrible story so the real one doesn't seem so bad?"

"No joke, Jill. And it gets worse. Sid Ford just took Celia in for questioning."

"*Celia?*"

"Jill, remember in the hospital earlier this year when she told us her first husband had died?"

"Yes, I remember."

"What she didn't tell us was that he had died of arsenic poisoning, and she was tried for the murder."

There was no answer on the other end.

"Jill, are you there?"

"Yes, I heard you." The words came out strained, breathy. "Allie, are you sure of all this?"

"Yes. She said she wasn't convicted, and when they let her go, she came here to live with Aunt Aggie."

"So Sid assumes that she did this to Stan," Jill said, as if talking to herself.

"I hate to say it, but it's an easy assumption."

"Easy, maybe, but not necessarily right. How long ago did they take her in?"

"A few minutes. They're on their way to Newpointe. Aunt Aggie's with her."

"Good," Jill said. "I'll be at the station when they get there."

"Thanks, Jill."

"Allie, remember something, okay? Remember the Celia we know. Don't jump to the same conclusions that Sid did. I've seen a lot of cases that aren't as they seem."

"Sure, I know. And she couldn't have done it. She loves Stan."

But even as she said the words, confusion was taking root in the back of her mind.

Chapter Seven

● ● ●

The fire truck was just pulling into its garage as Jill Clark parked her car in front of the adjacent police department and got out. She heard her name called and peered across the lawn. In the light from the street lamp, she saw Dan Nichols heading toward her. He was tall, six-four, at least, and built like an athlete. Even in the darkness, his green eyes were startling. As always, the heaviness in her heart lightened at the sight of him, and she waited with a smile on her face while he cut across the grass.

"Hey, Counselor," he said in that deep voice of his before he pressed a kiss on her lips. They'd grown close over the last few months, though they were taking things slow. Dan's reputation as a love-'em-and-leave-'em type kept Jill on her guard. "You didn't tell me you'd be making a trip over here tonight."

"Didn't know. Something's come up."

"Does it have anything to do with Stan Shepherd?"

"Yes, actually."

"Have they determined if it was poisoning?"

"I'm afraid so."

"Then . . . do they know who did it?"

"Not yet. They're bringing someone in for questioning."

He took a step back and regarded her shadow-laden face in what there was of the light. "You're not representing somebody who would poison a police officer, are you?"

She sighed. "Dan, I don't really think I can talk about this right now. I haven't been asked to take the case yet. But this particular person is innocent—there's not a doubt in my mind."

He frowned. "It's someone you know, isn't it? Who, Jill? I'll find out soon enough."

She thought about telling him, then decided against it. Yes, he would find out, but until she knew for sure that Celia was a suspect, the words weren't going to come out of her mouth.

Just then a squad car with lights flashing pulled to the curb, and Sid Ford got out. "I've got to go, Dan," she said. "I'll call you later."

He stood there watching as she hurried across the lawn to the car. Celia got out, followed by her Aunt Aggie, and Jill glanced back over her shoulder. Dan was standing there watching them, clearly trying to determine if Celia was the suspect. She didn't have time to worry about Celia's reputation now.

"Celia!" she said as she approached her friend with a hug. "Allie called me, and I came right down."

"Oh, thank goodness!" Celia's eyes were red and her nose was stopped up from crying. She was trembling. "Jill, I didn't do this! I didn't do it! I just want to get back to Stan and be with him—"

"Celia, I believe you. Do you want me to represent you?"

"Yes! Oh, please—"

She was beginning to sob again, and Aunt Aggie, who looked very tired, put her arm around her. "Don'tcha worry about money, Jill. I'll pay arrything."

"I'm not worried about that," Jill said, almost offended. She looked up at Sid, who looked almost as troubled as Celia. "Sid, I need to consult with my client."

"All right," he said. "Take the interrogation room."

"Let's go on in," Jill said.

As they walked up the sidewalk to the police station, Jill saw Dan standing in front of the door. "Celia?" he asked tentatively.

Jill shot a pleading look up at him. "It's all a mistake, Dan. Please don't let word get out. We'll have it all cleared up before daybreak."

"I won't say anything," he said. "Is there anything I can do?"

"Pray," Jill said as they went through the glass door.

• • •

By daybreak, Aunt Aggie Gaston looked almost as bad as Stan did lying in a coma. Though she had not been allowed in the interrogation room while Celia was being questioned, she had waited on a folding chair outside it. Stewing, she watched the buzz of minor activity in the squad room as drunk drivers were brought in, and a couple of kids arrested for disturbing the peace. One drunk driver was Mildred Bellows's husband, a fact that she stored away and decided to keep to herself. She recognized one of the kids as Lois and Jake Mattreaux's boy. He would probably call his Aunt Issie, one of the Newpointe paramedics, to bail him out so that he could keep it from his parents. Knowing Issie, she would comply. But Aggie made a mental note to let his parents know as soon as she had the chance, and to find out who the other boy was. He had probably told them he was spending the night with him, which accounted for them being out all night.

What was this old world coming to? she asked herself wearily. Kids staying out all night, husbands drinking till they almost killed someone, somebody poisoning another of her nephews-in-law . . .

The door to the interrogation room opened, and Sid came out and looked down at her. "You look awful, Aunt Aggie. Why don't you go on home and get some sleep?"

"I look awful 'cause I'm eighty-one years old."

"Not you, Aunt Aggie. You're the best-lookin' senior citizen in town, and you know it."

"Don't flatter me. I ain't buyin'. And I ain't goin' home till Celia come with me."

"Then it's gonna be a long wait, Aunt Aggie."

"Then you probably better avoid them mirrors, 'cause you won't be likin' what you see. Why you're tormentin' her this way, when all she want is to be with her husband?"

Sid looked more drained than before and leaned back against the wall opposite her. "Aunt Aggie, you know I'm not tormentin' her. I'm just doin' my job. I'm tryin' to figure out who poisoned my friend. How is he, anyway? Do you know?"

"'Course I know. I'm callin' the hospital ever' hour." She looked away, as if to end the conversation, then without looking at him, added, "Still in a coma."

Tears came to her eyes, and angry at the vulnerability, she wiped them away.

"We gotta get the prayer chain activated," Sid said quietly. "We gotta get people prayin'. Wonder if anybody's called Nick Foster."

Aggie shook her head in disbelief. The prayer chain. What a useless waste of phone calls. She had always suspected that the prayer chain was just a ruse for passing gossip, though she supposed that some of them were sincere. If it made those few feel better to think people were praying for them, she supposed there was no harm in it. And what good could Nick Foster—the bivocational pastor/firefighter—do? "Somebody called him by now, since half the fire department was at Stan and Celia's house."

"I might check just to make sure," he said.

"You don't want the prayer chain to miss this, do ya?" she asked, her wrinkled face tightening. "Fact that Celia been brought in for poisonin' her husband. Prayer chain got a *right* to know." The sarcasm was thick in her tone, and she noted with satisfaction that it seemed to sting him.

He set his hands on his hips and glared down at her with those big black eyes of his. "Aunt Aggie, do you honestly think I'm enjoyin' this? That I *liked* questionin' the wife of my best friend, and that I can't wait to tell everybody?"

"Wouldn't think it, if you listened to reason. He gon' strike again, you know. The killer. Still out there."

"I don't expect you to suspect your own niece," Sid said. "It's commendable that you'd back her up. I don't want to suspect her, either." He pushed off from the wall and started to go back into the room.

"What you're gon' do next, Sid? Drive them bamboo shoots up her fingernails? No matter how many times you ask her, the story ain't gon' change!"

"See you later, Aggie," he said.

The fact that he had dropped the "Aunt" from her name gave her some satisfaction, for she didn't want anybody who was an enemy of her niece calling her that.

She looked through the glass doors on the front of the building and saw that the sun was coming up. She couldn't believe they were still here.

Leaning her head back on the concrete wall behind her, she closed her eyes, but sleep did not come.

• • •

It was after eight A.M. when Sid and Jim Shoemaker, the police chief, finished questioning Celia. News was that Stan was still comatose, so part of the puzzle—the part only he could fill in—was still missing. When they began to leave the interrogation room one by one, Celia asked Sid, "Can I go back to the hospital now?"

"You're free to go anytime you want, but I'd appreciate it if you'd wait til we've examined the evidence they got from your house."

"What evidence?"

"The food. The dishes that were in the dishwasher. That kind of thing."

Jill, who looked as tired as the rest of them, checked her watch. "Sid, I want a copy of the lab report as soon as it's ready. Have you called to see if arsenic was found?"

"We didn't tape off their house till just a few hours ago. The evidence we collected ain't even at the lab yet. It just opened."

"Then what are you waiting for?" Jill asked. "If you really care about Stan, and if you ever cared about Celia, you'll get the evidence over there. If there's no trace of the arsenic in their food or dishes, then you'll know that he got it somewhere other than home. If you do find a trace of it there, maybe we can figure out where the food was bought. You remember how to do police work, don't you? Stan isn't the only one around here who knows how to investigate a crime, is he?"

Sid bristled. "Insultin' me ain't gon' get you nowhere, Jill. I know you're tired, but I am, too."

She blew out a frustrated breath and leaned back hard in her chair.

"Has anyone called to check on Stan?" Celia's question cut through the petty exchange and reminded them what this was about.

"Aunt Aggie has. No change."

"Maybe he needs to be in New Orleans. Maybe their facilities would be more up-to-date."

"I'm sure the doctor will have him transferred if it becomes necessary, Celia." Jill took in a deep breath. "While we're waiting for the lab results, I think my client needs to make a few phone calls."

Celia looked up at her. "What phone calls?"

"Isn't there anyone you want to call?" Jill asked. "Your parents? Your brother, maybe?"

She closed her eyes and pressed her fingertips on her eyelids. "Oh, no. It's my birthday. They were supposed to come to see me today. The first time they've ever seen my home. I was so hopeful . . ." She looked up, suddenly alarmed. "I need to call them before they leave Jackson. I don't want them to get here and find out that it's all happening again. They went years without speaking to me. It wasn't until a few months ago that we even spoke by phone. And then, yesterday, I thought we were about to reconcile completely."

Jim and R.J. exchanged looks, as if her estrangement from her family was the evidence they needed that she was a cold-blooded murderer.

"What happened yesterday?"

She groaned. "I told you, Jim, that Stan went to see them to try to convince them to come visit on my birthday. He thought it would make me happy."

"You told me he'd visited with your parents, but you didn't mention why."

"I didn't think it was relevant. My parents are John and Joanna Bradford, from Jackson, Mississippi. They own Bradford Oil."

"The rich Bradfords?" R.J. asked indelicately.

"Yes, they're the ones."

R.J. and Jim exchanged looks again. "Stan never told us you was rich," R.J. said. "You didn't seem to live no higher than any of us other police officers."

"*I'm* not rich," Celia said. "Didn't you hear me? I said that they turned against me during the last trial. They disowned me completely. Considered me dead." Angry new tears burst to her eyes as she spoke. "But I missed them. And Stan and I wanted to start a family, and I wanted my kids to know their grandparents."

Jill touched her hand, and she closed her eyes and tried to pull herself together.

"I had gotten them to talk to me, but things were still strained. Then Stan started calling them, and they listened to him. A couple of weeks ago, my brother came for a visit, and Stan asked him to help set up a meeting with my parents. He wanted my birthday to be special, so he went to see them yesterday. He got them to call me. We had a good talk, and I thought they were forgiving me—"

"Forgiving you for what?" Jill asked.

"For . . . for embarrassing the family name. For bringing shame on them. I don't know."

"So they called . . ." Jim prompted.

"They were going to visit me today—them and my brother, David, and I was so nervous and excited about it. I wanted everything to be perfect . . ." Her voice trailed off, and she wiped her eyes again. "I guess I'll have to call them and tell them, and they'll wash their hands of me again."

"I'll get Aunt Aggie to call," Jill said.

Celia shook her head. "She won't want to. Aunt Aggie's my great-aunt, and my mother is her niece. She hasn't spoken to her since the trial."

"But she can make her understand."

Celia shook her head. "No. They'll never buy it. They didn't the first time. It's taken years for them to get to the point where they'd even admit I was alive. Aunt Aggie and my brother were the only two family members who supported me."

"Your brother didn't have any clout with them?"

"Apparently not. He tried, but they're very proud and stubborn people."

Jill couldn't believe they could be so stubborn as to turn their backs on her again.

"Guys, could you leave her alone here and take a break until I get back from getting Aunt Aggie to make the phone calls?"

"I could use some breakfast," Jim said, standing and stretching.

"So could she," Jill said. "Why don't you get her something to eat?"

"I can't eat," Celia said. "I'm not feeling very well."

Jill sighed and waited for the two cops to leave. All of their nerves were shot, and she doubted that any of them would get any rest soon. She bent over the table and looked into Celia's eyes. "Celia, you need to eat."

"I'm queasy," she said. "If I eat, I'll throw it up. I know they said I hadn't been poisoned, and I'm sure I haven't, but I still feel sick, Jill."

"Can I get you anything?" Jill asked. "Some Pepto Bismol, maybe?"

Unaccountably, Celia closed her eyes and her face twisted and reddened as she began to cry again. She grabbed a tissue out of the box on the table and wiped at her nose. "That's what he wanted," she muttered. "Pepto Bismol. Like that would save him from arsenic poisoning, keep him out of that coma. Oh, why is this happening?"

Jill stood still, looking at her and wondering if she dared leave her alone in this state. "I'll stay here," she said softly. "I can talk to Aunt Aggie later."

Celia shook her head and waved a hand at her. "No, go. I'm fine. I need to be alone for a little while, anyway."

Jill didn't like the sound of that. She looked around the room, wondering if Celia intended to do herself harm. There was nothing in the room that she could use, but one never knew for sure. "Maybe that's not a good idea, Celia. I'll just stay."

Celia seemed to realize where Jill's thoughts were leading her. "Oh, you don't think I'm going to kill myself or something, do you? For heaven's sake, Jill, I just want to be alone to pray. I haven't had a minute alone in hours."

"Pray. Of course." Jill relaxed then and knew it was exactly what she would have expected of Celia if she'd been thinking clearly. In fact, it wouldn't hurt for her to do the same. "All right, Celia. I'll leave you alone."

Still weeping, Celia dropped her head in the circle of her arms as Jill left the room.

Chapter Eight

● ● ●

Jill found Aunt Aggie looking like death warmed over, and she realized how difficult it must be for a woman of her age to endure an all-nighter in a folding chair. The woman sat straight up with her purse in her lap and her feet flat on the floor, her eyes closed, as if she was sound asleep.

Jill bent over and touched her arm gently, reluctant to wake her if she slept. "Aunt Aggie?"

The old woman's eyes flew open, and she asked, "They done torturin' her yet?"

Jill shook her head. "No, they're not finished with her. We're waiting for the report to come back from the lab. In the meantime, I thought maybe you could call Celia's parents and tell them what's happened."

She gave Jill a bitterly disgusted look. "I ain't spoke one word to my niece since she turned her back on Celia, and I ain't startin' now."

"But Aunt Aggie, Celia said they were coming to visit her today, and she doesn't want them to hear about this after they get here. Please, won't you call them?"

"I'll call T-David, Celia's brother," she said. "Him I can talk to. But Celia's mama's hardheaded as a ram. I could go the rest of my life without talkin' to her, what she done to that poor girl."

Aggie got to her feet, resisting Jill's help, and started walking. "Which phone can we use?"

"Take that one," Jill said, pointing to an empty desk. "We'll use my credit card number."

Jill punched in the preliminary code, then gave the phone to Aunt Aggie. She dialed the number, rattling on as she did. "David lives in that mausoleum of a house with 'em . . . disgraceful how big it is . . . on three hundred acres . . . and he gots a whole wing to hisself. But sometimes his mama answers his line, and when she does, I just hang up . . ."

"Don't hang up this time, Aunt Aggie. Celia needs for you to do this."

Jill watched the tension on the old woman's face as she waited for the ring to be answered. When it was, she pulled her chin up and tightened her lips and said, "David, please. Well, where can I reach 'im? Yeah, Joanna, it's me." Her face was reddening, and she shot Jill a disgusted look. "No, that ain't why I'm callin'. I was glad you finally got over your bullheadedness to make up with your daughter. But Celia can't make it today, so don't come."

It was not how she would have handled it, Jill thought, irritated, but it was too late to do anything about it.

Aunt Aggie listened, her lips growing even thinner. "No, she ain't backed out, Joanna. But Stan, he's sick, in the hospital. Somebody tried to poison him."

Again, Jill's spirits sagged. There must be a better way to break the news, but delicacy had never been one of Aunt Aggie's traits.

Aunt Aggie closed her eyes, as though bracing herself for what came next, and when she opened them again Jill could see pure rage in her eyes. "No, Celia didn't do it, just like she didn't do it last time, but you never believe that 'cause you don't know your daughter. All you care about is yourself and your stupid, silly family name, which nobody cares nothin' about!"

Incredulous at how badly this was going, Jill snatched the phone out of Aunt Aggie's hand. The old woman surrendered it gladly.

"Uh . . . Mrs. Bradford? This is Jill Clark, a friend of Celia's."

"Where is my aunt?" the woman asked. Hers was a soft voice, very similar to Celia's, and she didn't sound like the shrew Aunt Aggie had made her out to be at all. "I need to talk to my aunt."

"Uh . . . she doesn't want to talk to you anymore, Mrs. Bradford. But I thought you should know that your daughter needs you now more than ever. Because of her first husband's cause of death, the police have been questioning her."

"Then they've arrested her again?"

"No. They're only questioning her." She could hear the muffled sob on the other end, something that surprised her. "I know it would help her tremendously if she had your moral support now, especially on her birthday. I'm an attorney and I'm doing everything I can to clear this up, but for now—"

"I should have known."

Jill hesitated. "Mrs. Bradford, you should have known what?"

"That this reconciliation, this reunion . . . was too good to be true." A moment of silence passed. "I had such hopes."

"You can still have a reunion."

"Is he dead?" The words seemed to come on a wave of emotion.

"No. He's in a coma."

"He was a nice man. I liked him very much. I could see why Celia loved him."

She ignored her use of past tense. "Yes, it's quite a tragedy. More so because of what Celia's going through."

"Thank you for calling, Miss Clark. I appreciate it."

Jill sat there for a moment, holding the line. "Is that all? Aren't you going to come?"

"No, I don't think so."

"But your daughter needs you."

"She has my aunt."

"Mrs. Bradford—"

The phone clicked in her ear, and Jill froze, still holding it.

"Hanged up on you, didn't she?" Aggie asked.

"Yes, she did."

"If there was a hell, it would be for folks like her."

"There is a hell, Aunt Aggie. And you don't want to wish it on your niece."

She watched as the old woman dug a handkerchief out of her pocket and dabbed at her eyes. Across the room, Sid got off of his own telephone and headed toward her.

"What did you find out?" she asked as he reached her.

He leaned over the desk, bracing himself with his hands. "There wasn't a trace of arsenic in any of the evidence we collected from the house," he said, "'cept for what Stan had … purged."

"All right, now we're getting somewhere," Jill said, springing up with renewed energy. "Sid, you have to see that if Celia had done this, there would have been some evidence."

"She didn't have to do it at home, Jill. She's experienced, remember? She knows how to cover her tracks."

"Cover her tracks?" Jill asked in a whisper, to keep from giving the gossip mill more fodder. "Give me a break! She'd have to be pretty stupid to think she was covering her tracks by poisoning her husband someplace else, with the *same* poison she was accused of using on her first husband! Don't you think she'd know that she would be the very first suspect?"

"Maybe that's what she is, Jill. Stupid. Or maybe she's just crazy. You ever thought of that? You'd better, because when I get through gatherin' all the evidence in this case, the insanity defense might be her only hope."

Before either of them knew what had happened, Aggie had leaped up and swung her purse across Sid's head, knocking him over.

"Man!" he shouted. "Why'd you do that?"

"Don't you talk 'bout my niece like that again!" the old woman shouted.

"That thing must weigh a ton!" Sid staggered back, holding the side of his head. "Whatcha got in there? Bricks? I could arrest you for assaultin' a police officer."

"You do it! Throw a eighty-one-year-old woman in jail, see what it gets you!"

He backed off, as if too exhausted to fight her anymore. "Guess this insanity thing runs in the blasted family."

Then mumbling under his breath, he headed for Jim Shoe-maker's office.

Jill caught up with him and blocked his entrance. "Sid, is my client under arrest?"

"That's what I'm goin' in to talk to the chief about."

"You don't have probable cause. You don't have a shred of evidence. All you have is an unsolved case from six years ago." Sid ignored her and tried to get around her.

"Sid, *think*. Why would she tell you it was arsenic if she *wanted* him dead? It would have taken days to discover that, postmortem, if they hadn't known to test him for it. Use your logic!"

"My logic tells me she could be a few bricks shy of a full load, Jill. That maybe she tried to kill him and got cold feet at the last minute. I'll leave that to the psychiatrists. All's I know is we got a police detective layin' half dead in the hospital, and she's the only suspect we got. I don't care how blonde, how pretty, or how married she is. If she's a killer, I'm gon' lock her up."

Jill wasn't about to leave it at that. As he started into Jim's office, she followed him in.

"Jim, since you're finished questioning my client, I'm telling her she can leave," she blurted before Sid could get anything out.

"Oh, no, you don't," Sid said. "Jim, I'm gon' book her."

Jim sank back in his seat. "You can't book her, Sid. We don't have any compelling evidence or any probable cause."

Jill shot him a satisfied look, but he didn't give up.

"Jim, who else coulda done it?" Sid demanded. "Look, she's my friend, too. I've always liked Celia. But the facts just stack up against her."

"What if you're wrong?" Jim asked. "And you have to explain to Stan why you locked up his wife when he needed her most? And on her birthday, to boot."

Jill leaned over his desk. "Jim, all she wants to do is go back to the hospital and be with him. She's scared to death. Let her go. You'll know where she is."

Jim nodded and looked up at Sid. "Tell her she can go home, but not to leave town."

"What about Slidell?" Jill asked. "That's where Stan is."

"Tell her not to go farther than Slidell. And we may have to question her more later."

Sid went to a filing cabinet and leaned his elbow on it. His anger was on simmer, working up to a low boil. Jim got up, rubbing his paunch. "Sid, the investigation continues. If you show me evidence that Celia did this, I won't hesitate to lock her up."

Sid nodded and started back out the door. "I got work to do."

Jill shook Jim's hand and thanked him, then went to tell Celia the good news.

Chapter Nine

• • •

They had moved Stan to a room by the time Celia got back to the hospital, and she hurried up to his floor. Hannah and Bart, her in-laws, were in there with him, watching a television set with the sound turned low. It was as if they watched out of politeness, since it was there and they didn't know what else to do with themselves. Hannah's mouse-brown hair was mashed flat on one side, as if she hadn't teased it back into shape since being awakened in the middle of the night. Bart hadn't shaved.

Hannah sprang up when Celia came through the door. As if she'd been holding back her tears just for Celia, her mother-in-law began to cry and hugged her fiercely. "How is he?" Celia asked.

"There's been no change, Celia. Where have you been? Allie said you were filling out a police report, but we didn't know it would take all night."

A police report. Good for Allie, Celia thought. "I didn't expect it to, either." She went to the bed and leaned tentatively over Stan. "Has he been awake at all?"

"No," Bart said. "Celia, if they kept you that long at the police station, you must know something. Do you know who could have poisoned Stan?"

Her eyes were misty as she looked up at him across the bed. "Bart, if I knew . . . oh, if I only knew . . . but I don't have a clue." She touched Stan's face gently. His stubble was thick. It surprised her. It seemed to her that all of his body functions should have stopped out of respect for his state. Hair growth had no place on a face as pale as death.

Tears came to her eyes. "He's not doing well, is he?"

"No, he's not. Tell us what happened," Bart said. "Last night, before they brought him in."

She raked her hair back from her face, wishing for a shower. "He was just really sick. Throwing up, his throat was hurting, he was really weak. I thought he just had a virus or something. But then he got really sick, and he passed out, and I called an ambulance . . ." Her voice trailed off in fatigued defeat.

"Stan, wake up, honey," she said close to his ear. "Wake up. Please, honey. It's my birthday. All I want is for you to open your eyes."

Hannah was still weeping, and she pulled a tissue out of the box on the table. "Happy birthday, Celia," she said softly.

Celia wiped her eyes. "Thanks." Distressed, she breathed in a sob. "Why won't he wake up? Haven't they done anything for him? Shouldn't it be working by now?"

Bart came around the bed and pulled both women into a strong hug. "We don't know," he whispered. "The doctor isn't sure how bad this is. It may have been a lethal dose."

"He's *not* gonna die," Celia said, pulling back and looking into her father-in-law's face. "Bart, he's not. They caught it in time. They just had to."

They all held each other and wept for a long time, until finally Celia urged them to go to the cafeteria and eat breakfast. They hadn't left Stan's side since he'd been brought to the room. Reluctantly, they agreed and left her alone with him.

When they had left, she sat beside Stan on his bed, talking to him and praying over him, stroking his chest and his face. But there was no response.

She tried to imagine his eyelashes fluttering, his eyelids opening, color coming back into his face. But the image was elusive. The fear of his death was so great that it couldn't be overridden. She thought of Nathan lying dead on an emergency room gurney, how she'd flown into hysterics until they'd had to sedate her. Finally, before the coroner had taken him, they had allowed her a few moments alone with him.

People said it was easier to cope when you had closure—when you could see the death and experience the finality of it. But it had all come too soon, too unexpectedly. There was no such thing as closure. Even the shock and the sedatives hadn't helped.

Now she clung to the sound of the heart monitor testifying to the life still left in Stan's body, to the stubble that felt like sandpaper under her palm, to the feverish heat of his skin against her lips ... heat that was so much better than cold.

She dropped her forehead on his chest and sank into her sobs, feeling the comfort of him even though he didn't move. If he'd awakened, he would have held her while she cried, as he'd done so many times since he'd met her, when she'd been trapped by grief over Nathan, or her parents, or the fear of some evil still out there without name or face.

But now that evil had descended once again, claiming Stan as its next casualty. She couldn't fathom how this could happen again.

After a while, Bart and Hannah burst into the room, startling her. Their faces had changed, and their eyes shone with rage. "Why didn't you tell us?" Bart demanded.

She looked up at them, confused. "Tell you what?"

"About your first husband." The words were uttered with horror. "That he died this way."

Her face drained of all its color, and she felt the heart-deep fatigue from crying buckets of tears. "I was going to tell you."

"Then it's true?" Hannah asked. "We didn't even know that you'd been married before. Did you lie to Stan, too?"

"No," she said. "I didn't lie to anyone. Stan knew the truth. I just didn't think it needed to be broadcast all over the place. I came here to escape the gossip." She left Stan's bedside and faced them with teary eyes. "But gossip has a way of regenerating, doesn't it? Who told you?"

"Simone, the 911 dispatcher," Bart said. "We called to see if they had a suspect yet, and she said you were the only one!"

Celia sank onto the vinyl couch.

"We were good to you," Hannah cried. "We treated you like our own daughter. How could you—" Her voice broke off, and she stepped closer to the bed. "I'm gonna have to ask you to leave."

"Leave? Hannah, he's my husband. I'm not going anywhere." She got up and walked toward them, intent on making them understand. "Yes, I was married before. Nathan was murdered, this same way. Hannah, Bart, you have to understand that the same person who did that must have done this, too. They set me up last time, and now it's happening again. You have to believe me. I didn't do it."

They both looked horror-stricken and confused. "I don't know what to believe," Hannah said. "Someone tried to murder my son. Simone says that you were charged with the first murder."

"Charged but not convicted. Hannah, you know me! You know what kind of person I am! Have I ever given you reason to think I'm a killer?"

"We didn't have all the facts," Bart said. "If we'd known that you'd been accused of murdering your first husband . . ."

"What?" she cut in. "You would have stood in the way of our marriage? That's why Stan decided not to tell you. You would have judged me unfairly. I'm *innocent*."

"We can't know that for sure," Hannah whispered through her tears. "All we know is that our son is fighting for his life, and we just . . . we don't know what to think about you anymore."

"But Hannah!"

"Go home," Bart said. "It isn't good for you to be here."

"I'm his wife! I need to be here."

"But if you're involved . . ." Hannah looked so distraught that Celia felt sorry for her. She was a tigress protecting her offspring. "Celia, we need for you to go home. Just . . . keep your distance for a while. Until we understand . . . everything."

"I don't want to leave him!" Celia cried. "Please, don't make me do this! He needs me. When he wakes up, he's going to look for me. He loves me, Hannah. Bart? Don't you know that he loves me?"

"We've never questioned that," Bart said, his lips trembling. "It's just that . . . these secrets, Celia. We have to sort them all out."

She suddenly felt nauseous, and her head hurt . . . and her heart ached.

She didn't know how much more she could take. Part of her felt that if she left Stan now, he would just fade away, and she'd never see him again. The other part felt that her very presence created strife and grief and angst. Her in-laws were not judgmental people. They weren't vindictive fault-finders.

They were just scared, and she couldn't say she blamed them. If she'd had reason to think that either of them had hurt Stan, she would have reacted the same way.

Finally, she kissed her husband good-bye, and wept as she left the room.

Chapter Ten

● ● ●

Marabeth Simmons dialed across town to Sue Ellen Hanover at the post office, and waited on hold until the postal clerk came to the phone. She tapped her inch-long nails on her Formica desktop, and straightened the sign at the front of her desk that said "Apartment Manager."

"U.S. Post Office," Sue Ellen said, though Marabeth knew that all she'd really had to say was "hello." Sometimes Sue Ellen thought more of herself than she should, and that post office job didn't help matters.

"Sue Ellen, this is Marabeth," she said. "Did you hear the news about Stan Shepherd?"

"What news?"

Marabeth could hear it in Sue Ellen's voice, the disappointment that Marabeth would have news that Sue Ellen hadn't gotten first. She delighted in the fact that this wasn't something Sue Ellen could have read in anybody else's mail. "He's half dead in Slidell. Poisoned."

"He *what?* I'm sure I would have heard something . . . Where did you hear this?"

"From Simone. I reckon she'd know, don't you? Seein' how Celia called 911 last night and all. And speakin' of Celia . . . You'll never guess who they think mighta did it. Celia Shepherd! That's who!"

As Sue Ellen gasped, the door to the apartment office opened, and a tall man with sandy hair and fern-green eyes walked in. "Uh . . . gotta go, Sue Ellen. I have a customer."

"But why would Celia poison her own husband?"

"Got me. Now, if you tell anybody I told you, I'll deny it. And don't let on that Simone told *me*, 'cause she'd lose her job and then where would we be?"

She dropped the phone in its cradle and looked up at the good-looking man. Suddenly, she wished she'd flossed after lunch. "May I help you?"

His grin was charming.

"Yeah, I'm Lee Barnett," he said in a voice that sounded remarkably like Elvis. "You're s'posed to be holdin' an apartment for me?"

She tried to think, but found that she was too flustered. She was too old for this, she told herself. At least twenty years older than the man ... but she'd kept her figure and had just had her hair done. Maybe he did find her attractive. Hadn't she seen an older woman/younger man relationship on *Sally Jesse* just yesterday? Nervously, she thumbed through her files. "Oh, yeah. It's apartment B-5. It's all ready for you if you'll just sign here."

He signed the lease, then glanced up at her. "Were you here when my friend chose this apartment?"

She shook her head. "No. I think our owner rented it through the phone. Musta been Monday, 'cause I'm off Mondays."

"I see."

She got the spare key off of the wall behind her and slid it across the desk, hoping he noticed her nails. "I hope you and your wife enjoy it."

He grinned, making her heart melt. "I ain't married."

"Oh." She hoped he didn't hear the delight in her voice. "When will you be moving in, Mr. Barnett?"

"Lee. Call me Lee."

Victory, she thought. He liked her.

"I'll be movin' in right now. Is the apartment furnished?"

Strange days, she thought, when a person didn't even know if the apartment he'd rented was furnished or not. "Yes, it is."

"All right, then. All I've got is a suitcase in the car. Guess I'll go on up."

She watched as he started to walk out, and she leaned forward with a smile. "You holler if you need anything, you hear?"

"Thank you. Thank you very much," he said with a wink, then left the office.

She sat back in her chair and sighed, then quickly picked up the phone and began to dial frantically. There was so much to tell, and so little time.

Chapter Eleven

● ● ●

W ell, *garçons*, does we order a pizza or does one o' you want
to try out your hand in the kitchen?" George Broussard
asked as he stood in front of the fire station's refrigerator, taking
grim inventory of the sparse contents. Aunt Aggie usually
brought her own groceries when she cooked for them.

"Guess we can do what every other fireman in the country
has to do and learn how to cook," Mark suggested.

Dan thought that over for a moment. "Pizza," he said finally.
"Maybe Stan will wake up and be okay, and Aggie'll be back
cooking for us by supper."

"What a selfish thought," Slater Finch accused. Then with
a grin, he added, "You think it could happen?"

The five firefighters, who'd spent most of the morning
fighting a fire over at Barker's Furniture Store and had worked
up some fierce appetites, erupted into a round of chuckles, but
the amusement quickly faded as they seemed to collectively
realize that they were laughing at their friend's expense. Stan
Shepherd could really die.

"Anybody called the hospital in the last hour?" Dan asked.

Mark got up and got a glass down from the cabinet. "I just
talked to Allie. She called and was told that he's still in the coma."

"Man," Slater said. "This is so bizarre. Anybody talked to
Celia? She must be a wreck."

Dan looked around, but no one seemed to know anything,
except maybe Mark, who didn't meet anyone's eye.

"She's probably still at the hospital. Poor kid probably
hasn't had a wink of sleep," Slater continued.

Dan didn't comment.

They heard the side door open, and hoping it was Aunt Aggie, everyone got up to see. Nick Foster, the pastor of Calvary Bible Church and a fellow firefighter scheduled to come on duty tonight, hurried in. "Hey, guys," he said.

Disappointed, most of them sat back down.

"Was it something I said?"

"No, not you," Dan said. "We were kind of hoping you were Aunt Aggie."

"Hungry, huh? I don't think she'll be coming today. Not until this thing with Celia is cleared up."

Mark and Dan jerked their eyes up to his, warning him to shut up, but it was too late.

"What thing with Celia?" Slater asked.

Silence fell over the room as the men who didn't know looked around at the eyes of those who seemed to. "Nick, what you're talkin' about?" George asked, closing the refrigerator with a jolt.

It was evident that Nick knew he'd spoken out of turn, and he looked from Dan to Mark, then back to George. "Uh . . . nothing. I meant . . ."

"Celia's sick, too?" George asked.

"No. She's just . . . upset. You know."

Slater narrowed his eyes and got slowly to his feet. "Are they suspectin' that Celia did this?"

"No, I'm sure they don't. It's just routine."

Dan rolled his eyes. The pastor was trying to tap-dance his way out of it. Dan felt sorry for him. It wasn't easy being a bivocational shepherd, and in a small town like this it was hard to know what was confidential and what was common knowledge. Nick would be beating himself up for days.

"So is Celia in jail?"

Dan decided to speak up, for he had talked to Jill earlier and knew they had let her go. "No, she's not in jail. Don't go getting all excited about this. They just questioned her about it.

But there's no evidence that she knew a thing about it. Jill's got them testing his coffee cup at work and taking food samples from the cafe he stopped at on his way out of town yesterday, and she's even got them searching Celia's parents' house in Jackson since Stan was there yesterday."

George sat slowly down in his seat. "You know, I gotta say I waked up more'n once durin' the night thinkin' how she knowed it was arsenic. How *did* she know?"

There was dead silence from Nick, Dan, and Mark. Finally, Mark spoke up. "It's probably going to hit the paper tonight," he said. "So I'll tell ya'll, but I expect you to keep it under your hats. Got it?"

They all agreed.

"It turns out Celia was married before, and her first husband was poisoned to death. Arsenic. Now, that doesn't mean—"

"She killed her first husband?" George asked on a whisper.

"No!" Dan said. "See what you've done, Mark? She was acquitted."

"Did Stan know about this?" Slater asked.

"She said he did," Mark told him.

"'Course, we won't know for sure till he wakes up," Slater pointed out.

"Look what you're doing!" Dan got up, angry. "You guys know Celia. You know she wouldn't do a thing like that. Already you're doubting her."

"Dan, what we really know about her?" the big Cajun asked. "Arrybody knows she ain't been in town that long."

"She's been here longer than you have! What do you want?"

"But I growed up here," George defended. "I knew most arrybody."

"And she came so mysteriously," Slater added. "Nobody knew nothin' about her except that she was Aggie's niece."

"That was enough! We all know and trust Aunt Aggie. And besides, Celia was a sweet, soft-spoken, gentle woman, and most of us liked her instantly."

"That had a lot to do with the fact that she's one of the prettiest gals in town," Slater said. "But for all we know, she could have been a cold-blooded murderer with a pretty face. For all Stan knew, either. And now look at 'im.'"

Nick intervened. "Guys, please. You can't burn her at the stake before you even hear all the facts. Celia's got a sweet heart, and it isn't capable of murder. You know it, and I know it."

"Doesn't matter," Dan said bitterly. "It makes juicy gossip, so they're going to run with it. If she gets hurt in the process, who cares, right, Slater?"

Slater swung around, red faced. "Yeah, Nichols? I guess you're just feelin' all superior because you had inside knowledge. Is Jill representin' her?"

"As a matter of fact she is. And I *don't* have inside knowledge. I just happened to be outside last night when Celia was brought in. I knew better than to say anything."

"Come on," Nick said in a sterner voice. "That's enough. We don't need this!" He turned to George, then to Mark and Dan, members of his church, all of whom seemed to be seething for one reason or another. "Celia is our sister. She's part of our congregation. She needs our prayers, not our indictments."

"Then she *has* been indicted?" Slater asked.

Dan wanted to hit him. "No, you fool, she *hasn't*, so why don't you just keep your mouth shut about it?"

Nick moaned as Slater got up, and the pastor reached out and grabbed the back of Slater's collar before he could react to Dan's fighting words. "Stop it, both of you!" he shouted. "We're coworkers here, and Dan, you should know better. I'm disappointed in you!"

Dan didn't like being treated like a child, so he just turned and headed out of the room. Behind him, he could hear Slater cursing his back.

Chapter Twelve

● ● ●

Aunt Aggie would never have left Celia alone, but when Jill assured her that she'd canceled all of her appointments for the day and needed to spend the afternoon with Celia anyway getting all the information she could on the first trial, Aggie decided, with Celia's blessings, to go to the hospital in Slidell.

She was glad she'd gotten a few hours' sleep, at least. Now maybe she wouldn't try beating up any more cops. She grimaced at the thought of how she'd slammed her purse into Sid Ford's head. If she hadn't been an old lady who'd been up all night, he probably would have thrown her in the slammer. Being old did have its perks, she supposed.

She pulled into the parking lot of the Slidell Memorial Hospital, carefully avoiding the "senior citizen" spaces marked near the wheelchair spaces close to the door. There was no reason she couldn't walk like everybody else, she told herself. The day she surrendered to her age was the day they would bury her.

She checked with the information desk to see where Stan was and found out he was on the sixth floor. The elevator took her there, and she got off and saw the crowd of off-duty police officers, a few firemen, the preacher, and a few people she didn't know, spilling out of the waiting room. No wonder Stan didn't want to wake up, she thought. A crowd like that would keep anybody in a coma.

Bypassing them, she headed straight for his room. After all, she was his wife's aunt, so if anyone was allowed in his room, she was. She reached his door and hesitated, wondering if she had the right room. There was an armed guard standing outside it, and she wondered who had hired him. With an air of authority, she walked right past him and pushed the door open.

He reached out and grabbed her arm, stopping her. "May I help you?"

"I want to see Stan," she said, indignant. "I'm his *tante*."

"You'll have to wait," he said. "I'll check with his parents."

His parents, she thought as he stepped inside the room. The ones who threw her Celia out. She had a bone to pick with them while she was here.

She waited for his parents to invite her in, but instead, the guard came back out. "Mrs. Shepherd said to tell you to wait in the waiting room with the others."

"What you mean, 'with the others'?" Aggie protested. "I ain't one of them others. I'm flesh and blood, practically." Realizing she was getting nowhere with the guard, she pushed past him, anyway. When he tried to grab her arm again, she felt for her purse and considered using it. Jerking away, she pushed into the room.

Bart and Hannah sat side by side on the vinyl sofa next to the bed, and she consoled herself with the fact that Hannah, who was at least twenty years her junior, looked worse than she. She stood up as Aggie entered, and Aggie started to tell her to sit down and rest before she keeled right over of natural causes.

"I'm sorry, Mr. and Mrs. Shepherd," the guard said behind her as he took Aggie's arm again. "I didn't think she would be so pushy. Looks can be deceiving."

"It's all right," Hannah said, prompting him to let go of her in the nick of time.

The guard disappeared back out the door, and ignoring both Hannah and Bart, Aggie went to Stan's bedside. He still looked as white as death, and had a breathing tube under his nose. An IV ran fluid into his veins, and a cardiac machine monitored his heart rhythm. Several other machines were attached to him, but Aunt Aggie couldn't identify them. She touched his forehead, pushing the hair back from his eyebrows. He needed a haircut, bless his heart. She should have brought her scissors.

"Aggie, don't touch him. Please." Bart's voice was just above a whisper.

"Please, Aggie," Hannah whispered across her son. "We want you to wait in the waiting room."

"What you're whisperin' for?" Aggie demanded loudly. "Ain't the goal to wake him up? No wonder he still in a coma."

"Aggie, please," Hannah said again. "Don't make us call the guard back in. You really need to leave."

Aggie gaped at them, indignant. "I got as much right in here as ya'll got. I love this boy arry bit as much as ya'll do!"

"He doesn't need visitors," Bart whispered harshly.

"Is it 'cause of Celia?" Aunt Aggie demanded. "'Cause what you done to that girl, sendin' her home like you done . . . oughta be a law. Now you tryin' to thow me out?"

"I'll call the guard if I have to."

Aggie wondered if this was the day she'd surrender to her age—and the burial part, too—as her heart began whamming into her chest. "You oughta be ashamed!" she threw back at them. "You know my Celia didn't do this! *She* saved his life! If she wants him dead, she'd have waited to call the ambulance! Let him croak, then act like she tryin' to save him."

"She lied to us," Hannah said through her teeth.

"How? When she told you a lie?"

"It's what she didn't tell us," Bart returned. "She didn't tell us that she'd killed her first husband!"

Aggie felt the weight of her purse and wondered if she could hit them with it from across the bed. She clutched her chest, as if that would slow her racing heart, and through her white caps said, "My Celia ain't never killed a bug! She ain't *never* lied to you! She didn't tell you she was *accused* of Nathan's death, 'cause she knowed folks like you wouldn't wait for the firin' squad. You'd mow her down before the words was even outa her mouth!"

"She betrayed us," Hannah said, livid tears springing to her red eyes. "Stan may die. He's our only son!"

"Read my lips," Aggie said through her dental work. "She … didn't … do it! 'Stead of bein' mad at her, be mad at the po-leece who's stopped lookin' for the killer. He still's out there, you know, the monster what really tried to kill Stan. It ain't the likes o' me that guard needs to keep out!"

"Until the police tell us differently, we want Celia to stay away," Hannah said. "And we aren't allowing any visitors at all."

"Well, ain't that con-*ven*-ient? She been good to ya'll people, and she make your son happier than he ever been. And this what you do to her!"

"Bart, do something," Hannah said.

He headed for the door and got the guard to come in. "Get her out," he ordered.

Aggie swung her purse like a lasso, aiming right between the guard's eyes. "You lay one hand on me, I'll lay you out just like him," she said, referring to Stan. "I *know* the way out." Then, straightening her dress and picking a dot of lint off of her skirt, she made her way to the door.

Just before she left the room, she turned back. "You be sorry for this one day," she said. "Destroyin' somebody never did nothin' but love your son. Someday she'll be the mama of your grandchildren."

Hannah didn't answer. She only turned back to her son.

Chapter Thirteen

● ● ●

H e's getting away with it."

Allie looked up at Celia, who sat with her arms hugging her knees on the big four-poster bed in Aggie's guest room. She looked so small there, so innocent. And so distraught. "Who?"

"Whoever it is," she said dully. "He's ripped my life at the seams twice, and gotten away with it both times."

"He's not going to get away with it," Allie said. "Jill's working on it right now. She's doing everything she can, Celia."

Celia wasn't buying. "For at least two years after Nathan died, I was so paranoid, Allie. I kept thinking the killer was stalking me, watching me, waiting to take my life, too. For a while, I almost hoped he would."

"I remember when you first came to Newpointe," Allie said. "You *did* seem timid, quiet. I thought you were just shy. Then you seemed to get over it, little by little."

Celia sighed and rubbed her tired eyes. "I knew he was still out there. That never went away. But when I got involved in the church and met Stan, I just started concentrating more on living than dying. I think that kept me alive." She looked down at her knees, clad in faded jeans. "I trusted him so much that I told him everything. And he trusted me unconditionally. He showed me how much God loved me, because he modeled it for me." Sick grief reddened her face, and she leaned her head back on the ornate headboard.

"What if he wakes up and they tell him I tried to kill him, Allie? What if they convince him that I've had some dormant murderous instinct just waiting to jump out?"

"He won't believe it, Celia. You know better. He believed you before. He'll know you didn't do it this time. And if he wakes up, maybe he'll know where he got the poison, and the whole thing will be cleared up."

"Or maybe he'll die, and it won't matter what they do to me."

Allie got up and went to the bed, sat down beside her. Out of habit, she rubbed her hand over her round stomach. Celia's eyes followed her hand.

"We wanted to start a family, Allie," she whispered. "That's why he started talking to my parents. He wanted to make things right, so our children would have grandparents on both sides. Today's my birthday, so he went to see them yesterday in hopes of getting them to agree to come for a visit today. I was starting to think it was all behind me, all of it, that God was returning the days that the locusts ate. I was starting to think he didn't let me die all those times I asked him to, because he had something wonderful waiting. But was this what he spared me for?"

Allie wiped the tears springing to her own eyes. "I don't know, Celia."

Celia reached for a tissue next to the bed and blew her nose. "I read about all those martyrs in the Bible who walked into furnaces and lions' dens and were crucified and beaten and beheaded ... and I can't help wishing that I had some greater purpose for my suffering, too. Does it feel better to suffer for a noble cause? Does injustice carry any peace if you're standing for some divine plan?"

Allie couldn't answer. She pushed the hair back from where it stuck to Celia's wet face.

"But there isn't any grand purpose here, Allie. There's no greater good. It's all just a mistake, but even if I'm not convicted of this, there will always be people who think of me as a murderess."

She slid off of the bed and went to the window to look out on Aunt Aggie's backyard. Allie got up and followed her, and saw Chester, Aunt Aggie's gardener, pruning a pear tree.

"Maybe God's just pruning you, Celia. Sometimes bad things happen because he's just trying to prune us. Make us bear more fruit." It was not what Celia wanted to hear, she realized, but it still could have some truth.

"I feel more like all my limbs have been amputated, right down to the trunk," Celia said. She turned back around. "I'm gonna be sick."

"No, you're not. You'll get through this, Celia—"

"No. I'm really gonna be sick." Allie stepped back as Celia dashed from the room, and she winced as she heard her retching into the toilet.

Allie went in behind her and held her hair back while she bent over the commode. She should have made her eat, she thought. But Celia had complained of queasiness, and now Allie wondered again if the doctors had overlooked the poison in Celia.

The doorbell rang, and Celia looked up at her. "Don't answer it. It's Jed from the newspaper. He keeps coming to the door trying to get a statement. This'll be all over tonight's paper."

"But it might be someone with news," Allie said. "I'll go see. Will you be all right?"

Celia got up and stood over the sink to splash water on her face. "Yeah. Don't let anybody in, Allie. I can't see anyone right now."

"Don't worry," Allie said, then hurried down the stairs to answer the door.

Allie saw the man through the peephole, and instantly thought he must be a news anchor from one of the New Orleans stations. He looked like a model, though he was small in stature, with perfectly coiffed blonde hair and large blue eyes. Behind him, a photographer who'd been planted on Aggie's lawn was photographing and questioning him, but he ignored him.

"Who is it?" she asked through the door.

"David Bradford," he said. "Celia's brother."

Allie caught her breath and let him in, then quickly closed the door on the photographer. "Celia's brother," she said, smiling at him. "I should have seen the resemblance."

David shot past the small talk. "How is she?"

"Well, she's . . . hanging in there. She'll be better now that you're here. I'm so glad you came. I'll go get her."

She left him standing there and rushed up the stairs. She found Celia brushing her teeth. "Celia, you have to come. It's a surprise. I think it'll cheer you up."

"Allie, I don't feel like company. Please . . ."

"No, come on. You'll be glad you did. I promise."

Celia stepped to the banister and peered over. Her brother David was coming up, and she caught her breath. "David!"

"Happy birthday," he said. She met him halfway down and threw her arms around him, and he squeezed her so tight that Allie thought he might crush her. David was only three or four inches taller than Celia, but the similarities were so striking that Allie wondered if they were twins.

"You didn't think I'd stay away, did you?" he said, pulling her back from him and getting a good look at her.

Celia nodded and touched her brother's cheek. "It's been a long time." She looked at Allie. "I guess you've met my baby brother, Allie?"

"*Baby* brother?" Allie asked.

"She's only three years older," David said. "Celia, look at you. Have you slept at all?"

She shook her head. "How could I? Can you believe this is happening again?"

"They searched our house," David said. "Took dishes and food and looked in every nook and cranny. You woulda thought we were criminals."

Celia led him into the parlor and sank down on a couch. He took the seat across from her. "I suppose Mom and Dad were embarrassed to death."

"You could say that. And just when they were ready to reconcile. The timing . . ."

"I know," she said.

He looked around the room, got up, and ambled to a table with family pictures. He picked up one of Celia as a child, dressed in pageant dress and striking a pose. "Where's Aunt Aggie?" he asked.

"She's gone to the hospital to see how Stan is doing."

He set the picture back down. "How is he?"

"I don't know," she said. "News hasn't changed. All we can get is that he's still in a coma. His parents don't want me there."

He slid his hands into his trouser pockets and settled his troubled eyes on her. "Who would do this? It's so weird. Stan was just at the house yesterday. He looked great. And he did a great job with Mom and Dad, Celia. You would have been so proud of him. He did what I haven't been able to do in all these years. He brought them around."

"Until this morning, when they reverted back to believing the worst about me."

"They're in shock, Celia. We all are."

"Tell me about it." She rubbed her temples and shook her head. "The police questioned me for hours this morning, trying to reconstruct yesterday—everywhere Stan may have eaten. David, did he eat anything when he was visiting yesterday?"

David thought for a moment, then shook his head. "No, he didn't eat anything. Cook brought out some cookies, but if I remember, he didn't take one. He mentioned having a sour stomach. He did drink some tea, but so did we all, and it all came out of a common pitcher. The police were still there when I left. Guess they have to test every place Stan was yesterday. Isn't arsenic the poison you can get from eating almonds or something?"

"No, that's cyanide," Celia said. "Did you see him eating almonds?"

"No, but I thought maybe he had picked some up on the way home. Did the police check his car for fast-food bags or anything?"

"Yes, they checked everything."

"Well, maybe there was a receipt in there that would tell us where he stopped, what he might have bought ..."

"They're working on tracing all those leads, but his car was pretty clean. There wasn't much to go on. It was after midnight before he got really bad," Celia said.

"Then it would have to be something he ate at home, wouldn't it? Just before he went to bed. Are you sure he didn't get up after you were asleep and eat something?"

"He didn't feel well when we went to bed. I don't think he would have eaten. Besides, they've tested the food we had in the house. *Nothing* had arsenic. No, wherever he got it, it wasn't at home," Celia said with certainty. "He got it on the road somewhere. During my trial, there were toxicology experts who said that arsenic could take up to twelve hours to work, so he could have gotten it almost anytime yesterday. But it's not a coincidence, David. Two of my husbands would not be poisoned with arsenic by accident. Somebody's trying to kill him, and we've got to find out who it is before they pull it off."

•   •   •

Across town, Jill Clark sat at her desk, rubbing the ache at the back of her neck as she held the phone to her ear. Someone at Judge Spencer's office in Jackson, Mississippi, had put her on hold almost ten minutes ago, but still, she waited.

While the Muzac played out an organ rendition of "Sweet Caroline," she scanned the legal pad on which she had taken copious notes at Aunt Aggie's house. Celia had easily answered all of her questions, holding nothing back. It was as if she thought that giving her enough puzzle pieces would help her to see the whole picture and quickly clear things up.

The Muzac stopped, and Jill sat up.

"Judge Spencer's office."

Frustrated, she rolled her eyes. "I was on hold for the court reporter," she said. "I'm calling in reference to a case Judge Spencer presided over. Jackson versus Celia Porter. It was six years ago."

"Hold, please."

She closed her eyes and moaned. It was so much easier to go down to the office and find it herself, but since the trial had been in Jackson, she was at their mercy. She turned the page of her notes and saw the names: Sheree Donolly and Lee Barnett. When she'd asked Celia if she'd ever had an idea who might have killed her first husband, she'd suggested these two names.

Sheree was a jilted girlfriend of Nathan's who bitterly resented Celia. Celia admitted that, if she'd been a killer, she would have gone after Celia, not Nathan. And why would she want to come back after all these years and kill Stan—someone she'd never even met? Celia had thought that too far-fetched to be true.

Still, Jill intended to check her out, see if there was any history of mental illness, any other crimes she may have been charged with.

Her eye moved to the notes she'd taken about Lee Barnett. He had been a computer programmer, upwardly mobile in his profession, Celia had told her, and she had dated him for a year. But he'd had more than one downfall. He drank too much, loved to party, and she'd caught him one too many times with another woman.

"Besides, it couldn't be him this time," Celia had said. "He's in jail."

"Jail?" Jill had asked her. "What for?"

"One of those nights he drank too much, he got into a fight and killed somebody. He was convicted of manslaughter."

"Was this before or after Nathan was murdered?"

"After," Celia had said. "Believe me, they did question him about Nathan's murder, but he'd been out of town at the time, and lots of people had seen him. A couple of years later he went to prison. I'm sure he's still there."

Jill wondered. She'd have to make sure.

The thing was, someone had set Celia up. This wasn't just about murder. Whoever did it wanted Celia to look guilty. They'd gone to great pains, twice now, to point to her.

Celia had told her about the stacks of evidence they'd had against her in the trial. Arsenic in the house, journals on her computer, in which she'd supposedly planned out the murder ... When she'd told her about them, Celia had sworn that she never used that computer and that she'd never even bought an insecticide for the house, much less arsenic.

Whoever the killer was, he'd done a good job. Jill supposed it was by the grace of God that the jury had acquitted her.

"Ann Hutchins."

The voice on the telephone startled her, but she tried to refocus her thoughts. "Yes. I'm calling to order a transcript of a trial that Judge Spencer presided over about six years ago. Were you his court reporter then?"

"Yes, I was," the woman told her. "What was the name of the case?"

"Jackson versus Celia Porter," she said. "Could you tell me if it would be possible to get that transcript today?"

"I doubt it," the reporter said. "You see, I rarely transcribe my notes unless one of the attorneys asks for it for an appeal. It should take a week or two for me to transcribe it."

"No," Jill groaned. "I can't wait. I need it today. A woman's life is at stake."

The woman sighed. "Well, hold on, and I'll see what I have on it."

Again, the Muzac. She dropped her forehead against her desktop, waiting.

In just a few minutes, the woman came back to the phone. "Hello? Ma'am?"

"Yes," Jill said. "I'm here."

"You're in luck. It seems that the defense attorney requested daily copies of the transcript during the trial, so I have it all done. Would you like me to mail it to you, or will you pick it up?"

She thought over the possibilities and realized she couldn't rely on anyone to get it to her quickly enough. No, she was too anxious. "I'll drive up and get it myself," she said. She looked at her watch. It was just after noon. "I'll be there around two-thirty."

"All right. I'll have it ready for you."

She hung up the phone, trying to think. She needed several things in Jackson today, she concluded. She needed to speak to the attorney who had defended Celia in the first trial, and she needed to find out if Lee Barnett was still in prison.

Quickly, she threw the legal pad into her briefcase and locked it shut. Her secretary, Sheila, one of the angriest but most competent women she'd ever known, shot her a questioning look.

"Call Celia at Aggie's house and tell her I'm on my way to Jackson to get some things I need from the clerk of the court, Sheila. Tell her I'll call her when I get back tonight."

Sheila muttered something under her breath, but since Jill couldn't hear it, she didn't worry about it. Sheila was always muttering. The fact that she was already dialing Aggie's number was all that really mattered.

• • •

Aunt Aggie pulled her lavender Cadillac into her driveway and saw the photographer and newspaper reporter who had been there when she left. She got out of her car and slammed the big door. "Shoo! Get on outa here, Jed!"

"Aunt Aggie, can you ask Celia to give us a statement?" the reporter whined. "Just a little one? Then we'll leave."

"Celia ain't givin' you nothin'. Now leave!"

"But Aunt Aggie, if I go back to the paper without *something*, Hank'll wring my neck. You don't know him when he's mad. And this is the biggest thing that's hit Newpointe in a while. Give a guy a break, will ya?"

As he droned on, Aggie marched up the steps to her front door, turning from flashes of the camera. "Hank gon' be real mad when he has to bail you out for trespassin'!"

She reached the door, and so did the photographer. He stood poised to snap a shot when she opened the door. She reached up and unsnapped the big lens protruding from the camera's front. "You tell Hank I'll give this back when my Celia's cleared," she said. "Now get off my prop'ty 'fore I have to start playin' dirty."

The photographer whined out his complaint, but she ignored him as she pushed through her front door.

She heard voices and looked into the living room. David, her nephew, was sitting there. "T-David!" she shouted. "*Sha!* You came!"

As they hugged, Celia asked, "Aunt Aggie, how is Stan?"

"Still out," Aunt Aggie said, her face changing again. "His looney-bin folks hired a guard to stand outside his room. Threw me right out, me."

"They threw you out?" David asked. "Why?"

Aunt Aggie hesitated. "They just real careful."

"That's not it," Celia said. "They don't trust you because of me. They believe that I did it, don't they?"

"Honey, ain't nobody thinkin' rational."

"That easily, they'd think the worst about their own daughter-in-law?" David asked.

"Why not?" Celia asked as tears pressed to her eyes again. "My own parents do. Why shouldn't his?"

David looked as if he didn't know what to say about his parents' insensitivity. "You know how Mom and Dad are. Image control is a big thing with them."

Aunt Aggie watched Celia's face draining of color. "You feel okay, Celia?"

Celia laid her head back on the sofa and took a deep breath. "Aunt Aggie, do you think they would even tell us if he died?"

"Oh, they'll tell us all right. That rat Sid'll change your charges from attempted murder to murder so fast, heads be spinnin'. They'd tell us."

"What if he wakes up?" she asked. "Will they let us know that?"

"Can't say," Aunt Aggie said. "But I ain't gon' let up callin' there till he does. And he will, *sha*, don't you worry."

"How did he look?"

"Pale. Monitors hooked up to him, IV, you got the picture. Medicine's workin' on him, darlin'. It'll work. I know it will."

"I wish you believed in prayer," Celia said on a whisper. "I could use someone praying for me today."

"I b'lieve in positive thinking," Aggie said. "That's all prayer is, anyway."

"No, it's not, Aunt Aggie. It's much more than that. I need someone to pray for me, not think about me."

"I'm praying for you," David said.

Aunt Aggie tried to hide her surprise. She'd never known David to be a praying man. She'd believed him to be one of the few in the family who didn't need religion. She'd half admired him for it. He took after her, she'd thought proudly. So now he'd changed his mind?

"I appreciate that, David," Celia said. She looked up, still as pale as a Mardi Gras ghost. "Uh ... excuse me."

She dashed out of the room to the bathroom, and moments later, Aggie heard her retching again. "That girl got some poison, too, whether they found it or not! She gon' have to black out, herself, 'fore they'll listen."

Slamming down her purse, she headed for the bathroom to help her niece.

Chapter Fourteen

● ● ●

Jill stared down at the trial transcript the clerk of the court had laid down in front of her. Jackson, Mississippi versus Celia Porter.

She flipped through the pages of transcript, saw the witnesses the prosecution had stacked against her. Expertly, she scanned the testimony, hoping to find the evidence they'd used against Celia. A computer journal, arsenic in the house, Nathan's affair ...

She froze on the testimony by Celia's friend, who claimed that the week of the murder, Celia had learned that Nathan was having an affair. So, that was the motive they'd come up with, Jill thought, feeling the blood rushing to her face. Celia hadn't mentioned that.

She flipped on through and found that the alleged girlfriend was Sheree Donolly. Hadn't Celia said she was a *former* girlfriend?

She turned to the back, looking for the closing remarks that would give her a nutshell summary of the case. Instead, she found a motion for dismissal with prejudice. Apparently, the judge had complied. Celia had not been acquitted at all. Something had happened to cause the judge to dismiss, and the "with prejudice" wording of the dismissal had kept the prosecutor from trying it again.

She realized that her face was turning red and her hands were trembling as she flipped through. She looked up to see the court reporter watching her curiously. She cleared her throat. "Uh ... thank you."

"Wasn't there something else you were looking for?"

She tried to clear her head and think. "Yes. Uh ... Lee Barnett. I'm not sure if Judge Spencer was the one who presided over that case, but he was convicted of manslaughter a few years ago. I'm not sure of the exact date. I need to know his sentence, if he's still incarcerated, that kind of thing."

"I'll see if that was one of ours," the woman said, taking the information down. "If not, I can find those things out, anyway." She disappeared into the records room.

Jill found a chair and sank down, and began reviewing the transcript again. She started from the last page of testimony and tried to trace her way back to whatever could have caused the charges to be dropped. It was too tedious and would take too long to get to the bottom of it, so she looked for the defense attorney's name, checked her watch, then pulled her cellular phone from her purse.

She called information, got the attorney's number, then quickly dialed it.

"Summers, Stockwell, and Graham."

"Yes, uh ... I need to speak to Robert Stockwell, please."

"May I tell him who's calling?"

"Jill Clark," she said. "I'm an attorney in Newpointe, Louisiana, and I'm representing a former client of his—she went by the name of Celia Porter. I need to talk to him about that trial."

The woman put her on hold, and within minutes, Robert Stockwell was on the phone. "This is Bob Stockwell."

"Mr. Stockwell, thank you for taking my call."

"No problem. My secretary said you were calling about Celia. How is she?"

"She's fine," Jill said. "Well, actually, she's not. You see, her husband was poisoned with arsenic last night, and she's been charged with attempted murder."

The man was dead silent, and if she hadn't heard him breathing, she would have sworn he'd hung up.

"Mr. Stockwell?"

"I don't believe it," he said. "Another husband poisoned?"

She knew the thoughts that must be coursing through his mind. Had he gotten a guilty woman off? Had he released her to kill again?

She knew her voice was too weak as she said, "She's innocent, Mr. Stockwell. I know she is. But I came to Jackson to get a copy of the transcript of her trial, and I'm a little confused about how the trial ended. I was under the impression that Celia had been acquitted."

"No, no. Is that what she told you?"

Jill honestly couldn't remember if she'd ever used that word. Maybe she'd talked around it, with words like "not convicted." She wasn't sure. "I . . . I don't think so," she said. "I may have just jumped to that conclusion based on the fact that there was no conviction. But could you clear this up for me? Why were the charges dropped?"

He seemed shaken, and hesitated for a moment longer. Finally, he cleared his throat. "About three weeks into the trial, we put a police officer on the stand who had been one of the first on the scene when Nathan's body was found. He swore that the supervising officer had made the comment that the wife is always guilty. And he had a string of other inflammatory remarks and innuendos about Celia. The jury was made up of eight women and four men, and during that testimony, you could see the anger on their faces."

"So you moved to dismiss the charges?" she asked.

"Yes. It was the perfect opportunity. The testimony had hurt the credibility of the investigation, since the man in charge seemed to want to nail her. Even the judge saw that we'd never get a guilty verdict from that jury after that, so he dismissed the charges and the trial ended."

She closed her eyes. "I wish you had let it go all the way. An acquittal would look a lot better right now."

"Afraid what the Newpointe police will think when they find out?"

Jill nodded silently. "I'm afraid they'll be as surprised as I was. One other thing, Mr. Stockwell. I noticed in scanning the testimony something about a computer journal. Could you tell me about that?"

"Yes," he said. "There were some computer files on the PC in their home. Some journal entries were made in which Celia allegedly wrote out her plans to poison Nathan because of his affair. Celia claimed she didn't even use that computer, that someone else had made those entries."

Jill let that sink in for a moment. "What can you tell me about the affair?"

"That was the motive the prosecution used. Apparently, Nathan did have a girlfriend, though, I have to tell you. I was with Celia when she first heard of this, and she was shocked. It was no act. I really didn't think she knew about it. But it came up every day of the trial. They turned it into a virtual soap opera. And when the girlfriend testified, it was quite a circus. She claimed Nathan told her the day before he died, that he'd asked Celia for a divorce and told her about his affair. Celia claims it never happened, and no one could verify if it was true one way or another." He paused for a moment, then added, "Celia should have told you these things. They're pertinent, don't you think?"

"Yes, she should have. But her state of mind isn't that great right now. She's very worried about her husband, and she hasn't slept. And I guess there could be an element of denial. It's bad enough to have your husband murdered, but while you're grieving, to be accused of that murder, and then be told that he was cheating on you?"

"Her second husband wasn't cheating, was he?"

Jill frowned. "No. Not at all."

"I was just thinking . . ."

"That maybe her toggle switch was flipped every time she faced rejection? Come on, Counselor. You knew the same Celia

I know, didn't you? Besides, she's sick with worry over her husband right now. All she can think about is getting to his side."

"He's not dead?"

"No. He's in a coma."

Silence again.

"Look, would you be willing to give me your file on that case? There might be something there that could help me to defend her."

"Certainly. I have several boxes in storage. I can have my secretary pull them and have them ready for you as soon as you can come by."

"All right. I'll be there before you close today." She paused, thought for a moment. "Look, Mr. Stockwell, I know what you're thinking. You're wondering if maybe you had her all wrong, if she really could have been a killer. But I can tell you that I've known her for the past few years, and she doesn't have this in her. That killer is still out there somewhere. He's simply struck again."

"But why? Why, after all these years? Why another of Celia's husbands?"

"That's the mystery," Jill said. "I'll let you know when I figure it out."

The clerk was just coming back as she clicked off her phone. Jill got up and went back to the counter.

"Judge Spencer didn't preside over the Barnett case," the woman said. "But I made a phone call and learned that he was incarcerated at the Rankin County Correctional Facility, just about fifteen minutes away. He was released about two weeks ago."

Jill caught her breath. *"What?"*

"That's right. He served five years, and last week—"

"Do you have an address?" she asked. "Is there a phone number for a family member I could call?"

"No, I don't think so," the woman said. "There's a former address, but this was five years ago. It's an apartment, so chances are, he won't be going back there."

"I'll take it," she said, and jotted it down.

"Was there anything else you needed?"

She couldn't think. Her heart was beating so hard that it drowned out the woman's words. "Uh ... thank you."

Somehow, she wrote out a check for the transcript, grabbed it, and made her way back to her car. It wasn't a coincidence, she told herself. It couldn't be a coincidence.

Lee Barnett had to be the killer.

Two hours later, armed with three boxes that contained all the work Robert Stockwell had done on Celia's case, Jill found Lee Barnett's address on the map, and navigated her way to it. It was a nice apartment on the Ross Barnett Reservoir—not at all a place where she'd expect a convict to have lived.

Instead of going to the apartment where Lee was supposed to have lived, she tried the office. A woman sat at a desk, the telephone against her ear. Jill stepped inside, and the woman motioned for her to sit down.

"Yeah. Apartment 15. Yeah. Okay, I'll tell 'em."

She hung up, made a notation on her desk calendar, then looked up at Jill. "Can I help you?"

"Yes. My name is Jill Clark. I'm an attorney from New-pointe, Louisiana, and I need some information." She knew the woman didn't have to tell her anything about her tenants, but she hoped her boldness and the fact that she was an attorney would disarm her.

"Okay," the woman said. "Are we bein' sued? Are you here to give me a subpoena? 'Cause we didn't have anything to do with that fire, and the inconvenience wasn't exactly our fault."

Jill wouldn't let herself smile. "No, nothing like that. I'm looking for Mr. Lee Barnett. This was his last known address, apartment 26. Could you tell me if he's still living here?"

The woman breathed a visible sigh of relief. "Thank good-ness. A lawsuit's all I need. Let me see. Nope. No Barnett in any of these apartments."

"Do you by any chance remember him? He would have been here, say, five years ago?"

"Nope. I've only been here two years."

Disappointed, Jill thanked her and left. What now?

Sheree Donolly. She needed to find and talk to the woman who claimed to have had an affair with Celia's husband. She thumbed through the transcript until she found Sheree's testimony. She'd given her address just after they'd sworn her in. She wrote the address down and studied the Jackson map. She navigated her way to the modest house in the Madison area, and pulled into the driveway.

Praying this visit would lead her closer to the truth, she went to the door.

A woman in her fifties answered. "Yes?"

Moved again, Jill thought. *Terrific.* "Hello, I'm Jill Clark. I'm looking for someone who used to live here. Sheree Donolly?"

"You're too late," the woman said. "She's in the hospital."

"The hospital?"

The woman seemed amused at Jill's surprise. "Don't look so worried. Didn't you know she was due?"

Jill felt as if she'd missed the first half of the conversation. "Due?"

"The baby. She had her baby yesterday."

Jill's eyebrows shot up. "Really? I didn't know she was pregnant."

The woman laughed. "And here I thought you were a good friend checking on her. I'm sorry . . . I'm her mother. Who did you say you were?"

"Jill Clark. Uh . . . Mrs. . . . ."

"Donolly," her mother said.

"Yes. Mrs. Donolly. Could you tell me Sheree's married name?"

The woman sighed. "Oh, she's not married, I hate to say. It's a real sore subject, but if you know Sheree, you're not surprised. She's my only daughter, but I don't approve of all she does. Still, I'm gonna enjoy that grandbaby. Sweetest little girl you ever saw. Go on up to the hospital and see 'em. I'm sure she'd love to see you."

Jill nodded, as if she'd do just that. "Mrs. Donolly, could you tell me what time of day Sheree went into the hospital yesterday?"

"Oh, she didn't go in yesterday. Went in the night before. Had hard labor for over twenty-four hours. Finally had a C-section."

Jill thanked the woman and let her think that her next stop would be the hospital, but she knew there was no point. If Sheree had been in labor on the day Stan was poisoned, she probably wasn't involved.

Lee Barnett was a much more probable suspect.

She checked her watch and saw that it was getting late. She needed to get back to Newpointe and confront Celia about the things she hadn't told her. She needed to be there in case the police pulled anything. She needed to be there in case Stan died.

Her heart sank. This was too much. She had never defended anyone against anything worse than drug dealing—except for one murder charge that was dropped within twenty-four hours. She wasn't sure she was equipped to defend Celia, and dismally, she realized that she wasn't equipped to track down Lee Barnett.

She started her car and headed back to I–55 south. She'd go straight to the police station and tell them what she'd learned. They would be getting a transcript of the trial themselves, but they probably hadn't gotten it yet. Maybe she could deflect their shock about the mistrial, then address their certainty that Celia was guilty by dropping the bomb about Lee Barnett's release. Hopefully they would take the baton and find him. Chances were, he was right there in Newpointe, watching the drama unfold.

She hoped they'd take her fears seriously, before he tried again.

Chapter Fifteen

● ● ●

The police station wasn't that busy this time of day, when the biggest crimes were being committed by speeding drivers on their way home from their daily commute to New Orleans. Jill found Sid slumped at his desk, and took a deep breath to sustain her. *Take the offensive*, she reminded herself. If she let Sid get the upper hand, he could probably even convince *her* that Celia was a raging murderer.

She had stopped by her office and made the police department another copy of the transcript, so that she could get the little surprises out of the way. She made her way across the room, between desks and around chairs, to where Sid sat.

"I have something for you." She dropped the transcript on his desk and plopped down wearily in the chair across from him.

"You look rough," Sid said.

"I feel rough. You don't look so good yourself."

"I did go home and get a couple hours of sleep." He sipped from a coffee mug that said something about cluttered desks being the sign of genius, and glanced down at the transcript. "Hey, where'd you get this?"

"I went to Jackson and got it."

"We were told it could take two weeks."

"No, the court reporter had it on file, because the defense attorney had requested daily copies of the transcript during the trial." She sat up rigid in the chair and locked eyes with him. It was very important that she choose her words carefully, so that the motive the prosecution had used and the way the trial ended wouldn't seem so important.

"I spoke to the defense attorney about the evidence that led to the dismissal, and he told me there had been a cop who'd said some despicable things about Celia—"

"Wait a minute." Sid's words cut her off, and he began flipping through the transcript. "Dismissal? I thought she was acquitted. That's what she said."

Jill knew she was going out on a limb, since she couldn't remember exactly *what* Celia had said. "I don't think she said that, Sid. What she told us is that she was not convicted. That was true."

She could see that Sid didn't like it. He turned to the back page of the transcript and found the motion to dismiss.

"I brought this to you so you'd be closer to clearing this up," she said. "And I also wanted to give you the name of a possible suspect that you need to check out. One of the guys questioned in the first murder was a man named Lee Barnett. He had an alibi, so the police didn't pursue it. But I find it interesting that just a couple of weeks ago he was released from prison after a five-year term for manslaughter."

Sid's bloodshot eyes returned to her. "Lee Barnett, you say?"

"Yes. Will you at least try to locate him? Find out where he was on the day of Stan's poisoning?"

Sid blew out a breath. "All right, Jill. I'll see what I can find out. But that don't explain why Celia led us to believe she was acquitted. That's important information, Jill. She coulda cleared that up any time, and you know it."

Jill knew it was true. She'd spent the last few hours fuming about that, herself. Still, she had to defend her. "She's beside herself worried about Stan, Sid. She's doing the best she can."

"To what? To cover up?"

"Look for Lee Barnett, Sid. I think that will answer a lot of our questions."

"Give me a motive," he said. "Why would this Barnett guy want to kill Stan right after he gets out of the slammer?"

"I don't know," she said. "But if you find him, maybe you'll find out."

"Don't hold your breath, Jill." He leaned up on the desk, bracing his elbows. "I know you gotta believe in your client and everything, but what if she's guilty?"

Jill didn't have the energy to fight him. She had to save it for Celia.

She headed out to her car just as she saw Dan's Acura pulling out of the Midtown fire station's parking lot. He spotted her and pulled his car over, got out, and came to her passenger door.

She smiled as he slipped in beside her.

"Hey there, Counselor," he said in that deep voice of his. Those stark green eyes had a smile in them, and he leaned over and pressed a chaste kiss on her lips.

"You smell good," she said, touching his face.

"I just showered," he told her. "We had a fire at the feed mill today, and I smelled like a smoke bomb. I'm off, so I was just about to start looking for you and see if you wanted to have a bite."

Jill remembered that she hadn't eaten at all today. She didn't have time for it, but if she took the time, maybe it would give her the energy she needed to confront Celia. "I can't spare much time," she said. "I've been in Jackson, and I really need to get over to Aunt Aggie's and talk to Celia."

"You gotta eat." He pushed a strand of hair out of her eyes. She wasn't sure why that jolt went through her every time he touched her. "Come on. We'll go to Maison de Manger and have a couple of po' boys."

Though the deli sounded like a five-star establishment to anyone not familiar with French, it was really a glorified fast-food place whose name really meant "House of Hunger." But it was one of the favorite places in Newpointe, third only to McDonald's and Burger King. "Okay," she said. "I'll meet you there."

She watched as he got out of the car and headed back to his own. A strong breeze whipped up his hair, and she bit her grin as he got into the car, flipped the visor, and finger-combed it back into place. Then he pulled the car out onto the street.

She suspected that his vanity had more to do with insecurity than pride. He hated his receding hairline. Though he'd never mentioned it to her, that seemed to be what kept him constantly looking at his reflection in windows and mirrors. That preoccupation served him well, though. She doubted he knew how good-looking he really was. His body testified to the amount of jogging and weight lifting he did, and if he wasn't aware of it, every woman in Newpointe was.

But it wasn't just his looks that attracted women, she thought. It was also his money. Dan was the only fireman she knew who owned acreage just outside of town and could afford a house that was bigger than the fire station itself. The word around town was that his father had moved heaven and earth to try to direct him into a more lucrative line of work, but Dan had a passion for fire, a passion that drew some firefighters no matter how little they got paid or how much they had to give up. His father had eventually given up and offered his blessings, along with a sizeable inheritance when he'd died two years ago. Dan Nichols would never hurt for money, which was just one more reason he was number one on the eligible list of every single woman in town. The fact that he showed any interest at all in her was a phenomenon she couldn't quite fathom.

She pulled into a parking space in front of the cafe that was perched on a bayou, and he was at her door in an instant. "Dan, have you heard any word on Stan?" she asked as they headed around to the back deck, where bullfrogs croaked and crickets chirped, and the breeze whispered through the cypress leaves.

"Nope. He's still in a coma."

She moaned.

"So what did you find out in Jackson?" he asked as they took a table.

Wearily, she set her chin in her palm. "Nothing. Everything. I really can't talk about it."

He looked offended, but he didn't press. "No problem. But don't expect me to tell you about the fire over at the feed mill."

She grinned, glad that she had taken the time to spend with Dan.

Chapter Sixteen

●●●

Joe's Place had a sparse crowd, and a smoky haze floated over the room that vibrated with the too-loud sounds of zydeco music. R.J. Albright sat at the end of the bar, relaxing for the first time since Stan Shepherd keeled over. He had thought of going home and falling into bed, but he'd decided that one drink might be in order just to help him unwind. He scanned the familiar faces in the room—the same ones that were here every night—and noted that there was no one here he particularly wanted to talk to.

The door opened and a stranger came in—a tall, sandy-haired guy who looked like a close cousin of Brad Pitt, only cleaner cut. After standing at the door for a moment and looking around, he headed for the bar and took a seat a few stools down from R.J.

Not too interested, R.J. went back to nursing his beer.

A newspaper lay folded on the counter between R.J. and the stranger, and R.J. saw the man glance down at the headline: Newpointe Detective Poisoned by Arsenic. He frowned and picked the paper up, unfolded it, and his eyes lingered on Celia's picture in the center of the article, next to one of Stan.

R.J. wondered if it was just his imagination or if the stranger's face drained of color.

"Where y'at?"

The man kept staring at the paper, but Joe, the bartender and proprietor, tried again.

"Where y'at, pal? You want somethin', or not?"

The man looked up into Joe's scruffy face, and for a moment, R.J. considered interpreting the Cajun greeting for him. Rapid-fire Cajun was a strange mixture of French and southern American, and not many outsiders could understand it.

"Uh . . . Gimme a beer." The man turned back to the paper, frowning as he read. Joe set a cold beer bottle on the counter in front of him, then waited for him to pay. As he reached into his wallet for his cash, R.J. saw a tattoo just under the man's shirt sleeve. It looked like a tally of some sort—four short lines and a fifth crossing diagonally through them. He'd tallied twelve.

R.J. breathed a laugh, wondering if the man kept a running score of the women in his life. The man pulled out a ten and set it on the counter. "Listen, you know anything about this case here?" he asked, pointing to the article.

Joe glanced down and rolled his eyes. "Don't arrybody? She killed her first husband, you know."

When Joe looked at him, R.J. nodded that it was true.

"When did this happen?"

"Last night. He ain't dead, though. They got him over to the hospital. He ain't woke up yet."

"And where's his wife? In jail?"

"Nope, not yet. She ain't been arrested yet."

"So she's home?"

"Guess so."

He looked back down at the article, reading the words with a little too much interest. "So where would that be?"

Joe had already turned away and was wiping the other side of the bar.

"'Scuse me," the man said louder. "Where does she live?"

Joe turned around. "Who?"

"Celia Shepherd."

Joe paused and glanced back at R.J., as if asking him if he'd heard all that. R.J. nodded.

The man saw the look pass between them and quickly tried to explain himself. "See, I know her. Or I used to. We went to school together."

"You from Jackson?" Joe asked him, growing interested now.

"That's right."

Joe leaned down on the counter. "What you know 'bout her first husband? The one died of arsenic?"

"I know she ain't a killer."

R.J. got up and hiked up his pants. Slowly, he ambled around to take the stool next to the stranger.

"R.J. Albright," he drawled, extending a hand.

The man shook. "Lee Barnett."

R.J. slipped onto the stool beside Lee, and brought his mug halfway to his mouth. "Celia Shepherd wouldn't be one o' them notches, would she?" he asked, pointing to the tattoo.

Barnett looked down at his arm, as though he'd forgotten the tattoo was there. "No, man. Those ain't for women. They're for deer."

"You shot twelve deer?"

"Fifteen, actually. But my tattoo's behind. It'd be more, but I ain't hunted in five years." He tapped the newspaper article with a calloused finger. "So do you know Celia Shepherd?"

R.J. nodded. "Stan's a good friend o' mine. Celia, too, I reckon. Downright shame."

"Is he gonna die?"

"Don't know. Hope not."

Barnett stared down at the article, reading over it again. He was still too shaken up . . . too concerned. He threw his beer back, as if trying to calm down.

"I always thought there was somethin' fishy about her," R.J. said. "She was too good-lookin' to marry a small-town boy like Stan. She looked Hollywood. We all knew there was somethin' wrong there."

Barnett stared down at the paper again, his eyes scanning the article.

"Where'd you say you knew her from?" R.J. asked.

"From Jackson," he said. "We went to high school together."

"Was she always devious?"

Barnett glanced up at him, his eyes laced with disgust. "Devious? No! She's always helpin' people. She may be a heart-breaker, but she ain't a killer."

R.J. and Joe exchanged looks. "She break *your* heart?" R.J. asked.

"Once. Long time ago." He gestured to Joe for another beer. When Joe slid it to him, he guzzled it a little too fast. "Ain't seen her in years."

"Is she what brings you to Newpointe?"

The question didn't amuse or surprise Barnett like R.J. might have expected. "I don't mess with married women. I came for the huntin'."

"She may not be married for long," R.J. said. "Not if Stan dies. And if he wakes up, he'll be smart to cut her loose."

Barnett threw back the second bottle. "Where did you say she was livin'?"

"You gonna get in touch with her?"

"Maybe. Just check on her. Give her some moral support."

"I wouldn't eat anything she fed you, pal. You might wake up dead, too."

The man's face was tense, thoughtful, as if reeling from what he'd just heard. "You don't have her phone number, do you?"

Again, Joe shot R.J. a look.

"Really, man. I need to get in touch with her. It's important. We go way back."

R.J. grinned and Barnett grinned back. Barnett had had enough to drink now that R.J. knew Barnett's talk would come a little more freely.

"Almost married her," Barnett confessed.

R.J.'s grin collapsed, and his eyes grew bigger. "You pullin' my leg?"

"Nope. We were tight."

"Oh, yeah?"

"Yeah."

"So why don't you know her number?"

He chuckled and brought his third bottle to his lips. "Been a while, and I'm new in town."

"So where you stayin', bein' so new to town?"

"Bonaparte Court apartments."

"You work in town?"

"Not yet."

"Then what brings you here?"

The man chuckled. "What are you? A cop?"

They all laughed raucously, and Barnett collapsed at his own humor. Man, he had trouble holding his liquor, R.J. thought. Three drinks and he was practically wasted.

As though the man realized it, he dug out another bill and paid Joe again, then slid off the stool. "It was nice chewing the fat with you two gentlemen," he said, "but I have an appointment."

"An appointment? It's almost dark. What kinda work you do, anyway?"

"Consultin'," he said.

"Consultin' about what?"

"Computers," Barnett said. "I'm a computer consultant. And I never let the clock dictate my hours."

"You stayin' in town for a while?" R.J. asked as he started back to the door.

"Maybe. Maybe not." He saluted them both, then hurried out the door.

R.J. set down his mug and looked at Joe. "I think maybe I need to get back over to the station and check out this fella." He paid his tab and hurried out the door.

Chapter Seventeen

● ● ●

Since she had gotten only a couple hours of sleep the night before, Jill was running on empty by the time she got to Aunt Aggie's house to talk to Celia. Doubts lurked like shadows in her heart, and questions shot through her mind with startling velocity. She sat in Aunt Aggie's pristine parlor, decorated with hundred-year-old antiques, delicate urns and fresh-cut flowers, and hanging plants in front of the large picture window. Celia sat in a Louis XIV chair with her back to the window. She seemed like nothing more than a silhouette against the harsh daylight, and her face captured the contrasting darkness of the room, revealing little. David sat in a matching chair on the other side of a marble-topped table. A small Tiffany lamp provided warm relief from the shadows, lighting one side of each of their faces. Still, it wasn't enough light to read Celia clearly.

"What is it, Jill?" Celia asked in a voice that revealed the fact that she'd spent much of the day crying. "You look almost mad at me. Are you turning on me, too?"

Jill shifted on the sofa and averted her eyes. "I have a few questions, Celia." The words came in a flat, metallic voice, between tight lips.

"Okay," Celia said. "Ask whatever you want. I have nothing to hide."

Jill met her eyes. "Why did you tell me that you were acquitted in the first trial?"

Celia didn't flinch. "I *didn't* tell you that."

Jill opened her mouth to speak, but an irritated, breathy sound escaped before the words did. "Celia, we all assumed it. Me, Sid ... You didn't correct us."

Celia dropped her feet to the floor and sat up straighter. As she leaned forward, her face came out of the shadows, and the colors of the Tiffany lamp gave it warm definition. "Did you use the word *acquittal?*" Celia asked. "I don't think you did. You didn't say anything at all untrue."

"Celia, you knew what I thought."

"Why does it matter?"

"It matters because if you were acquitted of a crime, then any evidence used in that trial is irrelevant in a subsequent trial. If you were charged with Stan's poisoning, the jury has no right to even know that you'd been charged with that before. But when the trial didn't come to a natural conclusion ..."

"Then I must be guilty? Is that it?"

"There's a difference between acquittal, Celia, and being let off on a technicality. The judge could allow that evidence."

Celia breathed a disbelieving laugh and got up. David braced his elbows on his knees and stared down at the floor between his feet. Jill watched Celia walk across the room, her arms crossed. It was a gesture that Jill was accustomed to—a defensive gesture that her clients often used. Especially the guilty ones.

"So what are you saying, Jill? That you don't believe me now that you found out I wasn't acquitted? You think I killed Nathan?"

She took a moment to consider that, then realized that she didn't—couldn't—think that. She just couldn't help being miffed that Celia hadn't been honest with her, and she needed to know the reason she had for hiding details about the case. "No, Celia. That's not it. I believe you're innocent. But you need to understand that you may be arrested for this, and if you are, your life is very much in my hands. I want to do everything in my power to help you. But that means that you have to help.

You can't leave things to my assumptions. You can't let me *think* things and not correct them."

"All right. I messed up! I wasn't thinking."

"You *have* to think, Celia. Your life, and maybe Stan's life, depend on it."

"Leave her alone," David said. "Can't you see she's upset? She's only had a couple of hours' sleep in two days, she's been throwing up, her husband's dying in the hospital—"

"Dying?" Jill asked on a whisper. "Has he taken a turn for the worse?"

"No!" Celia cried, shooting David a venomous look. "David, don't say that. He can't die."

He looked at her helplessly. "I'm just saying . . . you have enough on you without her badgering you like some half-baked criminal."

"She's not badgering me," Celia said, wearily walking back to her chair and sinking into it. "She's doing her job. It's a tough one. I'm sorry, Jill. I'll try to be more honest with you from now on. Please don't give up on me just because I didn't tell you everything."

"It's not me you have to worry about, Celia. Sid thinks he was duped, too. He thinks you were covering up."

"Why would I *do* that? I knew you'd get the trial transcript! I'm not stupid. I just had Stan on my mind, and I was so afraid of going through it all again . . ." She stopped and looked vacantly at the wall behind Jill. In her eyes, Jill saw the emotions struggling and the self-recriminations winning out. "All right, I guess I did know that you thought I was acquitted," she admitted finally, as the light from the lamp caught a tear in her eye. "But as far as I was concerned, I was. The judge dismissed the charges with prejudice. That means they can't try it again. I was off. I wasn't found guilty."

Jill reached into her briefcase and pulled out the transcript, set it in her own lap, and looked down at it. Her head was beginning to throb, and she rubbed her temples with her fingertips. "There's another thing."

"What?"

"Sheree Donolly." Jill looked up at her, gauging her reaction. Celia gave David an "I should have known" look, and he plopped back in his chair. "What about her?" David asked.

Jill kept her eyes on Celia. "Why didn't you tell me that she was having an affair with Nathan, and that the prosecution thought that was your motive for killing him?"

Jill wasn't sure if the red color on Celia's face came from the lamp or from the alarm at hearing that name again.

"Because ..." The word came out just above a whisper. "I don't think it's true."

"What? That they were having an affair? There were witnesses who said you knew about it."

"My husband loved me!" Celia's lips trembled, and she pushed her hair back from her face. "I didn't know about any affair until after he'd died. I still can't believe it, and I don't trust anything she said in that trial. Nathan and I, we had so many plans ... He wouldn't have done that, Jill. It was just a lie they used."

"You should have told me, Celia. Lie or not, I needed to know about it."

"Why? All you need is the truth, Jill. *I didn't do it.*"

Jill watched as Celia collapsed in tears, and David reached across the table and took her hand.

"Sheree and Nathan had a thing before he married Celia," David said. "Some people said it never really ended. That he only married Celia for her money."

Celia's face twisted more, and she turned to David, shaking her head. "It wasn't true, David. He loved me. We were happy."

"I know, Sis," he whispered. "They were," he went on, looking back at Jill. "At first, I kind of thought the rumors might be true, but he changed my mind. He was good to her. Our parents were crazy about him."

Jill didn't like those rumors. "What did you think, David, when you heard those things in the trial? Celia was biased, didn't want to believe them. But what about you?"

He let go of Celia's hand and looked down at his feet again, struggling with his answer.

"I need the truth, David. I know you want to spare Celia's feelings, but we need to cut to the heart of this."

David looked up at her. "I thought it was true. I had even seen him with Sheree a couple of times at the office."

"The office? You worked together?"

"Oh, yeah," he said. "When he married Celia, my dad gave him a position in our company. He was executive vice president of marketing. Couple of times, I stuck my head in his office to tell him something, and Sheree was there. Once I saw him in the car with her in the parking garage, coming back from somewhere."

Celia had heard this before, probably during the trial, so she didn't seem surprised. But she shook her head, denying it all.

"Did he offer any explanations?" Jill asked.

"Oh, yeah. Said she was trying to borrow money from him. He acted like she was bugging him to death, and he couldn't get rid of her. I bought it, at the time. But then, after all the testimony in the trial, I had to wonder."

"They were lies," Celia insisted again. "Why would those things be true, when they lied about my knowing? They said he'd asked me for a divorce just before the murder. That he'd told me about Sheree. That wasn't true. The night before he was murdered, we'd had a romantic dinner in Natchez, and we'd planned a trip to New England when the leaves changed. There wasn't any talk of divorce or another woman. They were all lies, and I won't believe them, when I already know how many other lies were set up in that whole case. Somebody out there wanted them to believe the lies, and they worked very hard to make them all sound believable."

Jill saw from the way Celia dropped her face into her hands and began sobbing that this was even more painful to her client than Jill had thought. She leaned back in her chair, too exhausted to comfort Celia. David sat there awkwardly, as if he wanted to comfort her but didn't know how. Jill wondered how *she* would feel if she found her husband dead, then was accused of murdering him, then learned that he'd been cheating on her? How would she feel if she'd had to spend months in jail, unable to get her own questions answered, unable to find the person who'd really done it?

Wearily, she got up and put her arms around the woman who was her friend, and remembered why she'd wanted to represent her in the first place. It was simple. She knew Celia was innocent.

Stooping in front of her, Jill made Celia look at her. "Celia, you have to tell me everything. But I know you didn't keep these things from me deliberately. The problem is that I'm afraid the police are going to grab this with both hands when they read the transcript. I tried to head it off by giving it to them myself, hoping they'd see that we weren't trying to hide anything. But when Sid gets finished, he's going to come to all the wrong conclusions."

Celia hiccuped a sob. "Oh, if only Stan would wake up. He would tell them. He knows I wouldn't do that. He may even know who did . . . where he ate . . . who he saw . . . maybe something tasted funny . . ." Her voice trailed off, and she covered her face again and shook her head hard. "But he may not even wake up." She rubbed her face and looked up, then touched her stomach and got to her feet. "Oh, no. I'm gonna be sick again."

She ran out to the bathroom, and Jill followed her tentatively. She stood at the bathroom door as Celia threw up. "Are you okay?" she asked after she had finished and was leaning against the wall.

"I guess."

"I think you should see a doctor, Celia. Arsenic or not, something isn't right."

Celia just kept leaning against the wall, but she didn't say anything.

Suddenly, Jill felt bone tired. Too tired to go on with this. Too tired to interpret her own instincts appropriately. "Celia, maybe I'll go by the hospital and check on Stan. But first, is there anything else I need to know? Anything at all?"

"No, Jill. Nothing."

"No more surprises?"

"Of course not." Celia led her out of the bathroom and back into the parlor. David was standing now, staring out the window, and Aunt Aggie had come in from the backyard and was waiting to see if Celia was all right.

Jill went back to the sofa, slid the transcript back into her briefcase, and snapped it shut. "Look, we'll start over in the morning, and maybe we can make some sense of all this. I really could use some sleep."

"Me, too," Celia said.

"Aunt Aggie, make her call the doctor. Something's wrong with her."

"First thing in the mornin'," Aunt Aggie said.

"I'm just gonna go on home after the hospital, okay?" Jill said, finally. "And I'll be here bright and early tomorrow." She looked at David. "Are you staying with them tonight?"

"Yes, why?"

"Because I feel better with a man in the house. We don't know who's out there, or what they want." As she said that, it occurred to her that David, with his slight build, might not be much of a deterrent. Still, his presence gave her some peace of mind.

As she stepped out into the humid night air, she took in a deep breath and wondered how this was going to end up. She hoped Celia didn't get a conviction this time. But Jill just wasn't sure that she was equipped to defend someone against murder.

Chapter Eighteen

● ● ●

The Wednesday night prayer meeting at Calvary Bible Church, which usually consisted only of its core group of active members, was unusually packed tonight. Allie and Mark Branning paused at the door of the fellowship hall, where supper cooked by some of the deacons' wives was being served. Every table was filled to capacity, and some of the teenaged boys were carrying folding chairs in for those in the overflow.

"Good grief." Mark stopped just inside the doorway, scanning the crowd. "I haven't seen some of these people since Easter. Are the children singing tonight?"

Though the children's musicals were always a big crowd sweller, what with all those proud parents and grandparents with their camcorders and cameras, Allie felt sure that wasn't the draw tonight. When there was drama in town, people came to church. It was the central clearinghouse for all of the gossip that had filtered its way from telephone line to telephone line.

Allie saw Dan Nichols sitting at the end of one of the tables with two seats vacant, and when he waved for them to take them, they headed toward him.

"I saved you a couple of seats if you want them," Dan said, running his fingers through his thinning hair. "The crowd really threw a wrench into supper, and the ladies are running around like chickens with their heads cut off back there trying to accommodate everybody. I already ate with Jill."

"We'll just get something later," Allie said, taking her seat next to Dan. "I'm not that hungry, anyway."

"Any word about Stan?"

Mark and Allie shot each other dismal looks before Mark spoke up. "We just came from the hospital. He's still not awake. It worries me. It worries me a lot."

"His parents are exhausted," Allie added. "I don't know how they'll get through this."

"Well, maybe tonight's prayer meeting will help them," Dan said.

"Maybe." She met Mark's eyes, but thankfully, he didn't take the opportunity to shoot Dan's hope down.

The piano on the stage at the far end of the room began to play, and Allie looked up to see Sue Ellen Hanover—the postal clerk—pounding the keys. Nick Foster got up and began leading those who had finished eating in a round of praise choruses. Since he liked to keep prayer meeting comfortable and relaxed, he held that service in the fellowship hall, where people could eat and fellowship among friends before they got down to business.

When they had finished singing the praise choruses, Nick took the microphone and began to read out the names of those who were sick, in the hospital, had special prayer requests, or had asked for intercession for friends or relatives. He seemed to fly through the names, as though he knew that the room hadn't been packed tonight for the usual fare. The fact that there were needy people out there who had requested earnest prayers, only to have them practically glossed over, bothered Allie. Nick had no business catering to the roomful of undevoted people salivating for a morsel of news.

"And now I come to the prayer request so many of you are interested in," the pastor said as if emceeing an awards ceremony. "Stan Shepherd."

The room got deathly quiet, and Nick looked up from his prayer list. His face was vulnerable, soft, and Allie could see the intense concern in his eyes. Maybe she was being too hard on him, she thought. Maybe he'd glossed over the others simply because of his desperate concern for Stan. That was understandable, even forgivable.

"I spoke to Bart and Hannah a couple of hours ago," he said, "and was told there's been no change in Stan's condition. He's still comatose, though they're administering medications to bind the arsenic in his system. When ... if ... he wakes up, there's potential for organ problems—kidney, liver, lungs ... and this was quite possibly a lethal dose of arsenic. And in the case of deadly doses like that, it can act as a carcinogen, so there's the danger of cancer eventually, if he does live."

Allie hadn't realized this, and tears flooded her eyes. Mark, too, seemed to melt beside her, and he set his arm across her shoulders and pulled her closer.

"But obviously, right now, the main concern is that he wake up at all. This coma is really taking its toll on Hannah and Bart. They need our prayers for energy, and strength, and peace. And I'd like to suggest that those of us who can, enter into fasting and deep prayer for Stan. This is really in God's hands." His voice broke, and he made himself go on. "Before we go to the Lord, are there any other prayer requests?"

Allie sat there for a moment as others in the congregation were silent, apparently too moved by the depth of Stan's need to call out any new requests. But she was stunned that no mention had been made of Celia. None at all.

She felt the heat blushing to her face, and awkwardly, she got to her feet. "Nick," she called out to get his attention.

All eyes turned to her.

She took a deep breath and set her hand on her belly. Her heart pounded, and she told herself to calm down. They wouldn't respond to her anger. "Nick, I think we've left someone very important off of the prayer list. Celia Shepherd needs prayers, too. And we need to pray that the would-be killer will be found as soon as possible before he tries this again."

"I heard Celia *was* the killer," Marabeth Simmons, one of the twice-a-year members, called out. "Word's all over town that she killed her first husband the same exact way."

"Still," the postal pianist said in a pious voice, "we should pray for her mental condition, for whatever would have caused her to do such a horrible thing."

A roar went up from the crowd as members discussed with one another what kind of mental condition could lead someone to kill two husbands in a row. Astounded, Allie looked around at her friends, her brothers and sisters in Christ, *Celia's* brothers and sisters in Christ.

"Celia is not crazy, and she did not try to kill Stan!" she shouted over the noise. "You all ought to be ashamed!"

The turmoil in the room died down as everyone grew quiet.

"Are you sayin' it's coincidence?" Marabeth asked. "You think it's just a *accident* that Stan got poisoned just like that first poor man?"

"No, I don't," Allie bit out. "And neither does Celia. There's obviously a killer who's struck twice, but it isn't Celia!"

"I heard they found the arsenic in her bathroom," somebody shouted out.

"That's a lie!" Mark said, springing to his feet. "I was there."

"How come she has all them secrets?" Sue Ellen Hanover asked.

"Would any of you have spilled your guts at your new church if you were trying to escape a year of torment?" Allie asked. "She found refuge here, and she found Christ, and she's ministered in her sweet way to more of you here than I can count!"

"Thank goodness I never ate that casserole she brought me after my gallbladder surgery," Jesse Pruitt said, "or I might be dead, too."

Allie shot a helpless, astounded look to Nick, and she saw the look on his face that he wore whenever he felt he'd failed. It was warranted, she thought. He *had* failed, and her look indicted him.

Nick finally tapped the microphone. "All right, all right. Let's calm down. We can't let our prayer meeting turn into a gossip session. The fact remains that both Celia and Stan, as well as Hannah and Bart, are part of our family. We need to love and pray for all of them."

Allie sank back down, her heart hammering. Mark took her hand. She saw from the way he looked up at Nick that he, too, was disappointed that their shepherd hadn't done a better job of defending one of their wounded sheep.

"He thinks she's guilty," Mark whispered. "He's buying it with all the rest of them."

"Poor Celia," Dan whispered.

As Nick began to lead them in prayer, Allie had the disturbing sensation that the Holy Spirit was nowhere near.

She only hoped he was watching over Celia.

Chapter Nineteen

● ● ●

Sid rubbed his raw eyes as he read the last page of the trial transcript Jill had given him. Man, he thought, leaning back hard in his chair. If he'd had any hope before that Celia was not the killer, the transcript dashed it. In the first trial, she'd had a motive, she'd had the arsenic in her possession in the form of rat poison, she'd confessed in her computer journal ... What else did anybody need?

But if they charged her with this crime, they needed probable cause. What motive would she have for killing Stan? Being looney didn't seem to be a good enough motive. But he was sure if he looked hard enough, he'd find something. The motive always surfaced eventually.

He set his elbows on his desk and rubbed his eyes, wishing it was two strangers whose lives he was investigating, instead of his best friend and his friend's wife.

He thought of all the time he'd spent with Celia at church, all the Sunday school classes and Bible studies they'd shared, all the insights she'd offered into the mind and heart of God. He'd never had any inkling that she wasn't as she seemed, or that lurking beneath that sweet exterior was an unstable woman.

But no one had suspected Judas, either, before he'd betrayed Christ. Even when Jesus told them that one of them would betray him, no one said, "It's gotta be Judas." Instead, they pointed to themselves, and asked, "Is it me, Lord?"

He had to remember that Celia *wasn't* as she seemed. She had a past, and she had secrets, and those secrets were stacked one inside another like those little dolls that got smaller and smaller. Except her secrets got bigger instead of smaller.

"Hey, Sid," LaTonya Mason called from across the room. "I verified that info on Lee Barnett." He looked up to see the rookie cop he'd put on the case. "It's true. He got out twelve days ago. Served his full term. I tracked down his mama in Jackson, but didn't get a answer. I'll try again later."

"Okay," Sid said. "Let me know what you find out. Did you do a rap sheet on him?"

"Yep. Had a coupla DWIs, and then the manslaughter charge."

Lost in thought, Sid hardly noticed when R.J. burst through the glass door. He was out of uniform since he'd finally gone off duty, and as he bounced to Sid's desk and pulled a chair up, Sid smelled the alcohol on his breath. "Man, somethin' just happened at Joe's Place, and I don't know if it means nothin', but I thought I'd tell you."

"What?"

"There was this guy in there spoutin' off about his relationship with Celia Shepherd. Claims they used to be an item. Had a little too much to drink, and told us he'd just got to town, got him an apartment, and kept askin' us where Celia was, if we had her phone number, that kind of thing."

Sid sat up straighter and narrowed his eyes. "Yeah?"

"Yeah. And I tried to get at why he's in town, and he said he was here for the huntin'. Then he said somethin' about bein' a computer consultant. Just kept wantin' to know where Celia was, like he had to see her."

Sid stared at him, the first bud of hope beginning to blossom in his heart. Could this stranger, rather than Celia, have poisoned Stan? "Did he know about the poisonin'?"

"It was right there in the paper in front of him. Seemed genuinely surprised, but it coulda been a act. I couldn't say for sure."

"Did you get his name?"

"Sure did," R.J. said. "And I was gonna run a check on him. Name's Lee Barnett."

Sid's jaw fell open. "Are you sure?"

"Yeah, why?"

He scraped his chair back and stood up. "Only because Lee Barnett just got out of prison a coupla weeks ago, and he was questioned in the murder of Celia's first husband. You don't happen to know where he's stayin', do you?"

"Sure. He said he has an apartment over at Bonaparte Court."

Sid grabbed his keys and almost knocked his chair over.

"Where ya goin', man?"

"To pick up Mr. Barnett," Sid said. "I got a few questions to ask him."

••••

Sid knocked on Marabeth Simmons's door at the Bonaparte Court apartments, for he knew no one would be in the office at this hour. He knew she would tell him where Lee Barnett's apartment was. There was very little that Marabeth could keep to herself, especially if she thought it was part of a police investigation.

She answered the door wearing a velveteen robe with fake fur around the collar. "Hey, there, Sid," she said.

"Hey, Marabeth. I'm here on police business. I need to know which apartment Lee Barnett is in. Do you know him?"

"Well, sure I know him," she said. "Cute as the dickens, if you don't mind my sayin' so. He ain't done nothin' wrong now, has he?"

"I don't know," Sid said. "Which apartment, Marabeth?"

"Well, he's in apartment B–5. Right up yonder." She pointed toward the man's door. Sid headed for the stairs.

"Are you gonna arrest him?" Marabeth asked. "I thought somethin' was funny about him. I was tellin' Sue Ellen over to the post office that it struck me odd that a man wouldn't know if his own apartment was furnished or not, but it takes all kinds. Don't reckon that's against any laws, though."

"No, ma'am."

"So . . . did he break some other law? Is that what you want with him?"

Sid started up the steps, and Vern Hargis—another officer who'd just pulled up in his squad car—followed him. "Thanks for your help, Marabeth."

She looked deflated that she hadn't gotten anything for the grapevine. But he didn't kid himself that she'd gone back into her apartment. He would have bet money that she was eavesdropping under the stairwell.

They went to the man's front door. There was a light on, so he hoped Barnett was home. He knocked hard.

After a moment, he heard him yelling, "I'm comin'!"

He answered so quickly that Sid thought he must have been expecting someone else. His expression crashed when he opened the door and saw the two cops. Sid wondered who he was waiting for.

"Yes?" he asked.

"Are you Lee Barnett?"

He hesitated. "Why?"

"I'm Lieutenant Sid Ford," Sid told him. "And this is Sergeant Vern Hargis. We need to ask you a few questions."

The man looked aggravated and crossed his arms with disgust. "Look, I served my time. I got out, fair and square. I ain't done anything wrong. I haven't had *time* to do anything wrong. What in the world would you have to ask me about?"

"We need to ask you about the murder attempt on Stan Shepherd's life."

His mouth fell open, and he rubbed the back of his neck as his face reddened. "Wait a minute." He took a moment to calm himself, then tried to speak again. "Look, I've never met the man. I've only heard his name. I didn't even know about the poisoning until I read it in the paper tonight."

He stepped back from the door, as if inviting them in. They went in, looked around. From the small living room, Sid could see into the bedroom. The bed was bare—no sheets or any- thing—and a suitcase lay open on the floor.

"I just got here today. Haven't had time to unpack or . . . buy sheets . . ." His voice seemed to trail off the further he got into the sentence. "Look, I got nothin' to hide."

"Then you won't mind coming down to the station with us so we can ask you a few questions," Sid suggested.

He breathed a nervous laugh. "Why can't you ask me here?"

"We'd rather take you to the station. It could take a while."

"Look, I don't *know* anything about the poisoning. Am I under arrest?"

"No, not at all. We'd appreciate your cooperation." As he spoke, Sid stepped over to the kitchen, glanced in. It didn't look like Barnett had even crossed the threshold.

"Is this your offhanded way of searching my apartment for somethin'?"

Sid turned back to him. "Searchin'? No, we ain't searchin'. You invited us in, remember? And now we're invitin' you down to the station."

He started to object, then stopped himself and seemed to think better of it. "All right," he said finally. "Let's go."

On the way to the police station, Sid glanced at the man in the backseat of his squad car and prayed silently that he held answers they needed. If he was the one who'd poisoned Stan, then Celia was off the hook. There was nothing Sid would like better. He would gladly eat crow and make his sincere apologies.

They reached the station, and he walked the man in. He was being amazingly cooperative, as if he feared what they might do to him. Sometimes, guilty people were too friendly, too cooperative, as if they thought their congenial manner would convince police there was no way such an upstanding citizen would break the law.

It didn't fly with Sid.

He led Lee Barnett into the interrogation room and offered him a chair. "Have a seat, Mr. Barnett. Can I get you anything? Coke? Coffee?"

"Coffee would be nice," he said. "I'm sure you know I ain't been out of prison long. Five years without alcohol, so the three beers I had tonight went straight to my head. I used to hold it better ..." His voice trailed off, as if he knew he was rambling.

Vern headed out to get the coffee for him. Sid took a seat across from him, surveying the man who looked clean-cut, not at all like an ex-con. He must have gotten his hair cut first thing, he thought. A new set of clothes, new shoes.

"So what do you want to ask me?" Barnett asked when Vern brought him his coffee. He busied himself mixing in the sugar and cream that Vern had brought in little packets, but his hands trembled as he did. "You said it was about the murder attempt. I'll say again, I don't know Stan Shepherd. I never laid eyes on him."

"But you do know Celia."

"Sure. But I ain't seen her in years."

"Then what brings you to Newpointe twelve days after your release?"

He could see the struggle on the man's face. There was something to that, but Sid wasn't sure they'd get at the truth.

"I'd heard it was a nice place. I wanted to do some huntin' outside of town."

"Did you know Celia lived here?"

"Yeah. I'd heard somethin' about it. But I knew she was married."

Sid shifted in his seat. "Mr. Barnett, what were you doing yesterday?"

Barnett frowned, as if trying to figure out where they were going with this. "I was at my mama's house. That's where I been stayin'. I been veggin' out watchin' videos and enjoyin' not havin' a schedule. We didn't have TVs in there, 'cause the governor took 'em outa the jails. I had a lot of catchin' up to do."

"Was anyone there besides your mother and you?"

"Yeah, my sister took the day off work and came by, and my little niece . . . and a neighbor of my mama's came by for lunch." He looked from Sid to Vern. "Why? You need them to verify my alibi? 'Cause they will. Only I don't like gettin' my mama all crazy worryin' that her son's broke the law again. She didn't deserve it the first time. It like to killed her."

Sid made a notation on his legal pad but didn't respond to Barnett's question. "Did you leave her house at any time yesterday?"

"I went to Wal-mart and bought a couple of shirts and a new pair of jeans."

"Anybody with you?"

"No. I went alone."

"Did you, at any time yesterday, see or talk to Stan Shepherd?"

He sat back hard in his chair and stared at them as the wheels seemed to turn in his head. "I just told you. I've never seen him before. I've also never spoken to him. I wouldn't know him if he spit in my face. Besides, I was in Jackson. I can prove it. I couldn't possibly have made it to Newpointe to poison some guy and then back to Jackson in the time I spent at Wal-mart."

Sid told himself that the man could be playing innocent, pretending he didn't know that Stan had been to Jackson yesterday. "Did you talk to anyone in particular at Wal-mart who might remember seeing you there?"

The stunned look on Barnett's face told Sid that he was getting the picture. He had to realize that they were pursuing this line of questioning because they considered him a suspect. Barnett shifted in his seat, cleared his throat, rubbed his hand across the stubble on his jaw. "You people think I did it, don't you?" He leaned forward on the table, his eyes riveted into Sid's. "Why would I do that? After waitin' five years to get back into the world, why would I jeopardize everything and risk get-tin' thrown back in?"

"You tell us."

"I don't believe this." He rubbed his face, thinking, and Sid watched as he seemed to search his mind for something. "I think I get it." He was breathing harder, and his face was red-dening. "Yeah, I'm gettin' it now."

"What do you mean?" Sid asked.

"I think I've been had." His lips compressed, and he shifted in his seat. "Yeah, I'm sure of it."

The man was trembling as he leaned up on the table and slapped his hand on it. "Monday, the day before I'm released, I'm sittin' there mindin' my own business, when I'm told the chaplain wants to see me. So I go down to the chapel, and she tells me that some priest dropped a letter by for her to give me. And guess who it's from?"

Now they were getting somewhere, Sid thought, bracing himself. "Who?"

"Celia Shepherd." He reached into his back pocket and pulled out his wallet. "I've got it right here. You'll see." He reached into the billfold and retrieved the folded letter. His hands continued to tremble as he unfolded it. "Oh, man. It was all too good to be true. There I was thinkin' that maybe she was unhappily married and had been thinkin' about me. I had this fantasy of my comin' here and her wantin' to resume things after all these years . . . Rich little Celia Bradford . . ."

He pushed the computer printed letter across the table, and Sid read it. His heart plummeted. That knot in his stomach tightened. He handed the letter to Vern.

Barnett's face was getting redder, and through his teeth, he said, "Man, she lured me here so I'd look like the suspi-cious one, so I'd take the heat. What is my life worth, right? Just pin me with it, and she gets off scot-free. Man, I didn't do it. I ain't even heard from her in years. Not a word. And then this."

Sid looked up, not sure if he was being conned. "Where's the check mentioned in the letter?"

"I cashed it, man. It was right where the priest said it was. In the locker at the bus station. Right combination, everything."

"And this priest. Who was he?"

"You know as much as I do. The letter's signed 'Father Edmund Mueller.' Must be at one of the Catholic churches here, I guess. I never saw the guy."

Sid ran the facts through his mind. Lee Barnett had been too quick to turn this back on Celia. Was it fact, or was the truth somewhere between what he'd thought and what Barnett was telling him? Maybe Barnett wasn't the killer, but he wasn't the innocent saint, either.

"You mentioned your fantasy about Celia resumin' things. You knew she was married. Was you plannin' to have an affair with her?"

Barnett turned his palms up. "Hey, I figured I'd take her any way I could get her. I ain't exactly in the position to make moral judgments after where I've been. But I didn't see her. I just took the bait and came, and I ain't heard from her yet. I couldn't figure out why she'd want me here, in Newpointe, unless she wanted to start somethin' up with me. But now I gotta say, I think it was because she'd been plannin' this. Probably waited till my time was up. She wanted me to be here, so it would look like I blew into town to poison him. I don't believe it! What did I ever do to her to deserve this?"

A while later, Sid left the interrogation room and went to do as much checking as he could to verify the things Barnett had said. The letter was typed and could have been written by anyone trying to set Celia up, but the personal check was a little more difficult to explain. He found LaTonya Mason and got her to try to get a copy of the check from the bank, while he called Marabeth Simmons to find out who came in to rent the apartment.

"Paula Bouchillon, the owner, done it all by phone on my day off," she said. "She told me she talked to Mr. Barnett on the phone two weeks ago and that he mailed the deposit in and said he'd come by when he got here and sign the lease, which he did."

That wasn't likely, Sid thought. Two weeks ago, Lee Barnett was in jail. "Tell me about the deposit. Did he send cash, a money order, what?"

"A check, I think," she said. "Let's see. I ain't deposited it yet. No, it's right here, with a copy of the lease."

Sid's heartbeat accelerated. "Whose name is on that check, Marabeth?"

He heard papers rustling, then she whispered, "Oh, glory be! You're not gon' believe this, Sid. Oh, my. Wait till I tell Sue Ellen. Even Simone won't believe this."

"What?" Sid asked. "Marabeth!"

"The check, Sid, is on Stan and Celia Shepherd's account. I can't believe I didn't see that before, but Paula give it to me to deposit just today, and I never looked at it. What does this mean, Sid? It's somethin' to do with the poisonin', ain't it?"

Sid wiped the perspiration on his forehead and was careful not to answer her question. "Look, I'm fixin' to send an officer over right away to pick up that check. Do me a favor and put it in an envelope, and give it to the officer, okay?"

"All right, but . . . Will we get it back?"

"I'm not sure, ma'am. But that check could be important evidence. We've got to have it."

He hung up the phone before she could ask anything else and called the dispatcher, knowing that she, too, was a live wire on the Newpointe gossip lines. "Simone, I need for the officer who's closest to the Bonaparte Court apartments to go by the office there and get an envelope for me from Marabeth. I need it ASAP."

While he held, she dispatched an officer to do what she'd been told, then she came back to the phone. "Sid, what's going on? Is this about Stan?"

"Just part of the investigation, Simone. When we solve the case, you'll be the first to know."

"Do you still suspect Celia?"

"Bye, Simone." He hung up, and dropped his face into his hands. What was going on? Had Celia faked a man's voice to secure the apartment, or more likely, had Lee Barnett had access to a phone somewhere in the prison? They were allowed to make phone calls from time to time, he knew. It was, at least, possible. If he and Celia had something going, maybe he had made the call, and she had sent the check. The average person couldn't fake a bank account. At least, not from prison.

It wasn't more than fifteen minutes before T.J. Porter came in brandishing the envelope. "This what you needed, Sid?"

"Yeah, thanks." He opened it and pulled out the check. Just as she'd said, it bore the names "Stan or Celia Shepherd." In the right bottom corner was Celia's signature. He rubbed his eyes, wishing from his heart that it wasn't so.

"What's going on?" T.J. asked.

"Just more pieces to the puzzle."

"What puzzle?"

"The puzzle of Celia Shepherd. Who is she, T.J.? *What* is she?"

"I heard you'd brought somebody new in for questioning. Find out anything?"

Sid took in a deep breath. "I'm not sure yet," he said. "He wants us to think he's a Boy Scout who's in the wrong place at the wrong time. But I don't think so."

"What *do* you think?"

"I think he's a possible suspect . . . but more likely, he's Celia Shepherd's motive."

Chapter Twenty

• • •

The police chief was livid when he saw the check with Celia's signature. "I can't believe this!" Jim Shoemaker said. "All this time, I was thinking we'd made a mistake. That any minute now we'd turn up evidence that would exonerate her. But it gets smellier and smellier. A boyfriend, that check, her past . . . It all adds up to Celia Shepherd being a killer." He slammed the side of his fist into a file cabinet with a clash, then swung around. "Look, I don't want us dragging our feet on this. If Celia's the killer, let's nail her. Get a warrant to search her house again, and find whatever evidence you can. Last night you were just trying to find what had made Stan sick. This time you're collecting evidence for the grand jury."

Sid leaned back hard in his chair. "What if we're wrong? What if there really is another killer out there—maybe even Lee Barnett—and Celia's innocent?"

Jim's eyes bore into him. "Do you think she is?"

"No."

"Then let's not waste our time chasing rabbits. My experience tells me you look at the most obvious first. Celia's the most obvious suspect. If she's guilty, something in that house will tell us so."

Sid left his office and radioed for one of the squad cars to come and pick him up. Chad Avery was the first to arrive. "Where we going?" he asked as Sid got in.

"To the Shepherd house. We have to search it again."

"You got a warrant?"

"I'm stopping by Judge DeLacy's office on the way." He radioed Simone and asked her to dispatch one more evidence technician to the Shepherd house.

"We gonna be pawing through food and upchuck again?" Chad asked when he cut the radio off.

"No. This time we're lookin' for somethin' even more substantial. Somethin' that'll tell us, once and for all, that Celia Shepherd intended to kill her husband."

Chapter Twenty-One

● ● ●

The condition of the Shepherd's house was just as they'd left it in the wee hours of the morning. Sid Ford looked around at the kitchen, cluttered with food containers and zip-lock bags that the police themselves had left out. "We've already done a pretty thorough search through the food," Sid told the three cops with him. "This time, we're lookin' for anything that has arsenic in it. Rat poison, bug spray, whatever we can find. Chad, you take the attic. Vern and T.J., you take the garage and the utility room, then search the rest of the house with me, under sinks, in cabinets . . . I'll concentrate on the laundry room. It's not a big house, so we can lick this pretty quick if we try. Remember, whatever you find, let me know. If it's the slightest bit suspicious, it's relevant."

They dispersed to their assignment areas, and Sid began to remove the contents of the cabinets in the laundry room one by one. He checked the ingredients of each box of detergent, smelling and feeling to make sure it was what it claimed to be. Because the laundry room was only large enough to hold the washer and dryer and a cabinet overhead, he finished quickly.

He went into the bedroom and saw the bed still unmade, and Celia's robe and pajamas in a heap on her closet floor, where she'd changed clothes quickly in hopes of flying to Slidell with Stan. He went to the closet, searched the floor, and saw only a few pairs of shoes. Standing, he checked the top shelf, and saw several white shirt boxes stacked there. He pulled one down and looked inside.

A baby's knitted sweater with matching booties and blanket were folded there. Lying on top of the little clothes was a pacifier with a ribbon and clip attached. Sid frowned. Were these for a baby gift? He could think of several church friends who were pregnant, including Allie Branning. It could have been intended for any of them. He set the box back in its place and reached for the next box. This time, he pulled out an expensive white christening gown with the price tag still attached. Unusual, he thought, for Celia to give such an extravagant gift.

He groped for the bag behind the boxes and looked inside. Several rolls of yarn the color of the knitted sweater were there, along with knitting needles and several other craft items he couldn't identify. Celia had knitted the sweater, booties, and blanket herself. He whistled under his breath. It was an odd paradox, he thought, that someone caring enough to knit an entire set like that for a friend would also be a killer.

Then he realized that the baby clothes might not be for a friend at all. Maybe they had been for her. If so, if she and Stan were planning to have a baby, why would she want to kill her husband?

Troubled, he put the bag back, restacked the boxes, and stared at them for a moment. It didn't add up. But he'd seen things that didn't add up before. Crazy people did crazy things for crazy reasons.

"Sid, I got somethin'!"

Chad's voice was coming from the attic stairs in the hallway, and Sid dashed toward it. "Whatcha got, Chad?"

"Just what we were lookin' for," Chad said victoriously, and brandished a box of rat poison.

Sid felt the blood flushing from his brown face, and he rubbed his jaw roughly. As much as he'd wanted evidence, the right evidence to convict Celia if she was guilty, he realized now that, in the back of his mind, he had wanted to find something, instead, that would prove to him that she wasn't the culprit. But the evidence was there.

With his gloved hands, he took the box from Chad and examined the ingredients. Arsenic trioxide was one of the first ones listed.

"That's it," he said in a dull voice. "The smokin' gun. Man, why would she do it?"

Chad looked as thrilled as if he'd just solved the Hoffa mystery. "Anybody else find anything?"

"Not yet."

Sid bagged the poison, and kept staring at it, trying to picture a scenario in which Celia would spoon this into Stan's food, then hide it in the attic. As clear as it was, it still didn't add up.

"What is it?" Chad asked.

Sid shrugged. "Nothin'. Just thinkin' how I hate this job sometimes."

"Not me," Chad said. "When things come t'gether like this, 'at's when I know I couldn't do nothin' else."

Chapter Twenty-Two

● ● ●

Since Mark and Allie had not eaten at church, as they usually did on Wednesday nights, they went to Maison de Manger and ordered sandwiches. Though the place was nothing more than a deli, it was decorated like a Bourbon Street bistro. Jazz music was piped in, and on the walls were photos of Louis Armstrong and various other jazz greats with whom the owner, Eddie Neubig, had once shared an acquaintance. It was Allie's favorite place because of the crawfish popcorn she could get as an appetizer, something she craved in the wee hours of morning.

They had invited Dan to join them, and he had seemed inclined to come with them, even though he'd already eaten, when he got a beep from Jill. He had gone to call her, so Mark and Allie had gone ahead to the restaurant.

Allie was finishing off her coveted crawfish popcorn when Dan and Jill came in together. Jill looked as if she'd gone days without sleep, but she was holding Dan's hand. Allie wasn't sure she'd ever seen Dan hold a woman's hand before. He'd once told her that he didn't like to date a woman over three times, because after that she thought of them as a couple. Allie had asked him how he'd ever get to be a couple with anyone if he cut it off at three dates. He'd grinned and said that was the idea.

She realized that he and Jill were long past three dates, unless he was creative with his counting and didn't consider something like this a real date. The fact that he held her hand seemed a monumental breach of the distance Dan so arrogantly liked to keep. She didn't know what Jill was doing, but it was apparently the right thing. Maybe it was the fact that she was so busy and often so unavailable. The challenge. Maybe Dan needed to be kept on his toes that way.

"Sorry I look like I've been drugged," Jill said, dropping into the booth and sliding over. "But I wanted to see you guys. Dan told me about prayer meeting. Thanks for standing up for Celia, Allie."

"How is she?" Allie asked as Dan slipped in beside Jill.

"Not good. Her brother is with her, which cheered her up some. But she's still not feeling very well. I'm afraid the doctors overlooked something that could be wrong with her in an attempt to rule out arsenic. And of course, she's miserably depressed and sick with worry about Stan."

"He's still not awake," Dan said. "I got his mother on the phone, and she sounded really discouraged."

The bell on the front door jingled as the door swung open again, and R.J. Albright, in his tent-sized uniform, came in and went to the bar to place his order. He glanced behind him and saw the four of them sitting there. He waved, quickly placed his order, then ambled across the room toward them.

"Slow night?" Mark asked him.

R.J. chuckled. "Hardly. I'm just now gettin' to supper."

"Oh, yeah?" Dan asked. "Something going on tonight?"

It was a common question among emergency personnel. No one ever wanted to miss anything big.

"We just searched the Shepherd house again," R.J. said. He saw Jill bristling, and said, "We had a warrant, Counselor."

"Well, I hope you're satisfied now that she didn't do it. There was no arsenic anywhere in that house, was there?"

R.J. grinned as if he had a secret that he couldn't tell. "I wouldn't say that," he said.

Her face changed as she gaped up at him. "Then what *would* you say?"

"I'd probably be better off not to say nothin'," he told her.

Jill's face was beginning to turn red. "R.J., I'm Celia's attorney. I have a right to know what you think you found."

"Talk to Sid, Jill," he said. "He's headin' up this investigation. I ain't sayin' no more."

He turned and waddled back between the tables, and for a moment, Allie thought she saw Jill's heart pumping through her shirt. "Excuse me," Jill said. "I have to make a phone call."

Dan got up and let her slide out, and she hurried out the door into the night.

"What do you think they found?" Mark asked Dan.

"Who knows?"

They waited quietly, perusing the menu with their minds on that conversation with R.J., while they waited for Jill to come back in.

Out in the privacy of her car, Jill dialed the police station and got Sid Ford's desk.

"Ford," he answered quickly.

"Sid, this is Jill Clark," she said. "I understand you searched the Shepherd house tonight."

There was a slight pause. "How'd you know?"

"What did you find?" she shot back.

Again, a pause.

"Sid, so help me . . ."

"We found arsenic hid in the attic, Jill."

Her heart lurched. "In what form?"

"Rat poison," he said.

"So maybe they had mice!"

"Maybe, and I'm sure you'll make it your life's work to prove they did. But we found what we were lookin' for, Jill. Evidence. And that ain't all of it. That Lee Barnett fellow you asked me to check on? Seems he just turned up in Newpointe. Moved into the Bonaparte Court apartments. And guess who paid the deposit and the first month's rent?"

"Who?"

"Celia."

"No," Jill said. "There must be some mistake."

"No mistake, Jill. Y'ask me, your client's got some explainin' to do. You should know that we're tryin' to get a warrant right now, Jill. We got no choice but to arrest her."

"Sid, there's a killer out there laughing at how stupid you guys are!"

"All right, Jill, that's enough."

"You're right! It is enough!"

"Hey, I didn't have to tell you. You oughta be thankin' me."

She clicked off the phone and flung it across her car, screaming with frustration. How was she going to tell Celia? She wasn't sure, but she knew that she had to tell her before the police showed up to arrest her.

Feeling even more drained than before, she went back into the deli. Dan, Mark, and Allie all looked hopefully up at her. Dan slid over, and she plopped into the booth.

"Celia's about to be arrested," she said, "so I've got to get over there."

"Oh, no." Allie's face became as pale as Jill imagined hers was.

Mark and Dan stared at each other across the table.

Finally, Dan spoke. "Jill, why? Have they found more evidence?"

"Looks that way."

"They found arsenic, didn't they? That's what R.J. was hinting at, wasn't it?"

She didn't answer. "This is Celia we're talking about. There's some explanation."

"What?" Dan asked. "I mean, her first husband is dead of the same thing; there was enough evidence to indict her for it the first time—"

"An indictment is not a conviction," Jill said through her teeth, her face turning red. "She wasn't convicted, and no one has the right to try her right here in Maison de Manger because of a box of rat poison that may have been there before she and Stan even bought the stupid house!"

"Is that what she said?"

"I haven't talked to her about it." She slid out of the booth. "I've got to go."

"Hey, come on," Mark said. "Dan didn't mean—"

"I can speak for myself," Dan cut in, irritated. "Jill knows I don't think Celia did it. All I meant was that people will think she did."

"You know what?" Jill bit out. "I'm going to prove all of them wrong, and when I'm finished, I'm not sure if Celia and Stan can go on living in this town. Celia will want to go where she can depend on people, and Stan won't want to be around people who think so little of his wife."

"Hey, calm down. You're strung a little too tight right now, acting like *we're* the enemy."

"You're right," she snapped. "I'm sorry. Just ... I've gotta go."

And as they stared after her, she rushed out to her car.

"Go after her," Allie told Dan as the door closed behind her.

Dan shook his head. "No way. I didn't do anything wrong."

"She's just tense and upset," Allie said. "This whole thing is on her shoulders."

Dan muttered, "You ask me, Stan's the one we ought to be feeling sorry for. Not Jill."

"Chill out, Dan," Mark said. "I know she ticked you off, but it's not worth ruining the whole relationship over."

"What relationship?" Dan asked.

Mark gaped at Allie. *"What relationship?"* Allie repeated. "Dan, don't give us that. You've broken your three-date limit with her, and you know it."

"There you go," he said. "You take someone out more than three times, everybody assumes you're a couple. Well, we're *not* a couple. I'm still a free agent. A *happy* free agent!"

"Seem real happy to me," Mark observed.

"I'm going home," Dan said, disgusted, and slipped out of the booth.

Allie and Mark just looked at each other as he slammed out of the cafe.

Chapter Twenty-Three

● ● ●

The doorbell didn't surprise Celia, for the local reporters had been trying to get a statement all day. "I might have to get out my rifle," Aunt Aggie said as she got up and scurried to the front window to peer out into the darkness. Celia looked over her shoulder and saw Jill standing under the porch light. Quickly, she opened the door.

Jill was pale, tired-looking, and heavy tension lined her face. Celia stood aside to let her in. "Jill, what's wrong?"

Jill hesitated, stared at the floor for a moment, then wearily met Celia's eyes. "I'm sorry to hit you with this so late, Celia, but there have been a few developments in the case you should know about."

"There have?" Celia asked hopefully. "What?"

Jill sat down on the chair in the foyer and rubbed her eyes. She hadn't had time to apply makeup this morning, and her eyes were red and bloodshot. "Tell me about Lee Barnett."

Celia frowned. "What about him?"

"When's the last time you spoke to him?"

She shrugged. "Years. He's in jail. Killed a man in a barroom brawl."

Jill was watching her, as if evaluating her for the truth, and Celia wondered why. What could Lee Barnett possibly have to do with any of this? "He got out a couple of weeks ago," she said. "And he's in town."

"In Newpointe?" Celia asked. "Why would he come here when he just got out of prison?"

"To be close to you."

Celia's eyes narrowed and she took a step backward. "Wait. *What?* No, that's impossible. He doesn't care anything about me."

"How do you know?"

"Well, why should he? I hadn't talked to him for a year or more even *before* he went to jail."

"He called the house, though." David had heard the exchange from the kitchen and came into the foyer now, dropping the statement like a lead ball that seemed to roll around in front of them.

"When?" Jill asked.

"Several times from jail. Asked for Celia, and I told him she didn't live there anymore."

Celia gaped at her brother. "You never told me that."

"I forgot about it. I knew you didn't want to talk to him."

Celia looked troubled as she turned her eyes back to Jill. "So he got out just days before Stan was poisoned, and he came here to Newpointe? Jill, you don't think *he* poisoned Stan?"

Jill obviously didn't know what to think. "You've got to admit, Celia, that it's an awfully convincing coincidence."

"So, did the police question him?"

"Oh, yeah. Then promptly let him go."

"Let him go?" David asked. "Why would they do that?"

"Because they aren't convinced he's a suspect. They think, instead, that he was Celia's motive."

"My *what?* Where did they get that?"

"The letter."

Celia could see that Jill was watching her eyes for some reaction, waiting for a sign of guilt. But Celia was clueless. She had no idea what Jill was talking about.

"What letter?"

"The one that he claims you wrote him, telling him you rented him an apartment at Bonaparte Court and that you wanted him to come here."

Celia could feel the blood draining out of her face. She struggled for the right words, but realized she needed to sit down. "Jill, you don't really believe that I wrote a letter like that ..."

"I don't, Celia, but the police aren't so sure. And then there's the matter of the two checks written on your bank account. One written to him, and one to the apartment manager."

"No! I didn't write those checks." She got up and paced across the floor, thinking. Suddenly, she swung around to Jill. "Our checkbook disappeared a couple of weeks ago. We thought we had misplaced it, so we just started with the next set we had in the box. Stan always kept it above the visor in his car, but it was just gone. Whoever poisoned Stan must have taken it!"

Jill sighed. "Celia, they searched your house tonight."

"Again?" Her nausea reasserted itself.

"Yes." Jill's answer was clipped and matter-of-fact. "And I might as well just get it all out. They found something in your attic, Celia."

"What?" she asked. "All we've got up there is junk, old clothes, stuff like that. What did they find?"

"Rat poison," Jill said. "The main ingredient was arsenic."

Celia shook her head and began backing away. "No. That was not in my house. We've never had a problem with mice. Why would we have rat poison?"

"Celia, I thought maybe the previous owners had left it there, but I talked to Sid and he said that it was a new box. It hadn't even collected dust."

"No!" she shouted, steadying herself. "He's doing it again. He's setting me up! Just like last time with the ... the journal entries ... the computer ... the arsenic they found that time ..." She turned to the wall and covered her head, as if she could protect herself from the cruel onslaught. "This can't be. We didn't have arsenic in my attic, Jill. I would have seen it. I would have known, and I wouldn't want that anywhere near my house!" She swung around and gaped at Jill with helpless, hopeless eyes. "Jill, you believe me, don't you? He hasn't gotten you convinced, too, has he?"

"Of course I believe you," she said, but Celia could see the doubt in her face.

"What about you, David?" Celia asked hopelessly. "Mom and Dad won't believe me, but you do, don't you?"

"Absolutely," he said.

"And Aunt Aggie? I'd die if you didn't believe me. I know the evidence looks bad, but—"

"I don't care about no evidence," she said. "Don't now, didn't then. I know my niece ain't no liar."

"Then what do we do?" Celia asked, wiping her face. "We have to start with the checks and the letter. It *can't* be my handwriting. If it looks like it, it must be forged."

"The only handwriting is your signature on the checks. The letter was typed."

"Well, see? Anybody could have written it! And the check could have been forged! If someone stole my checkbook, it wouldn't be that hard. All they'd need is my signature on something else, and they could copy it. They have to start by looking for my checkbook. Whoever has it is the one."

Jill got up and began pacing across the floor. "Celia, they're getting a warrant. They're going to arrest you tonight."

She turned back to Jill and shook her head frantically. "No. They can't. Not with those photographers out there. Everyone will know." She covered her mouth and took a deep breath. "No, I've got to go there myself. Turn myself in, so they won't have to come after me. Maybe ... maybe the judge will go easier on me, let me out on bond, if I do that."

Jill nodded. "We can do that."

"All right," she said, wiping her face with trembling hands. "Then let's do it."

Chapter Twenty-Four

● ● ●

Judge Louis DeLacy was a deacon in the Calvary Bible Church, the same church where Jill and Celia were members. Everyone in the congregation called him Louis, because he thought of himself as just another member of the Body, no greater than anyone else just because of the power the city had wielded him. But more important than that was the calling God had given him, the calling to mete out punishments to those who chose not to abide by the law. Normally, his job was fulfilling—satisfying, even, for he'd been responsible for keeping a number of drug dealers off the streets, disciplining drunk drivers no matter who they were, and putting away thieves and vandals.

But he couldn't remember a day when he'd dreaded his job more than today. He had been prepared for Celia's case when he'd arrived in his chambers this morning. He'd heard about Stan's hospitalization yesterday, but when he'd learned that Celia was a suspect, he'd felt sick. Both Stan and Celia were good friends, and he thought a great deal of her. She had worked alongside him to build a Habitat House for a needy family last year after their trailer had burned, and she had served on a committee that he led to raise money for a new organ. He'd had dinner at their house several times, whether alone or as part of a Sunday school class, and he'd attended Promise Keepers rallies nearly every year with Stan.

The thought that Celia would be considered a suspect for attempted murder was beyond his comprehension. Still, as Jill brought her in for her arraignment, he had to keep the emotion from his face and treat her like any other defendant. He tried to avoid meeting her eyes and focused on Jill instead, as the bailiff announced the case. He wanted to know how Stan was, but he wondered if he should address either of them personally. After a moment of thought, he decided that everyone in the room knew he was close to both women, and it wouldn't surprise them at all to know that he cared about Stan's condition.

"How's Stan?" he asked.

Celia looked up, but deferred to Jill.

"Not good," Jill said. "He's in a coma. Your honor, my client turned herself in the moment she heard of the warrant for her arrest. She had nothing to do with the poisoning. We'd like to request that these absurd charges be dropped."

Part of him reacted as a sympathetic friend who had trouble believing that Celia could be guilty. The other part of him, the part that had to keep a certain decorum in his courtroom, reacted with slight resentment.

Troubled, he rubbed his temples. "Then her plea is . . . ?"

"Not guilty," Celia said. "Absolutely not guilty."

"Judge," the prosecutor, Gus Taylor, cut in in a lazy voice, as if the whole process was so obvious that it was an insult to have to spell it out. "We have a solid case here. And we ask you not even to set bond—not for any amount—because of her past record. Her first husband died of arsenic poisoning, the same poison that's killing Stan right now."

Louis had read the account in the paper last night, but it still grieved him. This couldn't be true. It was too bizarre. What did she have? A double life?

"Your honor," Jill shot back, "I object to the prosecutor's sneaky and underhanded attempt to cast a bad light on my client by using information that is absolutely irrelevant to this case. My client has never been, nor will she ever be, convicted of any crime. Gus, were you absent the day they taught about relevance in law school?"

Louis tried to shake the troubling allegations from his mind. "She's right," he said. He cast a troubled gaze over the lot of them, from Jill to Celia to Gus, and then back to Celia again. There was more to this story, he told himself. If Celia's first husband had died of arsenic poisoning, that, indeed, was disturbing. But if there was no conviction, he could only determine that there hadn't been enough evidence. He didn't know what the evidence was here—now wasn't the time to hear it. His only purpose in this today was to set bond or deny it.

"Your honor, they also found rat poison in her attic. Its key ingredient was arsenic."

"Judge, you probably have rat poison in your attic, too, and it probably never occurred to you that it contained arsenic," Jill shot back.

He tried to think how he would have handled this case if Celia had been a stranger. Finally, he sighed. "I can't hold her," he told the prosecutor, "not with a record that's clean—"

"But your honor—" the prosecutor piped in.

"Unless she was found guilty, then any previous arrest is wiped off the slate," he said. "As far as the east is from the west, as someone said."

Jill looked at her feet and tried to suppress her grin. She doubted Gus knew who that someone was or what book it was quoted from.

"However, I can't drop the charges. I'll let you out on a hundred thousand dollars bond, Celia, but with the condition that you must not go near Stan or contact him in any way, even when he wakes up."

"*What?*" she asked.

Jill grabbed her arm to silence her. "We appreciate it, your honor."

He closed the file and handed it to the bailiff. "Next case?"

"But Louis," Celia cried, fighting as Jill tried to drag her out. "His parents won't let me see him now, but if . . . when he wakes up, if he wants to see me, I have to go. He needs me!"

Louis shot her a miserable look, then turned his eyes to the next file. He couldn't let his emotions get tangled up in this. He had to be objective. He had done the best he could.

• • •

Outside, Celia collapsed in a miserable heap on a bench against the wall, covering her head and wailing at the injustice of it all. Jill stooped down in front of her. "Celia, at least you can go home."

Aunt Aggie, who'd been sitting at the back of the courtroom, had come out and was now standing over them. "Home, nothin'. Celia ain't gon' be a open target for that killer, whoever he is. She comin' back to my house."

Celia was inconsolable. "Jill, you have to do something. You have to talk to the judge. I have to go to Stan when he wakes up."

"You can't," Jill said flatly. "Not until we get this cleared up."

"Then I might as well stay here. I don't have a hundred thousand dollars, anyway."

"That's not a problem. We'll get it from a bail bondsman. Celia, you don't want to stay here. At least if you're out we can find who did this. I need your help."

"Why is God *doing* this to me?"

Jill wished she had the answers. Her instinct was to tell her to trust him, but that was easy for her to say. Jill had never been accused of murder.

Chapter Twenty-Five

● ● ●

Celia Shepherd raised the candle as she walked into the black room. The flicker lit the room in a golden hue, and she saw the bed with the man lying on it. Her heart leapt, for she knew it was Stan, and she stepped closer, lifting the candle higher to cast the light on his face.

But he was dead.

She had known he was dead, even though her heart had chosen to deny it. She had believed the sheer power of her will would keep him alive, that her hopes would make him fight the poison in his blood. She had prayed so hard, wailing and begging and crying out to God . . .

"Celia! Celia! Wake up!"

Slowly, she emerged from the deep abyss of her sleep, and realized that she had been dreaming. There was no dark room, no candle, no body. Aunt Aggie stood over her, shaking her, and the afternoon sun radiated through her window.

"Celia, you got a phone call. Down to the hospital. They need to talk at you." *Hospital?* Celia managed to get her eyes open and sat up, wondering when she had fallen asleep. No wonder God didn't answer her prayers, if she couldn't even forsake sleep for something so important. "The hospital?" she asked. "Is Stan awake?"

"I don't know. Come on downstairs. They been waitin' a long time. I couldn't wake you up!"

For a moment she just sat there, paralyzed, her mind reeling with dread. What if they *weren't* calling to tell her he had awakened? What if he had died, just like in her dream? Slowly, she forced herself to get out of bed. She glanced at the clock on her bed table. Three P.M. She had lain down to pray and hadn't meant to fall asleep. She went barefoot down the stairs to the one telephone at the bottom of the staircase. By the time she reached the telephone, the cobwebs had sufficiently cleared themselves from her brain, and she was beginning to cry.

Her hand shook as she took the phone.

"Mrs. Shepherd? This is Frank Dupree at the Slidell Memorial Hospital Lab. We did some blood work on you Tuesday night?"

Her heart leapt, then took a nose dive. "This isn't about my husband?"

"No, I'm sorry. Actually, it's about you. We've finished running all of our tests on you, and we thought you'd like to know that one of them came up positive."

Her mind was still on Stan's condition, groping to find its way back to the phone call. She sat down in the chair next to the telephone table. "Wait . . . what?"

"Your blood test, Mrs. Shepherd . . ."

"But they said that night that they hadn't found arsenic in my blood."

"No, there's still no trace of arsenic. But the doctor ordered several tests. It's the pregnancy test that came up positive."

Celia's breath caught in her lungs, and her hand immediately fell to her stomach. "The *what?*"

"You're pregnant, Mrs. Shepherd. That explains the nausea."

She and Stan had been trying to have a baby for over two years, and now her heart raced at the thought that it was finally coming true. She had dreamed of this moment, when she got the news and would throw her arms around Stan and call him "Daddy."

Then she wilted as she realized that her baby may never know its daddy, because Stan might not wake up from his coma . . . that even if he did, the child could be born in prison and taken from her at birth.

She suddenly felt sick again. "Thank you," she said. "I appreciate your letting me know."

She didn't know how she managed to get the phone back in its cradle and make it to the bathroom on time. When she emerged, Aggie was waiting with a worried look on her face. "What they said, T-Celia? You been poisoned, too?"

Celia shook her head. She was shaking as she raked her hand through her disheveled hair. "No, Aunt Aggie. I'm pregnant." The word choked out on a wave of tears, and Aggie's face brightened, then instantly darkened.

"Why you cryin'? Ain't that what you want?"

"I want to tell Stan," Celia wept. "I want him to celebrate with me. We've waited so long for this moment, and I don't *understand* why it has to be like this . . ."

Aggie held her and let her cry, then walked her into the parlor and set her down on the sofa. "It's gon' be awright, *sha,*" she said. "I know it is. Somehow, this baby gon' make everything okay. Can you just see yourself sittin' in front of that jury with your belly out to here? Can only help in the sympathy department."

"I don't *need* sympathy. I need for them to catch the killer. I need for Stan to wake up and recover." She sat sideways on the couch, with her feet tucked beneath her, and dropped her face on the back of the sofa. "Oh, Aunt Aggie, what is he going to think when he does wake up? When he hears that his wife has been charged with his attempted murder? When he hears that he almost died of arsenic poisoning? Will he know that I didn't do it? Or will he doubt like everyone else is going to?"

"He'll know," Aunt Aggie said. "He'll fight tooth and nail to clear your name. You'll see."

She just wasn't sure. She wouldn't know until she talked to him, heard his voice, heard him defending her to those who would string her up. "Will you call the hospital and see how he's doing?"

"I just did 'fore I got you up. No change."

She groaned and wept into her hands for a moment longer. Finally, she said, "Aunt Aggie, I don't want anyone to know about the pregnancy. Not until I can tell Stan. I don't want him to read about it in the papers or hear about it from someone who thinks I did this. I want to tell him."

"Awright," the old woman said. "I won't say nothin'."

"You won't say anything about what?"

They looked up to see David standing at the doorway to the parlor, and Celia wiped her eyes and reached for a tissue in the gold tissue holder on the end table.

"Hey, David."

"What's going on, Celia? Something happened."

She blew her nose. "No, nothing. I'm just . . . a little depressed."

"Come on, Celia," he said, coming to sit next to her on the couch. "It's me. You've got me worried to death. Now, what is it?"

She looked at Aunt Aggie, and her aunt nodded, urging her to tell him. Finally, she realized that she wanted to. She wanted to share the news. At least she could tell those closest to her. She looked up at him through tear-filled eyes. "I'm pregnant."

There was no joy in his eyes as he gaped at her. "Pregnant?"

"Yes. That's why I've been sick off and on . . ." Her eyes filled again at his reaction. "David, what is it?"

"Well, it's just . . ." He got up and looked at Aunt Aggie, then turned back to Celia. "Celia, the timing couldn't be worse. Stan lying in a hospital, you being charged with his murder, a probable indictment . . ."

"I know that," she said, growing impatient. Did he really think she didn't know?

"Celia, you can't have this baby."

She looked up at him, stricken at the declaration, as if he'd made the decision and it was a done deal. "What do you mean?"

"I mean, you can't. It would be cruel to bring a child into the world in the middle of this."

She stared up at him. "David, are you suggesting abortion?"

"I'm just saying that this is going to complicate your life miserably."

"I can handle it."

"No, you can't. What do you think Stan will do when he finds out? Or his parents, for that matter?"

"Stan will defend me when he wakes up," she said with certainty. "And when I tell him about the baby, he's going to be happy."

"Right. And when they start feeding him all the lies about you, you think he's still gonna want you to have his baby? Celia, if you terminated it this time and waited until this was all cleared up and you and Stan were back together, it would be so much better."

She couldn't believe what she was hearing. Her hand went to her stomach again, and a burst of love surged through her. "God didn't make a mistake with this, David. This is my baby, and I've been praying and waiting for it."

"Did you pray to be a single mom? What if Stan dies, Celia?"

"That's enough!" Aunt Aggie got to her feet and stepped between them. "David, leave the child alone. She got enough worry."

"Aunt Aggie, you must agree with me. How can you condone this?"

"She had nothing to do with it!" Celia said, her voice rising. "It doesn't matter if she condones it or agrees with you. Neither of you has the right to decide anything for me." She got another tissue, blew her nose again. "I thought you might be happy, David."

"*You're* not even happy. When I came in here, you were sobbing, Celia. Don't tell me you weren't."

"I was crying over the circumstances. Not the baby. The baby is wanted. He or she is an answered prayer."

David seemed to realize he wasn't getting anywhere with her. He sank back onto the sofa. "It seems very romantic, Celia. But you're the one who'll be most hurt."

"I'm willing to take that chance." She wiped her face and looked down at her feet. "If you're going to support me, David, you'll have to support me in this, too. And you can't tell anyone. Either of you."

"Why not?"

"Because I want Stan to hear about it from me."

He stared at her as if struggling with the words, then finally gave up. "Okay, if that's what you want."

The phone rang, startling her, and Aggie went into the foyer to answer it. "Halo?"

Celia could hear her muttering something, and she reached for another tissue to blow her nose again. In a moment, Aggie was back in the doorway, fairly dancing as she got out the words. "He's awake, T-Celia! That was Allie, down to the hospital. She said he woke up!"

"Oh, thank God!" Celia got to her feet and began to weep, harder and deeper than she had all morning. "Oh, thank God!" She fell into Aunt Aggie's arms, then pulled David into the embrace with them. "Oh, I can't believe it. What did she say? How is he?"

"She wasn't sure," Aggie said. "But she knew you'd wanna know."

"Oh, I want to see him! I want to look into his eyes and tell him about the baby . . ."

"You have to," David said. "You have to get in there somehow and tell him. As long as you're not there, and his family is feeding him lies, he might believe them. You have to go see him."

"But I can't. The court order."

"Yes, you can, Celia. Stan needs to know about the baby."

He was right, she thought. She had to see him, to touch him, to kiss him. She had to tell him about the baby, and watch his eyes smile, and feel his arms around her. Then he would know that she couldn't have tried to kill him. Then he would tell them, and it would all be cleared up, and she could be with him as the baby grew . . .

"I'll figure out a way," Celia said on a whisper. "They won't be able to keep me away from him for long."

Chapter Twenty-Six

• • •

S tan Shepherd was still weak and felt as though he'd been dragged a hundred miles behind a pickup truck . . . then backed over. He felt so tired. So incredibly tired, but they all seemed to be so glad to see him awake that he hated to give in to the fatigue and close his eyes again.

But all the questions . . . they were asking so many, probably to evaluate whether he had brain damage. He tried to answer them, but the question he had for them seemed more pressing. Where was Celia? What had happened to him? Had they been in an accident? Was Celia hurt . . . or worse? Is that why no one wanted to tell him where she was?

"Celia," he whispered again, and his mother, standing on one side of the bed, offered him that cup of water with the straw that probed at his lips like some kind of medical instrument. He sipped obediently.

"Honey, don't try to talk."

"Stan, can you tell me your birth date? Your name and address? Your mother's maiden name?"

"Thought she said not to talk."

The doctor who stood over him wasn't amused. He was serious, so Stan tried to give him what he wanted. "April 22. Stan Shepherd. I live at 313 Burgundy Drive, Newpointe, Louisiana. Want the zip?"

The doctor smiled. "No, that won't be necessary. Detective, could you tell me the last thing you remember?"

That was a tough one. He closed his eyes and tried to think. Celia. He remembered Celia crying over him, calling 911 . . .

"I was sick."

"Yes. Do you remember when you began to feel sick?"

"I don't know." He began to get concerned and looked around the room again, taking grim inventory of the people watching him. Two doctors, a nurse, his father, his mother . . . "Where's Celia, Mom? Is she all right?"

"She's . . . not able to be here today. Just relax, darling."

He didn't like the sound of that. He turned back to the doctor. "How long have I been here?"

"Two days. You came in Tuesday night. It's Thursday now."

"Thursday? What happened to—" He tried to sit up, but realized he was too weak.

"You've been in a coma, Detective. You were poisoned."

"*Poisoned?* You've got to be kidding."

"No, I'm afraid not. It was arsenic poisoning."

Arsenic? He closed his eyes, trying to think. Arsenic. Like Nathan, Celia's first husband. Poisoned. He'd been in a coma . . . Had almost died.

His skin felt cold, damp, and he brought a trembling hand up to wipe his temples. "Where's my wife?"

Silence again.

His eyes filled. "Is she dead?"

"No, of course not," Hannah said quickly. "No, darling, nothing like that."

"Then what?" he asked, growing agitated. "Why won't anybody tell me where she is? I want to see her. She must be worried sick."

His father pushed between Hannah and a nurse, and set his hand on the railing of the bed. "Son, we don't know how to tell you this."

"Just spit it out," he snapped. "I want my wife."

"Celia's . . . not allowed to see you. There's a court order . . ."

"A court order? What kind of court would order a thing like that?"

"Son, did you know that Celia's first husband had died of arsenic poisoning, and that she was charged with that murder?"

Oh, so that was it. He closed his eyes again, racking his brain for some logical sequence of thoughts. That grogginess still hung on. Was it the arsenic, or the coma, or the damage that had been done to him? He forced his mind back to the question. Had he known about Celia's first husband?

"Yes," he said. "She told me before I married her. She told me everything. But she didn't do it, Dad."

"Son, I wish I could believe in her, but you were poisoned the same way. And there's evidence ..."

"What evidence? I want to talk to Jim Shoemaker. I want to talk to Sid." He struggled to sit up again, and this time half made it. "Do they think she did this to me? Have they arrested her?"

"Yes," his mother said. The word, uttered with such regret, shot to his heart like an arrow, knocking him back down.

"No," he said. "How could they be so stupid? Celia couldn't—wouldn't—do this!" His breath was coming harder. "Where is she? In jail? Get her out, Dad! I don't care what it costs or what you have to do. Get her out!"

"She's out," he said. "She was released on bond."

"I want to see her!" he managed to shout. "Now!"

"That's impossible, son. Judge DeLacy ordered her to stay away from you. There's a grand jury investigation going on, and she—"

"She didn't do it, Dad! She didn't!"

"Then who did?"

He fell back and laid his hand over his eyes, trying to think. "I don't know. But I know she didn't. Give me the phone."

Bart and Hannah looked at each other, but neither made a move. "Why?" Bart asked.

"I want to talk to my wife." His voice was a barely whispered rasp now, but he wouldn't give up. "She must be scared to death. She must be humiliated. Give me the phone, Dad."

"I can't do that, Son. I have to protect you."

"I don't *need* protecting from her! At least let me call the judge. He can't make that court order hold if I ask him to let me see her. I'm a grown man."

"You're a sick man," his father said. "You're still very, very sick. You're not out of the woods yet. You have to rest, and we can't take the chance of having her finish off the job . . ."

"*Give me a break!*" The words came with such passion that they almost took what was left of his voice. He couldn't believe they would do this to his wife. His body begged him to give in to sleep, to rest, to recovery, but his mind fought. He had to get up and get to her, wrap her in his arms and tell her it would be all right. Then he realized that it couldn't be all right, not while the killer was still out there. What if he poisoned her, too? What if she was an open target? "Call Jim and Sid. I have to talk to them," he said. "I have to make sure that someone protects her."

"When you're rested and feeling better," his mother said. "We'll call them then."

"No, not then," he said through his teeth. "Now. Mom, so help me, if you don't, you're gonna have to tie me down to keep me in this bed."

She shot his father a distressed look. "All right," Bart said finally. "We'll call them."

"Now. Call them now."

"Okay."

He closed his eyes as Bart picked up the phone. He didn't relax until he'd heard him ask them to come. Then, finally, he surrendered to the sleep pulling at him.

Chapter Twenty-Seven

● ● ●

Sid had managed to get a few hours' sleep, but it wasn't enough. He rubbed his eyes and tried to concentrate on the rap sheet he'd gotten on Lee Barnett. When the phone on his desk buzzed, he picked it up, preoccupied. "Yeah? Ford, here."

"Sid, this is Bart Shepherd. Stan's father."

"Yes, Mr. Shepherd," he said, coming to attention. "How are you?"

"I'm fine. More importantly, Stan is fine. Or, he's better. He's awake."

"All *right!*" With the exclamation, he leapt out of his chair, knocking it over. Everyone in the room turned to look at him. He picked the chair up and sat back down. "Does that mean he's out of the woods? What do the doctors say?"

"They think he's on his way to recovery, though we can't be sure yet how much damage the arsenic did. He's still very weak. But Sid, he wants to talk to you. You and Jim Shoemaker. You know how stubborn he can be and, well . . ." He dropped his voice. "He's a little upset. Do you think you can come?"

"Of course. Does he remember anything? Where he got the arsenic? Who may have given it to him?"

"No, but he's adamantly insisting that Celia isn't the one."

"I wish I could be that sure," Sid said, and Bart didn't reply. "Mr. Shepherd, I'll be there as soon as I can catch up with Jim, all right? Tell him we're glad he's awake, and that it's about time."

"I will."

He hung up the phone and punched the air, then got to his feet, doing a little dance. "Stan's awake! He's awake!"

The room erupted into cheers as Sid sashayed into the chief's office. Jim was on the telephone. He looked up at Sid, rubbed his eyes, then looked again. He put his hand over the phone. "What's going on?"

"Stan's awake, man! He wants to see us!"

Jim's mouth fell open, then into the phone, he said, "I'll call you back." He hung up the phone and got slowly to his feet. "Awake? Really?" He laughed out loud and high-fived Sid. "I don't believe it."

"That's right," Sid said, still strutting. "This ain't a homicide."

"Thank God."

"We gotta go, man. He wants to see us both, if you can break away from your chiefly duties long enough."

"You bet I can. Why does he want to see us? Does he remember anything pertinent?"

"I don't know," Sid said. "His daddy called and told me he was upset about Celia. Insistin' she didn't have nothin' to do with it."

Jim hesitated, and his grin faded. "Then this isn't a social visit. He wants to see what we've got on her."

Sid stopped dancing and stared at Jim as the unpleasant task before them sank in. "Guess you're right."

Jim got his keys off of the hook on his wall. "Sometimes we've got to play the bad guys," he said.

•   •   •

Stan heard the voices at the door, and he struggled to open his eyes. He saw the IV bag hanging next to his bed, felt the tube under his nose supplying oxygen, heard the beep of one of the monitors next to the bed.

His gaze drifted beyond the machinery to the door where his parents were talking quietly to someone. He squinted to make them out, and saw Sid and Jim standing just outside the door.

"Sid." The word was so weak that he could barely hear it himself. He tried to raise up. "Sid."

His mother turned around and saw that he was awake, and her tired face came alive. "There he is," she said, rushing to his side. "See, I told you he was awake. Stan, Sid and Jim are here like you asked."

"Help me sit up," he said.

She pressed the button that raised the bed up, and Stan reached out to shake his friends' hands. "Thanks for comin'," he said.

"Man, it's about time you woke up, givin' us the scare of our lives," Sid said. "I don't *ever* want to have to come find you on the floor again. What do you *mean* almost dyin' on us like that?"

"Sorry, man. Call me inconsiderate."

Jim was more staid as he stepped closer to the bed.

"Chief, how's it goin'?"

"Better, now that we don't have to upgrade this to a homicide."

"You've got the wrong person," Stan said. "Celia didn't do it."

Jim looked at Sid, and Sid shrugged. "We knew you'd think that, Stan. Nobody wants to think their wife did somethin' like this."

"You know Celia. How could you think that about her?"

"Too much evidence," Sid said. "There's nothin' else we can think."

He felt his pulse speeding up, felt his breath coming harder. It seemed to have a hair trigger. "You can't call yourself my friend . . . and try to set my wife up for something like this. There's a killer out there."

Sid sighed and pulled up a chair, turned it backward, and straddled it. "Look, man," he said, resting his chin on his fists. "If you want to know what we've got on her, we'll tell you. But it ain't pretty, Stan. It's gon' hurt you."

"What hurts me is that my wife can't come to see me. That she's probably worried sick. That she's being set up for the second time."

"Do you want to hear what we've got, or not?" Sid asked.

Stan looked his friend in the eye and realized how tired the man looked. He wondered if Sid had gotten any sleep at all since Stan collapsed. Had he spent all this time looking for the killer, or simply trying to build a case against Celia? "Yes, I want to hear," he said. "What do you think you have?"

"First, and most obvious, the fact that her first husband died the same way."

"He was murdered."

"Of course he was. And she was charged with that crime."

"And those charges were dismissed."

"Only due to a technicality. You know as well as I do that guilty people get off on technicalities all the time."

He was having trouble getting a breath, and his hands were shaking. He tried to calm down. "Look, my wife is as innocent as I am. She didn't kill her first husband, and she didn't try to kill me."

"There's more, Stan," Jim said. "Have you ever heard the name Lee Barnett?"

He shook his head. "No, I don't think so. Why?"

"Because he's one of Celia's old flames. Before she was married the first time, she was involved with him. He wound up in prison for manslaughter, barroom brawl sort of thing, and he got out two weeks ago."

"So have you checked him out? Maybe he poisoned me somehow."

"Maybe. Turns out that he came to Newpointe where he had an apartment waiting. He claims that Celia sent him a letter by way of a priest—"

"*Celia?*" he cut in. "He says she wrote to him? What priest?"

"We don't know. But he says she sent him a letter saying that she had an apartment here for him, and that he could get the key in a locker at the bus station, along with a check for $200."

"He's lying," Stan said without doubt.

"Marabeth Simmons said the deal was made by phone. The check that was sent in was one of your and Celia's checks. We saw it ourselves, Stan. It wasn't counterfeit."

"Lee Barnett is a liar. I don't know where he got the checks, but I can guarantee you that Celia did not write it."

"There's more," Sid said. "We searched your house again last night, looking for the checkbook, since Celia claims she doesn't have it. Do you know where it is, by the way?"

"No," he said. "If I had it, it would have been over the visor in my car."

"We searched your car, top to bottom. Not there."

"I don't know where it is," he said. "Maybe Lee Barnett has it. Stole it and forged her name."

"It looked like her signature, Stan."

His chest tightened, and a bead of perspiration rolled into his eye. "You said there was more."

"The arsenic. We found it in your attic, Stan. A brand new box. Hadn't even collected dust. It was rat poison, sitting behind a beam in your attic."

He tried to rise up. His face grew hot with the strain. "She didn't put it there," he said. "Celia's afraid to go in the attic. It gives her the creeps. I don't think she's ever been up there. She wouldn't have done it."

"Not even to cover up a murder?"

"Why wouldn't she have just flushed it down the toilet, burnt the box? Why would she bother to go hide the box in a place she would never have gone before?"

"We don't know why she did what she did, Stan. None of it's logical."

"Think like a cop," Stan said through his teeth. "If someone were going to set her up, he'd leave it where he knew you'd find it. Maybe it's this Lee Barnett. Go with the most obvious first, man."

"Celia's the most obvious," Sid said.

"Not to me! Not to anyone who knows her!"

His mother came to the bed and tried to push his shoulders back down. "Stan, you've got to calm down," she said.

"No!" he said, intent on making his point. "Sid, Jim, you've got to listen to me!"

Sid got up and leaned on Stan's bed rail. "Stan, Lee Barnett says she set him up so he'd take the fall when she poisoned you."

"I told you, I don't know who this guy is, but Lee Barnett is a liar."

"Maybe. He could have done all of this. But if that's the case, Celia may have put him up to it."

"No way!" He sat all the way up of his own volition and waved a shaky hand at Jim. "Jim, you get him off of her. You *tell* him that he's on the wrong track!"

His mother fought to lay him back down. "Stan, please—"

"Tell him he's wasting police hours going after the wrong person! My wife is a victim!"

Jim looked miserable. "Stan, we're exploring every avenue. We're not leaving any stones unturned."

"I don't want clichés, Jim! I want my wife. She's out there like a sitting duck, just waiting for this maniac to strike. I want her protected."

"Protected?" Jim asked. "What do you mean?"

"I mean, I want someone watching her. Twenty-four hours a day. I don't want anyone to go near her that isn't seen."

"Stan, we don't have the manpower for that. With you out—"

Stan grabbed Jim's collar and jerked his face close to his. "I've put years on this police force ..." He stopped to catch his breath "... and I've never once complained about having to work around the clock to solve crimes. I've been a good detective for you, Jim, and I've put my life on the line over and over. Now I need a favor. I want my wife protected. You owe that to me."

Jim took a step back, red faced, looking at him as if he was crazy. Stan supposed that arsenic poisoning gave him more license than usual. Instead of firing him on the spot, Jim only glared at him.

Stan blinked back the mist in his eyes. "What do you want, Jim? You want me to get down on my knees?"

Sid seemed startled by Stan's passion, and finally, he turned his long, dark face to the chief. "Jim, I could watch her."

"No," Jim said. "We don't have a detective. You're the most qualified evidence technician we've got. I need you on the case."

"We could take turns. Everybody could watch for a couple of hours each day. Get twelve of us to do that, and you got the whole day and night covered. We could do it, Jim. Then, if she is guilty, we'll see who she talks to and where she goes. It could work in our favor."

Stan ground his teeth together and shook his head. "I don't believe you guys."

Jim rubbed his stomach, a habit he'd developed shortly after becoming police chief. "Stan, I'll see what I can do."

"Do better than that, Jim," Stan said, "or you'll have to find yourself another detective."

"You wouldn't quit," Hannah cut in, laughing nervously. "Stan, you love your job."

"Watch me." His tone brooked no debate. "Promise me you'll put someone on her right away."

"I said I'd do what I can," Jim said, but both Stan and Sid stared at him, waiting for more than that. "Okay," he said finally. "I promise."

Stan relaxed back into his pillow, feeling suddenly tireder than he had felt since he came out of the coma. "Thank you." He tried to slow his breathing. "One other thing. I want to see her. This stupid court order ... Tell the judge to let her come. Tell him he can send a police escort, an armed guard, whatever. I just want to see her. I have to see her." His last words faded out on a whisper.

Sid and Jim stood looking at him as he tried to fight the heaviness in his eyelids.

Sid reached over and touched his limp hand. "I'm glad you're okay, man. Really glad. Even if you do hate my guts."

"I don't hate your guts," Stan whispered. "I hate what you're doing to my wife."

"And I hate what she did to you, if she did it."

Stan grabbed his hand and opened his eyes again. "Sid, you promise me that ... you'll work as hard ... to prove her innocent ... as you're working to prove her guilty."

"Sure, man," Sid said. "Believe it or not, I don't want Celia to be guilty."

He wanted to say more, but that heaviness was too overwhelming, and his eyes wanted so desperately to close. He told himself that they would keep their promises ... they had to. They would watch Celia, even if they thought she was guilty. She would be protected.

Knowing that, he let go and drifted back into the vortex of sleep.

Chapter Twenty-Eight

● ● ●

Celia stood in front of the mirror, brushing her hair up into a ponytail. She had no makeup on, and no inclination to use any, and her blue eyes were red-rimmed and bloodshot from crying. The news over the last twenty-four hours seemed to have come in waves. The things about Lee Barnett and the letter and the checks and the apartment. Her arrest. Her pregnancy. Finally, the news about Stan.

She had tried twice to call his room, but his parents had refused to put her through. They had claimed he was sleeping, which may have been true. But she knew from the chill in their voices that they wouldn't put her through even if he was awake. Who could blame them? She had been arrested for his poisoning. His parents saw her as a threat to Stan's life. Until she could prove to them—to everyone—that she was innocent, she had no hope of getting through.

Her blood pounded through her veins, and she trembled as she pulled her sunglasses from her purse and shoved them on. Would anyone who saw her recognize her? Would they know her from her pictures in the newspaper? The notorious, murderous wife?

She almost didn't care who saw her, but part of her knew that it wouldn't pay to be seen. She had a mission, and she intended to carry it out.

She grabbed her purse and started down the stairs. Aunt Aggie had gone to the fire station to cook for the men who claimed to be starving to death without her, and David was moving and shaking the oil business by phone downstairs. Maybe she could slip out without being noticed.

But David was off the phone and was sitting at the telephone table, poring over a photo album that Aunt Aggie kept there. It was futile trying to slip past him, so she stopped and looked over his shoulder.

He was staring down at a picture of them as children, sitting in a sandbox with little plastic buckets. Above that were three pageant pictures of her at age four or five, made up like a starlet and striking a pose in a thousand dollar dress with layers of petticoats. She must have been a winner, because she was wearing a tiara.

"Little Miss Southeastern Hinds County Magnolia Blossom . . . or some such nonsense. What a racket."

David nodded pensively. "You won everything. How many trophies did you have?"

"A roomful, for what it was worth. Does Mom still keep them out?"

He shook his head. "She boxed them up years ago."

Though the idea of such awards seemed so silly, they had been her identity for the first eighteen years of her life. The reminder that she'd been relegated to an obsolete memory in the attic only strengthened her resolve to go where she had to go.

He looked up at her and frowned at her ponytail and sunglasses. "Celia, where are you going?"

"Out for a little while," she said. "I just want to run a few errands, get some air."

He stared at her for a moment, then asked, "What are you driving?"

She wilted. For all her planning, she had forgotten that she didn't have her car here. It was still at her house.

"Uh . . . Well, I guess I forgot . . ."

He reached into his pocket for his keys. "Take the Beemer. No problem."

He tossed them up, and she caught them. "Are you sure it's all right?"

"Why wouldn't it be? Want me to go with you?"

She shook her head and wondered if she should tell him where she was going. It was only fair ... But then she decided against it, because he would surely talk her out of it. "No, I want to be alone."

"Okay. The court order didn't say you had to stay locked up in a house all day, did it?"

"No, it didn't."

"You're not going to see him, are you?"

"Who?"

He frowned, as if her question surprised him. "Stan, who else?"

She rallied and shook her head. "No. Not yet."

"All right then."

She left him alone and went out the back way, got into the big car that was a far cry from her little Civic. There had been a time when she had driven a Mercedes Roadster. It had been her first car. Funny how she hadn't missed it at all.

She backed out of the driveway, thankful that the photographer seemed to have left. He was probably back at the newspaper processing new pictures of Aunt Aggie's front door, and manufacturing new stories to tell the people of Newpointe about what was happening behind it.

She headed for the Bonaparte Court apartments, where Jill had said Lee Barnett was staying. She had thought about this all day—about the fact that Lee probably wouldn't hang around forever, not unless the police had warned him not to leave. She had to get to him before he left Newpointe. It was crucial.

She pulled into the parking lot of the apartment complex, found a space, then peered up at the doors and windows, wishing she had some idea which apartment he was in. No one had said.

She got out of the car and headed to the row of mailboxes beside the sidewalk, hoping to find some clue there. Most of

them had last names on them, but some didn't. There wasn't a
Barnett. Frustrated, she looked around the parking lot for
something familiar, maybe his car . . . a Mississippi plate . . .

There it was, a Mississippi tag on an old silver Grand Am—
the same one he'd driven when she'd known him.

It was in front of the B Building of eight apartments, so she
went back to the mailboxes, found the Bs, and saw that only
one of them didn't have a name. B–5. That had to be him, and
if it wasn't, she'd just try another one.

She heard a door close downstairs, and Marabeth Simmons
clomped down the walk back into the office. She hurried up the
steps of the B Building before the woman could see her. When
she was sure Marabeth had gone inside, she found B–5. Inside,
she heard the sound of a radio. She knocked on the door and
straightened her sunglasses.

"Yeah?" It was his voice. She would have known it anywhere. "Who is it?"

She shivered. "It's me, Lee. Open the door."

He opened it quickly, and she stared up at him. He had
changed since she'd last seen him. There was a tiny scar over
his top lip, and his hair was cut shorter, and he seemed
stronger, more muscular, as though he'd spent a lot of time
working out.

She suddenly wondered at the wisdom in coming here.

"Celia?"

She took off her sunglasses and looked up at him, wanting
him to look in her eyes and know for sure that it was she he was
ruining—a flesh-and-blood human who didn't deserve what was
happening. "Why are you here?" she asked him through compressed lips. "Why did you tell the police all those lies about me?"

He leaned out the door and looked from side to side.
"Come in," he said.

She breathed a furious laugh. "You've got to be kidding.
I'm not coming in there. I want to know why you're setting me

up, Lee. I want to know why you would want my husband dead
... what he ever did to you ... and I need to know if you killed
Nathan, and why ... why you would let me take the heat for it,
why you would hate me so much that—"

"You're nuts," he cut in. "I didn't kill Nathan, and I didn't poison this husband. And *I'm* the one being set up, not you! I'll hand
it to you, Celia. I didn't know you had it in you. You're smarter
than I thought, but not smart enough to make me your patsy."

Rage filled her, and it burst out as her hand swung up to
slap his face. It surprised him, and he grabbed her arms and
jerked her against him. She lurched free.

"Get your hands off of me!"

"Hey, *you* slapped me!" He dropped his hands to his sides.
"Why did you send for me, Celia? Why me? Why not some
other chump? I never did anything to you."

"I *didn't!*" she cried. "I didn't send for you. I don't even know
who did. I don't know where my checkbook is, and I don't know
who wrote those checks, and I don't know who sent the letter, and
I don't know any Catholic priest, and I *didn't poison my husband!*"
She was weeping now, hating herself for it. She heard a door close
downstairs and wondered if Marabeth had come back out.

She stepped back out of his reach and lowered her voice. "I
just came here to tell you one thing," she said. "If my husband
dies, they can do whatever they want to with me. I won't care.
But I want you to know that I'll move heaven and earth to make
sure you pay. You won't get away with it."

He stared at her, and the confusion in his eyes registered in
her heart. A long moment of electric silence screamed between
them. "You really *didn't* send the letter or the checks, did you?"
he finally asked.

"*No!* Why would I *do* something so destructive? *I love my
husband!*"

He looked down at his feet, working through the facts. And
suddenly she understood. Lee Barnett was innocent, too.
Could it be that they had both been framed?

"Celia, you're in a lot of trouble. I guess I am, too."

"Then why don't you just leave? Get out of town? Why are you still here?"

"Because the cops told me that I couldn't leave town until they'd finished investigating. I don't want to do anything that's gonna land me back in jail. And I've got this apartment paid for for a month . . ."

"But don't you see? If you're telling the truth, they *want* you to stay here. It was planned. Whoever it is, they *want* you here, because it makes people think all sorts of things about me. Can't you stay in town but go to a hotel or something? Get another apartment?"

"Why?"

"Because a killer set you up in this one! So far he's made you play into his hands. Don't you worry about that?"

She could see that he hadn't thought of that. "Well, maybe I could move. But I don't have much money left, and no prospects for a job."

She wiped her face again and shook her head with disbelief. She didn't know why, but she believed him. She had known him well, years ago, and while he was on the wild side, he wasn't conniving. She couldn't imagine that he was lying to her now.

"What can I do, Celia?" he asked. "Tell me what to do. I could go to the police and tell them that I talked to you, that you told me you hadn't sent the letter or the checks, but under the circumstances, they'd just think I was covering for you, that we had something going."

"Don't do anything," she said. "Please, don't do anything. Just stay out of it. Don't make it worse."

She was getting a headache and starting to feel nauseous again. She thought about the baby and touched her stomach. More tears pushed into her eyes. "I have to go," she said.

"You believe me, don't you?" he asked.

She dared not admit that she did. "I don't know what to believe," she said. "Just leave me alone, okay? Don't come near me or my husband, and don't ask about me or talk about me. Don't even say my name."

"What if I find something out? Can't I call then?"

"Call the police," she said. "But you won't find anything out. He's too smart. He's too good at what he does. He knows how to nail me. I just can't figure out why someone who hated me so much wouldn't want to kill *me* instead of my husband. But I guess that would be too kind. This way he can watch me suffer." She looked up at Lee, her eyes intense. "I don't know if you're the guy, Lee, but so help me, if you are, may the wrath of God fall on you so hard that you never find a place to hide from it."

She turned and stumbled down the steps, back to her car.

• • •

Out in the parking lot, Vern Hargis, who had been assigned to watch Celia, saw Marabeth duck back into her apartment. He wondered what she had heard. He pulled the cigarette out of his mouth and fingered the camera in his lap, wondering why his heart felt as if it had been punctured. He'd had a remnant of doubt about her guilt, but this certainly changed his mind. From what he'd seen, it looked as if they'd had some kind of lover's quarrel. Celia had slapped him, but the intimacy in their conversation had spoken volumes. It made him sick. Sid's instincts were right, as usual. Celia was no good.

He watched her get into the BMW that must belong to her rich brother, and she sat there for a moment before cranking it up. As he waited for her to pull out, he opened the shutter door of the camera and pulled the film out. The thought of processing the pictures didn't appeal to him. But it had to be done. Cops were about solving cases, and as far as he was concerned, this one was solved.

Poor Stan.

He wondered how he would take this.

He followed her at a distance and pulled his cell phone out of his glove box. Quickly, he dialed information and got Marabeth's number. He hoped she had call-waiting.

"Hello?" she said, breathless. "Sue Ellen?"

"No, Marabeth. It's Vern Hargis. You weren't by chance on the other line, were you?" He smirked even as he asked.

"Well, yes, I was."

"So what's the scoop? I know you just overheard a private conversation."

She hesitated. "Is this police business?"

"Well, yes, it is." His tone was mocking, but she didn't seem to notice.

"Well, you're just not gon' believe who just paid a visit to Mr. Lee Barnett."

"Marabeth, I already know. What did you hear?"

"Well, they were talkin' in low voices, see, so I couldn't hear too good." She lowered her voice to just above a whisper. "But I heard her askin' him to go to a hotel. Reckon she was gon' meet him there?"

Vern frowned. "What else?"

"They were talkin' about what to tell the cops. He said he was gon' tell ya'll that she didn't send the check for the apartment. I'm almost sure that's what he said. And he told her he'd cover for her, because they had somethin' goin'."

"Are you sure?"

"As sure as I can be. Vern, why aren't those two in jail? I'm not gon' be able to sleep tonight, worryin' that they'll find out I heard and come cut my throat."

"Then you'd better keep quiet about it, hadn't you?"

She didn't reply, but he knew she was weighing the cost of a cut throat versus the satisfaction of spreading the gossip. He knew she would take the risk.

When he'd hung up, he called Sid and told him the news. He only hoped Celia would head home so he could get the film developed.

Chapter Twenty-Nine

●●●

The zydeco sounds of celebration grated over the speakers in the Midtown fire station kitchen, where Aunt Aggie served blackened pork chops so spicy that the men broke out in a sweat just biting into them. She'd missed cooking for them, even if she knew that half of them suspected her Celia of terrible things. She had decided that they'd never know better if she didn't come down here to set them straight.

Ray Ford, the new fire chief, had even shown up to join them, as had some of the other firefighters who weren't even on duty. Ray planted a kiss on Aunt Aggie's cheek as she finished serving the plates. "I heard you been beatin' up on my brother, Aunt Aggie."

She didn't find that amusing. "He needed more'n me beatin' 'im. Needed a two-by-four right across the rump. Puttin' T-Celia in jail." She said it with such contempt that she fancied the bitterness dripped out of her mouth onto the food.

Slater Finch had already dug in, even before Nick Foster had blessed it. With his mouth full, he said, "How come Celia ain't Cajun, Aunt Aggie, if ya'll are relatives and all?"

"Celia's mama is my baby bro's girl. He went up to the college, you know, at LSU, and got 'im a education. Tried to pretend he warn't one o' us. Married a high-falutin' gal that talked Jackie Kennedy, and he thought he was *some*-body. Celia's mama never even knowed she was half Cajun, didn't know a word o' French."

"And I thought Cajun was so genetic that the kids were born talking that way," Slater said. "But let's get real. It ain't really

French. I mean, nobody from over in Paree could understand it. Just the same, though, I didn't know a body could choose."

"Can't choose," she said. "My baby bro was born a Cajun and he died a Cajun, whe'er he liked it or not."

Junior Reynolds took a bite of the pork and began to cough and grope for his glass. Everyone watched as he choked and teared up, his face reddening. Aunt Aggie reached for a glass of iced tea and hurried around the table to give it to him.

"Too hot for ya?" she asked, handing him the glass.

"What'd you do? Poison me, too?"

He reached for the glass, but instead of handing it to him, she turned it over and dumped it into his lap. He screamed out a curse and jumped out of his chair. "What's a matter with you? Are you crazy?"

"I didn't poison nobody, and didn't nobody in my family poison nobody, and if you don't want to eat my cookin', then you get that little empty-headed wife of yours to start bringin' you a samwich. In fact, maybe ya'll want samwiches. Maybe ya'll can make 'em yourselves!"

The others glowered at Junior as though they might lynch him on the spot.

Nick, ever the peacemaker, got up and went to Aunt Aggie's side. "Now, Aunt Aggie. Junior was teasin' you. He didn't mean it, did you, Junior?"

Junior stood there in his wet pants, his hands innocently on his hips as he looked remorsefully at Aunt Aggie. "I got a big mouth, Aunt Aggie. I'm sorry. Please don't make me eat my wife's cookin'. And I like your pork chops. They grow hair on a man's chest. We all like 'em."

Still not amused, she marched back around the table and grabbed her purse. "Ya'll can clean up after your own selves today. And I might not be back tonight, me."

"Aunt Aggie!" It was a chorus of protests, but Aunt Aggie compressed her lips and hightailed it out to her Cadillac before they quit being sorry.

The Branning's car was parked in the driveway when Aunt Aggie got home, and she figured they were inside talking to Celia. But then Celia pulled in, driving David's car, just as she was getting out.

"Where you been?" she asked her niece as Celia slid out of the BMW.

"I had to run an errand," she said. Her nose was red and her eyes glistened as if she'd just been crying.

"What errand? You shouldna been out by your lonesome, *sha*. Don't you know?"

"I had to, Aunt Aggie."

"Had to what? Where you went? Tell me, Celia."

She sighed. "I went to see Lee Barnett."

"*Coo!*" Aunt Aggie exclaimed. "He coulda hurt you. Coulda killed you! You crazy?"

"He didn't hurt me at all," she said. "I just had to confront him. Had to know what he's trying to do, why he's setting me up . . ."

"And what he say?"

"He said that he wasn't." She sighed. "Aunt Aggie, I think we've both been set up. I'm not sure that he's anything more than just a pawn. But when I think how well this killer knows me, that he'd know about Lee and how we dated once, and that he was in prison, and time everything so it would look like I was poisoning Stan so I could be with Lee . . . What else might he do?"

"Nothin'!" Aunt Aggie said. "He ain't gon' do nothin'." She looked up at the big house. "Reckon Allie's here. David inside?"

"Yes. He let me drive his car."

"We better go in, see if she knows somethin' about Stan."

Celia led the way into the house. There they found Allie, Mark, Dan Nichols, and David talking in the kitchen like old friends.

Aunt Aggie wished she'd made a pie this morning like she'd planned.

• • •

Celia was long past caring how she looked. She walked into the kitchen and saw Allie and Mark sitting with David at the table, Dan Nichols leaning against the counter. All eyes turned to her the moment she stepped into the room, and she met David's eyes, wondering what he'd told them.

"Hey, Sis," he said. "Did you have a good drive?"

She came in and set her purse down. "Yeah. I was feeling kind of cooped up. Has any of you seen Stan?"

"We have," Mark and Allie said simultaneously, then Mark went on. "He's not feeling too great, so his folks wouldn't let us see him too long."

"Is he okay?"

They exchanged looks. "Well, I don't think he's out of danger yet," Allie said. "There was some talk about dialysis . . . apparently some of his organs may have been damaged. But he talked to us for a minute before his parents ran us out."

Her face grew hot. "Damaged organs? How damaged? Can they be repaired? Could he die?"

Mark looked helpless. "We honestly don't know, Celia. We didn't get to talk to the doctors, and his parents weren't real forthcoming. What we found out came from the people in the waiting room."

"Did he know about me?" she asked, feeling as fragile as a crystal doll. "Had anyone told him why I wasn't there?"

"Yeah, he knew." Allie's tone was heavy with apology. "He asked me about you, Celia. Wanted to know if you were all right. That's when his parents ran us out."

Celia turned away from them as her eyes filled with tears. "Did you tell him I didn't do it, Allie? Did you tell him it's all a mistake?"

Allie reached for her and pulled her into a hug. "He knows that, Celia. He loves you."

Her face twisted and she wiped at her eyes. "But did you tell him?"

"Yes. But his parents got us out so fast I'm not sure he heard. Celia, don't blame them. They're exhausted. They've been with him since the beginning, and I doubt either of them has left the hospital. Now that he's awake, they're finally going home tonight to get a good night's sleep. Maybe after that they'll see things more clearly and realize you couldn't have done this."

She let that sink in for a moment, processing it. His parents were leaving. He wouldn't have them hovering over him tonight.

Celia looked at Allie. "Allie, would you go back to see him tonight? Take him a note from me? Maybe you could even call me from his room so I could talk to him."

Allie glanced at Mark, then brought her apologetic eyes back to her. "Celia, I can't. They're not allowing visitors after his parents leave tonight."

She sank back down and tried to think. "Is someone still guarding him?" she asked.

Mark spoke up. "If I'm not mistaken, several of the guys are taking turns guarding him. Three- or four-hour shifts each."

"Who's on tonight?" she asked.

"Well, I don't know," Allie said, and Celia could see the suspicion forming on her face. "Why?"

"Because . . ." She looked around at each of them. "I want to make sure he's being carefully watched. I don't want anyone sneaking in, especially if his parents won't be there."

"I know who'll be there," Mark said. "When I was up there, R.J. mentioned that Vern Hargis would be on the first shift tonight. I don't know what they consider the first shift, and I don't know who's taking over for him, but I think he'll be in good hands with Vern."

Vern Hargis. A chain smoker. He would need to take smoking breaks.

She pulled out a chair and sat down next to her brother. Dan frowned at her, as if contemplating something, and she looked up at him. "What is it, Dan?"

"You don't look so good, Celia. Are you feeling all right?"

"No, not really," she said. "I think I've had a touch of a virus. I'll be fine."

"You're pale," Allie said. "Celia, we'll go and let you lie down. We just wanted to tell you we had seen Stan, that he asked about you, that things are looking up."

"Thanks," she said.

"Are you gonna be all right?"

She nodded and wiped the tears beneath her eyes again. "Yeah, sure. I'll be fine."

"Celia, I'll check in with you a little later," Allie said. "You get some rest, okay? Jill's working hard on this. It'll be over soon."

"I hope so."

She watched as they all filed out of the room, and David led them to the door. She could hear Aunt Aggie telling them all not to rush off, but they did, anyway.

Celia sat staring at the table, trying to work out what she would do, trying to think of the pros and cons, trying to measure the consequences.

In moments, both Aunt Aggie and David were back in the kitchen. "You awright, *sha?*" Aunt Aggie asked.

She was getting tired of that question, so she ignored it. "I'm going to see him."

Aunt Aggie looked at David, and David pulled a chair out and sat down across from her. "What about the guard?" he asked.

"I'll get past him somehow," she bit out. "This might be my only chance. I have to go while his parents aren't there." She looked up at her Aunt Aggie. "The guard is Vern Hargis, Aunt Aggie. He's a chain smoker, isn't he?"

"Well, yeah, he is, but—"

"So I'll hide in the stairwell and watch until he goes out for a smoking break. I have to tell Stan about the baby," she said. "I have to tell him that I love him and that I didn't do it. I could look in his eyes and know that he believes me. I could see for myself that he's all right . . ."

"I'm goin' with you," Aunt Aggie announced.

Celia looked hopefully up at her. "You will?"

"I might can help. Let you know when Vern sneaks off."

The first hope she'd felt since she'd heard Stan had opened his eyes blossomed inside her. She looked at David. He was staring at the table, thinking.

After a moment, he met her eyes, still contemplating, working it all out. "We have to think this through, Celia. If they catch you, they'll assume that you came to finish him off. What if his parents change their minds and come back? What if a nurse comes in? What if that guard comes back before you expect him to?"

Her heart was pounding with anticipation. "I have to take the chance that his parents won't come back. But you gave me an idea. I need a nurse's uniform. If I have one, I can pretend to be a nurse. Of course, if Vern sees me, he'll know it's me. But if he's there when I come out, maybe I can get past him without looking at him."

David nodded, still concentrating. "All right, then. I'll drive you. That way I can wait in the car close to an exit, and we can drive away before anyone spots you."

"Sure you want to be an accessory?" she asked.

"Celia, you're my sister. I'll do what I can to make sure it doesn't turn out as bad as it could. Just promise me you won't take any stupid chances or get so anxious that you do something you'll regret."

"I promise." She threw her arms around his neck, kissed his cheek, then stood up to hug Aunt Aggie.

"I'll go t' Slidell and buy a uniform," Aunt Aggie told her. "Maybe a wig for me, so's I can set in that waitin' room and

Vern won't recognize me. I'll take off all my Mary Kay, and
slump over like some ole lady. Get me a cane and some o' them
ole lady shoes."

David grinned at her. "You're enjoying this a little too
much, Aunt Aggie."

She slapped playfully at him. "You hush. We got to do it
right. Now, Celia, you go on up and take a nap while I'm gone,
so's you'll look purty for your husband. Don't wanna go with
no swollen eyes and red nose."

Celia smiled. "Okay, Aunt Aggie. I'll do that."

She started out of the room. Behind her, she heard David
say, "We're all probably out of our minds."

Aunt Aggie laughed with delight as Celia started up the
stairs.

Chapter Thirty

● ● ●

Aunt Aggie had come home with enough paraphernalia to start a life of crime. Already she was practicing walking with the cane and a pair of brogans that, as far as she was concerned, gave the elderly a bad name. And she'd gotten Celia a nursing uniform, and had even purloined a security badge so she'd look like a bona fide employee.

"Where in the world did you get this?" Celia asked, studying the badge.

Aunt Aggie's eyes danced with delight. "I was down to the uniform shop, and a nurse come in t' try on a new uniform, and when she got undressed, she hanged her other uniform over the door. The sales lady, she warn't lookin', so I moseyed on over and seen it was for the Slidell Hospital, so I jes' unclipped the badge . . ."

"Aunt Aggie, you *stole* it!"

Aunt Aggie seemed quite proud of herself. "I borried it. I plan to give it back. On our way outa the hospital, you can drop it somewhere. Somebody'll get it back to her."

She looked down at it again. The woman in the picture had red hair and glasses. "Aunt Aggie, I don't look anything like her."

Again, Aunt Aggie's eyes danced. "Look a-here," she said, digging into a bag. She pulled out a red wig and a pair of wire-framed glasses, just like the woman in the picture wore.

Celia laughed. David tried to hold back his smile, though he wasn't doing a very good job. "I think it's official now. She really is crazy."

"Vern won't recognize you. You could prob'ly even go in right in front o' him. He'd never even know."

"Maybe that won't be necessary," she said. "Maybe he'll go smoke. But if he doesn't, we'll have plan B."

"So when are we going to perpetrate this unfortunate act we're planning?" David asked.

"After visiting hours," she said. "That way I can be sure his parents will be gone."

"All right," he said.

"Oh, I forgot to tell you," Aunt Aggie said as she put the supplies back into her bag. "We got somebody outside watchin' the house."

"What?" Celia asked, her eyes shooting back up to Aunt Aggie.

"Yep. Sittin' a ways down the road, thinkin' I'm too dumb to know, but I seen him. T.J. Porter, I think. Readin' the paper when I come by, like he always parks his car on the side o' the road to read the paper."

"Do you think he's following her?" David asked.

"Prob'ly. I ain't seen him before now."

Celia dropped the badge and covered her face with both hands. "Oh, no. What if he followed me to Lee Barnett's apartment?"

"*Lee Barnett's?*" David returned. "Are you telling me that you went to Lee Barnett's?"

"Yes," she said. "Earlier when I borrowed your car."

"Are you asking for trouble? Celia, what were you thinking?"

"I wanted to look him in the eye and find out why he was doing this to me. I wanted to know if he's the one who poisoned Stan . . . and why."

He dropped his face on the table, as if giving up. "I can't believe this. It's hopeless." He raised his head back up and braced his elbows on the table. Looking at her through splayed fingers, he said, "Okay. Let's just hope that no one did see you. It won't look good, Celia. The very guy they think you tried to off your husband for, and you're seen going in his apartment?"

"No, I didn't go in."

"What in the world did he say?"

"He said he didn't do it. That he was framed, too. That someone is setting us both up."

"Yeah, right."

She sighed. "He seemed genuine. But it's hard to tell with him. I don't know him anymore. I don't know how he's changed since prison."

David went to the front window and looked out onto the street. "Well, okay, so you went to Lee Barnett's, you might have been seen ... Well, we can't do anything about that now. But we definitely can't let them follow us to the hospital. So we'll go in my car, and I'll take my suitcase out there like I'm leaving, put it in the trunk. But how will we get you in the car without him seeing?"

"We'll get in before you open the garage door. We'll duck down, and then you can open the garage and make a fuss over loading your suitcase. Since the garage is attached to the house, he won't know we ever came out."

"Yeah, that'll work."

"We can do this," Celia said.

David released a long breath, then shook his head again. "I hope Stan will appreciate it."

••••

Stan was exhausted by the time his parents left that night, for a steady stream of visitors had come through to visit him. For much of the time, he'd lain there with his eyes closed, too weak to make conversation. The visitors had seemed satisfied just to see him.

Now, visiting hour was over, his parents were gone, and he felt more alone than he'd ever felt. He wanted Celia. If she were able, she would spend the night here with him, look after him, fill his loneliness. He couldn't understand why Judge DeLacy would have kept her from that.

An idea came into his mind even as defeat seemed to rush in, and he glanced over at the phone on his table. It was too far away, and he didn't think he could get up enough to reach it. If he could just get to it . . .

A nurse breezed in, carrying a tray of medications. "Are you awake, Mr. Shepherd? I would have thought you were sleeping."

"In a minute," he said. "Listen, could you hand me the phone? I can't reach it."

"Sure," she said. She rounded the bed and set the phone on his pillow. "How's that?"

"Great," he said. "Thanks."

Humming, she breezed out again.

His heart began to flutter as he picked up the phone and dialed out his home phone number. She couldn't come to him, but no court order said that he couldn't call her. He waited for the first, second, third rings . . .

Finally, the machine picked up. His own voice greeted him. He hung up.

Where was she?

Aunt Aggie's, he thought. Of course. She would have stayed with Aunt Aggie, since there was a killer out there somewhere, and she was, no doubt, depressed and upset, and Aunt Aggie would nurture and pamper her.

He dialed the old woman's number. It rang once, twice, three times. . . .

There was no machine, so he waited, thinking that they might be avoiding phone calls since they were probably getting hate calls and the press was probably hounding them. Oh, how he wished he could clear her of this quickly, so that people would leave her alone. He dropped the phone in its cradle and sank back into the pillow. He wanted so badly to talk to her. If only there was someone he could send, to ask her to call *him*.

The preacher, he thought. He could call Nick. Nick would help him. Surely, he knew that Celia hadn't done this. He could count on him. Besides, he could use a little spiritual guidance.

He dialed the number, and Nick answered on the second ring. "Hello?"

"Hey, man," Stan said, knowing he didn't sound like himself. "I hope it's not too late, but I need to talk."

"Stan?"

"Yeah, it's me."

Nick began to laugh. "You feel well enough to call me and talk? Man, our prayers are being answered, brother. I can't believe it's you."

"Believe it," he said. "Listen, Nick. I need a favor. I need you to get a message to Celia."

• • •

The plan for getting Aunt Aggie and Celia into David's car worked perfectly, and as they drove past the car parked down the street, they knew that he hadn't followed them. He was still watching the house, where lights were on, thinking that Celia was inside.

As they reached the Slidell Hospital, Celia began to tremble. This wasn't going to be easy. "How will you know where to pick us up?" she asked.

"I was just thinking about that," David told her. "What if I go in with you and find the stairwell you'll be coming down? I can park next to whichever exit you'll be coming out."

"Good idea. But you'll have to park, and we'll have to walk across the parking lot."

"I'll drop you off at the main entrance, and you head straight for the first stairwell you see. I'll meet you there after I park. And Aunt Aggie can go on up, okay Aunt Aggie?"

"I'm ready," the old woman said. Celia looked back at her and chuckled at how old she looked. She had donned her curly gray wig and glasses, and she was wearing a loose-fitting frock that she would have never been caught dead in.

"Aunt Aggie, do you think you'd look like that for real if you hadn't had those two face-lifts?"

"Never," Aunt Aggie said. "I take too good care o' myself."

They reached the hospital parking lot. "We'll go up and make sure which exit is closest to Stan's room," David said, as if thinking out loud, "and then I'll move the car."

He pulled up to the front entrance, and they both sat there for a moment.

"You sure you're ready for this?" he asked.

"Yes," Celia said. "I'm sure. Thanks, David. We couldn't have done this without you." She got out of the car, and Aunt Aggie got out, too. Not waiting for what appeared to be the decrepit old lady, she headed inside and around the hall behind the elevators, where she saw an exit sign. Quietly, she slipped into the stairwell there. There was an exit door right there, at the foot of the stairs, and she sat down on the bottom step and waited.

In just a few moments, David stepped inside. "Okay, let's go up," he whispered. "Aunt Aggie said Stan's in 306. We'll see how close this stairwell comes out."

They climbed three flights of stairs, then peered out the rectangular window on the third floor. "This room right across the hall is 310. I think this is as close as we'll get, don't you?" she asked.

"Probably," he said. "Okay, so you wait here, and I'll go move the car to this exit at the bottom of this stairwell. Remember, Sis, don't take long with him. Get in, say what you've gotta say, and get out."

"I will."

She watched as he trotted back down the stairs. Then she turned back to the window and waited for Aunt Aggie to come and tell her when Vern left for a smoking break.

• • •

The waiting room was almost empty this time of night, but no one paid Aunt Aggie any attention as she sat there where she could see right up the hall to Stan's room, where Vern Hargis had sat for the past hour reading a magazine.

He was getting nervous, jumpy, she realized, because he was shaking his foot and doing a two-fingered drum roll on his leg, and when he finally discarded the magazine and got up, she knew they were about to hit pay dirt. But where would he go?

She tried to see past him, down the hall. Was there a balcony somewhere that he could step out on? A window he could lean out of? A bathroom he could smoke in?

She saw an exit sign, and a door opened from the night. A nurse came in, holding her own cigarette pack, and Aunt Aggie's heart leaped.

"Don't you need a smoke, *sha?*" Aunt Aggie whispered under her breath.

As if he'd heard her, he looked longingly toward that exit. He seemed to consider whether he could smoke out there while still guarding the room. Her heart was hammering, and she fought the urge to yell for him to go on, smoke that cigarette, and hurry up about it.

But then her plan was thwarted when an orderly dressed in surgical scrubs ambled toward Stan's room.

"How ya doin'?" he asked Vern, and Vern nodded. The man pushed on in.

Aunt Aggie sat back in a slump, wondering what they were going to do now.

Chapter Thirty-One

● ● ●

Since you don't pay me overtime, you don't care if I go home now, do you?" Jill's secretary, Sheila, asked from the doorway of her office. "I mean, I could do like you and work around the clock, but like I said, I don't get overtime."

Jill didn't have time to trade quips with Sheila. She'd been going over depositions from the Nathan case and was too deep in concentration. "Sure. You can go home."

"'Cause it's after dark, you know."

"You were late coming in," Jill said, finally looking up at her.

"I figured you'd be sleeping late, since you've been working so hard."

"Even if I had, the phone would still need to be answered, Sheila, and there's lots of work to be done."

"Did you realize you didn't wear makeup today? I can't figure out if it makes you look older or younger."

Jill set her pen down and leaned back in the chair, staring at the woman. Sometimes she just wanted to throttle her . . . or worse . . . fire her. But she had done it once before only to find that there wasn't anyone else in town as qualified as she. She'd hired her back with the stipulation that she get an attitude adjustment, but apparently Sheila hadn't taken that too seriously.

"What?" Sheila asked, as if innocent of offending her boss.

"Did you expect me to respond to that, Sheila?"

"No, I was just making an observation."

"Thank you. I didn't wear makeup because I forgot. I had too much on my mind."

"Older, I think," Sheila finally decided. "Has Dan seen you like that?"

Jill turned the page of the deposition and began reading again. "Good-bye, Sheila."

The woman backed out of the room, and in moments, she heard the front door close. She was gone. Jill got up and stretched, then went in to the bathroom connected to her office and looked in the mirror. She did look awful. She couldn't believe she hadn't worn makeup, but she'd had all those questions about Celia on her mind . . . Sheila was right. She did look older. Old and unmarried. And if Dan saw her this way, he'd be even more repulsed then he'd been by her behavior last night.

She heard the door open and close again, and she went back to her desk, not wanting Sheila to catch her looking in the mirror. She didn't want Jill to have the satisfaction of thinking her comment had bothered her.

But it wasn't Sheila who appeared in the doorway. It was Sid.

"Got somethin' for you, Jill," he said.

Jill didn't want it. Whatever it was, it had to be bad news, and she wasn't up to it. She just stared at him.

He crossed the room and dropped a 5 x 7 snapshot down on her desk. "Now tell me Celia ain't guilty."

Jill looked down at the snapshot. Her face fell. It was of Celia and Lee Barnett, standing close with his hands on her arms. "What is this?"

"Your client went to see her boyfriend this afternoon," Sid said. "Because Stan made us promise to keep somebody on her for protection, Vern Hargis followed her there."

Jill frowned, studying the picture. Her heart was pounding out a dirge-like rhythm, and she wanted to cry. But that wouldn't do. "There's an explanation," she said weakly.

"Oh, yeah? Did *you* know she was goin' to see him?"

"No, but I'm sure . . ."

"That's cause she's fleecin' you, too, Jill. Wake up, woman."

Jill studied the picture and realized she couldn't see either of their faces. Just Celia's ponytail and Lee Barnett holding her. How could she have gone to see him in broad daylight, and necked with him right out in the open? Did she *want* to get caught? No, she told herself as reason took over. Something wasn't right.

She got to her feet and grabbed her briefcase with one hand and the snapshot with the other. "Excuse me, Sid. I need to go speak to my client."

"Be my guest," Sid said. "But don't eat nothin' she feeds you."

Chapter Thirty-Two

● ● ●

Stan was crushed when he realized that Nick had not been to see Celia since this whole ordeal had begun. He clutched the phone to his ear and tried to speak clearly. "What's wrong with you?" he asked. "You call yourself a preacher? My wife has been arrested for attempted murder . . . and you . . . you don't even visit her?"

He knew his words were too harsh, but he was too tired, too weak, to choose them any more carefully. Might as well just say what he thought. And what he thought was that Nick Foster had let Celia down.

"Stan, you're right. I should have gone. It's just that I didn't know if she wanted company . . ."

"That's lame, Nick. She needs support. Half this town probably thinks she tried to kill me. I never imagined you'd be in that half."

"I'm not! Stan, listen to me. I'll go right now. I do believe in her innocence. And you're right, I should have gone. I don't even know why I didn't. But I was working at the fire station, and then last night we had services, and—"

Stan knew he needed to calm down. His heart was beating too fast, and with all the medication being pumped into him to battle the effects of the arsenic, he couldn't afford to get too excited.

An orderly dressed in scrubs, with his surgical mask still up and his hat still on, came in and motioned for him to keep talking, so Stan didn't get off the phone.

"I'm sorry I jumped you," Stan said to Nick as the orderly went to the foot of the bed and checked his chart. He was holding an IV bag, and it hung from his finger as he flipped through the chart. "I just don't like having my wife treated like this. If there's even a chance that you believe she's guilty, or if she thinks you *think* she's guilty, so help me, Nick, I'll change churches so fast—"

"Stan, come on. I'm a preacher, not superman. I'm doing the best I can. I didn't know how to handle it. I've been praying for both of you, though. Stan, if you want me to go over to Aunt Aggie's, I will. I'll go tonight, wake her up, if you want."

"I do want," he said. The orderly came back around the bed and began changing the bag.

"So you want me to tell her to call you?"

"Yes, if the switchboard is still open. If it's not, tell her to answer it when I call. I think she and Aunt Aggie might be just letting it ring. If I don't hear something in the next half hour, I'll call her again."

"All right, Stan. Just relax, all right? I'll take care of it."

Stan hung up and regarded the bag the orderly had hung. "That bag wasn't empty, was it?"

"No, but it wasn't dripping right. I was told to change it."

Stan glanced at him. He was wearing big black glasses, and that mask made him nervous. He never liked not being able to see someone's face. "You just come out of surgery?"

The man shook his head and checked the drip. "Nope. They just made me wear the mask my whole shift tonight because of my cold. Don't want me passing any germs along."

He went back to the chart, made a notation, then started for the door. "You're all right now. Why don't you go to sleep?"

"I will," Stan said.

He lay there and let his eyes close, but as tired as he was, he didn't want to sleep. Not yet. Not until he heard from his wife. Not until he talked to Celia.

••• •

In the waiting room, Aunt Aggie saw the orderly leave the room. Vern had sat back down now and was reading that magazine again. As fidgety as he was, she finally realized that he wasn't going to smoke. He was too loyal to Stan. Celia would have to do the nurse bit and take her chances.

She got up from the vinyl sofa. Slumped over and leaning on her cane, she shuffled down the hall to the stairwell four rooms down from Stan's room.

Celia was sitting on a stair, waiting for her, and when Aunt Aggie stepped in, she sprang up. "Is he gone, Aunt Aggie? Is he smoking?"

"He ain't gon' smoke. He wants to, but he ain't gon' do it."

She took a deep breath. "Then I'll just have to pretend to be a nurse." She touched her red wig and straightened her glasses. "Will he recognize me, Aunt Aggie?"

"Not if you walk fast like you b'long there. He's readin' a magazine. I was you, I'd say hey to him and give 'im long enough to see your badge, then hurry past him. Don't look 'im in the eye. Jes' look up the hall like you're lookin' for somethin'."

She took in a deep breath. "All right. Wish me luck."

"Good luck."

She started out of the stairwell and didn't see anyone except Vern in the hall. Just as Aggie had told her, he was reading that magazine.

She walked quickly, and he looked up just as she drew near. She muttered, "Hey," and glanced up the hall.

"Hey." He glanced at her badge. Then he went back to reading.

She was inside Stan's door before she knew it.

She saw him lying there, with that IV in his arm and that oxygen tube under his nose, resting with his eyes closed, and that phone beside his head on the pillow. Who had he been talking to?

Her heart burst, and her eyes filled with tears, and she stepped closer to the bed. "Stan?"

His eyes opened, and he looked up at her.

She took off her glasses, and pulled the wig off, revealing her blonde bun. "It's me, honey."

He caught his breath and reached up for her, and she slid her arms around him and began to weep.

His embrace was weak, but his love wasn't, and as she pulled back to look at him, she saw the tears in his eyes.

"Are you all right?" he asked her.

"You're the one in a hospital bed." Her eyes filled again. "Are you in any pain?"

He ignored the question and touched her face. "They accused you."

"I didn't do it, Stan."

"Shhh, I know you didn't. We'll convince them. But you have to be careful. They're out there ..."

"You don't know who did this?" she asked him. "You don't remember who gave you the poison?"

"Can't imagine." He wiped her tears from her face. "But we have to find out."

"We're trying. Jill's trying. But Stan, I have some good news for you. You're not going to believe this." She was crying harder and could barely speak, but she forced the words out.

"Good news?" he asked. "Good news that makes you cry?"

"My emotions are on a roller coaster," she whispered. "Mostly down ... but this news ..."

"What are you doing?"

Celia swung around to the voice and saw Vern standing in the doorway. "Vern, please. I just wanted to talk—"

He shot across the room and grabbed her as he called for help on his walkie-talkie. She tried to wrestle free, but before she knew it he had the handcuffs snapped on her. "Vern, please. I didn't do anything. I just wanted to talk to him."

"You're under arrest again," Vern said. "You have the right to remain silent—"

"Vern, stop it!" Stan cried. "Let her go! She didn't do anything."

More security people came in, and Celia's face was raging hot as tears ran down her face. "What do you think I was going to do? Kill him? I just wanted to tell him something. I wanted to see him!"

Some nurses and a doctor ran in. "Mr. Shepherd, did she give you anything to eat?"

"No! Let her go!"

She was screaming and wailing now, and trying to fight free. "Please. Why would I kill my husband? Why would I want to kill the father of my baby? I'm pregnant, Stan! That's what I wanted to tell you!"

"Pregnant?" The word was weak, breathless.

"His blood pressure is dropping!"

"What?" she asked. "I didn't *do* anything!"

"Who changed this bag?" the nurse demanded. "Did you do it?" she asked Celia.

"No! I don't even know how!"

"Someone changed this bag! It was half full a little while ago when I checked it. Now it's full."

"It was the orderly," Stan got out weakly.

But his words were lost in the chaos that followed, and Celia realized that something was wrong. Had he been poisoned again?

"Help him!" she cried. But Vern wrestled her out of the room. And as tears streamed down her face, she realized she might never see her husband alive again.

Chapter Thirty-Three

● ● ●

When Jill had failed to find Celia at Aunt Aggie's, or any-where else, she'd been ready to erupt. She had finally given up and come home. The classical music CD piping through Jill's house calmed her spirit somewhat, though the questions of the day still churned in her mind. She made her-self a sandwich in the kitchen, a dollop of peanut butter between two slices of bread, then realized that she needed something healthier, something warm. But she'd had no time to go to the grocery store, no time to do any cooking.

Again, she walked to her answering machine and checked the messages to see if Dan had called. There was nothing there. Had he forgotten her in her busyness, she wondered? Was he still mad at her for the things she'd said last night? Was he waiting for her to call him?

He certainly had a reputation for arrogance, yet she couldn't help wondering after spending so much time with him if it wasn't a reputation built on fear. Something told her that Dan was afraid of rejection and abandonment, that his detach-ment from women had more to do with his own insecurities than with his desire to be alone. It was an insight that had come after a great deal of thought. She wasn't sure he would agree with her. She wasn't even sure she was right.

But she supposed that she should be thankful that they had been out more than his usual three times, and that he contin-ued to show interest. At least, he had until last night.

She went back to her briefcase and looked at the notes she had taken today when she'd visited Celia. She had been working around the clock to solve this case, racking her brain to figure out who could have poisoned Stan and Nathan. Now to learn that Celia was sneaking around, hiding things from her, was more than Jill could stand. She needed to talk to someone.

She thought of calling Allie, but she didn't want to cast more bad light on Celia. Besides, she had no business sharing the case with anyone.

She needed a friend. Just someone to eat with ...

Deciding to swallow her pride and take a chance, she picked up the phone and dialed Dan's number. He answered quickly.

"Hello?"

"Hi, Dan. It's Jill."

She could hear the sigh in his voice. Was it relief, or dread? "Jill."

"I hope I'm not bothering you," she said. "I wanted to apologize for last night. You're right. I was strung a little too tight. I was edgy, and I shouldn't have taken it out on you."

"No, you shouldn't have."

She sat there for a moment. Was he going to make her grovel? She began to get angry. "That's what I said."

"Okay."

She sat there a little longer, holding the phone to her ear and seriously considering hanging it up. What did he want from her?

"So ... did you get any sleep?"

The question seemed gentler, and her anger cooled a degree. "No, not really. And I've had a really rough day."

"Uh-oh. Then I guess I'd better not suggest a late dinner. We might butt heads again."

That balloon of anger seemed to deflate in her chest. "If I promise to behave better, would you go ahead and suggest dinner? I was just about to eat a peanut butter sandwich."

"You can do better than that, Jill," Dan said, all anger gone from his tone. "Let me take you out to eat."

She hesitated a moment. "It's after nine, and I don't know if I'm really up to going out. I thought maybe you could come over and I could make something—"

Before she could finish the sentence, he cut in. "You're not making anything, Jill. You've been working around the clock. I'll tell you what. I'll pick something up at Maison de Manger and bring it over. What would you like?"

She couldn't think. Her brain was too tired. "Surprise me."

"Will do," he said. "I'll see you in about half an hour."

She smiled. The night was looking up after all.

Jill spent the next half hour in a whirlwind, cleaning the mess that had accumulated in her house since Celia's arrest. She was not known for being a neat person. On a good day, she left her bed unmade, clothes thrown over a chair in her bedroom, and dishes in the sink. But in the past few days, dust had collected, dirty laundry had gathered in a heap on her bedroom floor, and stacks of unread mail spilled over her kitchen counter. She rushed as fast as she could to get the place clean before Dan showed up.

By the time he arrived, her house was passable, though not spotless by anyone's standards. They ate together, talking quietly, and she enjoyed the warmth and sustenance of the food he had brought, for she hadn't had a real meal since the last time she'd eaten with him. She'd have to watch it, she thought, or she would start associating comfort and well-being with his presence.

"So how's the case going?" he asked.

She sighed. "Not good. I'm hitting a lot of dead ends. I've spent most of today going over depositions from the first trial and making phone calls, trying to track down people who knew anything about the Nathan case. It's slow going."

He touched her hand and fondled her fingers, sending a jolt through her body. She wasn't used to affection of any kind. But she told herself that she could get used to it from Dan.

"You'll be fine," he said. "I have a lot of faith in you. Your instincts are great."

She sat there a moment, letting the words sink in. Her instincts. Weren't those what were pulling her down now? She wasn't sure whether her instincts were urging her toward trusting in Celia's innocence, or sending up alarm signals in her brain. To her, doubting Celia meant failure. Celia had been a good enough friend to her to deserve her trust.

"What's wrong?" Dan asked.

She met his eyes and wondered how much he could see. "I guess this case has just got me down."

"You're not worried, are you?"

She averted her eyes. "A little. There were some new developments today. I can't really discuss them, but it doesn't look good for Celia."

Dan frowned. "You're not starting to think she did it, are you?"

"No, not at all. Of course not."

"But what?" he asked.

"But Sid does, and that's important. It's important for me to stand behind Celia and to do everything in my power to make Sid think twice about keeping her on the suspect list. But it's getting harder all the time."

"They've found more evidence?" he asked.

She stared at him, knowing she couldn't elaborate, but needing so badly to talk. Thankfully, the doorbell rang.

She got up and hurried to it, wondering who it could be, dreading the bad news that seemed almost inevitable. She opened the door and saw Nick Foster standing there. "Nick, hi."

He looked worried, distracted, as if he hadn't come to pay a social visit. "Jill, can I talk to you for a minute?"

"Sure," she said. She ushered him in, and he saw Dan and reached out to shake his hand.

"I'm sorry to interrupt, but I'm worried about Celia."

Jill's expression changed. "What do you mean?"

He took off his glasses and rubbed his eyes. "Stan called me a little while ago," he said. "He wanted me to go by Aunt Aggie's and tell Celia to call him, because he really wanted to talk to her and they weren't answering the phone."

"Really?" Jill asked, her eyebrows rising. "That's a good sign."

"Of course it is," Nick said. "Stan doesn't think Celia had anything to do with this. In fact, as weak as he is, he had plenty of energy to lambaste me for not being there for her. And he's right. I just . . . I don't know what to think about her, Jill."

Jill understood more than he knew. She touched his shoulder gently. "Nick, we all have to keep an open mind and just pray hard for Celia."

"I know. And sometimes I really just have a hard time following the Spirit, and I wonder if I ought to even be in this profession at all."

Dan got up from the table and set his hand on Nick's shoulder. "Nick, you're a good fireman, but you're the best preacher I know. Don't start getting all down on yourself."

"The best preacher?" Nick almost laughed, but he obviously didn't find it amusing. "You haven't had much experience with them, then, have you?" He sighed. "Well, anyway, that doesn't matter. The reason I came is that I went by Aunt Aggie's, and no one's home."

"Still?" Jill asked. "Are you sure?"

"That's right," Nick said. "I knocked on the front door, went around to the back door. There were lights on in the house, but no answer. I went to a pay phone and called, still no answer. Finally, I went over to Celia's, thinking maybe she'd gone home, but there was no one there, either."

Jill frowned. "Where could they be?"

"I don't know," Nick said. "But I thought she might be over here." He glanced at the food on the table. "I guess I was wrong. I don't know what to do now. I guess I should call Stan back and tell him I can't find her."

Jill didn't like what she was hearing. She thought of Lee Barnett, then quickly tried to squelch the thought. But it hung on. Celia had already gone to see him once—what was to stop her from going again? No, certainly not. Just because Celia had gone to him once didn't mean she'd do it again. She went to the telephone and dialed Aunt Aggie's, then waited as it rang and rang and rang. No answer.

"Where could she be?"

Dan thought for a moment, then met her eyes. "The hospital?"

Jill froze. "No. No way. She knows better."

"If she wanted to talk to Stan as much as he wanted to talk to her," Nick said. "I wouldn't put it past her."

Jill closed her eyes. "It's the worst thing she could do right now. I don't think she would have tried it without talking to me first." But hadn't she gone to see Barnett this morning without talking to Jill? That had been self-destructive, but Celia hadn't cared. Right now, Celia was desperate, and she was only interested in the bottom line. Jill just wasn't sure what that bottom line was.

"Maybe I'd better call Stan and see if he's heard from her." She went to the telephone, but before she could pick it up, it rang. Quickly, she snatched it up. "Hello?"

"Jill, this is Sid Ford." The words were rapid-fire, distant, as if he was calling from a cellular phone.

"Sid, what's wrong?"

"I'm on my way to Slidell Hospital," he said. "Your girl was just caught in Stan's room."

"*What?*" Jill asked. Then rallying, she said, "Sid, don't jump to conclusions. She just wanted to see him."

"Jump to conclusions?" he shot back. "Jill, they found arsenic in his IV bag. *Somebody* put it there."

She was speechless.

"Jill did you hear me?"

"I heard you," she said.

"Use your head, Jill. Think. She breaks the court order to come there in the first place, finagles a way in usin' a disguise, and when she's caught they discover that arsenic is in her husband's bag. Nobody else could have put it there, Jill."

Jill sank into a chair. Dan and Nick stood over her, waiting to hear what was going on. "Where is she?"

"Vern's haulin' her in right now," Sid said. "But I'm goin' there to talk to Stan."

"I'll meet her at the police station," Jill said.

"You do what you want," Sid said. "But don't expect bond tonight. I've already been in touch with the judge and given him an earful. Louis is with us on this."

Jill closed her eyes.

"I thought you'd want to know," Sid said, and cut off the phone.

Jill lowered the phone but kept holding it in her hand.

"What is it?" Dan asked.

"You were right," she said. "That's exactly where Celia was."

"At the hospital?"

"Yeah. And she got caught." She didn't tell him about the arsenic. That was something that he wasn't going to hear from her. "It's gonna be another long night," she said. "I've got to get to the police station, guys."

"Of course you do," Dan said. "I'll follow you there."

She didn't have any energy to argue as she grabbed her briefcase and headed for the door.

Chapter Thirty-Four

● ● ●

Aunt Aggie had been sitting in the hospital waiting room when she saw Vern get up restlessly and peer into the room. She had braced herself. She knew what would come next.

And then she'd heard shouting, and security people began running to the room, and then nurses and doctors, like Stan had done one of those Code Blue things. When they had dragged Celia out of the room, crying and screaming, Aunt Aggie had been torn between beating Vern off with her cane, and taking the stairs down as fast as she could. Since Vern had gotten Celia onto the elevator before she'd made up her mind, she'd chosen the stairs.

She was out of breath by the time she got all the way down, and just as he'd promised, David was sitting in his car right beside the exit. He saw the look on her face and leaned over to open the passenger door.

"Aunt Aggie, what's wrong?"

"They got her!" She climbed into the car like a thief escaping a bank robbery. She pulled her wig off and threw it down, leaving her own white hair sticking out all over. "Come in and caught her!"

David cursed. "Where is she?"

"They takin' her to Newpointe, I guess. Maybe Slidell. Hurry 'round and maybe we'll catch up with 'em. We can follow 'em, see where they take her. But what if they see us?"

The sound of sirens began to get closer, and David shook his head. "Aunt Aggie, if they do see us, so what? *We* weren't

under a court order. You and I were allowed to come here."
Aunt Aggie saw several police cars pull in front of the building,
and the cops got out and hustled in. "What did they do, call out
the cavalry? All she did was break a stupid court order."

"The commotion!" Aunt Aggie said, dropping her head
back against the seat. "You shoulda seen it! The screamin' and
runnin' and wailin' and doctors and nurses . . ."

"I should have talked her out of this. Aunt Aggie, they'll put
her back in jail."

"*I* shoulda talked her out of it, too. But I didn't think we'd
get caught. She didn't hurt nobody."

They saw Vern leading a crying Celia out the front door
and put her roughly into the squad car. Several other cops clus-
tered around the car.

Aunt Aggie started to cry. "I got to help her. I got to go
over there and tell 'em to leave her alone, that she didn't do
nothin' but visit her husband . . . Give me that cane back."

"No, Aunt Aggie. I don't need my sister *and* my aunt in jail.
You're not going over there swinging your cane at a bunch of
cops. Now, just sit here for a minute. I think we can do more
good if we follow her to the police station and try to bail her out."

"Awright," Aunt Aggie agreed. But in her heart she wasn't
sure if it was the right thing to do.

•   •   •

Up in the room, Stan felt weak, disoriented, and he was having trouble breathing again, and those stomach cramps
were starting. Doctors and nurses poked and prodded him,
drawing blood and taking vitals, and he kept muttering,
"Orderly. Not Celia. Orderly."

Someone in a lab coat stood over him, talking to the doctors and cops as if he wasn't in the room. "The IV bag was poisoned with arsenic. It also had a pinprick in it, so she must have

injected the arsenic solution into the bag. Either she brought the bag in and switched it, or she injected it right here."

"No," he said. "No, you're wrong." But they weren't listening.

He tried to think what the orderly looked like. He needed to give them a description. But he'd had on that surgical mask ... said he had a cold ... and the surgical hat, and scrubs, and those glasses. He hadn't looked at him that closely, had only glanced up at him.

"Stan ..."

He looked up and saw Sid standing over him. How had he gotten here so fast? He realized vaguely that a lot had happened. Things were fading in and out, and time had slipped by. Had they medicated him? Had the arsenic damaged his brain?

"Stan, tell me what she did when she came in here."

Yes, he thought. He wanted to tell him. He shored up every ounce of energy he still had. "She told me she was pregnant," he whispered. He grabbed Sid's shirt and tugged him down. "She didn't do anything to the bag, Sid. It was an orderly. Someone came in before her ... changed the bag."

"Someone? Who?"

"An orderly. Scrubs. Mask."

Sid looked up at R.J. standing across the bed, and Stan grabbed his shirt, too. "R.J., she didn't do it."

"What *did* she do, then? What did she say?"

"I told you ... that she was pregnant. That she loved me ..." He could feel the emotions rushing from his heart straight into his face. "Then Vern came in ..."

"Stan, I know you don't think she did anything, but were you awake when she came in?"

"Yes. I was waiting for her to call."

"Call? Had you been in touch with her?"

"No, but I sent Nick ... to tell her to call me." Tears rolled down his temples.

"Are you sure you weren't asleep when she came in? She might have done something to the bag before she woke you."

"She *didn't*. Why aren't you looking for that orderly?"

Again, Sid and R.J. exchanged looks. "Stan, I don't blame you for trying to cover for your wife, but one minute you didn't have arsenic in your IV bag, and the next minute you did. She was here, man, and she wasn't supposed to be." He leaned over him and patted Stan's shoulder. "Man, I know it hurts. I know how awful this must be. But you can't deny what's happenin'. Maybe if she really is pregnant, the hormones have done some kind o' number on her brain cells. Maybe she can't even help herself. But she did it, man. It's so obvious."

He could feel the heat in his face. "She *didn't*. Where are they taking her?"

"To Newpointe. Stan, we need your help. Did she say anything else? Was she carrying anything? A purse? A bag? Did she bring anything in?"

"No. Find the orderly." The words came through his teeth, with as much strength as he could muster. "Find him, Sid. Let my wife go. She's innocent."

Again, the two cops exchanged looks. Finally, Sid nodded to R.J., who then pulled a snapshot out of his pocket.

"What's that?" Stan whispered.

"It's a picture. Evidence that Celia's involved. Stan, you told us to guard her and follow her, so we did. And earlier today, when it was Vern's shift, he followed her to Lee Barnett's place."

"Who?"

"Lee Barnett. The convict we told you about who was recently released. Her old flame. She went there to see him this afternoon. And Vern got this picture." He looked sympathetically at Stan before he handed him the snapshot. "I'm sorry, man. I don't want to show you this."

Stan felt the wallop in his heart, but he forced his hand up and took the picture. He didn't want to see it. Didn't even want to look. But he made himself.

There stood Celia in Lee Barnett's arms, right outside in broad daylight.

His heart crashed. Suddenly, he couldn't find words, couldn't think . . .

"I'm sorry, man," Sid said gently. "Stan, I'd rather be tortured than to make you look at that picture. I didn't want to show you. But tonight she came in here and poisoned you for the second time, and I'll be hanged if I'm gonna let her get away with it. And that means that I can't let you keep thinkin' that she's the victim. *You* are, man. *She's* the criminal."

"There's a reason." He didn't know how he got the thought to formulate, much less the words, but some nagging voice in the back of his heart told him it was true. "There's a reason . . . it's not the way it looks . . . It may not even be her. I can't see her face."

"It was her, Stan. Vern saw her. He followed her there, watched her go to his door . . ."

"Did he hear what she said to this . . . Barnett guy?"

"No, but Marabeth Simmons did. She heard them talkin' about checkin' into a hotel, and about what to tell the cops, and he told her he'd cover for her. Maybe they were plannin' what just happened."

Stan looked as if he'd just been walloped in the stomach.

"Did she go into his apartment?"

"No."

"They just stood outside like this, talking about murder in voices loud enough to be heard, in broad daylight?"

"No, of course not. They were talking in low voices, but Marabeth was able to make out some of it."

"Marabeth Simmons is one of the two biggest busybodies in Newpointe, and you believe *her* over *Celia?*"

"Stan, look at the picture, man. She went there. Ain't what you see there evidence enough?"

Stan stared at the ceiling, unable to speak.

"Stan, you got to listen, man."

"Get out."

Sid looked stunned by the words. "What?"

"Get out."

The nurse in the room came to his bedside, checked his blood pressure reading, then nodded to the two cops. "You'd better go."

Sid took a step back and nodded to R.J. The other cop walked toward the door, but Sid hung behind.

"Man, I don't want you holdin' this against me."

"She didn't do it."

"I think she did. And when I go, and you're layin' in here by yourself, your body tryin' to filter out that arsenic for the second time, I think you'll believe it, too. It ain't a coincidence that her first husband died of the same thing, that she was the suspect, that she was with you the first time you were poisoned *and* the second time. No coincidence, man. But I'm goin', if you want me to. Take care o' yourself, man. R.J.'s gonna be here for a while, right outside the door. He ain't gon' let nobody in without writin' their name down—doctors and nurses included."

"How about orderlies?" Stan asked through his anger. "There's one in this hospital that poisoned my bag."

"Orderlies, too. Don't worry about it, man."

Stan closed his eyes after Sid left the room, yet he fought the sleep from the drugs they had given him to combat the poison. He thought of that picture again, of his wife in Lee Barnett's arms. Was it true?

No, of course it wasn't. It couldn't be.

But pictures didn't lie. Or did they? Didn't they lie all the time? She hadn't gone into the apartment, after all.

He tried to picture Barnett's face again, and what he could see of the orderly's face. Was it the same face? Had Barnett been working with her? Could it be possible?

Tears filled his eyes as he remembered her announcement to him. A baby. Was there really a baby? What would happen to it now? Was she in jail? Was she guilty, as everyone seemed to think? Or was this all just a terrible mistake?

He didn't know, but he laid his arm over his eyes and began to sob as the confusing torrent of thoughts washed over him. What if it was true? What if his wife really did want him dead?

Chapter Thirty-Five

● ● ●

Nick hadn't been back home long when the telephone rang. Wearily, he picked it up. "Hello?"

"Nick?" The voice was weak, and he recognized it to be Stan's.

"Stan, is that you?"

"Yeah, it's me. Listen, uh ... something happened tonight."

"Yeah. Celia wasn't at Aunt Aggie's when I went to tell her to call you, and then I went over to Jill's and I was there when she got the call that Celia had been caught in your room."

"Yeah." His voice cracked, and Nick could tell that he was struggling with emotion. "Uh ... look man. I could use some help tonight."

Nick swallowed. "Sure. I'll do anything, Stan, just tell me what you need."

"Do you think you could come over to the hospital? Pay me a little ministerial visit?"

"Of course. I can leave right now."

"That'd be great." His voice cracked, and the silence was eloquent. "I'd appreciate that, man."

"Stan, are you all right?"

"No, I don't think so."

"Is there anything I can bring you?"

Stan was quiet again. When he finally found a word, it was wrought with emotion. "Hope?"

Nick's heart sank. Once again, he was being asked to give something he didn't possess. "I'll do what I can, buddy," he said. "I'll be right over."

Stan's parents had come back to the hospital by the time Nick got there at 10:30, and his mother had red patches under her eyes, as if she'd been weeping as hard as she'd ever wept in her life. She clucked over him like a mother hen, arranging his pillows and straightening his covers, while his father paced the room back and forth with simmering anger so intense that Nick could almost see it smoking out his ears.

Stan looked weaker than Nick had expected. Dark shadows lurked under his red-rimmed, puffy eyes, and Nick imagined that he had been weeping, as Nick himself would have done had he been betrayed in such a colossal way.

"How ya doin', man?" he said, shaking his friend's hand.

Stan's eyes immediately filled with tears again. "Mom, Dad, would you mind giving me a few minutes alone with Nick?"

His mother wiped at her own eyes. "Of course. We'll be in the waiting room if you need us."

He waited as they both left the room. Nick got a chair and pulled it up to the side of the bed, sat down, and leaned forward. "Her visit . . . was it traumatic for you?"

Again, Stan's eyes filled. "Actually, it was nice. It was right after I'd talked to you on the phone. I hung up and closed my eyes and was waiting to hear back, and there she was, with this silly wig on, and glasses, and a nurse's uniform—" His voice cracked, and he covered his face with both hands.

"What happened?" Nick whispered.

"She got caught," Stan forced out. "And then they found arsenic in my IV bag."

"Arsenic?" Nick asked. "There was arsenic in your IV?"

"Somebody put it there," he said. "And I'd swear to you it was the orderly that came in while I was on the phone with you. Only, I can't identify him. He had a surgical mask over his face, and he had on glasses and a surgical cap. Why would he come in like that, if he wasn't trying to make sure I couldn't ID him? Said he had a cold. But no one believes me. They think I'm covering for her."

"What do *you* think, Stan?" Nick asked.

Stan looked up at the ceiling. "Nick, I would lay my hand on a Bible and swear to you that my wife did not do this. But—"

That "but" was heavy and set itself down between them like a big lead box. "But?" Nick asked.

"But the picture." His mouth twisted, and he covered it with the back of his wrist.

"What picture?" Nick asked.

"The picture of her with that man. That Lee Barnett. The convict."

Nick frowned. "Wait a minute. She was with him?"

"Seems that way," Stan said. "Vern followed her. Took pictures."

Nick was stunned, and for a moment he couldn't speak. Finally, he managed to whisper, "I can't believe it."

"I saw the picture myself." He covered his eyes with the heels of his hands and balled his fingers into fists. "I don't know what's going on with her, but it's suspicious."

"But . . . the orderly. What about the orderly?"

"The hospital staff swears that everyone on shift has been accounted for, and that none of them changed the bag. But I know he was here. I saw him change it. Who *was* that and why does he want me dead?"

Nick searched his heart and all of his wisdom for an answer that would satisfy Stan, but he had too many questions himself. He looked helplessly at his friend, and shook his head. "I don't know what to say, buddy. I don't know what to do for you."

Stan kept the heels of his hands pressed against his eyes. "Tell me that my wife doesn't want me dead," he said. "Tell me that the baby she's carrying isn't going to suffer."

"Baby?" Nick sat erect. "Stan, you didn't tell me—"

"*She* just told *me*," he cried.

Nick groped for the right words, but could find none. For the thousandth time since this case had begun, he sought the wisdom of the Holy Spirit, but he still felt inadequate, useless.

"I can pray for you, Stan," Nick said, wiping his own tears. "That's all I know to do. Just pray."

"That's enough."

Nick touched his shoulder and began to pray, for answers to their questions, for peace, for truth, for healing, for restoration, for reconciliation. When the amen came, he saw that Stan was calmer. Stan removed his hands from his face and looked at him.

Nick's heart broke. His own face twisted, and he rubbed at his jaw. "I've got to be honest with you, Stan. I don't know what to do for her ... but I know that she is still a member of my flock. Whether she's innocent or guilty, she needs God. And she needs friends."

"I don't know if there's some dark room in her brain that holds some deadly secret," Stan said, "but even if she did poison me, Nick, even if she poisoned Nathan ..." His voice broke and his face twisted. "Even if she did those things, I still can't stand the thought of her sitting in jail alone ..."

Nick nodded, knowing that feeling himself. "I'll go to her tonight, Stan. She may just be a lost sheep in my flock. Jesus would have searched high and low for her ... for the one lost sheep. If she did this, there's something wrong here, Stan. Some mental illness, or something that can be explained. Or she could be totally innocent, in which case she really needs a friend."

"Help her, Nick."

Nick nodded. "I will. I'll go see her when I leave here, if they'll let me."

"And keep praying," Stan said.

"I'll keep praying," Nick promised. "It's all I can do. It's all I have." Nick wiped his eyes. "If there were a fire, I'd put it out. If there were a heart attack, I know CPR. If there were a wreck, I'd use the jaws of life. For a thing like this, I just pray."

"That's better than CPR or the jaws of life. You're doing fine, Nick."

Nick swallowed back his own emotion as he got to his feet. "Get some rest, okay? Try not to think. I'll talk to you tomorrow and let you know how my visit with Celia went."

"All right, Nick. Thanks."

Nick hated to leave him, but Stan's parents returned to the room as soon as he stepped into the hall. He got onto the elevator, let the doors close, and stood there for a long moment before pushing a button. Silently, he prayed for the power and wisdom to do the right thing.

Of its own accord, the elevator began to move, down, down, down, until the doors opened on the lobby, where someone waited to get on. He stepped off, realizing that God was telling him to move, take action, get going . . .

He headed out to his car to do *something*, hoping that it was the right thing.

Chapter Thirty-Six

● ● ●

"Why did you do it?"

Jill's monotone question dripped with suspicion, and Celia knew she was close to losing Jill's trust.

"Because I wanted to see him." The tears were gone. She had cried enough to fill a bayou, and now she was empty, dead, numb. She leaned on the table in the interrogation room where she'd been drilled just a few days before, and set her dull eyes on her lawyer and friend. "I wanted to tell him about the baby."

Jill's face changed. "Baby? What baby?"

"I'm pregnant, Jill."

Jill stared at her for a moment, as if not sure what to believe. "Are you sure?"

"Yes. This morning the hospital called. The blood they took the other night? It was negative for arsenic poisoning, but it was positive for pregnancy. That's why I've been sick."

The merest hint of a smile tugged at Jill's lips, and she drew in a breath. "Oh, Celia."

"That's why I went, Jill. I had to tell him. He had a right to know, and I didn't want him to hear it from the police or newspapers. It's our baby, and we've wanted it so much." Though she hadn't thought it was possible, tears stung her eyes again.

Jill contemplated that for a moment, staring at her, either assessing her sanity or her honesty. She was definitely losing her, Celia thought.

"Celia, someone poisoned Stan tonight. His IV bag had arsenic again."

Celia's heart jolted, and she straightened. "I was afraid of that. The nurse said the bag had been changed . . ."

"They think you did it."

Her face twisted as she tried to grasp some logical train of thought. "How is he? Did it get into his bloodstream? Is he all right?"

"He's okay. They don't think much got in, and they're doing what they can. He's still conscious, so that's a good sign."

"Thank God," she whispered. Then, shaking herself out of her shock, she focused on Jill again. "Did they ask him if I did it? He would tell them. I didn't touch his bag. I wasn't there long enough. Somebody else—"

"He claims there was an orderly there before you who switched the bags, but Sid isn't buying. He thinks he's trying to cover for you."

She got to her feet in the small room and looked down at her lawyer. "Why would a man cover for someone who was trying to kill him? Stan *knows* I didn't do it!"

Jill looked away. There was something else, and Celia could see her wrestling with it.

"What is it, Jill?"

Jill stood up, picked up the pencil on the table, and began tapping it on the palm of her hand. Finally, she stopped and looked her dead in the eye. "Celia, why didn't you tell me that you went to see Lee Barnett today?"

Celia wilted. "You would have gotten angry, told me it was stupid. Same reason I didn't tell you I was going to the hospital."

"I would have been right."

"I know." She dropped her face into her hands.

"They have a picture."

Celia looked up at her without much interest. "What kind of picture?"

"They had someone following you, Celia. They followed you to Barnett's apartment. They took pictures."

The fact that she'd been followed irritated her, but it didn't surprise her greatly. They had seen someone sitting outside Aunt Aggie's house when they'd left for the hospital. "So they got pictures," she said. "All I did was stand outside his door and ask him questions. There wasn't anything incriminating, except the fact that I slapped him. I guess I could be guilty of assault. But I don't think I was there for more than ten minutes."

"They have a picture of you in his arms."

"*In his arms?*" she shouted, springing to her feet. "*What?*"

Jill was silent, watching her, waiting for an explanation.

Celia didn't have one. "Jill, you've got to believe me. I was *never* in his arms. They faked the picture . . . doctored it somehow. I want to see it."

Jill nodded. "I can get it for you."

"Do it!" Celia cried.

Jill opened the door and stuck her head out, and Celia heard her talking to someone. She sank down at the table and dropped her face into her hands. There was no way . . . *no way* . . . anyone had gotten a picture of her in Lee Barnett's arms. She had been yelling at him, had slapped him . . .

Jill came back into the room, holding the snapshot. "Here it is, Celia," she said, and tossed it down in front of her on the table.

Celia picked it up and felt the heat fevering across her face. She opened her mouth, but no sound came out. After a moment, she brought her hand to her forehead. "Jill . . . you've got to believe me . . . I was so full of rage . . . I hit him, and he grabbed me and shook me, and I told him to let me go . . . He had his hands on me maybe five seconds . . . *Not an embrace!* What about the other pictures? Didn't they get me slapping him? Is this all they got?"

"It's the only one they're using for evidence."

"I don't *believe* this." She sucked in a sob. "Did they show Stan?"

"I'm not sure."

She dropped her head into the circle of her arms. "What is he thinking about me? Oh, why is this happening?"

Jill sat down next to her and touched her hand, but when Celia looked up she could see the confusion in her lawyer's eyes. "Celia, I don't think they're going to let you back out. I'm going to do what I can, but I don't think they're going to set bond this time."

"You wouldn't, if you were the judge, would you?" Celia asked bitterly.

Jill didn't answer.

She raised up and wiped her eyes. "Look, Jill, if you don't want to represent me, I understand. I mean, the evidence is insurmountable. You're not even sure you know who I am."

Jill stared at her, and for a moment, Celia was sure she would take her chance to give up the case. But Jill surprised her.

"I know who you are." Tears came to her eyes, and she shook her head. "I'm confused, Celia. I don't know who's doing this, or how they're doing it. I don't know why there's been so much evidence against you. I don't know why someone would want to kill your husbands and not you—and to put you through such a nightmare yourself. I can't imagine. I don't know what Lee Barnett's part was in this. I don't know who else to trust, because I think whoever it is might be right under our nose. It scares me. But there is one thing I do know for sure. I believe you."

Celia accepted that with tearful relief. "Thank you." She tried to pull herself together. "No one else will, you know. They'll alienate you, too, just for representing me. You'll be as popular in this town as Oswald's lawyer. Are you sure you're up to it?"

"I'm up to it," Jill said. "But you might need a more experienced criminal lawyer than I. If you'd rather hire someone else, I'll understand."

"With what?" Celia asked. "I don't have any money."

"Aunt Aggie would pay."

"No, I want you. You know me. No one else does."

"Okay, then." She squeezed her hand. "Celia, are you going to be all right in jail?"

"Oh, yeah," Celia said. "No problem. Been there, done that. I can handle jail, as long as I know it's temporary. 'Course, it might not be."

The look on Jill's face told Celia that this was the first time that she'd faced such a serious case . . . a case that really would decide someone's lifelong fate. She hated to give her that burden. Then she thought of Aunt Aggie, and David . . .

"Where are my aunt and brother?" she asked quietly.

Jill nodded toward the door. "They're being questioned."

"Are they going to be charged with anything?"

"Not if I can help it. Something was said about accessory to attempted murder, but I think it was just a threat. Don't worry about them. I'll take care of it."

"I don't know how much more Aunt Aggie can take. She's hardly gotten any sleep lately. She's too old for this."

"She's stronger than both of us put together," Jill said with a slight smile. "And as for their putting her in jail, they'd have such a protest by the fire department that they'd have to let her back out in time for lunch tomorrow."

"I guess you're right."

"Just hold on, Celia. I'm doing everything I can, okay? You may have to stay here a night or two, but maybe we can get you out before much more time passes."

Celia had heard that before.

Chapter Thirty-Seven

●●●

The moment Aunt Aggie and David had walked into the New-pointe Police Department, they were descended on as if they were criminals about to turn themselves in. They took Aunt Aggie into one interrogation room and David into another and began to question them separately about the incident. Aunt Aggie was livid.

"Yeah, I helped her sneak in the hospital, and I helped her get in that room, and if you wanna lock me up for that, then I ain't fightin' you."

Vern Hargis shot a look at Chief Shoemaker. "We just want to know what happened, Aunt Aggie."

"I tole you already. She wanted to see her husband!"

"But the judge told her not to. There was a court order."

"Aw, she don't care about no court order. She missed her husband. He's layin' in the hospital dyin', he finally come awake, and she want to see him. You bet I'm gon' help her."

Vern rolled his eyes. "Aunt Aggie, there was arsenic found in his IV bag. Celia tried to kill him again."

Aunt Aggie's heart tightened into a fist, and she shot to her feet. "Celia didn't poison him! I don't know who did, but Celia didn't."

"Aunt Aggie, you have to admit—it's hard to believe it was just a coincidence that he was poisoned a second time when she just happened to be there."

Aunt Aggie's mind raced. The answer was there—she had seen so much as she'd sat there waiting for Vern to go take a smoke. Suddenly, it came to her. "That orderly had a bag with 'im! He was carryin' it just as plain as day. Just a few minutes 'fore I went to get Celia! Vern, don't you remember? Didn't you see 'im? And Celia, she was empty-handed."

Vern looked troubled. "I'm not sure, Aunt Aggie. There was an orderly, but I didn't see him carrying anything."

"Why'd he have his mask on, then? That hat? I didn't think of it then, but he was the killer! Vern, if you'da stopped him, we'd have 'im now!"

Jim got to his feet. "That true, Vern? Did you check that orderly's identification?"

Vern shifted uncomfortably. "I saw it, Jim. He had a badge on. I didn't stop him and examine it, but ..." He looked up at Aunt Aggie. "Celia was wearing a badge, too. Where did she get it?"

"I took it," Aunt Aggie said, lifting her chin proudly. "Stole it myself right offa somebody's uniform at the uniform shop today."

The two men looked at each other again as if they didn't believe a word she was saying. "Whassa matter, you don't think a ole lady can steal?"

"We didn't think you were a thief, Aunt Aggie. Sue us."

Aunt Aggie wished she had her cane with her so she could knock them upside the head. "I wanted to help her. She deserved to see Stan. She had stuff she needed to tell him."

"Stuff about the murder attempt?"

"No, nothin' about no murder attempt! She don't know nothin' about no murder attempt!"

Vern was getting impatient. "Aunt Aggie, we need your cooperation. We need you to sit down and relax, and quit ranting and raving."

"Rantin' and ravin'? You ain't seen nothin.' You got my Celia locked up in jail like she some half-baked killer, and you think I'm rantin' and ravin'?"

"Aunt Aggie, I don't want to have to lock you up with her."

"Do it!" Aunt Aggie challenged. "Go ahead, lock me up." She held out her wrists for them to cuff, but they only looked amused. It made her madder than ever.

"Aunt Aggie, we're not locking you up. However, we have to inform you that you are an accessory to a murder attempt."

"Accessory? You don't know what you talkin' about. Alls I did was sit in a waitin' room and tell my Celia when she could come in. You're just mad cause you didn't recognize her when she come through."

"Yeah, I'm mad," Vern said. "I'm mad that she poisoned him right under my nose. Call it a vendetta if you want to, but I'm gonna make sure that she goes down for it."

Aunt Aggie kicked a chair, hurting her foot, but she would have died before she would let them know it.

"Tell us about David," he said. "What was his part in all this?"

"He drove the stinkin' car," she said. "Dropped us off, come in to see where we'd come out, then sit there and waited at that exit."

"Then he's an accessory, too," Vern said.

"It wasn't against no court order for me and David to be at that hospital," she said. "We didn't break no laws."

"It's against the law to poison a man twice."

"Didn't nobody I know poison Stan!" She could feel her blood pressure rising, ready to explode out the top of her head. "If we're accessories, then you're one, too, Vern. You let the killer walk right in and change that bag, without so much as readin' his badge. Y'ask me, you might be in on this whole thing your own self."

"Oh, for Pete's sake ..." Vern muttered. He threw his pen against the wall and stood up, aggravated beyond measure. "I'm gonna let her go, Jim. She's just wasting our time."

"And Celia? What you gon' do with her?" Aunt Aggie asked.

"She's staying," Jim said. "The judge would be crazy to let her out again."

"Then I'm stayin', too."

Vern gaped at her. "No, you're not, Aunt Aggie. You're going home, if I have to take you myself."

"You can't let a criminal like me back out on the streets," Aunt Aggie said. "Not when I could go around accessorizin' more murders, stealin' and whatnot."

"Aunt Aggie, I'm not locking you up! Go home!"

She sat back down and put her purse stubbornly in her lap, determined not to move. "Then I want to press charges."

"Against who?" Vern shot back.

"Against me. For stealin' that badge. I confess. Go get one o' them court reporters in here and I'll give 'em my statement."

Jim began to chuckle with frustration. "Aunt Aggie, we're not going to lock you up for stealing a badge."

"Why not? What kinda po-lice department you call this? If you can't get locked up confessin' to a crime . . ."

"The judge wouldn't give you more than a slap on the hand for stealing a badge off of a uniform."

She could feel her face reddening, and her heart hammered with anger. She got up and looked Vern squarely in the eye. "What about assaultin' a po-lice officer?"

Jim chuckled again, but Vern didn't find it funny. "Aunt Aggie, you don't want to do that."

"Why not? I done it before. Ask Sid Ford if I ain't."

Jim nodded confirmation, and Vern rolled his eyes. "Aunt Aggie, I told you. Go home."

"Make me."

Vern's face twisted with disgust. "What are you? Six years old? Give it up, Aunt Aggie! You can sit in here all night if you want. I'm through with you." With that, he turned to leave.

Aunt Aggie couldn't think of anything she hated worse than not being taken seriously. Suddenly, she decided to make sure she got her way.

She swung her purse in a circle from its handle, just like a lasso, then sent it flying across the room. It hit the back of Vern's head, and he swung around, his eyes livid. "Are you crazy?"

"That's twice now I assaulted a po-lice officer. Add that to stealin', and accessorizin' murder, and you got plenty o' reason to lock me up. I *demand* to be locked up!"

Vern's nostrils were flaring, not a pretty sight. "Demand? You demand it? All right, Aunt Aggie. I'll lock you up. But you won't be in the cell with Celia, if that's what you hoped. You can both sit there alone and think about what you've done."

Aunt Aggie wasn't afraid. She'd been in the women's part of the jail to visit people before, and she knew that there were only four small cells. If she and Celia weren't roommates, at least they could talk to each other, and she could make sure she was all right. She held out her hands to accept the cuffs. "I'm ready."

Vern looked as if he could scream. "I'm not cuffing you, Aunt Aggie."

She was a little disappointed. Something about walking through the police station in handcuffs appealed to her. The uproar it would cause, the rumors, the outrage . . .

He opened the door and took her arm, led her out. David was waiting for her.

"They lockin' me up," she yelled to him, louder than she needed to. "Throwin' me in the pokey."

David's jaw fell open. "You've got to be kidding. For *what?*"

Vern seemed too embarrassed to answer, so Aunt Aggie obliged. "Assaultin' a po-lice officer. Couldn't get 'em to do it for nothin' else."

David turned his outraged eyes on Vern, then on Jim Shoemaker. "This is ludicrous! What is the matter with you people? Locking up my sister, and now my eighty-one-year-old aunt? Are you absolutely out of your minds?"

Jim's amusement had passed, and he was beginning to lose his patience. "If you want to make it a threesome, we can oblige you, too."

"*None* of us did anything!" he shouted. "My sister is being framed. And Aunt Aggie ... well, give me a break. You know what she wants. She's looking out for my sister, but for crying out loud, she doesn't need to go to jail, too. Look, I'll just take her home, and—" He reached for her, but Aunt Aggie jerked back from him.

"David, so help me, I'll wallop you, too, if you interfere. Justice is bein' served. I got to serve my time."

David's face was crimson. "You've done some crazy things, Aunt Aggie, but this beats everything."

Aunt Aggie couldn't help smiling. "It does, don't it? How 'bout that? Now you run on home. If my fire boys call to see where I am, you tell 'em I can't cook for 'em till they let me outa jail, now, you hear? They'll understand."

David looked at Vern with disgust. "They'll tar and feather you. They'll raid the place to get her out."

"I'll take my chances," Vern said, then pulled Aunt Aggie into the hall leading down to the basement where the jail cells were.

Chapter Thirty-Eight

• • •

Though it was getting late when Jill left the police station, she walked next door to the fire station to see if Dan was working. She found him in the weight room bench-pressing, and stood at the door watching him for a moment before he saw her.

She didn't know why she was here, really. She should be able to handle this. She'd had difficult cases before. Granted, none of them had left her client's life hanging in the balance. And she'd never had so many surprises in a case, surprises that shouldn't have been . . .

But she did believe Celia. She did.

Tears pushed into her eyes, and she sniffed. Dan heard her and looked up. "Jill." He got up, as if self-conscious about what he was doing, and wiped his face on a towel. "I didn't know you were here. It's late."

She shrugged. "Yeah, I was just at the police station. Thought I'd come see if you were here."

"You're upset," he said, looking into her eyes. "Come sit down. Tell me what's wrong."

She let him lead her to a folding chair, and he took the weight bench across from her. "Nothing, really," she said. "I just . . . uh . . . I'm having some problems with Celia's case. I don't know quite what to do."

"Has something happened?"

She contemplated telling him. How much was attorney-client privilege? How much was guaranteed to be in the paper tomorrow, anyway? How much would the fire department know in just the next few minutes when the cops started talking?

"Celia's back in jail."

"What? Why?"

She got up and walked across the room, picked up a small barbell, set it back down. "She broke a court order and went to see Stan tonight. It just so happens that, after she got caught, they discovered that someone had injected arsenic into his IV bag."

Dan got slowly to his feet, his mouth open.

"He's okay. I mean, this new poison didn't have much time to get into his system. They caught it in time."

"Jill—"

"I know," she said, stemming his response. "I know how it looks. Believe me ... I know. She's in jail. They probably won't let her out. And I don't know how I'll fight this."

Forgetting the sweat he'd worked up, he put his arms around her and pressed her head against his shoulder. She rested in that embrace, thankful that something had the power to bring her that much relief, that much comfort.

"What is she saying?" Dan asked.

Jill pulled back and looked up at him. "That she didn't do it. Even Stan ... he's saying that an orderly came in before her and switched the bags ... Sid is convinced he's covering for her. But that doesn't make sense. She would know she'd get caught. Why would she do that?"

"It's an awful coincidence, Jill," he said. "For this person to come in and poison him again, and it just happens to be right before she comes? That's hard to buy."

"She didn't do it." The words were said so weakly that she hardly believed them herself. "She didn't, Dan. It may look like it to everyone else, but not to us."

He let her go and sat slowly down. "I want to believe her. I know what it's like to have people accuse you because of how things look. This town is bad about that. I haven't forgotten how they almost strung me up. You were the only one who believed in me."

"I may be the only one who believes in her. But I have to."

He met her eyes. "What if you're wrong?"

"Then I'll be wrong. But she's my friend, and now she's my client. I have to get rid of whatever doubts I have."

"Then you admit you have some?"

She looked at him for a long moment. "I don't want to, Dan. I don't want to have doubts about my friend. I look in her eyes, and I believe her. But then when I walk away, and I start adding things up . . ."

"You start to realize you're human?"

"I haven't got time to be human," she said.

Chapter Thirty-Nine

● ● ●

Issie Mattreaux hated to be stood up. She sat alone at the bar at Joe's Place, nursing a glass of wine and feeling sorry for herself. She might have known the guy who was meeting her here wouldn't show. She'd met him on one of her calls today, when he'd found his cousin in a hypoglycemic coma. He had called 911 and had been impressed when she so easily revived the patient with glucose. She'd spent the next half hour bantering with him, and when he'd finally asked her out, she'd had high hopes. He'd had to work late, so he'd asked her to meet him at ten o'clock. But it was already eleven, so he was an hour late, and she knew better than to kid herself any longer.

From the corner of her eye she noticed a man across the room looking at her, and she turned and met his eyes. He wasn't bad looking. In fact, he looked better than most of the men who frequented this place—even better than the guy who'd stood her up. She smiled at him; he smiled back. After a moment, he got up and came to claim the stool next to her. "Buy you a drink?" he asked.

She lifted hers slightly. "Got one."

He smiled. "Can I buy you the next one?"

She considered that a moment, then lifted her glass and finished it off. "Sure."

He grinned and waited for the waiter. "How about another one for the lady?"

Joe seemed to sneer at him, and Issie frowned. It wasn't Joe's way to be rude to his customers. There must be something wrong. She glanced up at the man. "I'm Issie Mat-treaux," she said.

He nodded. "Lee Barnett."

The name sounded familiar. She ran it through her mind, trying to process it. "You new in town?" she asked.

"Yeah," he said. "Just been here a few days."

Suddenly it came back to her. The gossip at the fire station, about the man in Celia's past. No wonder Joe was giving him the cold shoulder. Joe brought her the drink and she thought of refusing it, but then decided she needed it. "I've heard things about you," she said, bringing it to her lips.

"Yeah," he said. "I guess everybody has, but they're not true."

She looked up at him. "How do you know what I've heard?"

"Because they're sayin' that I had somethin' to do with Stan Shepherd's poisonin', and that I'm involved with his wife."

"Aren't you?"

He sat there a moment, as if contemplating the question. "Tell you the truth, I'm not sure."

"Not sure? That's interesting."

"Well, see, I thought I was. I thought there was this letter from her, and a check . . ."

He'd had too much to drink, she could tell, because his speech was slurred. She wondered how many he'd put away.

"But I don't think she wrote that letter, and I don't think she wrote those checks."

"Then who did?"

"Got me. That's the ten million dollar question. Matter of fact, it could be a life or death question."

"If you're not involved with her, then how come you're staying around town?" she asked.

He shrugged. "They won't let me leave till the investigation's over. But I'm tellin' you, I didn't do anything."

Something told her to get up and leave, to walk right out, but she was lonely, and she had nothing to do at home. She decided to stay. What could it hurt? She took another drink of her wine, set it down, ran her finger along the rim.

"You a friend of Celia's?" he asked.

"I know her."

"What about Stan?"

She nodded. "Yeah, I know him better. I'm a paramedic. I work with him from time to time."

"Paramedic, huh? So you go around saving lives?"

The question irritated her. "Sometimes. I almost lost Stan Shepherd." She regarded him, watching for his reaction. He was handsome, just the type she could picture Celia dating years ago. She wondered if there really was anything between them. Something about that possibility piqued her interest in him. She wasn't sure why that was, didn't want to explore it. But when a man had an attractive woman interested in him, he seemed more valuable in her eyes. As if to counter her attraction, she said, "So I hear you were in prison."

He swiveled on his stool and looked out over the crowd. "Not the kind of thing I like for a girl to know about me the first time I meet her, but yeah, it's true."

She sipped her drink. "Got involved in a barroom brawl and killed somebody?"

"Word travels fast."

She picked a fish-shaped cracker out of the bowl on the bar and nibbled on it. "So if you could kill somebody in a bar, what would keep you from killing somebody with poison?"

"Prison," he said simply. "The best deterrent I know. I'm not going back."

She finished off the cracker, took another sip, then glanced at him again. "It's just suspicious, you know. You being here, where Celia is. Showing up right around the time Stan was poisoned."

He leaned his elbow on the bar and lowered his voice. "I think it was supposed to be suspicious," he said. "That's what this is all about. We're both being framed."

"She's the one in jail," Issie pointed out. "You're sitting in a bar hitting on me."

He pulled back a little and grinned at her. "Hitting on you? I thought I was making conversation."

A grin tugged at one side of her lips. "You bought me a drink, didn't you?"

He laughed softly. "Yeah, I bought you a drink."

"That usually means that you're being hit on."

"Yeah, well, I've been out of circulation for a while," he said. "I don't know the rules anymore."

She breathed a humorless laugh. "Oh, you know the rules. Who are you kidding?" She was playing with him, she realized, and she wondered if she had had too much to drink, herself. But there was something about his eyes. Something exciting, something fun, a thrill she hadn't had the opportunity to experience in a long time. The forbidden.

He seemed to read her thoughts. "This place is awfully smoky," he said in a deep voice too close to her ear. "What do you say we go someplace else?"

"Someplace like what?" she asked innocently.

"I don't know. You tell me. You're the one who knows Newpointe."

Her senses came alive as she thought of the possibilities. They could go to Maison de Manger and get a bite, or they could go for a walk along the bayou behind the fire station. Or they could drive down to Lake Pontchartrain, or go to her apartment, or his . . .

She'd heard about his apartment, that Celia had set him up there, and she wondered what it looked like. Then her common sense ruled that out, and she realized that it was stupid. She couldn't be caught alone in an ex-con's apartment, not when he was suspected of murder, no matter how much she'd had to drink.

"I think I'll just stay right here," she said.

He grinned again. "Okay. I'll stay here with you. It's safer. I can't attack you if we're in a crowd."

She grinned. "You couldn't attack me, anyway."

"Tough guy, huh?"

She nodded. "I can hold my own." It was true. She'd had self-defense training, and was stronger than she looked. More than a dozen times lately she'd had to lift an unconscious grown man onto a gurney. She felt quite sure she could fight one off if she had to.

"If you're so tough, then why are you so afraid to go anywhere with me? It can be someplace public, you know."

"I know." She winked. "But I think I'll stay right here."

"Okay," he said. "Maybe we can get to know each other even in all the smoke and noise."

"Do you like to dance?" she asked.

He grinned. "Haven't done it in five years. There weren't many cotillions in prison, but we can give it a whirl."

She set her glass down. "All right," she said. "Let's have at it."

Chapter Forty

● ● ●

There were only four small cells in the women's portion of the Newpointe city jail. They were each five by ten, with a small cot with a flat mattress, and a sink and commode behind a partition. Celia lay on her cot, fighting her nausea. She didn't need that sick feeling on top of the despair closing in on her, but it was there, nonetheless, reminding her that there was a baby involved, that this was no longer just about her life and her integrity. Now she was also defending her child.

She got up and went to the sink, bent over, and splashed water on her face. At least the sink was clean. It could be worse. The commode, too, had been recently cleaned, and a sterile smell wafted in the air.

She sighed and sat back down on the bed, wishing for something to occupy her mind, to keep her from thinking of the horror on Stan's face as they had dragged her out of his room. He still loved her; she knew that without a doubt. But she wasn't sure he believed in her anymore, not after someone had poisoned him.

But didn't he know that it wasn't her? He had to.

She tried to rest in that knowledge, but it was difficult.

The door to the hall opened, and she heard footsteps. Were they coming for her? Had Jill maneuvered a way to get her out this time?

"T-Celia?" It was Aunt Aggie's voice, and Celia sat up and looked through the bars.

"Aunt Aggie?" She saw Vern ushering the old woman past. "Aunt Aggie, what are you doing?"

"I'm locking her up," Vern said.

Aunt Aggie was smiling, as if she were the victor. Celia realized her aunt had given them reason to incarcerate her so that Celia wouldn't be alone. Horrified, she tried to appeal to Vern. "Vern, this is ridiculous. Aunt Aggie, I can handle this. I've done it before. Now go home."

"Too late," Vern said.

"What did she do?" Celia demanded.

"Knocked me upside the head, for one thing," Vern said.

"I deserved to be locked up," Aunt Aggie said proudly. "I'm a thief, and I'm dangerous."

"Dangerous? Come on, Vern, she's eighty-one years old."

"She asked for it, Celia." He opened the door in the cell next to her and pushed Aunt Aggie in. "If there was some way I could put her in a different section of the jail, I would, so you two couldn't talk. But we got regulations, and this is the only place we keep the women."

Aunt Aggie walked into her cell and sat primly down on her cot. He slammed the bars. "Good night, ladies," he said.

Aunt Aggie's eyes were intent on Celia through the bars. Celia gaped at her as Vern left the area.

"Aunt Aggie, what in the world are you up to?"

"I didn't want you bein' alone down here," the old woman said. "I couldna slept tonight. Couldn't bear it."

"Aunt Aggie, I'm fine."

"Well, I'm fine, too. Now we'll be fine together."

Celia's throat filled with emotion over the lengths her aunt would go to protect her. "Aunt Aggie, you don't deserve to be here."

"And you don't either."

"But I can handle it."

"So can I."

Celia shot her a frustrated look. Aunt Aggie stood up and leaned her head on the bars. "Look, *sha*. I can't do nothin' about it now. I'm here and you're here, and we're both here for the night. Can we at least make the best of it?"

Celia reached through the bars and held her aunt's hand. "I love you, you crazy thing."

"I love you, too," Aunt Aggie said matter-of-factly. "Now what can I do for you?"

Celia almost laughed. "Aunt Aggie, short of naming the killer, there is *nothing* you can do."

"Well, I can't do that," she said. "But I knew you'd wanna talk to Stan. I can help you with that."

"Talk to Stan?" she asked. "How can I do that?"

Aunt Aggie looked as if she had a delightful secret. "What if I told you I had a phone with me?"

"Aunt Aggie, that's impossible. You came in here empty-handed. They had to have checked your purse in."

"Don't mean I can't hide no phone."

Celia's eyes twinkled. "You can't be serious. You smuggled a telephone in here?"

"There're advantages to age, you know. They don't dare frisk an old lady."

Celia couldn't help laughing. "Oh, Aunt Aggie."

"I ain't promisin' you can get through. I don't know when the switchboard closes, but you can try." She pulled up her skirt, pulled out the elastic band on her panty hose, and fished out the cellular phone tucked down in them.

"Aunt Aggie, you amaze me."

"I amaze myself, *sha*." She thrust the phone through the bars.

"What if we get caught with this? It's not gonna look good."

"Then don't get caught. Just make the call and hurry it up."

Celia looked at the phone, almost reluctant to take it. But it would be wonderful if she could call Stan, just to see if he was all right, and to tell him once again that she had had nothing to do with the poisonings, and tell him again about the baby. Her hands trembled as she took the phone, flipped up the top, and dialed information.

"No need to do that," Aunt Aggie said. "I know the number. I been callin' it enough since this whole thing started."

Celia dialed the number Aunt Aggie called out, then brought the phone to her ear and waited.

"Slidell Memorial Hospital, may I help you?"

Her heart leapt. "Uh, yes, could you connect me to Stan Shepherd's room, please?"

She waited for the woman to tell her that the switchboard was closed, that it was too late, but she didn't. Instead, the phone began to ring.

"They connectin' you?" Aunt Aggie asked hopefully.

Celia's eyes were wide as she waited. "Yes."

After a couple of rings, someone picked up the phone. "Hello?"

It was his mother, and for a moment, she thought of hanging up. But she needed to talk to him, and it was worth whatever chance she had to take. "Hannah?"

Hannah hesitated. "Yes?"

"Hannah, it's me. Celia. Please don't hang up! I need to talk to Stan . . . Please."

Hannah's voice was tight as she answered. "He has nothing to say to you, and if you call here again—"

"Stan knows I didn't do it. He saw me there. I didn't change his bag. He knows. Please, Hannah. Just let me talk to him for a minute. Tell him it's me."

There was silence. She closed her eyes and prayed that Hannah was giving Stan the phone. Finally, Hannah said, "He saw the picture of you with that man, Celia. His eyes are opening. He doesn't have anything to say to you."

"That picture . . ." Her voice broke off, and she groped for words. "It wasn't what it seemed, Hannah. Please . . ." She sobbed, then tried to rally. "Is he all right? Did much of the poison get into his system this time? What are the doctors saying?"

The phone clicked in her ear, and she realized that Hannah had cut her off. "Hannah, don't hang up!" But it was too late.

She handed the phone back to Aunt Aggie, dropped onto the cot, and covered her face with both hands. "Oh, Aunt Aggie. I've lost him. He believes them! He believes them!"

Aunt Aggie took the phone back and tucked it into her skirt. "He don't believe 'em, *sha*. Don't you believe his mama."

"No, Aunt Aggie," Celia said. "They showed him the picture. He thinks I'm trying to kill him!" Celia curled up into a fetal position, her face still covered, and sobbed into her hands. "Oh, Aunt Aggie, what am I gonna do? What am I gonna do?"

But Aunt Aggie was uncharacteristically speechless as Celia wailed out her pain.

Chapter Forty-One

● ● ●

In the hospital, Stan covered his eyes with his wrist, and his mother leaned over him. "Honey, are you all right?"

He shook his head. "I wanted to talk to her, Mom."

"To what end?" his mother asked. "Stan, she's dangerous. Physically and emotionally. I don't want you listening to her lies. Look at you. You didn't even talk to her, and you're all upset."

He took in a ragged breath and wiped his face roughly. "It's been a long day, Mom. A lot's happened."

"I know it has, Stan."

He closed his eyes and pretended to sleep, but he knew sleep wasn't going to come tonight. It was too hard. How could Celia have betrayed him? And was it true about the baby, or had she lied to further manipulate him? What was going on with her? How could he have been so blind?

He thought again of that picture of her in Lee Barnett's arms and fought the despair.

His mother picked up the phone and began to dial. He wiped his face and looked up at her. "Who are you calling, Mom?"

"The Newpointe police. I'm going to tell Sid Ford that Celia called. I thought she was in jail."

"No, Mom," he said. "Don't tell him."

She looked at him as if he was crazy. "I certainly am."

With all his effort, he pulled himself up, reached for the telephone, and took it out of her hand. "Hang it up, Mom," he insisted. "Now."

She hung up the phone. Deflated, she headed into the bathroom to get ready for sleep.

Stan realized that his mother had every right, every reason, to report the phone call. But as it was, he couldn't stand the thought of Celia sitting in that jail cell. He had long thought that they needed to do something to improve the women's portion of the jail, but it was rarely used. He'd never had anyone he cared about down there before. Now something inside him ached at the thought that she was sleeping on that thin mattress, using that toilet, that sink . . . He hoped someone had had the presence of mind to clean it before she'd gone down there.

Then he wondered why he cared. If his wife had truly tried to kill him, shouldn't he hope the worst for her? No, somehow he couldn't. His heart ached. It was broken into tiny pieces, and he doubted he would ever put it back together again. How would he ever trust again? How would he ever believe? Marriage was supposed to be for better or for worse. Had things been so bad, against his knowledge, that she hadn't been able to endure it? He tried to relax the torment from his face, to hide it from his mother as she came out of the bathroom, so she would leave him alone. But part of him didn't want to be alone.

He'd never felt more alone in his life. And he wondered what the cost would be of continuing to love Celia, especially if he didn't believe her.

Chapter Forty-Two

● ● ●

The police station was still buzzing at eleven-fifteen when Nick showed up to see Celia. Phones were ringing and printers were printing. A drunk man yelled curses to a cop who was booking him, and a woman with a black eye and bloody mouth sat at a cop's desk wailing that she couldn't press charges against her husband.

Nick's soul swelled at the depravity of his own generation, and he clutched the Bible in his hand, wishing he'd brought one for each of them. Reminding himself of his purpose for coming, he scanned the desks for Sid Ford. There he was at the back of the room, talking to Jim Shoemaker. He wondered if those men ever slept.

He cut between the desks and made his way back. "Sid," he said, hating to interrupt.

Sid glanced back at him. "Oh, hey, Nick. How ya doin'?"

"I'm interrupting," he said, shaking both of their hands. "Sorry, Jim. Do you mind if I talk to Sid for a minute?"

Jim told Sid to come into his office when he'd finished with Nick, and he left them alone.

"Sid, I need to see Celia," Nick said in a quiet voice.

Sid shook his head. "Sorry, man. It's after visitin' hours."

"Please, Sid. Stan asked me to come and see her. It's spiritual business that I need to take care of."

"I'm sorry," Sid said. "We ain't makin' no exceptions."

"Sid, I'm your preacher. You can help me out just this once. Bend the rules a little."

"No way, man. We been jerked around enough tonight."

"Jerked around? You think I'm jerking you around?"

"Yeah, I think you are," Sid said. "I think you're pullin' rank on me."

"Rank? We're not even in the same department."

"Rank with the Lord," Sid said. "Just because you're my preacher, I'm s'posed to bend the rules."

"Sid, if it was you in jail, you'd want me to visit."

"If it was me in jail I would deserve a visit," he said. "You can come back tomorrow when it's visitin' time. But right now we need to let her and Aunt Aggie stew."

"Aunt Aggie?" Nick asked. "*She's* in jail?"

"Yeah," Sid said defensively. "And don't you get on my case about that. Second time she assaulted a police officer, they threw the book at her."

"An eighty-one-year-old woman?"

"You got a problem with that?" Sid threw back.

Nick saw that he wasn't going to get anywhere with him. "All right, Sid, look. If you won't let me visit, at least take this Bible down to her. That's the least you could do. She has the right to a Bible."

Sid took the Bible, as if he knew Nick was right. "I'll get it to her when I got time."

"No, Sid," Nick pleaded. "Do it now. For Stan. He wanted me to come and see about her, make sure she was all right. If you won't let me in, at least, for his sake, take her the Bible."

"All right, but I gotta tell you somethin', Preacher. I'm gettin' sick and tired of all this. I don't like folks poisonin' my friends. When you start tryin' to kill a police officer, I take it real personal. And I ain't fixin' to coddle Celia Shepherd, or even her demented aunt, for that matter."

"I'm not asking you to coddle them, Sid. I'm just asking you to give them what they're entitled to."

"Aunt Aggie don't want no Bible."

"No, I realize that. But Celia might. Please, just get it to her right away."

Sid rolled his eyes, but he started back to the basement door.

"Are you taking it now?" Nick asked.

"What does it look like?" Sid shouted.

Nick had to be satisfied with that, and finally, he turned and left.

He walked out of the police station, looked up at the stars, and wondered for the thousandth time what he was doing being a preacher. Silently, he asked the Lord what he could do for Stan, Celia ... if he should do anything. He started to go back to his car, but the night was cool and serene. In the midst of all this turmoil, it was a welcome relief.

He decided to walk for a few minutes, and he set out past the fire station, down to the corner. Across the street, he saw Joe's Place. He could hear the music spilling out of the doors. The parking lot was full.

Many of the patrons were part of his flock, but he'd had little impact on their nighttime behavior. He wondered what he could do, what he could say, to make them understand that life wasn't found in the confines of a smoky bar.

The door opened, and a triangle of light spilled out along with a cloud of smoke. He saw Issie Mattreaux coming out with a man swaggering behind her. Something drew him across the street, and he stood at the edge of the parking lot, watching, listening—his nerves on red alert.

•   •   •

Issie had every intention of letting Barnett come home with her, even though it was against her better judgment. He'd had too much to drink, but so had she. The alternative choice of going home alone was too boring to consider. Lee Barnett could add some excitement to a stressful but mundane existence. Besides, he was a good-looking man, and any woman in town would have thrown caution to the wind for him. She was sure of it.

She opened her car door and tossed her purse in, then turned back to the big, virile man with romance on his mind.

"So . . . you wanna come to my place, or do I come to yours?" the man muttered as his lips hovered over hers.

"Maybe I'll come to yours," she whispered. "That way I won't have to throw you out when I'm tired of you."

He chuckled under his breath. "You won't get tired of me."

As if to prove it, he leaned in to kiss her, but almost lost his balance. She caught him, and he grabbed both her shoulders and gave her a punishing kiss.

Issie tried to push him away. Too many people could come out of the bar and see her with Barnett, and by tomorrow, rumors would fly. No, she preferred to show her affections privately.

She tried to break free, but he wouldn't be deterred. Turning her head to break the kiss, she said, "Not here, Lee. Not now."

"Why not?" He tried to put her into the car, but she kept pushing him away.

"Someone will see us."

"So?"

"So . . . I said no!" Her voice was getting louder. "Stop it!"

She heard footsteps on the gravel, and someone grabbed Barnett by the back of the collar, pulled him away from her, and flung him to the ground. Issie realized her "rescuer" was Nick Foster.

"Nick!"

Nick left Lee lying disoriented on the ground and swung around to her. "Are you all right?"

"Yes," she said. "He was . . ."

"Who do you think you are?" Barnett called out from the ground.

Nick spun around. "I was about to ask you the same question."

Suddenly, Issie felt ashamed that the preacher had seen her in such a compromising position. She decided to play the victim.

"He had a little too much to drink," she said, feigning distress. "I should have known better than to walk out to the parking lot with him by myself." She looked up at him, widening her eyes as innocently as she was able. "Thank goodness you came along."

Barnett staggered to his feet and brushed off his jeans. "Look, I don't want any trouble. I just met Issie here in the bar, and we were havin' a couple of drinks. I walked her out to her car . . . no big deal." He shot Issie a look. "You didn't tell me you had a boyfriend."

"He's not my boyfriend," Issie said, unable to meet Nick's eye.

"What is he then? Your father?"

She could see that the barb stung Nick. He was a little older than Issie. But not old enough to be her father.

"I'm actually her preacher," he said.

"Preacher?" The man's eyebrows shot up as if he was impressed. "You really a preacher?" Suddenly, it seemed he'd forgotten that the man had just flung him to the ground. He took a drunken step toward him. "You know a priest around here named Mueller? Edmund Mueller?"

Nick frowned, wondering what in the world he was talking about. "I don't know any Mueller."

"Oh, yeah, you got to," he said. "A priest. Don't you preacher types hang together? You gotta know him. He came to visit me. Celia Shepherd's priest."

Nick shook his head. "*I'm* Celia's pastor, and my name is Nick Foster."

Barnett squinted at him for a long moment. "You sure?"

"Yeah, I'm sure."

Barnett looked thoroughly confused, and he stood there a moment, looked down at his feet, and shook his head.

"Who are you?" Nick asked.

Barnett kept staring at his feet, and Issie became slightly annoyed that he'd forgotten her so easily. Instead, he seemed to be struggling to understand something about some nonexistent priest. The perplexity and vulnerability on his face revealed something almost sad. It reminded her of herself.

"Who is he?" Nick asked her.

Issie took a deep breath. "Lee Barnett. The one they're saying is involved with Celia."

Nick's face seemed to drain of color, then quickly redden again. The flashing neon sign in front of Joe's Place seemed to punctuate his surprise.

"Look, you just go on home," Nick told the man, "and I'll make sure Issie gets home all right."

"Yeah." Barnett still seemed confused. "I'd appreciate that." He tapped his pockets, presumably for his keys, and began to wobble away.

The ease with which he dismissed her stung Issie, and biting back the feeling of rejection, she got into the car and closed the door. She turned the key to start it, but Nick knocked on the window and motioned for her to wait. Time for the sermon, she thought, cutting the car back off as Nick came around to the passenger side.

Nick got into the car and sat there for a moment, not sure what to say. Should he be a preacher now, or just a man? Or was there really any difference in the two?

Issie seemed self-conscious when she met his eyes. "I really appreciate your coming along, Nick. I always think I can handle things. I'm not exactly a wimp, but he was coming on a little strong."

Nick stared at her. Her face was lit only by the red neon lights on the front wall of Joe's Place. "What are you doing, Issie?"

"What do you mean?"

"I mean, what do you want? What would make a beautiful woman who has everything going for her come here every night alone, drinking and picking up strange guys?"

He could see her visibly wilt beneath the words. He hated it. He'd much rather use words that built her up, but he couldn't find any at the moment.

"Nick, just because I don't have the same values and beliefs that you have, doesn't mean that I'm some kind of terrible person. There's a thing called tolerance, you know."

Nick shook his head. "Some things shouldn't be tolerated."

"Oh, yeah?" she asked. "Like what?"

"Like promiscuity. Drunkenness. Explaining away your sin as if it was something that happens to you instead of something you choose."

He could see that she didn't take that well.

Her mouth fell open, and she tried to speak but failed. After a moment, she rallied. "Come on, Nick. If I wanted a sermon, I'd go to church."

"I'm sorry," Nick told her. "I didn't mean to preach."

"I guess you can't help yourself."

He sat there for a moment, wondering if he could. Was his preaching really a calling, or was it something *he* had just wanted to do in his zeal for Christ? Maybe it was one of those plans he had made, *then* asked Christ to come along, instead of waiting for the calling itself. He had been so sure at first, but now he wasn't sure.

"Don't you ever feel like letting your hair down?" Issie asked. "Just kicking your shoes off and drinking a little and dancing until the cows come home? Haven't you ever just wanted to spit out a couple of cuss words and follow your feelings?"

Nick thought back over his youth, when he had done all of those things. It had been an empty youth, and he hadn't really felt alive until the day he'd found Christ. "I have temptations," he said, "because I'm human. It goes with the territory. And sometimes I follow those temptations, and I sin. But you know what happens to me when I do?"

Issie rolled her eyes. "You get struck by lightning."

"No," he said. "Worse. I feel horrible about myself. I can't rest until I've repented."

"Oh, of course." Issie seemed amused. "That guilt thing that you right-wing extremists have. You love guilt."

He was saddened by the label she used like a weapon, as if she hoped it would wound him.

"It's like you think guilt will absolve you of everything."

"Oh, no," Nick said. "You've got us all wrong. Guilt doesn't absolve us of anything. And if we feel guilt, it's because we're guilty."

"Guilty? Just because you stumble now and then? Nick, give yourself a break. If nobody's hurt—"

"Nobody's hurt?" he asked with disbelief. "A man died because I stumble, Issie. He gave his life so I wouldn't have to drown in guilt."

Issie seemed lost for a moment, but then he saw the understanding dawn in her eyes. "I thought Jesus said he came to save the world, not condemn it."

"That's exactly what he said. And that's what he did, when he died for me. He saved me. See, I was already condemned, when I was going to bars every night, when I was promiscuous ..."

Those big eyes widened again. "You?"

"Me. I was condemned then. Without Christ, everybody's condemned."

"Oh, yeah," she said sarcastically. "Right straight into hell."

Nick shook his head. "I wish you believed it."

"Why?" she asked angrily. "Why do you care?"

His eyes drove deep into her, and she shifted with discomfort. "I care because I can see your potential, Issie."

"Potential? For what?"

"I see you in emergencies," he said. "I see you when you save people's lives. I see the way you throw yourself into your work as if every case was your only case, as if every person you're called to help is a life-or-death situation. I see goodness inside of you, Issie."

"Yeah, right," she said. "And what else?"

"I also see self-destruction, and I don't know where that comes from."

"And sin?" she mocked.

He thought about that for a moment. "You remind me of myself."

"Yourself?" she asked. "Oh, please."

"That's right. Ten years ago, before I knew Christ, I was just like you."

She stared at him for a moment, her expression heavy with a million thoughts. "I think it's nice, Nick, that you were able to turn your life around and find a purpose for it. I think it's great that you don't have to feel that guilt anymore. And I'm glad that you have the discipline not to fall back into the lifestyle you had. But I'm not like you."

"Thank goodness," Nick said.

A moment of smothering silence followed, but finally, she smiled slightly. "Actually, I would think that if I could be like you, it would be a nice thing to be." She sighed and averted her eyes. "A lot of ladies in town are vying for you, Nick. You and Dan Nichols."

He laughed, embarrassed. "That's ridiculous."

"Ridiculous? I think you know better than that."

"But you don't agree with them?"

Her smile was too pretty for his own good. "It's not that I don't agree with them. It's a question of type."

"Yeah, I guess the preacher's the last person in the world you'd ever be interested in."

"And I guess a party girl like me couldn't be farther from your dream of the perfect woman."

Their smiles faded, but neither of them refuted what the other had said.

"Want me to follow you home?" he asked.

She shook her head. "Better not."

"What if that Barnett fellow shows up tonight?"

"I didn't tell him where I live."

"Be careful of him," he said. "We don't know his part in Stan's poisoning. He could be the killer."

"I'm aware of that."

"Then what were you doing with him?"

Her expression fell. "Tell you the truth, I don't know," she said.

He could see the darkness in her soul, the despair, the loneliness, and he wondered what had caused it, where it had come from. Part of him understood what it was in her life that drove her to the bar every night. He had experienced it himself, working as a firefighter. They had thankless, dangerous jobs, with fierce stresses and little pay. They saw things others didn't have to see, and went home with the nightmares. It was tough when you had to go home alone. He knew.

He wished she had something more than Joe's Place to sustain her.

"Well, guess I better go," he said.

"Yeah." She started her car. "Hey, listen. Thanks for the rescue. And thanks for the sermon, too."

He smiled. "Anytime. But I'm best on Sunday mornings."

She breathed a laugh. "Well, maybe some day I'll get around to coming."

"If you have absolutely nothing else to do?"

"Something like that."

He opened the door and got out. "Lock up, okay?"

"Will do."

He backed up from the car and waited until she did it, and slowly ambled back across the street to where his car was parked. Why was it that Issie Mattreaux kept popping up in front of him? There were dozens of women in town who frequented bars and nurtured their promiscuity as if it were a religion that would bring some meaning to their lives. Why was it that she had such an effect on him? He didn't know, but he decided that it was wrong. She was not for him, and he needed to get her out of his mind.

He got into his car and watched as she pulled out of the parking lot and headed home. Before he cranked his car he said a prayer for her protection, a prayer for her rescue. The rescue of her soul.

Chapter Forty-Three

● ● ●

Shortly after the lights in the Newpointe jail went off, Aunt Aggie fell asleep. Sleep was a luxury not available to Celia, however, for as much as she would have liked to drift into a never-never-land of rest and dreams, she was unable to turn off the thoughts that kept her awake. If what Stan's mother had said was true, Stan had turned against her. He had decided to believe the lies.

Crushing despair almost smothered Celia as she lay curled up on her cot. A memory came back to her, vividly clear and precise, of another cell and how she had longed for an extra blanket and wished for an escape. It was almost too similar to be true. Her husband had been murdered, her family had turned against her, and someone was trying to frame her for something she had not done.

The difference was that, the first time, she'd had nowhere to turn. Through grace, God had shown her where to turn this time. But it was so hard doing what she knew she should. It was difficult to put her life in God's hands, when she had no idea why he'd allowed such a travesty of justice again, what good he could make come of it, and how he could ever use her for his kingdom again with this stigma attached to her.

The door to the hallway opened, spilling in some light from the stairwell, and she glanced over at Aggie, thinking that probably David had convinced the judge to set bail. Thank goodness the old woman would not have to stay. The overhead light flicked on.

She sat up as Sid Ford paused at her cell instead of going to Aunt Aggie's.

"I got somethin' for you," he said in a quiet, though grudging, voice.

Celia stood up, feeling weak. "What?"

"A Bible," he said. "Nick Foster came by and wanted to see you, but it was past visitin' time. I told him I'd bring you this Bible anyway."

She looked at the Bible in Sid's hand and slowly walked toward him to take it through the bars. "Thank you, Sid," she said.

He couldn't look her in the eye. "No problem." He glanced over at Aunt Aggie. "She all right? She ain't dead or nothin', is she?"

"No, she's just sleeping. She's very tired."

"Ain't we all?"

He started away from her, and she stepped to the bars, wrapping her hand around one of them. "Sid?"

He stopped but didn't look back at her. "Yeah?"

"I really appreciate the Bible. I needed it more than anything tonight. Would you mind leaving the light on so I can read it? It's just us here, and Aunt Aggie's sleeping soundly. I'd really like to read, if it's not too much trouble."

He didn't say anything, just walked through the door and closed it behind him. But the light didn't go back off.

Celia went back to her bed and looked down at the Bible in her hands. It was a godsend, she thought. An answered prayer. She was so thankful for it, but she didn't know where to begin to find the sustenance and comfort she knew waited for her there. She wished she'd spent more time studying God's Word.

She pressed the Bible against her heart, pulled her knees up, and pressed her forehead against them. "Oh, Father," she whispered. "You and Aunt Aggie are the only ones who aren't doubting me right now." She squeezed her eyes shut from the onslaught of tears. "Lord, you know what's going on," she whispered. "You know I didn't poison Stan. You know I love him. You know I'm innocent. Father, show me what to do. Show me how to fight this battle. Show me how to find peace and trust that you will deliver me from this evil." She wept as she prayed, her very heart uttering the words that her mouth could not say, and she felt God listening. His comfort embraced her like loving arms, and she wept, without words, without question, without answers.

Suddenly, the word *Jehosaphat* came to her mind. She opened her eyes and leaned her head back on the wall. "Jehosaphat," she whispered. "I don't even remember who he is." He was in the Old Testament. A king or something, but what had he to do with her?

She drew in a cleansing breath and decided that maybe God was speaking to her in his soft, still voice. Maybe she needed to read the story of Jehosaphat again. She looked into the concordance, found him listed, and turned to 2 Chronicles. She read how faithful Jehosaphat was as king of Judah, how he sought the God of his father, how he followed his commandments. She read how God had blessed him, raised him up, made him prosperous, how he had great riches and honor. How he established a God-fearing government and brought his people back to the Lord.

Still not certain how this applied to her, if at all, she kept reading, hungrily searching the Word, burying herself in the sustenance of it, the goodness of the story, the love inherent in the plot. She read how the sons of Moab and the sons of Ammon, and the Meunites, came to make war against Jehosaphat. And how he was afraid, because of their numbers. Suddenly, her heart began to pound harder. God was showing her another man who'd had a battle to fight, a battle that seemed impossible. He hadn't known how to fight, either. She read further and saw that Jehosaphat turned to God, and not to the counsel of men, and how he trusted in God. Then she came to chapter 20, verse 15, and she read the words that the Lord gave to the king, the words that sealed his strategy and gave his nation peace.

"Do not be afraid or discouraged because of this vast army. For the battle is not yours, but God's."

Her heart jolted, and her eyes filled with tears again. She sat staring at the words, soaking them in, breathing them, letting them seep into the pores and the chambers of her heart.

"Do not be afraid or discouraged ... the battle is not yours, but God's."

She looked up at the ceiling as if she could see the Lord through the beams. The battle wasn't hers. She hadn't invited it. Had done nothing to deserve it. She had not entered into it willingly. She had been thrust into it. And now God was telling her that she didn't have to claw and fight her way out. It was the Lord's battle.

A tremendous peace fell over her, and she began to weep, this time not of despair but of joy and the comfort that only the Lord could provide.

The battle is not yours, but God's. What wonderful words. What a bountiful provision. If the battle was not hers, then she need only wait. The Lord would provide somehow. He would reveal the truth.

She read on and saw how God had delivered Judah from the hands of their enemies, how Jehosaphat praised God and said, "Give thanks to the LORD, for his love endures forever."

That was what she would do tonight.

The lights flickered and went out, and Celia sat in the darkness for a moment, letting her eyes adjust, but no fear came upon her as she had expected. Aunt Aggie still slept in her cell, and Celia stayed on her bed, her Bible in her lap. Though she could no longer read it, she touched the pages as if life emanated from them. "The word of God is living and active. Sharper than any double-edged sword, it penetrates even to dividing soul and spirit, joints and marrow; it judges the thoughts and attitudes of the heart." The verse Stan had taught her years ago played over and over in her mind. He could judge her intentions, her thoughts, and he knew she had no murderous intent. He could also judge others' hearts. He knew who the killer was. He knew who had doubted her wrongfully. He knew how this would turn out. He knew what she would endure. But there would be a purpose, because she belonged to him.

She didn't intend it, didn't plan it, but suddenly a soft chorus came from her mouth, and she began to sing and praise God. Softly, but with all her heart.

In the darkness, Celia could see Aunt Aggie beginning to stir, and she sat partially up and looked at her niece through the bars. "Celia, you okay, *sha?*"

"I'm just fine, Aunt Aggie. Just fine."

"What you singin' about?"

"I'm sorry I woke you."

"You singin' about Jesus?" Aunt Aggie asked.

"Yes."

She couldn't see her in the darkness, but she could imagine Aunt Aggie rolling her eyes and shaking her head with what she considered the futility of it all. Poor Aunt Aggie.

"Oh, Aunt Aggie, something wonderful happened."

"What is it?"

"Sid Ford brought me a Bible. Nick Foster sent it. And I was praying and asking God for a sign, and he led me to a passage that told me the battle is not ours, but God's. Isn't that wonderful?"

Aunt Aggie's silence indicated how perplexed she was. She wouldn't see why this was wonderful at all. Celia almost laughed.

"Don't you see, Aunt Aggie? It means I don't have to fight. God knows I'm innocent. He's gonna take care of me and my baby. So I was just sitting here singing a praise song to God."

Aunt Aggie, once again, was at a loss for words. The dark-ness punctuated the silence between them. Finally the old woman said, "I'm glad your religion is givin' you some comfort."

Celia knew Aunt Aggie thought that was all it was. A false assurance that she put in some meaningless context of rules and circumstances that had no life to them at all. Again, she began to sing.

Aunt Aggie was silent at the end of the chorus. But Celia was smiling. "You'll see, Aunt Aggie. God's going to deliver me through this."

"I know you're gon' be all right," the old woman said. "I don't think God's gon' have nothin' to do with it, but you'll be all right if I got anything to say about it."

"The battle's not yours, either, Aunt Aggie," Celia said. "It's not Jill's, and it's not David's, and it's not mine. The battle is the Lord's."

"Well, if you don't mind, I'm still gon' keep payin' Jill to do what she can," Aunt Aggie said cynically.

Celia heard the sheets rustle as the old woman lay back down. But Celia wasn't finished praising the Lord. Quietly, softly, she began to sing again.

Chapter Forty-Four

● ● ●

In Slidell, Stan lay awake in the darkness of his hospital room, watching his mother sleep on the vinyl couch beside him. He closed his eyes and tried to pray. But he kept seeing the picture of Lee Barnett holding Celia, hearing her cry out that she was carrying his baby, hearing Sid and R.J. telling him how certain they were that Celia had tried to kill him.

"Lord, I don't know what to think," he cried out in his heart. "Tell me what to think. Tell me what to believe."

She was sitting in a jail cell, and the thought haunted him. Even if she was a murderer, cold-blooded, evil, he still couldn't stand the thought of her in jail. He wondered if Nick had gotten in to see her, if he had taken her the Bible. He wished he could have spoken to her when she called, heard her out. Maybe something she said could have brought some explanation, some understanding. There were so many "should have's", so many "if only's." He couldn't sort them all out.

He closed his eyes and let the tears seep down his temples and into his hair. He didn't know what was going to become of him after all the damage from the arsenic was assessed. He didn't know if he would ever be the same. His marriage certainly would not. The injustice of it all, the tremendous betrayal, the despair that seemed so smothering overcame him, and again his heart cried out to God. "Tell me what to do, Lord. Tell me what to do."

The words he had learned as a child in Bible drill came back to him. "Trust in the LORD with all your heart and lean not on your own understanding."

Was that the answer? Was the Word of God speaking to him, reminding him what he was to do? Hadn't he known it all along? All he had to do was trust in the Lord with *all* his heart and lean not on his own understanding. Maybe that was the mistake he was making. But how did one keep oneself from trusting his own understanding when things seemed so clear? He didn't want her to be guilty, but he couldn't imagine that she wasn't. Not now. Not after what he had seen. Not after what he had been told. Still, he couldn't stop loving her. How did one end a love that had been such a vital part of his life for so long?

Trust in the LORD with all your heart and lean not on your own understanding. The words played like a recording in his mind, over and over and over. Yet he was not able to let go of his own understanding. Not yet.

Chapter Forty-Five

● ● ●

Thoughts of Jill woke Dan early the next morning. He didn't like waking up with a woman on his mind. It wasn't like him. He didn't know what it was about her that had gotten under his skin, but he decided that he needed to see her.

It was seven A.M., but he tried to call her at home. There was no answer, only her machine. He hung up without leaving a message. Maybe she was at work.

He dialed the number of her office, and the machine picked up. Her secretary wasn't in yet, but maybe Jill was there, working away, ignoring the telephone. He decided to leave a message.

"Jill, this is Dan. Are you there?" He waited a second, and the phone clicked.

"Hey, Dan. I'm here."

"Oh." Suddenly, he wasn't sure what he wanted to say. He felt ridiculous having tracked her down like this, like it was some emergency, when all he wanted was to talk to her. "I didn't think I'd catch you there this early."

"Did you try me at home first?" she asked.

He hated to tell her that he had. It wasn't his style to track women down, like one of those desperate on-the-prowlers whose very existence seemed to hang on the affections of beautiful women. "I was just calling to see if you'd like to have breakfast." It was the first he'd thought of it, but he had to come up with something.

"Breakfast?" She hedged. "Uh . . . Dan, I'm a little busy right now."

"Busy?" This was the first time a woman had been too busy to spend time with him. He hesitated, trying to come up with a response. "Of course you are. I figured you were. Maybe another time." He waited for her to tell him when, to give him a rain check . . . maybe lunch. But she didn't.

"Dan, I'm just really swamped right now. I'm trying to gather my thoughts before I face the judge this morning. I'm doing everything I can to get Celia out. Then I wanted to run to the hospital in Slidell to see Stan. I just heard he's having dialysis today to flush his kidneys of the toxins. It's gonna be a busy day."

"I understand," he said. "No time to eat."

She seemed preoccupied, distant. "Look, we'll catch up with each other later, okay?"

"Sure," he said. "No problem." He hung up and felt as low as he'd ever felt in his life. This was exactly why he avoided serious relationships. He hated the rejection. Hated the groveling. Hated the feeling that he wasn't good enough. He hated the memories it brought back of his childhood.

He tried to push the thoughts out of his mind as he went up to his bedroom and changed into his running clothes. But he couldn't forget that smothering feeling of rejection. His parents, too busy to spend time with him, leaving him with a nanny while they shuttled off to Aspen to spend Christmas. His parents entertaining and making him stay upstairs, so they wouldn't be disturbed. His parents shipping him off to camp for the summer, a ritzy, cushy camp for rich kids whose parents didn't want them around. No, he hated that feeling of rejection, and he wouldn't tolerate it again. He hated that feeling of having to garner someone's approval, someone who hardly even cared that he existed. No, he wouldn't endure that again, not for any price.

He decided not to brood. Instead, he ran five miles, pushing himself past his own limits, forcing the poisons of rejection out of his system. He didn't know what he was so agitated about. He'd never declared his love to Jill Clark, and she'd never declared hers to him. Though people had started to speak of them as a couple, there was no exclusivity, no "understanding." If things just faded out, no one would think less of him. That was the way relationships worked with him. They would just think that he had grown tired of her and decided to move on.

Was he really that pompous? he asked himself as he got back home. Was it really his pride that was eating at him, rather than his disappointment that things were ending this way? Yes, he admitted. But knowing it didn't change things. Prayer was what he needed, he realized with a jolt of humility. Prayer and a shower.

He chose the shower first and put the prayer off until later.

Chapter Forty-Six

● ● ●

Judge Louis DeLacy had released Aunt Aggie early the morning after her incarceration, as soon as he was told how she'd wound up in jail. He was not about to allow her to spend another moment there, he said. She was tearful as she left Celia in the jail cell, promising to visit as often as they would allow her to.

Celia's peace remained, and manifested itself as compassion for Nick when he finally got in to see her. He looked tired and uncertain, and she saw the doubt about her in his eyes. She realized vaguely that if she had seen that look in his eyes yesterday, she would have been crushed. But today, she knew better than to blame him. She hugged him as he came into her cell, and pointed him to the only chair in the room. She sat across from him on the cot.

"I know what you must be thinking, Nick," she said. "I know everybody in town must think I'm absolutely guilty. I mean, how could I not be, with all the evidence against me?"

"I don't think you're guilty, Celia," Nick said weakly.

It was obvious that he was lying. She hated seeing him in this position, and almost wished he hadn't come. "Don't lie, Nick. Not for me."

He drew in a deep breath, and his face changed. Suddenly, she saw the real Nick, the one who wasn't acting, the one who was honest even when it hurt. "Okay, Celia," he said. "I'll be straight with you. I don't know what to think about you anymore."

She had believed she was ready for that, but when they came, the words still stung her. "Why would you think anything other than what you've always thought?"

"Because I haven't always known the whole story."

"Yes, you have," she said. "What you haven't known is all the old allegations. But they weren't truth. What you've known about me is truth."

She could tell that he struggled between his ministerial facade and the humanity within him. It was what she loved about Nick—the fact that he was so spiritual, yet so human . . . so close to God . . . yet so like herself.

"I have to ask you something," Nick said.

"Anything, Nick. I don't have any secrets."

"Well, you seem to have had some. A lot of things no one knew about you until all this blew up."

"I understand how that could make you suspicious," she said. "But you've got to understand that I had a right to start fresh. I was wrongly accused. I didn't need to drag that around for the rest of my life. If I had done something wrong to deserve that, fine. But I didn't. So I left it behind me and I pressed on."

"I can see that," Nick said. "But the question I want to ask you is more immediate, and even more personal. It's about Lee Barnett."

"What about him?" she asked.

His eyes were direct, probing, as he asked the question. "Why did you go see him yesterday?"

Her heart jolted. How had Nick found that out? Had the police been talking out of turn? Had they been gossiping her business all over town?

"How did you know about that?"

"Stan told me."

Her heart crashed, and despair hovered over it, waiting for an opening so it could move in and fill her with the darkness she'd stumbled through yesterday. But then she told herself that it was no surprise. She knew he had seen the picture.

It was still the Lord's battle, not hers. The realization enabled her to hold the despair at bay.

"Nick, I'm gonna tell you what happened yesterday, and I'm not telling you to defend myself, because I'm innocent and I don't *need* to defend myself. But I want you to know the real story."

Nick waited.

"I went to Lee Barnett because I wanted to find out what he was up to," she said. "I didn't step one foot in his apartment. I didn't touch him except to slap him once when I got so angry that I couldn't hold it in any longer. He grabbed me and shook me, and that must be when Vern snapped the picture. Now, if anyone wants to know the truth about that encounter, I suggest they go to Vern and ask him what he saw before and after that embrace. Put that picture in context. Ask him to see what else is on that film. Look at our faces, Nick."

Nick was quiet as the words sank in. He seemed to be listening, seriously wanting to believe her. She desperately wanted him to.

"Nick, please tell Stan the truth. He must know in his heart that I didn't do this."

Nick looked down at his feet, and she could see that he still struggled with what to believe about her.

Her expression crashed. "Nick, I am so sorry for you."

"For me?" he asked.

"Yes," she said. "When this is all over and I've been acquitted of any guilt, and you see how hard someone has worked to set me up, it'll be one more time when you beat yourself up for not doing the right thing."

He sat there, his face vulnerable, exposed. She knew what was going through his mind. He had to be thinking about all the times he had failed. All the inadequacies, all the mistakes. It was what made him such a good preacher ... and what made him so human.

"I'm gonna forgive you, Nick," she whispered. "And when you feel guilty for doubting me, I want you to remember that, if it weren't for your teaching, I may never have come to Christ. Yes, Stan led me, but you closed the deal, Nick. I'm tremendously grateful to you. So when you find out that I'm innocent, that everything I've said is true, and you get mad at yourself, I want you to remember that what you did for me five years ago was a whole lot more important than this."

Nick's eyes filled with tears, and he set his elbows on his knees and cupped his face in his hands. Finally, he looked up at her. "Celia, I love you. I want to believe you. I want to know that you know Christ, that all of this has not been a terrible act. Because if it is, then my judgment is horrible and my discernment is pretty lousy. I need to believe you."

"Then do it," she said. "Believe me."

He looked into her eyes, long and hard, and she knew that in his mind he probably prayed for eyes like God's eyes, to see into her and know if she lied. And suddenly she realized that God had told him in words that she had not been able to utter that she was innocent.

The tension in his face melted away, and more tears filled his eyes. He seemed to straighten, and his eyes were softer as he regarded her. "I believe you, Celia. I do."

"Then help Stan to believe me," she said. "Please Nick. I need you to help Stan believe me."

"I'll do everything I can," he told her. "I promise."

She gave him a hug, and he started to get up. "Nick? Tell him to trust in the Lord with all his might. And then he can trust in me."

Nick nodded and left her alone.

Chapter Forty-Seven

● ● ●

The dialysis did wonders for Stan, making him feel better than he'd felt since he'd been poisoned. It seemed that no major damage had been done to his organs, though the arsenic had taken its toll on him, and it would be weeks, maybe months, before he was restored to his former energy level.

They released him from the hospital with strict orders for his mother, who was going to care for him at home. Because his parents were sensitive to his need to return to some form of normalcy, they decided to move into his own house with him so he could sleep in his own bed and be surrounded by his own things. Newpointe police officers would continue their rotational guard of him.

Nick caught him in the corridor as they wheeled him out in his obligatory wheelchair. Stan's father tried to intervene, but Stan insisted on a moment with him alone. Nick wheeled him back into his room and sat down in front of him. "I spoke to Celia this morning," he said. "Stan, I know things look grim for your marriage, but I want you to reconsider your trust in her."

Stan almost laughed. "This is a role reversal, isn't it? Last time we talked, I was the one telling you to stop doubting her."

"I did doubt her," Nick said. "You were right. But when I met with her, I could tell that she wasn't lying. She's not guilty, Stan. You've got to trust her."

He closed his eyes. "How is she doing?"

"She's good," he said. "Better than I could have imagined. She said to tell you to trust in the Lord."

Stan's eyes came open. "Trust in the Lord?" he asked. "Is that exactly what she said?"

"Yep. Exactly."

Stan remembered the verse the Lord had given him just last night. *Trust in the Lord* . . .

It sounded like something Celia would say. That childlike faith came so easily to her. That bottom line that made it a done deal, even when others would have sought counsel and groped around for meaning and understanding. Celia didn't need much. A simple verse of Scripture.

"I know you can't get around much," Nick said. "But if you felt like going to visit her later, I could take you. We could put you in a wheelchair and you wouldn't have to walk . . ."

Hope blossomed with the idea, but then the image of her in Lee Barnett's arms—that irretractable image that would not let go—stopped him. "I'll think about it."

Nick gave him a skeptical look.

"No really," Stan said. "I just need to pray about it. I need to think."

"All right." Nick took his hand, shook it firmly. "Get some rest, okay? I'll be praying for you. And if you need me, anytime, man, I'm there."

The sight of his house as they pulled into the driveway brought a fresh onslaught of grief. Stan sat in the front seat of his father's car, wishing he could go in and find Celia waiting there, as she always was, full of news about her day, fluttering around him trying to help him unwind from whatever case he'd been absorbed in. The thought that he may never have that again was too much to bear. For a moment, he made no move to get out of the car, just sat there, staring at the door from the garage into the kitchen.

He tried to grapple with the logic of avoiding her. If he did, wouldn't he be sealing his fate, discarding his marriage, throwing her to the wolves? And what if she really was innocent? Could he live with himself if he'd turned against her?

Maybe Nick was right. Maybe he did need to see her. If he could just touch her, look in her eyes . . . he would know the truth. He knew he would. He'd been lied to countless times during his career as a cop, and his detective instincts hadn't been damaged by the arsenic. He would know, if he saw her. It would be obvious to him.

He got out of the car, staggering slightly, and his mother helped him walk to the door. "You sure you don't need the wheelchair, hon?" she asked.

"I'm sure. I can make it."

T.J. Porter was the guard on duty, and he parked his squad car out front and carried his bag in as his father pulled the wheelchair out of the trunk of the car. He waited as he gave his mother the key, and she unlocked the door leading in from the garage. It opened, and he stepped inside, his eyes scanning the kitchen, which was still in disarray from the investigation. Slowly, he walked through the kitchen into the living room.

"What's that?" his mother asked, and he followed her eyes to an envelope on the floor right inside the front door. "Looks like someone slipped it under the door." She picked it up, and her face changed. "It's addressed to Celia."

Something hardened in his chest as he took it, and he sank onto the closest chair and sat down. His hands trembled as he opened the envelope and pulled out the paper. He scanned the typed print, then shot a look at the bottom, to the signature of Lee Barnett.

His heart plunged again, and he began to read.

"Dear Celia," it said. "I look forward to being with you as soon as things are worked out. Please call me as soon as you have the chance. I miss you, and I love you. Lee Barnett."

Stan tossed the letter on the table next to him and dropped his face in his hands.

His father was just coming in, and his mother picked up the letter. "Bart, it's from Lee Barnett," she said. "For Celia."

Silence stood like a lethal gas around them, as all eyes turned to Stan. He began to weep.

His mother's eyes were full of tears, too. "Let's get him to bed," she said.

His father came over and pulled him up from the chair. Stan did as they wanted him to do, for he had no energy to fight them.

Chapter Forty-Eight

● ● ●

Stan awoke in his own bed several hours later. He could smell Celia's scent on the pillow next to him, and the fragrance sent sweet relief washing over him. Groggy, he turned over and slid his hand to her side of the bed, reaching for her, but the coldness of the sheets jolted him back to reality.

That image of her with Lee Barnett filled the big screen of his mind again, and the words of the letter echoed. Barnett had told her he loved her, as if the two of them had exchanged those words many times before. But when? How could she have been carrying on an affair without Stan's knowing it?

Something didn't ring true. The note slipped under the door was enough of a red flag. If, indeed, Celia had been seeing Lee Barnett, wouldn't he know that she was staying with her Aunt Aggie? Why would he have slipped a note under their door, unless he knew that Stan would be the one to find it?

Why would Celia have killed her first husband, why would she have tried to kill him, why would she claim she was pregnant, why would she have an affair with a man barely out of prison, why would she have lied all these years about her love for Stan? What would she possibly have to gain? None of it made any sense.

He got up and walked weakly into the living room. His father was sound asleep in his recliner. Some World War II movie was playing on the television. His mother had lain down on the couch and was sleeping. He felt sorry for them. They hadn't gotten much sleep lately, and the one night they had tried to go home to rest they had been called back because of the second murder attempt.

Stan decided not to wake them. He sat down in an easy chair adjacent to the couch. The letter was lying on the table next to it, and he picked it up and read it again. He thought of the explanation Celia had given—that someone had written a check and sent it to him, that there was a letter that she had not written, that it had her signature. It was typed, just as this one was. Why would he type it?

The possibility suddenly occurred to him that he could go straight to the source—look in the man's face and ask him those questions. Wouldn't he know if the man wanted him dead? Wouldn't he be able to see if there were lies in his eyes? As a detective, he was more astute than most. His instincts paid off well. Maybe he would be able to tell.

The cops who were working on the case now were passionately involved, because he was the victim, their one detective, their friend, their brother. Someone needed to be equally passionate on the other side. Celia had no one. Not even him.

Maybe, just because of the years of happiness she had brought him, he owed it to her to go to Barnett and see what he could determine.

He quietly went into the foyer and slipped out the front door. T.J. Porter was sitting on a lawn chair beside the front door. He got up as soon as he saw Stan. "Stan, should you be up?"

"I'm okay," he said, already out of breath. "Look, I need a favor."

"What favor?"

"I need for you to take me somewhere."

"Where?"

"I want you to take me to the Bonaparte Court apartments."

T.J. looked at him like he was crazy. "Stan, sit down."

Stan sat with relief in the folding lawn chair and looked up at the huge man.

"Stan, this isn't a good idea, man. You don't need to be out. You just got out of the hospital. You can barely walk."

"I can make it. Just get me there."

"Why? What purpose would it serve?"

"Nothing illegal," Stan said. "I want to talk to Lee Barnett. I want to look him in the eye and talk to him."

T.J. ran his fingers through his hair and shook his head. "I can't do it, Stan. I'm sorry."

"Why not?"

"Because I've been told to guard you."

"You weren't told to imprison me, you were told to protect me. Now, you can go along and protect me."

"But Sid said—"

"I don't care what Sid said. I'm still on the police force. And Sid is my subordinate. So are you."

"But Stan, you can't pull rank when you're so sick. You're not on active duty right now."

"I don't recall taking a leave of absence. I'm on sick leave. That's all. Now, I order you, as your superior, to take me where I want to go."

T.J. looked miserably divided. "What about your parents?"

"My parents are fine," he said. "It's me the killer's after, not them. As long as you're guarding me, you're doing your job."

T.J. breathed a heavy, defeated sigh. "All right, Stan, get in the car."

Stan went to the car, opened the door, and sank into the front seat. T.J. got in on the other side and pulled out of the driveway. "Did you tell your folks?"

"They're sleeping," Stan said. "I'll be back before they even wake up."

He leaned his head back on the seat and closed his eyes as T.J. drove. Silently, he prayed that he would be able to see clearly what was going on. If his wife was an adulteress, he needed to know. If she was a killer, he needed to know that, too. If Lee Barnett had anything at all to do with this, he had to see it.

It took only ten minutes to reach the Bonaparte Court apartments on Rue Matin, and T.J. pulled into the parking space closest to Barnett's apartment. Stan gave him a look. "Do you know which apartment it is?"

"Right there," T.J. said, pointing to the one on the second floor. "B–5. We've been patrolling it at least hourly. Stan, I don't know how you'll get up those stairs."

"Don't worry about it," Stan said. "I'll make it."

"I'm coming with you."

Stan thought that over for a moment, then decided it probably was a good idea. "Yeah, if I'm facing my killer, then I probably do need an armed guard."

T.J. got out, came around to the passenger side, and helped Stan out of his seat. "Stan, it won't be easy getting you up those stairs, buddy."

"I can do it," Stan said. "Just give me a little time."

He took the steps one at a time, stopping to rest on each one. T.J. put his arm around his waist and helped him up the final few steps. He was sweating and had to stop to catch his breath before they got to the door.

"You sure you want to do this, buddy?" T.J. asked.

"I'm sure."

They reached the door, and T.J. rapped hard on it. For a moment, there was no answer, then a muffled, "Who is it?"

"Po-lice," T.J. said.

Stan shot him a look. "You didn't have to tell him that."

"That's exactly who we are," T.J. said. "Best way to get him to open the door that I know of."

"Or to make him run out the back window," Stan said. But there was no need to worry. The door opened and Stan found himself facing Lee Barnett for the first time. He stared at the man. His hair was unwashed, his face unshaven. Dark shadows defined his bloodshot eyes, as if he were hung over. He wasn't wearing a shirt, and Stan saw the tally marks tattooed on his arm.

Could Celia really be involved with a man like this?

"Yeah, what do you people want now?" Lee asked.

"My name is Stan Shepherd," Stan said.

Lee's face changed and his eyes opened wider. "You're outa the hospital?" he asked.

Stan gazed intently into his eyes, looking for some sign of evil. Was this the orderly in the surgical mask and glasses? He wasn't sure. "Yeah, I'm out. I want to talk to you."

"Is this police business?" Barnett asked. "Or personal?"

"A little of both," Stan said.

Barnett backed up from the door. "Well, I guess you oughta come in, then," he said. Stan looked at T.J., who seemed a little uncertain about whether they should go inside. T.J. patted his weapon, then nodded that it was probably all right. The two men went inside.

Barnett nodded toward the couch, and Stan gratefully sank down. "I thought you were practically dead," Barnett said.

Stan nodded pensively. "Somebody would like to see me that way."

"Sounds like it." Barnett took the seat across from them. "I think I know why you're here."

Stan waited. Often silence was the best catalyst he knew to get someone talking.

"You're here to ask if I'm the one who poisoned you."

Stan waited for him to go on, to hang himself.

"Well, I'm not." He said the words without flinching, without averting his eyes. He looked intently at Stan, as if determined to make him believe.

Stan reached into his back pocket and pulled out the envelope that he'd found under the door today. "You know anything about this?" he asked.

Barnett eyed the envelope, and so did T.J. "No, what is it?"

His response seemed genuine, but Stan watched him nonetheless, waiting for some flicker of deceit. He pulled the letter out. "It's a letter to my wife. Has your signature on it."

Barnett got up, grabbed the letter, and peered down at it. "Now how would I have typed this? And anyway, that isn't my signature. I don't write like that."

Stan watched him carefully. "Can you prove you didn't write it?"

Barnett held his hands up. "Can anybody prove anything? All I can tell you is that I don't have a typewriter *or* a computer. How would I have printed this out? You can search this apartment high and low. I don't have that much stuff here, anyway."

Stan nodded to T.J. and the big cop got up and began to go through the rooms, looking for some sign of a typewriter or computer.

"I'll tell you somethin' else," Barnett said. "I can guarantee you that's not my signature." He pulled out a driver's license that had been issued the day after he'd gotten out of prison, and handed it to Stan. "See, that's my signature, right there. Nothin' like the one on that letter."

"Then who wrote this and why did they put it under my door?"

Barnett almost laughed. "Don't you see? It's just part of the game they're playing."

"Who's playing?"

"Whoever this is that's tryin' to set me up." Barnett was beginning to break out in a sweat, and he leaned back in the chair. "Look, I understand where you're comin' from. You're the one who almost bought the farm, and you're prob'ly not feeling so good right now. But I didn't have a thing to do with this, and neither did Celia."

Stan might have predicted that Barnett would defend her, but it still hurt. He sat for a moment, trying to compose himself, trying to fight the emotions overcoming him. He was a cop, he told himself, and he was here as a cop, no matter how he felt.

"She came here yesterday," Barnett said matter-of-factly. Stan wondered why Barnett would volunteer that if, indeed, anything was going on. "She was mad as a hornet. It was the first time I'd seen her since before I went to prison, and she looked awful. She was furious at me, man, and I could tell just from lookin' at her that she didn't have nothin' to do with poisonin' you."

Stan kept staring at Barnett. "What about the letter she sent you? The checks?"

"Apparently it wasn't her." He got up and paced around the floor. "Some fictitious priest named Father Mueller brought the letter to the prison chaplain. I ain't been able to find him, and now I'm wonderin' if it wasn't the killer himself."

T.J. came back in and shook his head. There was nothing with which Barnett could have typed the letter. That didn't rule out one of those all-purpose office shops. There wasn't one in Newpointe, but he could have gone to Slidell or New Orleans.

"Look, man, there wasn't a happier guy alive than I was a coupla weeks ago when I got that letter and those checks and thought they were from Celia. I tell you what, talk about redemption. I thought maybe there really was a God, and he had sent Celia to rescue me. But then I got here, and everything started breakin' loose, and I realized that I'd been had, that some jerk out there didn't care if a ex-con got blamed for doin' somethin' he hadn't done. And, to tell you the truth, when I first realized I'd been set up, I thought Celia set me up. I thought she'd probably tried to off you, then pinned it on me since I was convenient. But yesterday when she came to see me, I knew better."

"Did she come into your apartment?" Stan asked.

"No, of course not. She wouldn't be that stupid. Don't forget I just got out of prison. She wouldn't trust me."

Stan's mouth trembled slightly, and he pulled the snapshot from his pocket and stared down at it. Then he held it up where Barnett could see. "Explain this."

Barnett took the picture, squinted down at it, then began to laugh. "Oh, this is priceless."

Stan couldn't find the humor.

"I musta held her for a split second, right after she slapped the fire outa me. It was in self-defense, man. I can't believe this guy got that picture at exactly that moment. He's a master. He'd get rich as a paparazzo." He studied it with a look of amusement. "Come on, man, give me a break. Look at my face in the picture. It's not exactly tender."

"I can't see much of it," Stan said. "I can't see any of hers."

Dismissively, he thrust the picture back at Stan. "Well, if you *had* seen hers, you would have seen that she was cryin' and her face was beet red. Let me tell you somethin'. She can pack a wallop when she wants to."

Stan would have found that amusing, if it hadn't been so sad. He knew all too well how much of an emotional wallop she could pack. He stared down at the picture, then looked at the letter and back up to Barnett. "You know there's no law against having an affair with another man's wife," he said. "You can't go to jail for it. If you're having an affair with my wife, I need to know that now. I need to know whether my wife is involved in this in any way."

Lee Barnett gaped at him. "And you claim to love her?"

Stan didn't appreciate the question.

"No, really, I mean it, man," Barnett said. "You're the guy who's supposed to love and cherish her, right? I mean, you married her. You've lived with her all this time. You know her better than anybody else. But here I am, ain't laid eyes on her in years, and I see her one time and I know for sure she's tellin' the truth. Man, if she ain't after an affair, maybe she ought to be."

If Stan had had more strength, he might have lunged for him, but there was too much truth in the words.

"Look, I know there's evidence. Apparently, there's evidence against me, too, and you're holding two pieces of it in your hands. But I can swear to you that that don't mean a thing. I ain't foolin' around with your wife, she ain't in love with me, she didn't poison you, she didn't set me up, she didn't come here to have a secret rendezvous with me yesterday, none of those things. But somebody wants to kill you, man. And I don't know why, but he wants it to look like Celia did it, and he wants it to look like she did it for me." He chuckled slightly. "If it weren't so scary, I might be a little flattered."

"Flattered?"

"Yeah, that the cops would think that somebody could care enough about me to kill her husband over me."

Stan's eyes narrowed as he tried to process that admission.

"Trust me, detective. There ain't nobody in the world who would do that for me. And nobody in the world I'd go to prison for, either."

Every instinct in Stan's body told him Barnett was being straight with him. He'd always trusted those instincts. He had no reason not to trust them now. He got to his feet and nodded to T.J. T.J. started across the room to the door.

"I appreciate your time," Stan said.

"You believe me, don't you?" Barnett asked.

Stan didn't want to commit himself. "I'll think about it all."

"Think about it hard," Barnett said. "Look, I ain't in love with your wife, but I don't much like the idea of her sitting in jail for something she didn't do. It just ain't right. I had to go to prison for something I *did* do, and it was bad enough. I can just imagine what it would be like if you were innocent."

He held the door and turned to T.J. "Hey, do I have to stay in town? I was told I couldn't leave town, but I'd really like to get back to Jackson. I don't know anybody here, and I'm not havin' good luck, and it's not where I want to be."

"You'd better stick around, buddy, until you're told you can leave."

"Terrific. At first, I thought it wouldn't hurt, that the apartment was paid for, so who cares? But I don't like it here. It's a hostile environment, and I'm not getting very far. Maybe I oughta take Celia's advice and stay in a hotel or somethin'. I feel like a sittin' duck. I just ain't got any money to pay for nothin' else."

Stan turned around at the word *hotel* and stared at the man. Hadn't Marabeth Simmons mentioned them talking about a hotel? Maybe it had been in that context.

Stan sighed and started down the stairs.

Barnett stepped outside of his door. "Hey, you take it easy now. That arsenic, it ain't nothin' to play with."

Stan stopped on the steps and turned around, looked up at him again. "Did she tell you she was pregnant?"

Barnett's eyebrows shot up in mild surprise. "Who? Celia? *Pregnant?*"

He studied the man's eyes for some sign of deceit, but again, the most he could find was indifference. "Yeah, Celia."

"No, is she?"

Stan didn't answer, and finally, he turned away again. He took the remaining steps down, carefully. When he reached the bottom, he looked up. Barnett was leaning against the rail, staring down at him with a slight frown as if worried he might fall. He nodded good-bye and Barnett gave him a half-wave before going back in.

Stan got into the car, and T.J. went around to the driver's side and cranked it up. "So what do you think?" T.J. asked.

"He didn't do it."

T.J. rolled his eyes. "Then how do you explain all the evidence that says he was involved?"

Stan stared at his friend. "I think he just explained it."

"And you believe him?"

"I'd stake my whole career on it. And my marriage."

"Are you sure, Stan?"

"She's innocent." His mouth twisted. He put his hand over his face and wept into it.

T.J. reached out and touched his shoulder. "You okay, man?"

"No, I'm not okay. My wife is in jail because of something she didn't do, and for a little while, I believed she did it. I can't believe I bought into it. Whoever's doing this, they're evil, and I played right into their hands."

"Man, don't go off the deep end. You don't know for sure that Celia's innocent."

"Well, until I know for sure she's guilty, I'm gonna believe she's innocent."

T.J. sat there for a moment, letting the car idle. "You ready to go home, buddy?" he asked.

Stan shook his head. "I'm not going home."

"Man, you're sick. You need to be in bed."

"Take me to the station."

"The station? What are you gonna do? Go back to work?"

"No," Stan said. "I'm gonna visit my wife."

Chapter Forty-Nine

● ● ●

The noise in the police department came to an abrupt halt as Stan stepped through the door. All eyes seemed to turn to him, even those of the criminals being booked. Sid Ford got to his feet and began to laugh as his eyes misted over.

"Man, *there* you are! Your folks was worried sick about you. What you doin' here, man? You s'posed to be in bed."

"They let him out," T.J. said, "and now he's trying to investigate this crime himself."

Sid approached Stan and shook his hand as if he were fragile. "Man, you need to be at home in bed. You need to let us take care of this. We're gettin' to the bottom of it. Let me call your mama back and tell her you're here."

"You're on the wrong track," Stan said weakly, "but we can talk about that later." He tried to catch his breath. "Right now I came for another reason."

"Another reason?" Sid asked. "What?"

T.J. shot Sid a look. "He wants to see Celia."

"No, man!" Sid took a step back, shaking his head. "You don't wanna do that. That's gon' be too hard on you! You know it is."

"I want to see my wife," Stan said. "You can't stop me."

"Man, there's a court order sayin'—"

"There's not a court order telling *me* to do anything," Stan said. "If I want to see my wife, I can. Sid, I don't think you want me to pull rank on you."

Sid held his hands out to stem the threat. "Man, you don't have to go that far. I'm just tryin' to protect you."

"I'm sick of people trying to protect me in the wrong way. My wife doesn't deserve to be locked up. I want to see her."

"You ain't gon' talk us into lettin' her out."

"I know that," Stan said. "Just take me to the jail."

Sid rolled his eyes, as if he couldn't believe he was being asked to do such a ludicrous thing. But finally, he led him to the basement.

Stan stepped carefully down the stairs, stopping every few steps to catch his breath. Sid reached the door to the women's jail before he did, so he tried to hurry the rest of the way down.

"Sure you're up to this, man?" Sid asked. "You don't look good."

"Yeah . . . I'm fine . . ."

Sid opened the door and Stan stepped in. He looked from one cell to the next, but didn't see Celia. Then he heard a gut-wrenching sound from behind the partition surrounding her toilet. Celia was throwing up.

Stan stepped up to the bars and looked into the dimly lit cell. A Bible lay open on the cot, and her shoes were beside it. He heard her retching again, then the toilet flushed.

"She throwin' up?" Sid asked.

Stan couldn't answer, for there was a lump of emotion the size of Texas in his throat. Had she been sick like this the whole time? Didn't anyone care? Suddenly, a fierce, protective instinct came over him. "Open the door," he ordered Sid.

"Stan, don't you think you better talk to her through the bars? I mean, we ain't talkin' about somebody stable."

"Open it," he said again.

Sid registered his disapproval with a loud sigh and opened the cell. "I'm waitin' right by the door, man. Holler if you need me."

But Stan wasn't listening. Weakly, he headed across the cell and stepped around the partition. Celia was on her knees in front of the toilet, and as he stepped up behind her, she began retching again. Stan leaned over her, gathered her hair, and pulled it back out of her way.

As soon as she was able, she looked up to see who had come to her aid. Surprise widened her eyes, and the gray color of her complexion quickly flushed with pink tones. She got to her feet, and as tears flooded her eyes, whispered, "Stan?"

He hadn't expected to be so overcome with love, not after all the doubts, but his eyes filled with tears and he pulled her to her feet. "Are you all right?" he whispered. "Let me help you."

He led her to the sink and she bent over it to rinse her mouth out, then fell back into his arms. She wept against his shirt, her body shuddering. After a while, she managed to whisper, "I'm fine now." She pulled back and looked up at him. "What about you? You look terrible, honey. You need to be in bed." She touched his cheek. "You've lost weight . . . and you're skin . . . it's yellow. Why are you here? Why aren't you in bed?"

"I had to see you." He felt himself wobbling unsteadily, and she led him to the cot and made him sit down. She sat next to him, sideways so she could face him, and he combed his fingers through her hair as remorse and shame welled up inside him and filled his eyes with tears. "Can you ever forgive me?"

"Me?" she asked. "What for?"

"For doubting. They showed me that picture, and told me about Lee Barnett, and the arsenic in the attic, and all the other stuff, and I bought into it, Celia. I'm so sorry."

Her face twisted and grew redder. "How do you know they're not right?"

"Because . . ." He wiped his face with a rough hand. "None of it makes any sense. I look at you . . . and I know who you are . . ." His voice broke off and he embraced her again. "Please forgive me."

"I do," she whispered. "Of course I do."

"Who did this, Celia?" he asked. "Who could it be?"

"I don't know," she said. "I've racked my brain for years, even before you were poisoned. I have no idea. I really don't. I suppose it could be Lee Barnett, but it didn't seem like it was, when I went to visit him. I can't understand his motive, if it's him. Why would he do something that would land him right back in prison? It doesn't make any sense."

He shook his head. "No, I don't think he did it. I just went to see him myself."

Her eyebrows rose. "You did?"

"Yes. I think he's being used somehow." His eyes took her in, drinking in her beauty, her sweetness, and he touched her face. "Celia, the other night when you came to the hospital, you said something."

She smiled slightly. "Yes."

"About a baby?"

Her tears spilled over again. "Mm-hmm."

"That's why you were throwing up?"

She nodded.

His mouth trembled. "When did you find out?"

"Remember, I had been nauseated for a few days, even before you were poisoned. That night they took blood samples from me, determined I wasn't poisoned, so I didn't know what it was. But a couple of days later, they called and told me that I was pregnant."

Stan's face twisted as new tears reddened his eyes. "An answered prayer," he said. "Funny, I never dreamed it would be answered quite this way."

"Me, either," Celia said. "But it's gonna be all right."

"How can you say that? They think you tried to kill me."

"But *you* don't think I tried to kill you, and that's the most important thing," she said. "Stan, God already knows who's doing this. It's gonna be all right. I promise."

"But I don't want you in here," he said. "I don't want you in jail. This place was built for criminals, not for my wife."

"I know how you feel. I'd feel the same way if you were in here. But Stan, it's really okay. I'm spending all my time soaking up the Bible. I needed this time. As long as I'm in here, I'm safe, and maybe you are, too. If somebody's trying to set me up, they can't do it while I'm in jail."

He breathed in a deep shuddering sigh. "Celia, I would have done anything to keep this from happening."

"So would I," she said. "But right now all we can do is try to figure out what's going on. The best thing you can do for me is to get plenty of rest and get well. We're gonna have a lot to do over the next nine months."

He laughed softly. "Yeah, I guess we are." He thought of the nursery they were planning to add on to their little house when she got pregnant, how he was going to do most of the work himself. The wallpaper they'd picked out, the little sleigh crib they had their eye on . . . He thought of all the decisions—pink, or blue, or yellow, or green . . . He thought of that camcorder he was going to have to buy . . . and then he thought of the fact that his wife might have to stay in jail until the trial that could take forever to come about. That this baby could come home from the hospital without its mother. He couldn't stand the thought.

"Look at me, Stan," she whispered. "We've got to trust in the Lord. He gave us this baby. He's not going to forsake us now. David said the timing was all wrong, that it wasn't fair to the child, that I should have an abortion, like that would be more fair—"

"An *abortion?*"

"He doesn't understand. He doesn't know that God's timing isn't flawed. But this is our baby, no matter how or when God gave him to us."

He pressed his forehead against hers and closed his eyes. Again, her simple faith astounded him. He had once believed he had that kind of faith, but now he wasn't so sure. She slid her arms around his neck again, and he held her as tightly as his weakness would allow.

Finally, Sid ambled back to the cell door and rapped on the bars. "Come on, Stan. I can't stand here all day."

"Then leave us," Stan said.

"I can't do that, man."

Reluctantly, Stan got up and kissed his wife, wiped the tears from her face. "I'll be back soon, and I'm gonna have some answers," he said.

"Remember one thing," she whispered. "The battle's not ours, but the Lord's. He'll fight it for us."

Her faith had always been so absolute, and now he found himself grateful for it. She was right, and in the deepest part of his soul, he knew it was true.

Walking away and leaving her in that cell was the hardest thing he had ever done, but he vowed as he did that he would get her out as soon as God permitted.

• • •

Sid walked Stan and T.J. back out to the car and helped him get in. "You get back on home and rest now."

Stan knew that he'd pushed the limits of his energy level, and the only thing he could do was go home and collapse in bed for a while. But as he rested his head on the back of his seat, he looked up at Sid. "I'm calling a meeting for tonight."

Sid frowned. "A meeting? What you mean, man?"

"A meeting," Stan repeated. "My house, seven o'clock." His words were heavy, labored.

"Who you want at this meeting?"

"You, Vern, Jim, Jill, Gus, the prosecutor, and whoever else is involved in this case in any way."

"Man, you can't get involved in this. You're too close. It's too personal."

"Consider it an interview as part of the investigation," Stan said. "Your star witness wants to talk. Will you be there, or won't you?"

"Yeah, I'll be there, but I can't speak for nobody else. I mean, Vern . . ."

"Tell him to bring the rest of the snapshots he got from following Celia yesterday. I want to see every last one of them."

Sid shrank back. "What you tryin' to do? You tryin' to get in the way of this investigation?"

"Nope. I'm trying to see that it's done right."

"Man, he was straight."

"Well, it's funny that he'd pick that one shot out of the entire meeting."

"What do you think, man, that he's in on some kinda conspiracy to cover up? You suspectin' me, too, now?"

"No."

"Man, you know we're good cops. You know we're doin' a good job."

"All I know is my wife is sitting in jail for something she didn't do. My house. Seven o'clock." With the last bit of energy he had, he pulled the door shut. Sid straightened and stepped back on the curb.

"Home?" T.J. asked.

"Home," Stan said.

"Man, your parents called the station two or three times to see what you were doing and when you're coming home."

"I'm a big boy," Stan said. "They'll get used to it."

He sank his head back onto the neck rest and thought how weary he was of all these people who didn't have a clue. He only hoped he could set them straight before much more time passed.

• • •

Jill was in her office when Stan called. She could hear the weariness in his voice, but he pressed on, nonetheless.

"Jill, I'm calling a meeting at my house for tonight at seven o'clock," he said.

Jill frowned. "A meeting? What for?"

"I want everybody who's involved in this case to get together. I just came from seeing Celia. I also saw Lee Barnett today."

"Stan! Aren't you supposed to be in bed?"

"Things have to be done, Jill. They're botching the whole investigation. Can you be there or not?"

"Of course, Stan. Of course I'll be there. You saw Celia? Stan, did you two talk? Do you—?"

"I know she's innocent," he said. "I want to get her out as soon as possible."

"So what's this meeting about?"

"We're going to put our heads together and figure out what's going on," he said. "And then we're going to make a plan."

"What kind of plan?"

"I don't know yet," Stan said. "But something to draw the killer out. We've got to figure out who this is before Celia has to suffer anymore."

Chapter Fifty

● ● ●

Stan was feeling weaker than ever when seven o'clock rolled around. His mother fussed around him as if he were a child. She had come close, at least twice, to calling everyone and canceling the meeting. But when he'd been adamant to the point of asking her to leave if she couldn't tolerate his actions, she'd settled down.

Now he sat with his feet up in the recliner in his living room, his head resting back on the chair. He'd had little appetite, though he'd forced himself to eat something, just so his mother would be satisfied.

When the doorbell rang, his mother answered. Jill breezed in. "Am I the first one here?"

"Yes," Hannah said. "Jill, I wish you could talk him out of this. It's madness. He's not up to having people over . . ."

"Mother!" Stan snapped, and she decided to shut up and leave the room

Jill stood in front of him, looking down at him with concern. "Stan, how are you feeling?"

"I'm okay."

"We really don't want you to wind up back in the hospital. We're so thankful that you've been able to come home."

"I said I'm okay."

His tone warned her to change the subject, so she set her briefcase down and took the seat next to him. "I went by a little while ago to see Celia."

His tone changed. "You did?"

"Yeah. Her spirits were so much higher than the last time I saw her, thanks to your visit today."

Stan's mother reappeared from the kitchen, a horrified look on her face. "Stan, you went to see Celia? In *jail?* Is that where you were?"

"That's right."

"Stan, what were you thinking?"

"That I wanted to visit my wife."

Thankfully, the doorbell rang again before Hannah could react, and flustered, she went to open it. Sid Ford walked in, followed by Vern and Chief Shoemaker. A few minutes later, Gus Taylor, the prosecutor, showed up.

"We're all here," Sid said. "What you want to talk about?"

He invited them all to sit, then he dropped his footrest and forced himself to sit up straight. "The reason I called this meeting," he said, "is that there are some things we all need to get to the bottom of."

Trying to take the lead, Jim shifted in his seat. "Stan, I know that things are hard for you right now. It must be terrible to be told that your own wife may have been involved in your murder attempt. But you gotta know that we're doing everything we can."

"No, you're not," Stan said matter-of-factly. "I know absolutely that you aren't doing everything you can. The only thing you've managed to do so far is to torment my wife. There's still a killer out there, and nobody's doing a blasted thing to find him."

"Stan, we've got a ton of evidence," Gus said.

"Yeah, let's talk about that evidence," Stan said, breathing hard. "Vern, that meeting you saw between Barnett and my wife. Tell us about it, why don't you?"

Vern looked uncomfortable. "Well, you know, I was followin' her like I was told. We were doin' it 'cause you asked us to."

"Don't change the subject. Just answer the question."

Vern looked offended. "Well, I didn't know I was in a courtroom."

Stan's eyes drilled into him, waiting for him to answer.

"Just what I told you. I was followin' her, she went to visit Lee Barnett, and I took some pictures."

"I want to see the rest of the pictures on that roll of film," Stan said.

"I told him to bring 'em," Sid said.

Vern pulled the pictures out of his pocket and shuffled through them. "There aren't any that are very helpful in the case. I don't know why—"

"Just give them to me," Stan said. Jill got up and moved her chair closer to him as he flipped through them. It was all so clear, in context. He could see the fury on Celia's face now, the tears, the hands balled into fists. He could see her talking through her teeth in outrage. He could see the blurred arm as she slapped him . . .

"Vern, Sid . . ." He took a long breath and tried to steady his voice. "Why didn't you flash any of *these* pictures in my face when I was in the hospital? These pictures that would have shown that she didn't go there for some kind of romantic tête-à-tête."

"I showed you what I considered evidence, Stan."

Sid shook his head. "Man, I saw them pictures before. They don't mean nothin'. So they could have been havin' a fight."

"Or she could have gone there for the very reason she said she did," Stan said. "To pin Lee Barnett down about what he's doing in town and whether he tried to kill me. These pictures bear that out."

"You don't find it the least bit suspicious that she went to him in the first place?" Gus asked.

"Stan, I know this is the last thing you want to believe," Jim threw in. "I know it's as painful as all get-out. But you're not thinking clearly. You're sick, and you're hurt, and if you were back at work doing this same investigation on somebody else's attempted murder, I guarantee you you'd make the same assumptions they've made."

"I wouldn't do the smorgasbord approach to collecting evidence," he said. "Picking and choosing a little here ... a little there ... disregarding all the evidence that doesn't support my theory. That's shoddy police work, Jim, and you know it."

The plump man got up, unable to stay seated. He rubbed his belly as if it burned and paced across the room. "Look, Stan, I've taken a personal interest in this case because it's you. You know I don't usually get involved in investigations. But somebody tried to kill a police officer, and I'll be cursed if I'm not gonna follow the most obvious trail, no matter who that leads us to."

"I feel the same way," Gus said. Jill sprang to her feet, facing off with him. "What if the most obvious trail is just that—obvious—because someone wants it to be? Gus, what if the killer has some perverted reason for wanting to see Celia locked up for the rest of her life? I mean, he's done it once before already, but she got off. What if he's carefully laid a trail—the arsenic in the attic, the checks to Barnett, the letter from Celia."

"And the letter left under my door today," Stan added.

"What letter?" Sid asked.

Stan spoke up. "The letter that was signed Lee Barnett, only it wasn't his handwriting."

"Maybe it was a for-real letter, man. Let me see it."

"No," Stan said. "Just think, Sid. You know Celia. Does she seem stupid to you?"

"No. I can't say she does. A little looney, maybe, in light of all this, but not stupid."

"Then why would she do such stupid things? Why would Barnett?"

"Man, you don't wanna go there. Barnett's so stupid that he gets drunk at Joe's Place every night and spouts off at the mouth about everything in his head. Tried to pick Issie Mattreaux up last night. Everybody who was in Joe's Place is talkin' about it. That's how stupid he is."

Stan didn't know how to counter that. If Lee Barnett could have proved to have some self-control, some savvy, some sense, maybe they would listen. But Barnett obviously wasn't helping any.

Jill looked down at him, as if waiting for a comeback, but he found himself without one. What now? Where did they go from here?

"Look, I have an idea," Jill said, turning back to the others. "It's the best one I've been able to come up with to draw the real killer out, and if it's Celia, even prove that it's her."

"Celia?" Stan shot back. "You're her lawyer. You're supposed to believe her!"

"I do," she shouted over him. "Just listen. This will satisfy everybody. Those of us who think she's innocent will be able to identify the real killer, and those of you who think she's guilty will be able to prove she is if she is."

"What?" Gus asked skeptically.

She sat down, and looked down at her feet, and Stan became aware that she wasn't at all sure of her idea. Still, she went on.

"It's kind of far-fetched, but just hear me out, okay?"

"Shoot," Jim said. "We don't have to go for it."

"No, you don't. Not unless you're serious about doing the right thing." No one said anything in response, so she leaned forward and went on. "For the moment, let's assume that Celia is innocent, and that there's a killer out there trying to set her up for a second time. He can't act while Celia's in jail, right? I mean, if he attempts to kill Stan again while she's locked up, it's clear to everyone that she couldn't be the culprit. Am I right?"

The others in the room looked at her with dull eyes. "We're not letting her out, if that's what you're getting at," Gus said.

"Just listen," Jill went on. "On the flip side of that, if she were by some chance guilty—"

Stan groaned and shook his head.

"—then she still can't act until she's out. So either way, we'll never be able to be absolutely sure who the killer is as long as she's in jail. Now, I know that Celia has to stay in jail, that she's been denied bond. Believe me, I realize that. But there is one scenario in which she could be let out for a couple of days. If she had a death in the family, the judge would probably let her out for the funeral."

"You gon' kill somebody in her family so she can get out for a day?" Sid asked.

Jill shot him a murderous look. "Right, Sid. I thought we'd just shoot her mother so we could get on with things. Give me a break."

"Well, what else are you suggestin'?"

"I'm suggesting that we *stage* someone's death. Specifically, Aunt Aggie's. That we make it look like Aunt Aggie had a heart attack and died. Do the obituary, get a coffin, have a funeral, the works. The only people who would know about it are those of us in this room, Aunt Aggie, and the judge, who would have to agree because I couldn't lie to him."

"Aunt Aggie's on Celia's side. She'd do anything to get Celia off."

"That's because she's certain she's innocent. If I told her this would prove it, and draw out the killer, I guarantee you she'd go along with it. But just in case, you could post a guard to be with her twenty-four hours so she doesn't tip Celia off."

"I don't get it," Stan said. "How would this help?"

"If we could get her out of jail for one night, and make sure word got out, then it's possible the killer will try again. It would be his perfect opportunity to seal her fate. Or, if it's Celia, and she's dead set on killing Stan, as you seem to think—so desperate that she would have gone into his hospital room and changed his IV bag, knowing she'd get caught—then she'll try again. Either way, we win. When the killer strikes, you'll have people there waiting for him . . . or her."

There was dead silence in the room as each of the men contemplated the idea. Finally, Sid spoke up. "What about Stan? How does he figure into all this?"

"We'd hide him," she said. "Use a decoy. Put somebody in his bed, fill the house with guards. Tell people he's not well enough to attend the funeral. Celia still couldn't go near him because of the court order. Meanwhile, he would be safely hidden where no one could get to him."

"So we're gonna scam the whole town?" Jim asked. "Make them all think Aunt Aggie died? The mayor'll have my hide. The fire department'll tar and feather us when they find out the truth. Not to mention how Aunt Aggie'll react."

"Aunt Aggie loves Celia," Stan said. "She'll do anything to help her. But I'm not so crazy about Celia having to grieve Aunt Aggie's death. She's had too much on her, and now there's the pregnancy. I don't want her to face any added stress."

"Pregnancy?" Gus asked. "What do you mean—"

"My wife is pregnant!" he said. "And if you baboons weren't so intent on this witch hunt, you'd have noticed that she's throwing up constantly."

Jim looked at Sid. "Did you know about this?"

Sid shrugged. "Not till this afternoon when I saw her barfin'."

"She said something about it yesterday," Vern said. "When I was dragging her out of his hospital room, but I figured she was just blowing smoke."

"I just found out yesterday, myself," Jill said. "She asked me to keep it to myself so the media wouldn't have a field day with it."

"Why wouldn't she want the press to know, if it's Stan's baby?" Vern suggested. "I mean, if she has nothing to hide—"

"Vern?" Stan cut in.

"Yeah?"

"Why don't you shut up?"

Vern looked wounded.

Stan turned back to the others. "As I was saying . . . she'd grieve. Hard. I don't want her to have to go through that."

"Celia will be all right," Jill assured him. "Please, Stan. It's the only answer I can see, unless the killer does something on his own to convince these guys that it's not Celia. You got any better ideas?"

Stan didn't. He rubbed his eyes, wishing God would miraculously expose the criminal and relieve Celia of all of this. But maybe that wasn't how God intended to work.

"What do you say, guys?" she asked.

Jim looked from Gus to Sid. Gus nodded, and Sid shrugged. "Talk to the judge, Jill," Gus said. "If Louis goes along with it, I will."

"I'll talk to him tonight," she said. "I'll go to his house." She looked back at Stan, her eyes dancing. "I think this will work, Stan."

Somehow, Stan thought the solution might just cause more problems.

Chapter Fifty-One

● ● ●

Judge Louis DeLacy paced across the brick floor of his country kitchen, his hands crammed into the pockets of his baggy jeans. He stared down at the brand new Nikes he wore, frowning as he listened to Jill's plan. He didn't react until she had finished.

Finally, he shoved up the sleeves of his sweatshirt and focused on her.

"I like Celia," he said. "I've been sick about having to put her in jail. And with what you've told me about her pregnancy ..." He shook his head and ran his fingers through his salt and pepper hair. "I don't like having a pregnant woman in jail. It's a touchy situation. But I have to be objective, Jill, and I can't make special exceptions for people just because I know them or go to church with them."

"Louis, I'm not asking you to make a special exception," Jill said. "I'm asking you to do what you'd do for anybody who's in jail and has a death in the family. It's routine for you to give weekend passes for funerals."

"I give weekend passes to those who have to go out of town to attend the funeral," he said. "And it depends on the crime. I don't give them to people charged with attempted murder."

"Celia is not a murderer, Louis. You know that. I'm just trying to prove it. Trust me. I won't let her out of my sight. And the cops aren't going to let her out of their sight, either. You know she can't do anything. But if we're lucky, we can prove whether she's innocent or guilty."

He went to the coffee pot that had just finished perking and poured it into two cups. He handed one to Jill and sipped thoughtfully.

"I could let her out for the funeral," he said, "but as for spending the night, I just don't think that's necessary."

"None of it's necessary, since no one's really dead. That's the whole point! If she doesn't spend the night, then it's not likely that the killer is going to strike. If she's only out for a two-hour period . . . don't you see? He has to do something that can be blamed on her."

"But what excuse can I give for letting her out overnight when the funeral is right here in town? There'll be an uproar."

"Since when did you care more about what people think, than about justice?"

Louis shot her a look. "This isn't about justice. It's about a deception."

"It's about a deception that *leads* to justice," Jill said. "We're trying to make sure the real killer is found." Abandoning her coffee, she got up and moved closer to him. She leaned on the counter next to him and lowered her voice for impact. "Louis, I believe with all my heart that Celia is innocent and that the killer is out there, waiting for another chance to set her up. Stan believes it, too, and it's his life that's at stake. Come on, Louis, please. If you've ever trusted me, if you've ever seen any wisdom at all in me, if you've ever believed that I have good instincts, *and you know I do*, please trust me on this."

He puffed his cheeks and blew out his frustration. "So what day are you proposing to do this?"

Jill's heart leapt. Was he about to grant permission? "As soon as possible. We'd have to set it all up with Aunt Aggie, get everything in place. Maybe tomorrow?"

He thought for a moment longer, then breathed a laugh. "Aunt Aggie'll never go for it. Who would? Who would want to convince the whole town that they're dead when they aren't?"

"She'll get a kick out of it," Jill said, her eyes dancing. "Come on. If she doesn't go for it, we won't do it. But I'll convince her."

Louis grinned and turned back to the counter to shovel some sugar into his cup. "Somehow I think you could."

Her eyes sparkled. "Then you'll agree to it?"

Again, silence passed as he considered it. "I guess so," he said finally. "I don't know any other way to put an end to all this craziness. Let's just hope it works."

After getting Louis's order for Celia's weekend pass, Jill headed for Aunt Aggie's house. David answered the door.

"Hi, David," Jill said, walking into the house. "Is Aunt Aggie here?"

"Sure," he said. "She just got back from the fire station." He stuck his head in the kitchen and called for her, then turned back to Jill. "Any news?"

"No," she said, as though disappointed. "None at all."

"I saw Celia a couple of hours ago," he said. "She seemed okay. Apparently Stan's on her side now."

"Yeah, it really buoyed her spirits."

Aunt Aggie rustled in wearing a hot pink wind suit. "Jill, come in. You got news?"

"No, Aunt Aggie. I'm afraid not." She considered telling both of them about the plan, but somehow feared that David, the more practical of the two, might not go along with it. She couldn't take that chance. "Listen, I was just at Stan's a little while ago, and he would like to see you, if you have time."

"Stan? Sure I got time," Aunt Aggie said. "He wanna see me now? This late?"

Jill looked at her watch. She hadn't realized it was almost nine. "Now would be good, if you have some time. His sleep schedule's a little messed up. I figure we can humor him if you're not too tired."

"Lemme get my purse." She headed back into the kitchen, then reemerged quickly. "David, I won't be long."

"So what he wanna talk to me about?" Aunt Aggie asked as they headed out to the car.

"About Celia," Jill said.

Aunt Aggie got in and Jill went around to the other side. "'Course about Celia," the old woman said. "But what? Is somethin' happenin'?"

Jill pulled out of the driveway and looked over at the woman who waited so anxiously to hear what was going on. "Actually, Aunt Aggie, I lied to get you out of the house. We're not really going to see Stan. I had something I needed to discuss with you, and I didn't want to do it in front of David."

"What you got to say to me you can't say in front of T-David?" Aunt Aggie asked.

"Oh, it's not David. It's just that I promised this would be very secretive. We have a plan, Aunt Aggie."

"A plan?"

Jill pulled her car over to the side of the road and regarded the old woman. "Aunt Aggie, I've thought of a plan that will draw the real killer out and clear Celia. There's just one catch. I need your help."

"You got it," the old woman said. "I'll do anything it takes to find out who that killer is and clear my Celia."

"I thought you would," she said. "But it's a lot to ask. An awful lot."

"I *said* I'd do anything."

Jill braced herself. "You're gonna have to die."

The look on the old woman's face would have been comical if they hadn't been dealing with such a serious subject. "Say what?"

"Not really die," Jill clarified. "Just *pretend* to die."

"I'm sorry, Jill, I ain't follerin' you."

She tried to think of a better way to explain it. "Aunt Aggie, what we need to do is to pretend that you've died suddenly of a heart attack. All we have to do is tell key people at Joe's Place, the fire department, and the beauty shop, and the next thing we know it'll be all over town. We start making funeral arrangements, get a coffin—"

"Wait a minute!" Aunt Aggie shrieked. "You're scarin' me."

"I know, Aunt Aggie," Jill said, softening her voice. "I'm just trying to get to the good part."

"Thank goodness you don't think *that's* the good part."

Jill almost laughed. "Aunt Aggie, the judge is going to give Celia a pass for two days, one night. When she gets out, we're counting on the killer coming out and trying to make another attempt that Celia can be blamed for, at which point, we'll have plenty of police officers waiting to arrest him. The flip side is that *they* believe *Celia* did it. They figure that if she had any intention of killing Stan, she'd probably try it while she had the chance."

"She didn't kill nobody!"

"I know that, Aunt Aggie. And the truth is, she'd be stupid to try the two days she's out of jail, but they're thinking she's crazy, anyway, and she might try. Anyway, I've convinced them to try this. It's the only answer."

"Well, we ain't gon' tell Celia I'm dead, are we?"

"Yes, we are."

"No! We can't do that. It'll break her heart. No, I won't let you tell her that."

"Aunt Aggie, she has to believe she got a bona fide weekend pass or no one's gonna believe that she's really innocent. We have to let them think she has the opportunity to act, and if she's a murderer, she really will. What I know will happen is that the real killer will realize this is another opportunity to make it look like Celia did it, and he'll act. We'll be able to catch him, Aunt Aggie. Once and for all."

Aunt Aggie thought about that for a moment. "So you say they gon' be a funeral?"

"Yes. The whole works. We have to make it look real."

She sat staring out into the night for several moments. "I want to go to the funeral," she said.

Jill frowned. "Aunt Aggie, you can't be there. It's your funeral."

"I want to hide someplace and watch," she said. "I always wondered what my funeral'd be like. Want to see it for myself."

"Aunt Aggie, that's ridiculous. I don't think you want to be there and see Celia crying and the firemen grieving—"

Aunt Aggie's chin came up. "I ain't doin' it 'less I can be there."

Jill gaped at her. "Aunt Aggie, are you serious?"

"Serious as a heart attack," Aunt Aggie said. "That is what I'm gon' have, ain't it? A heart attack?"

Jill almost chuckled. "I guess." She sighed. "Well, if you insist, I guess it's okay to have you there, provided we let Sid and Jim know. And you can't tell anyone, do you understand? Not even David. Not Celia's parents. Nobody. They have to all think you're dead."

"When can I come back to life?" she asked.

"As soon as the two days are up, we'll announce to the world that Aunt Aggie's alive. It'll be like a resurrection. People will be so happy they'll be rejoicing in the street. The fire department will probably shut down in celebration."

Aunt Aggie grinned. She liked that idea. "It will be a surprise, won't it?"

"Absolutely."

"Maybe people start 'preciatin' an old woman."

"Without a doubt," Jill said.

Aunt Aggie looked up at her with playful eyes. "Well, let's get to it," she said. "My heart's startin' to feel a little weak."

"Good, Aunt Aggie," Jill said. "By this time tomorrow it should give completely out."

Chapter Fifty-Two

• • •

The sting was set up by the following day, and Aunt Aggie was told that her time had come. Jill had hoped to have her drop dead in a private place, where she could be pronounced dead without the aid of firemen, police officers, and paramedics, who could tell in a moment that there was nothing wrong with the old woman, who had more strength and energy than the average thirty-year-old.

Jill had visions of calling the funeral director and telling him that they needed a coffin and funeral arrangements, but that she would take care of the body herself, thank you very much. It almost seemed funny now that she had ever believed she could pull this off. Finally, Sid Ford convinced her to bring the funeral director in on the sting. There was just no way around it. Otherwise, Aunt Aggie would be found out the moment the mortician found a pulse.

To make matters worse, the private death that Jill had envisioned threatened to go no further than her imagination, for Aunt Aggie had visions of much grander things. She wanted to drop dead in the town square, on the corner of Jacquard and Purchase Streets, have a huge fuss made over her, and have all the protective services show up on the scene. She wanted to go out with red and blue lights flashing around her, sirens blaring, and wailing and gnashing of teeth. It had taken some doing for Jill to convince her that they could never pull that off.

"You can't will your heart to stop beating for show, Aunt Aggie," Jill reminded her. "The paramedics will know you're not in arrest."

291

"Aw, I could die on the way to the hospital," Aunt Aggie said. "Nobody'd know no different."

"The paramedics would know," Jill insisted. "You really can't fool them."

"I can die in the hospital, then!"

"Aunt Aggie, you'll be surrounded by doctors. They're not stupid. They know when somebody's dead!"

Aunt Aggie looked as if Jill was spoiling all her fun. "Well, then, what you wanna do? Jes' have me die quiet without nobody knowin' about it?"

"Aunt Aggie, *everybody* will know about it. That's the point!"

At long last, she had convinced Aunt Aggie to die in Slidell, presumably on her way to a doctor's appointment regarding the chest pains she'd been having. That way, the paramedics of Newpointe couldn't ream Jill about not calling them in to help. They could all assume they *had* called an ambulance and tried to revive her. Sid even managed to bring a discreet Slidell surgeon in on the scam to pronounce her dead. The mortician, who served as the town's medical examiner as well, took care of the death certificate. No one knew any better, and they had managed to evade any direct questions about the death. Now it was time to tell Celia.

Jill went to the police station and paced in front of the door down to the jail, trying to think of the words she would use, the level of emotion she would muster. How could she spare Celia any more pain than necessary? She shook her head. It just wasn't possible. She tried to think of the realistic order in which they would have done things, had Aunt Aggie really died. She would have told David, first of all. He was the one staying in her home, expecting her to return. She hadn't done that. She caught her breath and decided that she was messing this up already. Quickly, she started back up the stairs and across the police room to the front door.

Sid stopped her. "You done it already?"

"No," she whispered. "I just remembered that I haven't told David. I've got to do this right or it won't look real."

"You ain't wimpin' out, are you?"

"No, of course not," she said. "I'll be back shortly."

He nodded and looked toward the door to the basement jail cells. "Man, I don't know about you, but I'm a little nervous."

"Yeah, I am, too," Jill said. "This feels really wrong, even though it was my idea."

"Yeah, and pretty soon you got to lie to the preacher."

Jill felt nauseous. "Look, I'm gonna go tell David, and then I'll bring him back here with me, to break the news to Celia, all right?"

"Okay," he said.

"Hopefully we can hold off letting anyone else know until they've been told."

Jill hurried out to her car, cranked it. Dan Nichols was outside washing the pumper, and he looked over at her and waved. She gave a distracted wave back.

He ambled over to the car, but she cranked it anyway, too preoccupied to talk.

"What's goin' on?" he asked.

She couldn't look him in the eye.

"Are you okay?"

"Yeah, I'm fine. Look, I've got some stuff I've got to take care of. I'm kind of in a hurry."

He looked crestfallen, then quickly rallied and that prideful look passed over his face as though he couldn't care less. "Sure, whatever. Talk to you later."

She rolled up the window and pulled out of her parking space, her heart sinking further. How many lies would she have to tell before this weekend was over? She didn't know if setting Celia free was going to be worth it all. Was it ever right to lie?

She headed to Aunt Aggie's house and pulled into the drive-way. The old woman's Cadillac was still parked in the parking lot at Jill's office. David was here, though, probably waiting for Aunt Aggie to get home. Again, she felt nauseous, but she pushed it away. A lawyer's job was never easy, never cut and dried, never particularly clean. It had been her idea, after all. Whispering under her breath, "Lord forgive me," she got out of the car and headed to the door. Tears were coming to her eyes already, and it was no act. She couldn't believe she was about to hurt so many people.

The pain they were going to feel was already welling inside of her. Again, she pushed it down and knocked on the front door.

••• •

David was stunned by the news. For a moment, he just stared at Jill, his face a portrait of shock. He looked around him, as if he didn't know what to do with himself. "I can't believe this."

"I know. It was a shock to us all." Jill hated herself as she muttered the words, but decided she was going to join the Newpointe theater as soon as all this was over. She was a natural.

"They didn't try to revive her? Give her CPR? Anything?"

"They did," Jill said. "David, her death was instant. She didn't respond."

"But they could have defibrillated her. They could have done something!"

She looked at her feet. "It was too late."

David sank back into his chair, his eyes glazing over.

"David, I really hated to come and tell you this," she said. "I guess since Celia's in jail, you're the one who's going to have to make all the arrangements."

He just looked at her, his eyes vacantly searching her face. Did he suspect that she was lying? If he did, she would have to confess, tell him the truth. But that could be a mistake. The fewer people who knew about the sting, the better it would work out.

"Look, I'd be happy to handle all the funeral arrangements for you."

"No," he said. "No, I can do it." He shook his head and looked at the telephone. "I guess I need to call my parents."

"Of course," she said.

He got up. "So many things to do. Where should I begin?"

"I guess with the funeral."

"All right. Do they have her . . . her . . ."

He struggled with the word "body," and Jill relieved him of it. "Yes, they have her there now."

He closed his eyes. He was getting pale. She wondered if he could manage this alone. "Well, I guess I'll call them, make an appointment. I guess that's what you do when this kind of thing happens." He sank back into his chair again. "I never thought Aunt Aggie would die. She seemed so invincible."

"None of us is invincible," she said.

He glanced over at her. "Have you told Celia?"

"No, actually, I was hoping you would go with me to do that."

He rubbed his face with both hands, then his eyes, and looked at her over his fingertips. "Yeah, I guess that would be best, wouldn't it?"

He drew in a deep breath and got to this feet. "It was all that rich cooking, you know. That's what did it."

"Aunt Aggie seemed healthy."

"But that rich cooking. I've tried to tell her for years."

Jill looked down at her hands.

He shook his head, then slapped his hands on his thighs. "Well, I guess we'd better tell Celia before somebody else does."

"Yeah. I don't think too many people know yet, but we don't want her to hear it from anyone else."

"She won't even be able to come to the funeral. This is just too much."

"I've already spoken to the judge. He's going to let her have a weekend pass," she said. "They often do that in the case of a funeral."

"Yeah, but with a murder charge?"

"I convinced him."

"Well, that's something." He looked around the room as if trying to collect his thoughts, then shook his head sadly. "Let's go and get this over with."

Chapter Fifty-Three

● ● ●

Jill saw the look of apprehension on Celia's face as she and David waited for the jail door to be unlocked. So far, her performance had been Oscar caliber, she told herself. David had bought into it, and already Celia looked as if she were fighting Armageddon in her heart. Did she think she'd brought her news of the end of the world?

Tears were already welling in Celia's eyes, and she took a step back.

"Celia, we have something to tell you," Jill said.

"No," she said, sucking in a sob. "No, don't."

"Celia—"

"It's Stan, isn't it?" Celia blurted.

Relieved that the news at least wasn't as bad as that, depending on one's perspective, Jill shook her head. "No, honey, of course not. Stan's doing fine. In fact, they can't keep him in bed."

It was as if a black cloud suddenly floated away and the sun shone through again. She let out a huge breath of relief and the tears began to roll down her cheeks. "From the looks on your faces, I thought you were going to tell me he's dead. I just don't know what I'd do . . ."

Jill hated to bring that cloud back, so she focused on the floor, trying to find the words she had rehearsed earlier today. Somehow, they seemed inadequate and cruel.

The shadow passed back over Celia's face. "What is it?" She turned her eyes from Jill to David. "David, something's wrong. What?"

David drew in a deep breath. "Celia, I don't know how to tell you this."

"Just say it," she said, almost angrily. "Spit it out. What's going on?"

"It's Aunt Aggie," Jill said.

"Aunt Aggie?" Celia repeated. "What—"

"Aunt Aggie died this morning."

"NO!" The word came out of her with such power that Jill took a step backward. Celia covered her head with her arms and began to wail as she fell down on her bed.

Tears burst into Jill's eyes. She had never hated herself so much. She went to the bed and tried to put her arms around Celia, but the small woman was moaning and sobbing and curling up into a ball, as if stretching to her full height was just too painful after such a blow.

"I'm sorry, Celia," Jill said over the moans. "So sorry."

Celia unfolded then and threw her arms around Jill, and clung to her as her body racked with pain.

"What happened?" she managed to squeak out.

David came closer to the bed, but looked awkward, inadequate. Jill realized that he, too, was grieving, and that this was probably just as hard for him. "She probably died the best way she could, Celia. She just had a heart attack and was dead instantly."

Celia let go of Jill and turned on her side, pulling her knees up to her chest as her arms covered her head again. A sound like that of a wounded animal came from her throat, and Jill almost considered backing out of the charade. Could she really go through with this and cause Celia such pain?

Suddenly Celia sprang up and slid off the bed, rushed to the toilet behind the partition in the cell. Jill heard her heaving into the commode. She followed her in and tried to help her.

When Celia had stopped throwing up, she sat on the floor and leaned back against the cold concrete wall. "It's my fault," she wept. "It's just as if I killed her myself."

Jill got down on her knees next to Celia and put an arm around her. "What do you mean?"

"It was the stress of all this stupid stuff! She couldn't take it. We thought she could take anything, but all the stress . . ."

She might have known that Celia would blame herself, but she hadn't anticipated it. "Celia, you couldn't do anything about that. None of this is your fault."

"She just . . . can't be gone! She . . . can't be!" Jill held her again for a long moment, and finally she got her to her feet and walked her back to the bed. David was leaned back against the wall now, hands in his pockets, looking as dismal as Celia seemed to feel.

"We've managed to get you a weekend pass for the funeral," Jill said finally. "David's making all the arrangements, but they're letting you out tomorrow. You can go to the funeral, spend the night at Aunt Aggie's, then come back the next morning."

The word *funeral* seemed to plunge Celia into deeper grief, and she lay back down and hugged her pillow to her face.

"You have to stay with me the whole time," Jill went on. "I swore to Louis that I wouldn't let you out of my sight."

Celia's shoulders shook as the pain rampaged through her.

Finally, she moved the pillow and turned on her back, looked up at the ceiling with wet, red eyes. "How's Stan taking it?" she whispered.

Jill looked at her vacantly for a moment. "I haven't told him yet. I wanted to tell you first."

She nodded. "Just break it to him easy, okay? He loves her, too, and he's suffered so much . . ." She broke down again, and finally, David came closer to her cot, as if trying to find a way to comfort her. Celia raised up and met him halfway. The two hugged.

"It's gonna be okay," he whispered.

"No, it's not," Celia muttered as she wept against his shoulder. "Aunt Aggie wasn't a Christian."

David didn't seem to know what to say to that.

After a moment, David let her go. "I have a funeral to arrange," he said. "You have any special requests?"

Celia couldn't answer.

"Maybe some of the firemen could speak about her?" Jill suggested. "They loved her so much."

"That's a good idea," David said. "We'll do that. Any special music?"

Celia threw up her hands. "I don't know."

"We'll think of something," Jill said.

"I want Nick to do the funeral," Celia offered suddenly. "She didn't have her own minister, and he knew her best."

"That's what I was thinking, too," Jill said.

She gazed at Celia, wishing she could ease some of the pain. But what would she say? *She'll only be dead a couple of days, Celia.* It was all ludicrous, yet it had to work.

As they left, Jill looked back over her shoulder through the bars that locked her friend in. Celia was on her side, clutching the pillow and weeping her heart out. Silently, Jill prayed that this cruel deception would somehow turn out for good.

••• •

When they had gone, Celia buried her face in the pillow as great sobs tore through her. She tried to pray, but the despair was too great, the grief too intense. She felt as empty and limp as a rag doll with no stuffing as she approached the throne of God. She had nothing to give, and no words to say. What did one say to the Lord about a loved one who didn't believe? She had failed. She had let Aunt Aggie down.

Why hadn't she tried harder to lead Aunt Aggie to Christ? Why hadn't she convinced the old woman of what she needed to do before she died? Why had she believed there was plenty of time left? But at the foot of that cross where her Savior hung for her failings, she found no condemnation, no judgment, no accusation. Instead, she felt the warm arms of God around her, holding her, whispering soothing words in her ear, letting her weep out her heart, offering his comfort. It was a phenomenon she hadn't experienced many times in her life. Usually when she went to God, she had supplications, petitions. Usually, she had problems and urgent requests. Hardly ever had she come to him speechless, without a word that she could offer, without anything of herself to give, without anything to ask. It was too late; Aunt Aggie was gone. What more was there?

Miraculously, God's comfort led to sleep, and she dozed on the flat mattress, numbing herself to the pain of Aunt Aggie's death.

Chapter Fifty-Four

● ● ●

The visitation for Aunt Aggie was at the Cain and Addison Funeral Home the night before the funeral, and Aunt Aggie insisted upon attending. Jill tried to talk her out of it, but the old woman would not be swayed. She wanted to see how people would take to her death, she said. She wanted to see who her real friends were.

The funeral director, who was in on the sting, was able to change her mind, however, for he had no place adequate to hide her where she could see and hear what was going on, without being seen and heard herself. Finally, she convinced Jill to set up a camcorder in the room, stuffed in a spray where no one could see it. Jill promised that if Aunt Aggie stayed away, she'd show her the video the moment visitation was over. Aunt Aggie had reluctantly agreed.

Now Jill sat with the old woman as they played back the hardest two hours of Jill's life, during which David and his and Celia's parents, along with various and sundry other relatives that no one in Newpointe had ever seen before, stood shaking hands of well-wishers and teary-eyed friends. Aggie stayed in Jill's house with her, and no one knew she was there. Outside, Vern sat in his unmarked car, watching to make sure Aunt Aggie didn't slip away to fill Celia in somehow.

"I can't believe they don't have no open casket," Aunt Aggie said. "Woman who preserves herself good as me at my age oughta have a viewin'."

Jill wondered if the woman had finally gone senile. "Aunt Aggie, if we opened the casket, they'd see that you weren't there."

Aunt Aggie's eyes danced with the possibilities. "I could be there," she said. "Matter of fact, that might be the best way t' tell what's goin' on. Lay up in that coffin and hear what folks is sayin' 'bout me."

"Aunt Aggie, they could see you breathing. What if someone touched you and you were warm?"

"I ain't been warm in ten years," she said. "I freeze to death most times. Ain't the circulation, though, cause these arteries ain't got no clogs. It's just my tempa-ture. Feel of me, see if that don't feel like death."

Jill took her hand and confirmed that it was, indeed, cold. "Aunt Aggie, what am I gonna do with you? I promise, at your next funeral, we'll open the casket."

Satisfied at that, Aunt Aggie sat back and watched some more of the video. The firemen were coming in with red eyes and noses, not knowing what to say to the people they'd never met before who represented Aunt Aggie's family. "They shoulda let Celia out for the visitation," she said. "So's I wouldn't be mourned over by a bunch of mealymouthed, greedy souls. Ain't seen most o' them in fifteen years. Ain't heard from 'em in ten. That one right there, old bat, she's my sister-in-law, Celia's *grandmere*. Turned away from Celia when all the others did. Crazy as a loon now, though. Don't know a shoe from a hat. What'd they do? Parked her in a nursin' home, waitin' for her to die. Don't know why they even brang her here."

Jill looked at her, stricken. She had wondered who the old woman was with the vacant eyes, and now she was disappointed to see how detached Aunt Aggie was from all of them. "Don't you care, Aunt Aggie? Haven't you missed her? Your own sister?"

"Nope. I hold grudges, Jill. I'll hold this one till I die."

Jill gazed at the screen. "I always wanted a sister."

The old woman grew quieter. "Still wish Celia was there."

"We talked about it, and didn't think it was appropriate, even if they had let her out a day early."

"Not appropriate to come to her Aunt Aggie's visitation?"

"Of course it would be appropriate for her to attend under any other circumstances, Aunt Aggie, but since half the town thinks of her as a killer, she just didn't think it would be very comfortable. Besides, she's really torn up about your death. It would be hard for her to be there."

Reminded of her niece's grief, Aunt Aggie's eyes misted over. "Bless her heart. I hate to put her through that."

"I hate it, too. Oh, boy, you have no idea how I hate it. The lies, the deceit . . . it's not my thing."

As the last of the visitors left the room, she heard the voices of the relatives that remained behind, milling around the small room. She heard the low voices of Celia's parents, and then David came over and put his arms on both their shoulders, hugged them tightly. Celia's mother was crying quietly.

"You'd almost think they *cared* I was dead," Aunt Aggie said. "But they're jes waitin' for probate."

"Do you think?" Jill asked.

"Can't be nothin' else," Aunt Aggie said. "They never picked up the phone to call me when I was alive."

Jill grinned at her use of the past tense. "It seems to me that you wouldn't have taken it real well if they had. Don't forget I was there the last time you spoke to Celia's mother. I wouldn't want to get on your bad side, Aunt Aggie. You do have a bite."

Aunt Aggie pshawed. "Aw, that's only 'cause I can't stand her."

Jill watched the woman in the video crying harder. "She obviously does care about you. Maybe she's not such a bad person."

Again, she harrumphed. "She's selfish and mean-spirited, and she don't care nothin' about her daughter. That says it all to me."

"What about when she was younger, before she had children? Did you two get along then?"

Aunt Aggie grew pensive, as if trying to remember. "We did," she said. "She was a cute little ole thing, and I loved her.

It wadn't till she turned her back on her own kin that I turned my back on her."

She watched as the camera recorded her niece and her husband wiping their eyes and crying quietly. "She's pretty," Jill said. "I can see where Celia gets her looks."

"Purty on the outside, maybe," Aunt Aggie said. "That's about it."

"You know, she didn't have to come for the visitation *or* the funeral. She didn't have to stand there listening to all the well-wishers. She could have just shown up at the last minute before the funeral, paid her last respects, and left."

"I tole you why she's here. Probate."

Jill didn't want to be quite that cynical. "Maybe David made her realize how much she needed to be here. Maybe he's working on a reconciliation between them and Celia."

"Maybe," Aunt Aggie said. "Reckon he's a good boy, after all."

"After all?"

"He's a little greedy. Cares a little too much about money. Means too much to him, all them things. Money never did make me no better 'n nobody else, but don't ever'body know that."

"Maybe now that you're supposedly gone, and everybody's grieving and hearts are broken, maybe this will be the start of something new. Maybe Celia's parents will come to see that she isn't guilty, and they'll reconcile, and you can let go of your grudge and forgive them …"

"I ain't holdin' my breath," the old woman said. "I wouldn't advise you to."

Chapter Fifty-Five

● ● ●

Celia avoided the second visitation that was held before the funeral the next morning. She was released from jail a couple of hours before, and went to Aunt Aggie's house to shower and change. The sight of the old woman's things—everything she loved—created a fresh void in her heart. She ached with the pain of it.

David was there with her, and Jill was staying in one of the guest rooms. Already, dozens of friends had brought food over, and the firemen had contributed greatly to the wealth of culinary delights. It seemed that they had appreciated her cooking for them so much, that now in her death, they felt they owed it to her to bring food for them. She wondered if they had realized that she was getting out of jail for the funeral, or if they expected David to eat it all alone, since her parents were staying in a hotel.

She wept in the shower as she got ready for the funeral, then threw up in the toilet as she got out. This grief wasn't good for the baby, she thought.

She looked in the mirror and saw how pale she was, saw the dark circles under her eyes. People would look at her and think she was certainly a murderer. If only Stan could be there. But that was one of the conditions of her release. She could have no contact with him while she was out. The idea upset her terribly. But there was nothing that could be done. Besides, she'd been told that Stan needed to rest, that he had no strength or energy to come to the funeral, anyway. She remembered how he had come to her cell just yesterday, how weak and breathless he'd been. She hoped he wasn't taking the death too hard.

She went downstairs and saw David pacing across the living room floor, back and forth, back and forth. It had been a trying time for him, she thought. He'd lost almost a week of work already, no small feat in a job as high-pressured as his, and had stood by her wholeheartedly now for Aggie's death. He'd had to take care of all the arrangements, all the food being delivered, all the flowers, all the well-wishers. She wondered if it was taking its toll on him.

"David, you look tired," she said from the staircase.

He turned back to her, stared at her for a moment. "*You* look like death warmed over. Are you sick again?"

"Just a little. It'll pass. It always does."

"You know, this isn't going to be easy," he said. "You have enough stress with the funeral and Stan and the murder charges, without all this nausea. Celia, I know you hate it when I bring this up. But be realistic. Think of your health. I checked, and I found out that Newpointe has a Planned Parenthood clinic."

She was too tired, too depressed, to realize what he was suggesting.

He sighed. "They could see you today, Celia. I could take you there, and at least that part of this ordeal would be behind you. You wouldn't have to worry about what was going to happen to a baby that might be born in prison . . ."

She stared at him, stricken, as if he'd just poured alcohol on an open wound. She touched her stomach. "David, this is your niece or nephew. How could you suggest that to me again?"

"Celia, a person can only take so much. You may think you're Wonder Woman, but you're not."

"I'm stronger than you think," she said. "And I trust God with this baby." Her mouth quivered with the words, and she turned back to the table to get her purse together. She swallowed a sob, then whispered, "Not another word about that, David. Not one more word."

He looked as if he didn't know if he could agree to that. "All right. I just hope you don't start throwing up at the funeral. It's going to be very hard, once you get there with the family—"

"I know," she told him. "I'm gonna get there, and Mom and Dad will either ignore me completely or comment on the gall it took for their killer daughter to show up for their aunt's funeral."

"They won't," he said. "I've already talked to them."

"Oh, then you expected it to happen, too?"

"Well, the thing about where you were gonna sit at the funeral . . . all that stuff."

Her expression crashed. "You mean they didn't want me to sit with the family at the funeral?"

He hesitated, as if he hadn't meant to spill the beans. "Look, I nipped it in the bud, okay? I let them know that you had more of a right to be there than they did. You were her favorite."

"I wasn't her favorite," she said. "I was just the one who needed her most."

"Yeah, Aunt Aggie was real big on need. She liked the way you needed her."

She didn't want to think about how adept Aunt Aggie had been at filling those needs.

Jill came down the stairs, dressed in black and wearing makeup for the first time in days. "Ready to go?" she asked.

Celia nodded and opened the door. Immediately, she was assaulted by a reporter and a photographer who stood on the front lawn. Quickly, she pulled back into the house and closed the door. "What are they doing here?"

"They must have heard you were getting out," David said. "They were at the funeral home last night, snaking around asking everyone questions about their opinions of these murder attempts."

"You're kidding! People were talking to them? My friends?"

"Celia, I don't know if you still have any friends in this town. Not any real ones, anyway. And yeah, a few were talking to them. It's in the paper today."

"Oh, no. Where is it?"

"You don't have time to read it," Jill told her. "Come on, Celia, we're just gonna have to walk through them. Just hold your head up and ignore them."

David opened the door again. She stepped out onto the porch. The camera began to flash again, and she turned her head and started toward the car.

"Celia! Is it true that your aunt died of arsenic poisoning?"

She swung around. *"What?"*

"Is it true that arsenic killed your aunt?"

She looked at David, then at Jill, as if wondering if the suggestion bore some truth. "No!" Jill said. "She died of a heart attack."

"That's what we were all told, but rumor has it that they're just calling it a heart attack to cover for the arsenic."

"And of course you're suggesting that I did it?" Celia asked.

"Did you?"

Amazed, she got into the car, slammed the door behind her, and locked it. David got in on the other side. Jill went to her own car.

"How could they think I could kill my poor dear aunt with arsenic?"

"Well, they think you killed your poor dear first husband with arsenic."

He was irritable, she could see, and she wrote it off to fatigue and stress. He'd had enough of this, and he hadn't deserved any of it. In the back of her mind, a niggling thought came. What if David was doubting her, wondering if she was guilty, questioning his support of her?

She wept silently as they drove to the funeral home and parked in the back. Already, the parking lot was full. Jill got out of her car and walked in with them. When Celia stepped into the hallway, she saw the dozens of people standing there. They all turned to look at her when she came in. She saw faces that used to be friendly, but this time they were hostile, and they turned away and began whispering. Jill gave her a hug and joined the crowd. Celia followed David into the family room, but was immediately confronted by her parents sitting on a bench across from the door.

She stopped cold. Their eyes met, and she felt the chill from both of them. "Mom, Dad?"

"Hello, Celia," her mother said, and her father only nodded.

It was as if they were strangers, she thought, as if her mother had never changed her diaper, patched her skinned knee, sung her a lullaby when she couldn't sleep. It was as if her father had never taught her to ride her bike or tie her shoes, or helped her with her geometry. As if her mother had never delighted in taking her shopping, or teaching her to put on makeup, or brushing her hair. She turned away, not willing to give them the satisfaction of seeing her cry. There were other relatives in the room, relatives she had seen occasionally over the years, and they, too, looked at her as if she were a malignancy in the midst of their family.

She thought of running back out into the hall, but she couldn't face those people again. She was trapped.

When Nick came in, he shot straight to her. "Celia, how are you?"

Relief flooded over her like a soothing tide. She reached out and hugged him desperately.

"I'm so sorry," he whispered in her ear. "So very sorry."

She turned her wet face up to him. "The worst part is that she didn't know Christ," she whispered. "I didn't work hard enough to lead her to him. I thought there was plenty of time."

"So did I," Nick said. "Believe me, I haven't slept a wink since I heard about her death. I've been beating myself up like you wouldn't believe. Don't do that to yourself. The truth is, it was her choice. We both tried."

She sucked in a sob. "But it's so tragic."

"That it is," he said. "This is gonna be the hardest funeral I've ever done."

He hugged her quickly again, then whispered in her ear. "Stan said to send you his love."

The words were like an injection of hope and promise, of joy and peace, and even comfort. "How's he doing?"

"He's doing well," he said. "He's really tired and weak, and the doctor apparently advised him to stay at home. I hear he got out a little too much yesterday and was seen around town a couple of places. It must have taken a lot out of him. The doctor warned him that he was gonna put him back in the hospital if he didn't start taking it easier." He looked at her with concerned eyes. "How are you doing?"

"I'm fine," she said. "Just a little tired. And my family . . . well . . . they're not too thrilled to have me here."

"Yeah, I know. I've kind of encountered that, already."

She hated the fact that her own preacher had to know of her family's indifference toward her. Nick let go of her and stepped toward her parents. "If you're all ready, the music has begun and all of the congregation are filtering in. If you don't mind, I'd like to lead us in a prayer."

Her parents were not praying people, she knew, but in a time like this, she supposed that everyone prayed. She wondered if they ever prayed for her.

They formed a circle, but it was a broken circle. No one was bound by held hands. Even their eyes did not meet. Nick led them in a prayer that was short, but poignant, and Celia found herself crying again, harder. She didn't know when the tears were ever going to end.

When it was time, they walked into the chapel and took their places in a secluded section of the room where people couldn't stare at them. She was thankful for that. She sat at the end of the row, next to David, with no one on the other side of her.

She wished for a Kleenex. Had Stan been here, he would have had some in his pocket. He always remembered to bring them to funerals and weddings, because he knew how easily she cried. He would have held her close and reminded her that she was loved. He would have helped unwind the knots in her stomach, and nursed the bruises on her heart. He would have made the pain easier to bear.

But he wasn't here, and no one had brought Kleenex for her. No one held her hand. No one offered comfort.

So she returned to the silent, strong arms of the Creator who'd comforted her last night in places too deep for human love to reach. And in his arms, she found hope and peace where she'd been certain there was none.

Chapter Fifty-Six

● ● ●

From up in the closed-off balcony of the funeral home that smelled like rotting wood and dust, Aunt Aggie sat watching the funeral. She had to sit at the back, in the shadows, so that Nick could not see her from the pulpit. Sid Ford stood by the balcony door, presumably to keep anyone from coming in and spotting Aunt Aggie, though Aggie felt sure he was mostly there to keep her under control, in case she got a notion to yell something down to the mourners. She had been here for hours, for they didn't want her to take the chance of being seen coming or going.

She could see the congregation through a lattice railing, though they couldn't see her. She could see the uniformed firemen designated as pall bearers sitting in the front row, and the others scattered around the room, wiping their own eyes. Someone from Celia's church sang a hymn that Aunt Aggie couldn't identify. She wondered if Jill had suggested it.

Mark Branning got up to say a few words, and Aunt Aggie leaned forward, listening hard. She didn't want to miss a syllable.

Mark wiped his eyes as he reached the podium, and he was quiet for a moment, as if trying to find his voice. "We all at Midtown fire station loved Aunt Aggie," he said. "She was one of the sweetest, most caring women we've ever known, and she was a heck of a cook."

She heard some soft chuckles around the room, and she smiled.

"Aunt Aggie didn't put up with much, but she was fiercely loyal to the people she loved. I respected that about her. I'm gonna miss her." His voice broke. "There's gonna be a huge void in this town. But I wanted to tell a few stories about the Aunt Aggie that I knew. Last summer, Aunt Aggie ..."

She heard a commotion somewhere in the congregation beneath her, and Mark's voice faded out. She fought the temptation to get up and lean over the balcony railing to have a look. Instead, she stood up in the shadows, straining to see. Several people were standing up, and she couldn't see who they were hovering around. Someone was sick.

"Uh ... excuse me." Mark's voice rippled with panic. "My wife ... will someone call our doctor, please?"

Mark dashed from the podium, and Nick took his place. "Allie seems to be in labor," Nick said. "We need to get her to the hospital."

Aunt Aggie caught her breath. Allie Branning had the gall to go into labor during her funeral? Couldn't she have waited just another hour? She wasn't due for another month, after all. She pushed the resentment back down, then told herself that was ridiculous. When a baby was ready to be born, it was ready to be born. Couldn't nobody stop it.

She saw Mark walking her out a side door, saw several people run out with them. Aunt Aggie sat back down, trying not to resent being upstaged.

After a few minutes, the crowd's roar died down, and Nick took over. "Well, I guess Mark won't be making those comments, after all. But I have some things to say. Aggie Gaston was a woman unlike any woman I've ever known," Nick began. "Everyone in town called her Aunt Aggie, though only Celia Shepherd was related to her."

Aunt Aggie smiled. It was brave how he'd mentioned Celia's name, even though he knew a murmur would follow. And it did.

"Aunt Aggie was a giver. She was one of the kindest, gentlest, most giving people that I've ever known. Twice a day, she brought meals to the firefighters on duty at Midtown. Why? Because she thought they needed what she called 'good eats.' She led a long, prosperous, contented life," he said.

She could see how carefully he was choosing his words. It was hard for a preacher to preach a funeral for someone who didn't believe. She almost felt sorry for him. Too bad they couldn't have had the sense to find an atheist to preach her funeral. Either an atheist or a liar, who could pretend they'd all see her again someday in heaven, if that's what they wanted to hear. But she supposed that wasn't done.

She wondered if this was gonna be one of those times when Nick was gonna look everybody in the eye and tell them what a pity it was that Aunt Aggie wasn't going to heaven. Would her death become the launch point for a fire-and-brimstone sermon?

"I wish Aunt Aggie could have known the abundant life offered in Jesus Christ," he said solemnly. "'Cause I think she would have been a glorious servant for the Lord. With her giving spirit, and her love for so many people, and the wisdom that came with her age, and her inner beauty—not to mention her outer beauty. I know that she could have made great strides in the kingdom of God."

"There he goes," she whispered to herself. The God stuff had to come sooner or later, she supposed.

"Her greatest sorrow in life," he said, "was when her dear niece Celia was accused of attempting to kill her husband. But Aunt Aggie needn't have worried," Nick went on, "because Celia has the peace of the Lord. And even though she was sitting in a jail cell all alone, she had the joy of the Lord, because she was in tune with him, and he was speaking to her.

"When I first heard about all the stuff with Celia and Stan," he said—as if he was talking to a room full of close friends—"I thought that it was possible that Celia was guilty. But then I went to see her, and I saw the Holy Spirit in her eyes, in her face, and I saw Jesus in her heart and in her attitude. I saw peace, the kind that someone who's entered into a new level of spirituality can attest to. I saw a woman who knew God and, despite the circumstances, was trusting him." He looked around at the other faces in the room. "I wish Aunt Aggie had trusted God, because he loved her dearly. I wish she had known how precious that love of God can be." His voice broke, and he looked down at his notes. He was having trouble going on.

Aunt Aggie watched, captivated. Something in her heart deflated, and she wished she hadn't come. Jill had been right. It was crazy. What had she expected? She had wanted grief . . . didn't everybody want to know they were missed when they died? But she hadn't quite expected the grief that had to do with her religious beliefs—or lack thereof. A heavy weight came over her, making her feel suddenly very, very old and very tired. The finality of this whole death business began to dawn on her, and she realized many of the tears being shed in the room were not because she was such a wonderful person, but because she didn't believe in God. She thought of standing up and shouting out to everyone in the room that death hadn't conquered her yet, and that it didn't matter if she believed, that she was happy, and she was good, and she was a philanthropist and generous with everything she had, and that she met people's needs when she saw them. What more did they want from a person?

But she didn't. She sat quietly, as she had promised she would, because she wanted so much for Celia to be cleared. Still, she felt a tightness over her chest, and wondered if she died right here, right now, if they'd let this dismal funeral suffice. Was this all there was after a life well-lived?

She saw Celia sitting at the end of the family pew, being shunned by the rest of them. She couldn't wait to give Celia's parents a piece of her mind when she resurrected, tell them what she thought of them, coming to her funeral and acting all mournful, then treating her Celia like a leper.

Soon the funeral was over, and she realized that Nick hadn't had much good news to offer the crowd on her behalf. He couldn't tell them that they would see her again, because he didn't know that they would. She thought it probably would have been nice for him to say anyway.

It was she who felt the worst, sitting here, viewing something that most people never had the chance to see. She wasn't enjoying this like she thought she would. In fact, she was ready to go home, to try to wipe out of her mind all the things she had seen and heard here today. But she couldn't leave. She had to sit through until the end, hear every word. It had been her choice, after all.

She glanced at Celia again and wished her little heart wasn't breaking over some imaginary spiritual condition that Aunt Aggie had never understood. And then she thought of Celia that night when Aggie had been in jail, too, singing a hymn, telling her that things were going to be all right, as if she'd forgotten she'd been accused of trying to kill the man she loved most in the world. Aunt Aggie just couldn't fathom it. Either Celia was stupid, or she had been brainwashed so deeply that every fiber of her own being believed in the things she said she believed. And suddenly, Aunt Aggie realized that it wasn't with every fiber of her being that she believed there wasn't a God. The idea of God was just something beyond her grasp, something she had never experienced before, something she thought was a bunch of hooey. For the first time, it occurred to her that these people, who were crying at her funeral because they thought they'd never see her again, might know something she didn't know.

She wiped at a tear in her own eye, surprised that she would cry at her own funeral, when she'd expected to laugh her head off. She hoped Jill would come quickly to get her after the service. She didn't know how much more of this she could take.

The funeral broke up, and in moments, Jill was in the balcony with her. "Aunt Aggie, the funeral director said there's a van out on the side with blackened windows. He's gonna be driving it, and you can sit in the back if you want to go to the burial site."

She shook her head. "No, I think I've had enough."

"Really?" Jill asked. "Well, I thought you'd want . . ."

"No, never mind. I'll jes' stay here and wait till you come back."

"All right. It shouldn't be that long. Just stay right here and don't come out, and no one will see you. Sid is staying with you."

Jill ran back out, and Aunt Aggie could hear below her as everyone filed out of the room, talking quietly, no doubt, about the tragedy of her death and the scandal of Celia's plight. She stared down at that pulpit where Nick had done her eulogy. This was good experience, she told herself. As soon as she came back to life, she was going to write her own eulogy, maybe videotape it, so nobody would have to endure the likes of this again. Yes, it was a very good experience, she thought. She just wasn't sure why it didn't feel so good.

Chapter Fifty-Seven

● ● ●

Lee Barnett was the first person Issie saw when she walked into Joe's Place that night. She told herself that she hadn't gone there to see him, that she just wanted a drink to unwind after the funeral, but that didn't explain the elation she felt when he spotted her and patted the empty stool next to him. She felt like the high school cheerleader who had a crush on the town's bad boy.

As she took the stool, he ordered her a glass of wine, the same brand she'd been drinking the other night. "How's it going there?" he asked.

"Fine," she said, trying to seem nonchalant about seeing him.

He grinned. "Don't pretend you're not glad to see me. You know you are. I could see it in your face when you came in."

Something about that bold appraisal charmed her. "You're pretty confident for somebody in a lot of trouble."

"I'm not in trouble," he said. "Haven't you heard? I met with Celia's husband. Convinced him I'm a Boy Scout. 'Cause I am, you know."

She smiled. "Yep. That was my first thought about you. A real Boy Scout. Especially the other night when my preacher had to rescue me from you."

"Another few minutes, and I'm the one would've needed rescuing," he said.

She started to tell him he had a lot of gall, but she hadn't exactly been fighting him off. Besides, she liked gall in a man.

She sipped on the wine Joe put in front of her, and decided to change the subject. "So did you hear about Aggie Gaston?"

"Who?"

"Celia's aunt. She died. She was buried today."

"Arsenic poisoning?" Lee asked.

Issie frowned and shook her head. "No, she had a heart attack."

Lee nodded. "Good."

"Good?"

"I mean, I'm glad it's not arsenic. There's a little too much of that going around, if you know what I mean."

Issie supposed he was right.

• • •

Across the crowd of people, R.J. sat at the back table pretending to read the paper. He knew he wasn't fooling anybody. Lee Barnett had seen him come in, and he knew he was being watched. Still, he kept up the pretense, if not for Barnett, then for everyone else in the room. His cellular phone vibrated, and he pulled it out of his hip pocket. "Albright."

"Where are you?" It was Sid's voice.

"Joe's Place."

"Albright, are you drinkin' on the job?"

"No," he said, shoving the empty beer bottle across the table as if Sid could see through the phone.

"Where's Barnett?" Sid asked.

"Right here. Got my eye on him. Thing is, he knows I'm watching him."

"Well, that's a big help."

R.J. bristled at the sarcastic tone, as if he didn't have enough police savvy to do the right thing. "I was just fixin' to leave," he said. "You don't have to tell me how to do my job, Sid. I think I can handle it."

He clicked off the phone and dropped it back in his pocket, then left the paper on the table and got up to leave. Barnett, who was bantering flirtatiously with Issie Mattreaux, winked at him as he left. R.J. felt like throttling him. He didn't like being taunted, even silently. He went out across the street and headed to his car parked in the police parking lot. He could see the front door from there. With the aid of his binoculars, he could watch Barnett come out, then follow him to wherever he went. *Fun detail*, he thought sarcastically. It was going to be a long night.

•   •   •

Two hours later, Lee Barnett had had too much to drink. Once again, he'd passed his limit, and he knew it. But he was doing so well with Issie Mattreaux. The knockout brunette was laughing and flirting, and he knew that he had a much better chance of getting her to go home with him tonight than he'd had the time before, and he'd been really close then.

He leaned into her, too close, he knew, but she allowed it. He reached out and stroked her arm.

"Hands off," she said in a teasing voice. "I'm not into public displays of affection. The town's already buzzing about Issie spending time with Celia's ex-con."

"How about private displays?" he asked against her ear.

She didn't say no, so he took that as a yes.

"Come on, Issie. Who are you kidding? You know you want to go home with me."

"You're awfully cocky for somebody who'd let a preacher knock him down."

She was still teasing, but he was less amused. "Hey, I can take on the preacher."

"Yeah, if you're not drunk, maybe."

"I ain't drunk," he argued, sliding one hand under her hair to cup the back of her neck. "I'm in love."

She laughed then. "In love? Is that what you call it?" She took his wrist and removed his hand.

He grinned. "If you don't want me touchin' you in public, then let's go someplace private. I'm gettin' tired of these games."

"I'm thinking about it," she said.

He put his heavy arm around her and pulled her too roughly against him. He knew instantly it was a mistake because she fell off her stool with a clatter. Quickly, he helped her right herself and she got back on the stool. The look on her face had changed.

"I'm sorry," he said, stroking her back. "I didn't mean—"

"I think she told you to let her go."

The voice of the man sitting next to Issie thundered over his own voice, and Barnett didn't like it.

"Stay out of this, pal. This is between me and the lady."

"You ain't treatin' her like much of a lady," the guy said.

Issie looked over her shoulder and tried to calm the guy down. "It's okay, Billy, I can handle it."

"Yeah, she can handle it, *Billy*," Barnett said, jerking her against him again to make his point.

Billy dove from his stool, and his fist came across Lee's jaw, knocking him back against a table. The people around it stood up, and a woman screamed.

Humiliated, Barnett got to his feet and lurched for the guy. But Billy was ready for him, and they wound up on the floor, wrestling like children. Barnett found himself with his thumbs against the guy's throat, and it brought back a memory. A memory of something that had landed him in prison for five years. Quickly, he let go of his neck.

He hadn't realized how long he'd been struggling with the man until the door burst open and the cop who'd been there earlier came in. He broke up the fight and pulled Lee to his feet. "You're under arrest, Barnett," he said. "You have the right to remain silent . . ."

"No, man!" Lee said. "I ain't goin' back to prison. Man, I served my time. I didn't do nothin'. I was sittin' here mindin' my own business."

"Save it for somebody who's interested," the cop said and dragged him out of the establishment in handcuffs.

As the cop half-dragged him across the street to the jail, Lee thought how ironic all this was. He couldn't believe it. It was just too stupid to be true. *He* was too stupid to be true.

After they'd booked him and thrown him in the jail cell, he stood nodding his head. Yep. He deserved to be exactly where he was. He kicked the cot, almost breaking his foot, then hopped around cursing venomously until the others in the jail began cursing back at him.

Chapter Fifty-Eight

● ● ●

While Aunt Aggie spent the night in hiding, Jill stayed in Aunt Aggie's house with Celia. David had decided to have dinner with his parents before they headed back to Jackson.

Still fully dressed, Jill lay in the guest room next to Aunt Aggie's room, where Celia was going to sleep tonight. Every muscle in her body was tense as she waited for her plan to work. The killer had to strike tonight. If he didn't, she didn't know what she would try next. She checked her cell phone to make sure it was still powered, and wished Sid would call.

It was already past midnight, and Jill could still hear Celia weeping in the bedroom. The pain Celia was going through broke Jill's heart. She hoped the joy of seeing her aunt revived would be enough to make Celia forgive her. The forgiveness would come hard, though, if her plan didn't work tonight.

The cell phone vibrated, and she bolted upright. Maybe they had caught the killer already. Maybe it was over. Quickly, she clicked it on.

"Jill?" It was Sid's voice.

"Yeah, it's me," she whispered. "What is it? Has anything happened?"

"Nothin' here," he said. "But somethin' else I thought you might be interested in."

"What?"

"Lee Barnett. He got arrested tonight at Joe's Place. Seems he had too much to drink and got in a fight. Disorderly conduct."

"Oh, no!" she whispered. "Sid, what if he's the killer? He can't make a move if he's stuck in jail! The whole sting could blow up in our faces if the killer's not free to strike."

Sid wasn't buying. "We ain't callin' this off, Jill. He's in jail and I can't do nothin' about it."

"You can let him back out," Jill said through her teeth. "Sid, *think!* You're messing this whole thing up!"

"I didn't mess nothin' up. He got arrested fair and square. Remember, most of my cops ain't in on this sting."

She began pacing the floor. "I know that," she whispered harshly. "But isn't there someone who could go bail him out? Without him, we're in serious trouble here."

"Jill, I'm tellin' you, your client is our killer. She's the only one we gotta watch."

"Celia is in Aunt Aggie's room crying her heart out. She's not going anywhere. Do you realize we only have tonight? Please, Sid. You know the judge'll go along with setting bail to keep the sting from being sabotaged. I'll call him myself."

"You gon' have to," Sid said, "'cause I ain't callin' him. I don't like this."

"Well, you don't have a choice! As long as somebody meets bail, that guy's out on the street where he can do the harm we need for him to do."

Sid moaned.

"You let me know the moment something happens," she said. "By the way, where is Stan?"

"Took him and his folks and Aunt Aggie to my house. Nobody knows. We took every precaution. I'm at Stan's. His and his parents' cars are still here. No reason for nobody to think he ain't in here, sound asleep."

"All right," Jill said. "Let me know the minute something happens." She went out into the hall and peered into Aunt Aggie's room, just to make sure Celia hadn't overheard. Her client was sitting in the dark on the pillowed window seat, gazing out into the stars. She was still crying, but she was quieter now. Jill wished Celia would fall asleep.

She went back into her room and quickly dialed information to get Louis DeLacy's phone number. It rang several times before he answered. "Hello?"

The judge had been sleeping, but Jill didn't let that stop her. "Louis? Jill Clark. We have a problem."

"What problem, Jill?"

"They've arrested the major suspect—other than Celia—for disorderly conduct."

"What? Of all the cockamamy . . ."

"He's in jail, Louis. I need for you to set bail so somebody can get him out. I'll pay it myself. Just please, help me. If he isn't out, we'll never know if he's the real killer."

"Oh, for heaven's sake. I'll set it at fifty dollars, Jill, and I'll go to the police station right now and take care of it. But I can't bail him out. That would look too suspicious. And I don't want you leaving Celia."

"I'll find someone to do it. Thank you, Judge."

She hung up and punched out the number for Midtown station. She hated calling the fire department this late at night, when the guys were probably asleep, but it couldn't be helped.

"Midtown fire station," someone said.

She hesitated. "May I speak to Dan Nichols, please?" she whispered.

The man didn't hear her well enough. "Excuse me?"

"Dan Nichols," she repeated just above a whisper.

A few minutes passed, and finally, a groggy-sounding Dan came to the phone. "Hello?"

"Dan, it's me," she said.

"Jill? I can hardly hear you. Where are you? Are you all right?"

"I'm fine," she said, "but I need a favor."

He paused. "Jill, what's going on?"

"Please, will you just do me a favor? This is very serious. I need for you to do me this favor without asking any questions, I need for you to do it as soon as possible, and I need for you to keep quiet about it."

"What is it?"

"Lee Barnett was arrested tonight for brawling at Joe's Place. His bail is going to be set at fifty dollars. I need for you to give it about twenty minutes, enough time for the judge to officially set bail, then go get him out. I promise, I'll pay you back with interest, and I'll explain everything for you tomorrow. But I need for you to do this."

Again, there was silence. "Jill, why would you help him? Where are you?"

"I can't explain right now. Please, trust me. This is very, very important."

"Since when have you been Lee Barnett's advocate?"

"I'm not. Please, Dan, will you trust me and do it? Can I count on you?"

He hesitated again. "I guess so, Jill, but tomorrow I would like to hear the story."

"I promise you will," she said. "And trust me, it's a doozy."

Chapter Fifty-Nine

• • •

Dan Nichols paid the bail, then waited around for Lee Barnett to emerge from jail. When he did, he looked as mad as a rabid dog.

The cop who brought him up pointed him to Dan, and Barnett swaggered over. "You the one bailed me out?"

"That's right," Dan said.

"I owe you," he said. "I just don't have it right now. I haven't gotten a job yet."

"Don't worry about it." Dan started walking toward the door, unwilling to get too chummy with the man who might very well have poisoned Stan. What Jill was up to was beyond him.

"Hey, I appreciate it, man! Nice to have a friend in town."

Dan glanced back and started to tell him that he wasn't his friend, but he decided to leave it alone. Instead, he just headed back to the fire station.

‣ ‣ ‣

From where he was parked outside, R.J. watched Barnett walk back across the street to Joe's Place, where his car was parked. He couldn't believe the judge had set bail already, and to make matters even worse, he'd been assigned to follow him again. R.J. didn't see the point, if every time he arrested a guy, they let him go. He supposed if they wanted to waste his time, it was their prerogative.

He watched him pull out of the parking lot, and realized he could bust the guy again for drunk driving, if he wanted to. But he didn't. He watched him drive in a roundabout way through Newpointe, as if he couldn't remember which way would take him home. R.J. followed him as he drove through town, waiting for him to make a move.

They came to a busy intersection at the corner of First Street and LaSalle Boulevard, and a car got between them as the light turned red. R.J. tried to keep his eyes on the taillights of the Grand Am, but soon he lost sight of it. Had he gone left or right? He honestly didn't know.

He cursed and gunned his engine as the light turned green. He passed the car in front of him, cursing again, and tried to catch up to Lee Barnett. But it was too late. Barnett was out of sight.

Chapter Sixty

● ● ●

Sid began to get nervous as he sat in the dark in Stan's bedroom. If they could anticipate how the killer would strike, it would be so much easier. But so far, the only method had been poison. Would the killer come in and try to inject more poison into Stan, or would they bring a gun this time and just shoot him outright? He didn't know what to be prepared for.

Police officers were staked in the trees all around the house where they could see anyone who approached the house the moment he arrived. But they had to catch the killer in the act or there would never be a conviction for anything more than breaking and entering. They had to be able to prove they had the right person.

He looked over at the bed, where they'd put a dummy under the covers. In the dark, it looked as if someone slept there. He hoped that all they'd gone through in the last two days was not in vain. He hadn't been crazy about this idea at first, but it had grown on him. And as they'd planned out the farce, he had begun to hope it would work. If Celia was the killer, and he felt sure that she was, they would be able to prove it unequivocally tonight, to everyone, including Stan.

His telephone—which he brought instead of his radio because of the noise level that would alert any intruder—vibrated on his hip, and he grabbed it up and put it to his ear. "Yeah?" he whispered.

"Someone's coming," one of the guys outside said. "We almost missed them. But whoever it is is on foot, headed toward the house from the woods behind it."

"Is it a man or a woman?"

"Hard to tell. They're wearing a black ski mask."

Sid closed his eyes and hunkered back against the corner. "Are they armed?"

"Can't tell. Whoever it is is almost to the house."

Sid aimed his weapon, waiting.

He got up and went to the door of the bedroom, where he could see the back door. There was no sound, none at all, and he waited for a scratching or breaking glass, anything that would indicate the door was being broken into. Instead, the door came open easily, as if the intruder had a key.

It *had* to be Celia!

He sank back into the bedroom, waiting. What would she do next?

But the prowler didn't come toward the bedroom. Sid waited as agonizing moments ticked by. He heard nothing. If people had truly been asleep in this house, no one would have been awakened. He inched to the door again and peered out. There was no sign of whoever had come in. The uncertainty of what was going on made him very nervous. Should he leave the bedroom and find the person, wherever they were hiding? Should he go ahead and make an arrest? If it was Celia, wouldn't this be enough evidence to convict her, or would she just convince the judge that she had come into her own home not meaning any harm?

Something told him to sit still, not to move.

Then he heard the slight squeak of the back door opening again. He inched back to the casing and saw the person stealing out. Quickly, he grabbed his phone.

"She's comin' back out! Don't let her get away!"

"Did she try anything?"

"Nothin'. Didn't even come in the bedroom. Man, somethin's up, but I don't know what."

"Did she plant a bomb . . . start a fire?"

"I don't know, but I ain't likin' this. Just grab her. Don't let her get away, whatever you do! I'll be searchin' the house."

"I'm on it." He heard the phone click off and looked out the window. His phone vibrated again.

"Chad's in pursuit, but she took off through the woods. Chad's followin' on foot, and we have some patrol cars comin' out on the other side."

"How did she get away?" Sid yelled into the phone.

"Just went the other way. We weren't expectin'—"

"You *idiots!*" Sid screamed. "Catch her or all your jobs are on the line." He flicked on the lights and began to go through the rooms one by one, looking for anything that might look suspicious. There was no fire, none that he could detect, no smoke of any kind. He began to sweat. It was hot in here, getting hotter. Why was the heater on?

He went from room to room with his gun, looking around, desperately trying to determine what the intruder had done. In the living room, he began to smell gas. Slowly, he walked to the fireplace, where the smell was strongest. There was a gas starter in the bricks, and he pulled his latex gloves out of his pocket, put them on quickly, and tested the chrome key. It had been turned on full blast, letting gas flow through the air. Whoever might have been in the house sleeping would never have woken up.

So there *had* been a murder attempt!

He ran outside. "All right, we've got an attempt," he said. "She turned on the gas starter in the fireplace, tryin' to kill everybody in the house with gas poisonin'."

"You gotta be kidding."

"Don't go in there. Call the fire department."

"Maybe we could get fingerprints on the starter's key, or on the door."

"First we gotta catch her, and we gotta do it now."

R.J.'s unmarked car screeched up to the curb, and Sid jumped in. R.J., who'd been out looking for Barnett, had heard all the commotion on the radio and decided to come this way.

"Man, turn this thing around and go to the street behind them woods!"

"What's goin' on?" R.J. asked. "I heard somethin' about gas leaks and Celia runnin' through the woods. How'd she get away with the place surrounded?"

"Ask *them*," Sid said, disgusted. "Just step on it."

R.J. turned his blue light on and hurried around the streets until he came out on the other side. Already, four police cars were parked there with blue lights flashing. The canine force was out, and he could hear their two dogs barking as they hurried through the woods. He got out of the car.

"Hey, Sid, we got something!" someone called, and he hurried over.

There was a BMW parked there, pulled slightly in among the trees.

"This car has to belong to the person involved."

Sid's heart lunged. "That's Celia's brother's car. That's what she's been drivin' since all this started."

The cops all stared at him, as if they didn't want to hear it. "Come on, man. We gotta find her."

"Well, did you call to see if she's slipped away from Jill?" R.J. asked.

"No," Sid said, kicking himself. Quickly, he dialed the number. Jill answered the phone. "Yeah?"

"Jill, it's Sid."

"Has something happened?"

"Sure has. Look, has Celia left the house?"

"No, she's still in Aunt Aggie's room."

"All right, do me a favor. Get up, go to her room, talk to her. I want to make sure you see her face-to-face."

"Why? You think I'm hearing a tape recording of her crying or something? I hear her, Sid."

"Jill, just do it!"

He listened to the silence for a moment as she went to the other room. He heard her calling, "Celia?"

In reply, he heard Celia's voice. "Yeah?"

"You okay?" she asked. "Can't you get to sleep?"

"I'm okay. Don't worry about me."

"All right." Silence again as Jill went back to her room. "Sid, she's fine. You heard her," she whispered.

Sid turned back to the BMW. "Then do you have any clue where David is?"

"David? Well, he had dinner with his parents, then came back and went to bed."

"Go look in his room, Jill. I need to know where he is."

"Okay." He heard her knocking on the door, and calling out, "David? David, it's Jill. I need to talk to you." No answer.

Then Sid heard Celia's voice again. "Jill, what is it?"

"I need to talk to David," she said. "It's very important. He's not answering."

"Maybe he's sound asleep."

Jill banged again loudly. "David! Wake up!"

Still no answer. She opened the door. The bed was still made up, and the clothes he'd been wearing lay in a heap on the floor. David was gone.

"Where is he?" Jill asked Celia, panicked.

Sid heard the silence, then, "I guess he went out again. Must not have wanted to wake us up."

Jill was breathless as she came back to the phone. "Sid, he's gone." She ran to the back door and looked in the garage. "His car's gone, too."

"That's what I thought," Sid said. "Jill, I think we may have found the killer. And you're right. It ain't Celia."

• • •

Celia stood in David's room as Jill finished her phone call. From the panic in her friend's voice, she knew Jill thought that David was the killer. But that was ludicrous. He was her brother, and he loved her. He had done nothing but support her through this whole ordeal.

She went to the bed and picked up the photo album that lay there. It was the same one she'd seen him studying the other day. She opened it and saw a page full of her baby pictures. Her parents held her like a pageant trophy and smiled with such pride and delight that no one would have dreamed that they'd someday disown her.

She turned the page and saw herself at three, dressed in a flowing white gown with baby's breath in her hair, holding her newborn baby brother. It seemed more a picture of her than of him. She scanned the snapshots one by one, noting the way the camera zoomed in on her, leaving him as an afterthought.

She thumbed past the pageant years, where she was pictured in a fortune's worth of dresses and tiaras. David appeared in some of them, always to the side or in the background, sulking while she hammed it up. She wondered why he seemed so interested in those pictures now. They couldn't hold fond memories for him. She wouldn't blame him if they drew out resentment and bitterness in him.

But enough to kill? No, she thought. That was ridiculous. Whatever Jill was so upset about, it couldn't be that.

But a chill came over her as she realized that something wasn't adding up. If he was resentful and nursing childhood wounds, why did he act like the loving brother who would stick by her through thick and thin? Why had he put his workaholism aside to spend a week with her in her time of need?

She saw his briefcase lying on a table, and something compelled her to open it. She saw the usual items—his laptop computer, some paperwork that meant nothing to her, a day planner. She unzipped the pocket on the side and pulled out three pens. On the other side, she saw various notepads and Post-it notes haphazardly stuck down in the pocket. She pulled them out, but as she did, her fingers brushed something under the lining. She pulled it to see if there was another pocket. The lining came free ...

She slid her fingers into the opening and pulled out what was hidden there.

Her heart froze.

It was the checkbook she'd been looking for.

She tried to catch her breath, but her chest seemed too heavy. She stumbled out of the room as her mind raced. It made no sense. David wouldn't—*couldn't*—have poisoned Stan.

She heard Jill in the kitchen talking to Sid in a panicked voice. Something about gas leaks and David's car in the trees ...

Her heart sprinted as she tried to think. Had something happened to Stan?

She managed to move herself into the kitchen, just as Jill hung up.

"Is Stan all right?" she rasped.

Jill turned back to her, and her face changed. "Celia, you look awfully pale. Sit down." Celia did as she was told, but she kept her eyes fixed on Jill. "He's fine," Jill said. "But there was another murder attempt, Celia. They're looking for David."

Celia looked down at the checkbook in her trembling hands.

Jill saw it. Gently, she took it out of her hands and opened it. "Celia, where did you find this?"

Celia frowned, desperately trying to think of a reason why David would have had it. "It was ... in his briefcase ... hidden in the lining ..."

Jill's eyes widened, and slowly, she stooped in front of Celia and looked in her eyes. "Celia, I know this is hard for you. But I think your brother may be the killer."

"No," she said, beginning to cry. "There's an explanation. I know there is. You can't jump to conclusions. Maybe ... maybe someone put it there, to set *him* up."

Jill lifted Celia's chin and made her look at her. "Celia, David and Aunt Aggie were the only two who knew when you'd be at the hospital when the IV bag was changed. David was there the whole time. He was with Stan the day he was poisoned. He had the checkbook."

"No!" Celia got up and pushed past Jill, shaking her head frantically.

Jill was red-faced as she clicked her phone back on and dialed. "Sid, it's me. Listen, you're not going to believe this."

Celia couldn't listen. Sobbing, she ran out of the room as Jill told Sid that David was a killer.

She went to Jill's purse, which sat on a chair in the parlor, and pulled out her keys. Quietly, she went down the hall to the back door and slipped out. She got into Jill's car, cranked it, and pulled out of the driveway before Jill even knew she was gone.

Chapter Sixty-One

● ● ●

Fighting back his panic, David ran through the thick woods behind Stan's house, tripping over vines, swiping at spider webs and hanging moss. A bayou cut between him and his car, and he tore through the brush and the brambles, ducking under limbs and leaping over fallen branches, until he reached the edge of the bayou. He plunged into it, hoping the water would throw the dogs off his scent, but the murky water wasn't deep enough. It only reached his waist, and his shoes clung to the mud bottom like suction cups, slowing his progress across. He couldn't see where he was going, and a tree branch stopped him, knocking him back, but he rallied. Knocking the Spanish moss out of his way, he sloshed through the murky water, trying to follow the bayou to Clearview Street, where a bridge crossed. Maybe he could hide under the bridge until they gave up on him, or until the dogs got to him first.

Behind him, he could hear them closing in, and he thought of diving under and swimming, but the water was too muddy and dark, and it wasn't deep enough. He shivered at the thought of alligators lurking nearby, watching him though he couldn't see them, or snakes curling through the water, wrapping around his legs . . .

He saw a flashlight beam up ahead, and he tried to turn back, but there was another one to his right and another one behind him. The dogs, held back by their leashes, howled and barked as they led the cops straight to him.

He took a deep breath and plunged under water and began to swim with all his might along the bottom of the bayou.

When he came up for air, the dogs sounded farther away. He forced himself to go under again. He swam until it got too shallow, then sloshed up onto the grass of the bank. The sirens sounded miles away now. He saw the lights of a house and headed toward it. A man's bicycle was parked on the patio.

He kicked at the stand, flung his leg over, and took off into the night, pedaling the bicycle as fast as he could as the sirens grew farther away. They were still looking for him in the bayou. If he could just get out of these wet clothes and call the police to report his car stolen, he knew he could still make them think that Celia was the one who'd broken into Stan's house tonight. They had believed everything else he'd thrown at them.

He reached the Bonaparte Court apartments and looked up at the apartment he had rented for Lee Barnett. The light was off—Barnett wasn't home. Perfect. He parked the bike under the stairwell and hurried up the steps. He pulled his keys from his wet jeans pocket and found the apartment key. He was glad he'd had a copy made.

He opened the door and slipped inside, paying no heed to the mud he left on the carpet as he headed for the bedroom. He turned on the light and saw Barnett's suitcase lying on the floor in the corner, near a pile of dirty clothes. He dug through and found a pair of jeans, then discarded them. They'd never fit. Barnett was taller and broader than he.

He found a pair of gray gym shorts and a T-shirt. Good enough. Quickly, he stripped of the wet clothes, left them on the floor, then hurried into the shower. He rinsed the mud and muck off of his skin, and quickly shampooed the bayou out of his hair. He got out and dried off, then got dressed. The clothes fit fine.

He picked up Barnett's blow dryer and dried his hair, then ran back to the suitcase for socks. He pulled them on, carefully avoiding the wet, muddy places on the carpet. Shoes, he thought, looking around. He needed shoes.

A pair of Nikes lay on their sides beside the bed, like a gift waiting to be worn. He slipped them on. They were a size too big, but they served the purpose.

He grabbed a towel and hurried out the front door, grinning as he ran back down the stairs. He wiped off the seat on the bike, dropped the towel, then took off into the night. Now all he had to do was get to a phone and report his car stolen. He'd claim that Celia and Lee Barnett took it and left him stranded, that it had taken him this long to get to a phone to report it.

They'd buy into it, because it was evidence. And everybody knew that evidence superseded common sense. And when they came to check out Lee Barnett's apartment, they'd find the wet, bayou-soiled clothes. There was only one conclusion they could jump to.

He laughed as he rode down Rue Matin and turned onto Jefferson Avenue. The Newpointe Inn, where his parents were staying, was up on the left, so he pulled into the parking lot, abandoned the bicycle, and dashed inside. He rode up on the elevator, then ran down the hall to their room.

He banged on the door, knowing he was waking them up.

"Who is it?" his father asked through the door.

"David," he said. "Let me in, Dad."

His father opened the door, and he hurried in, breathless. "You're not gonna believe what she's done now," he said as he headed for the phone. "She stole my car. Celia and that ex-con. Left me out on the street. I had to walk all the way here."

"What?" his mother asked, coming out of the bedroom as she tied the belt of her robe.

He held up a hand to stem their outbursts, and waited as 911 answered.

"911, may I help you?"

"Yeah, this is David Bradford. My car was stolen a little over an hour ago. My sister, Celia Shepherd, took it and left me on the street. I had to walk to a phone." He paused, waiting for the dispatcher to recognize his name. Surely they had an APB out on him.

"Mr. Bradford, where are you right now?" the woman asked.

"I'm at the Newpointe Inn, in my parents' suite. Look, I don't know what she might do. She said she was going to finish off her husband. Oh, and Lee Barnett was with her. I've been defending her, but I can't anymore. She's crazy. She even mentioned something about coming after our own parents, that it was time they paid for disowning her . . ."

His parents gasped, and his father put his arms around his mother to comfort her. They were scared to death, buying the whole thing hook, line, and sinker.

The dispatcher put him on hold, and he could imagine how they were tracing the call to make sure he was where he said he was, how she was relaying the conversation to someone who would weigh what he'd come to believe against the evidence. Again, the evidence would rule.

"We'll have an officer there shortly, Mr. Bradford," the woman said. "Do not leave."

"Oh, I'm not going anywhere. But maybe they ought to start looking for her before she kills Stan. There's no telling what she might do."

He hung up and got to his feet. His parents were gaping at him, horrified, and his mother was crying. He went to hug her, like a dutiful son. "It's okay, Mom. The police are on their way. Dad, do you still keep a gun with you when you travel?"

"Just a small caliber pistol," he said. "But yes, it's in my bag."

"Go get it," he said. "We might need it if Celia gets here before they do."

His father disappeared into the bedroom, and Joanna began to weep into her hand. "What's gotten into her? She seemed so rational at the funeral. I started to think that . . . maybe . . . she wasn't really—"

"She can turn it on and off, Mom. I've been with her all week, and you wouldn't believe the desperate, crazy mood swings. It's like Dr. Jekyll and Mr. Hyde. She's sick."

His father came in with the gun, and David took it from him and put it in the waistband of his gym shorts, then pulled the T-shirt out to hang over it. "I'll have it, just in case I need it."

Someone knocked on the door, and his mother made a frightened sound and backed against his father. David went to peer out the peephole. "It's the cops," he said, and both of his parents dropped onto the couch with relief.

Chapter Sixty-Two

● ● ●

Lee Barnett pulled his car into a parking space near his apartment and realized that he was parked crooked. He didn't care. He could straighten it out in the morning. Right now, he needed to get to bed and sleep off the booze he'd put away before he was arrested.

He had been too drunk to find his way home, and he'd spent the past hour just driving around town trying to figure out which way to go. Once, he'd run his car off the road into a small ditch. It had taken him twenty minutes to get it out, with the help of a couple of teenagers who'd pushed it while he'd steered it back onto the road.

Now he was here, and he slapped at his pockets for his keys, then remembered they were still in the ignition. He laughed at himself, then got out and staggered toward the steps. He made his way up and went in, turned on the light, and saw the muddy prints across his living room carpet. In his drunken state, he thought he had made them.

He went into the bedroom and failed to notice the wet clothes on the floor. Instead, he stepped out of his shoes, cursed at the wet carpet, and fell onto the bed. He closed his eyes, thankful that he'd finally made it here.

The doorbell rang, followed by a loud knock, and he heard someone shout, "Police, open up!"

He frowned and sat up. What did they want with him now?

He cursed again, got up, and stumbled for the front door. He threw it open. "What?"

"We have a warrant to search your apartment," the cop said.

He stepped back from the door as they came in. "Wet carpet," someone said, and Lee found a chair and dropped into it.

"The clothes are here!" someone shouted from the bedroom. "This is exactly what he was wearing."

He looked up as one of the cops began to handcuff him. "Mr. Barnett, you're under arrest. You have the right to remain silent—"

"You already did this tonight. I got bailed out, remember? I can't get arrested twice for the same fight, can I?"

But the man just kept reading him his rights as they led him out to the police car.

Chapter Sixty-Three

● ● ●

Sid shook his head, puzzled by the news of the theft of David's car and Lee Barnett's arrest. He'd had it figured out, and now, in just a few minutes' time, his theory had been shot all to pieces.

Still, he decided that Stan might not be safe. He headed to Jill's house, where Stan and Aunt Aggie were staying. While he drove, he called Jill back.

"Hello?" She sounded shaken, anxious.

"Jill, I'm on my way to see Stan and Aunt Aggie. I ain't sure what's goin' on or if we got the right man. One minute I'm sure it's David, and then we find David calmly sittin' in his folks' hotel room with some story about a car theft that Celia and Lee Barnett perpetrated, even though I know Celia's there with you."

"She's not," Jill cut in.

He didn't hear. "And the next minute we're findin' wet clothes in Lee Barnett's apartment, even though the guys at the station say that right now he's wearin' the same thing he had on when he was arrested earlier tonight—"

"Sid, I said she's not here."

His words ground to an abrupt halt. "Who? Celia? Jill, where in the world is she?"

"She left. Took my car, while I was talking to you. I just realized she wasn't up in her room."

Sid felt the heat of a volcano prickling through his skin. "Jill, are you sure you ain't been lyin' to me about her bein' there? Cause if what David says is true—"

"It isn't true, Sid!" she shouted. "She was here! But she found that checkbook, and heard that David had gotten away, and she just left!"

"I don't believe this. She sure don't make it easy to clear her."

"Sid, listen to me. David's doing it again. He's getting away with it. If you found the wet clothes in Lee Barnett's apartment, couldn't he have put them there? I mean, if he's the killer, he'd have the key to that apartment. He'd be the one who rented it in the first place!"

"That's far-fetched, Jill. I ain't buyin'."

"But he had the checkbook, Sid. And he's saying that Celia and Lee Barnett stole his clothes? Lee was in jail, and then someone was following him, weren't they? They would know if he'd gone and turned on the gas starter at Stan's house."

"R.J. lost him," Sid said. "There was about an hour there when we didn't know where he was."

"And you believe that in that time he went home, changed clothes, picked up Celia, stole David's car, broke into Stan's house, waded down the bayou, went home, and changed back into what he'd been wearing before? Come on, Sid!"

"All I know is that David Bradford ain't wet. He's sittin' in his folks' hotel room dry as a bone. The guys just took the report of the stolen car and left him. I talked to 'em myself."

"They left him there? Are you telling me that he's free to go back out?"

Sid realized that probably wasn't the wisest thing, after all. He was confused. He didn't know what to think. "Look, I'm at your house. I'm gon' go in and talk to Stan. Maybe he can help me sort all this out. Meanwhile, I'm gon' have to put an APB out on Celia. You say she's in your car?"

"Yes, although I can't see how that could be, if she stole David's car."

"Maybe she stole your car because she couldn't go back to David's, since we'd found it."

"Sid, for this to be true, I'd have to be lying about her being with me all night. Are you calling me a liar?"

"She's your friend, Jill. You're tryin' to keep her outa trouble."

"I'm not a liar, Sid!"

Sid cut the phone off and dropped it on his seat, then got out of the car and dashed to the front door.

• • •

Stan answered the door, and saw Sid standing there. "What's going on?" Stan asked. "I heard sirens over an hour ago. I tried to call the station to find out what was going on, but I got put on hold—"

"Somebody broke into your house and turned on the gas starter in your fireplace, so you'd die in your sleep."

Stan's eyebrows lifted. "And you were there, right? Caught him?"

"No," Sid said. "We botched it up, man. Whoever it was got away. We found David Bradford's car on the other side of the woods, and thought sure it was him. And Celia claims she found the checkbook in his briefcase, but she's disappeared, and I don't even know if Jill was tellin' the truth about her bein' at Aunt Aggie's all night, and David's reported his car stolen, claimin' Celia and Lee Barnett took it, and we found wet clothes in Barnett's floor, even though he really couldn't have had time to do all this since the time he was in jail for the bar fight . . . and whoever the killer is would have a key to Barnett's apartment anyway . . ."

"Wait a minute," Stan said, cutting him off. "David said that Celia and Lee Barnett stole his car?"

"Yes," Sid said.

He backed off, trying to think. David had the checkbook. David's car was at the scene of the crime. David had lied about Celia stealing his car.

"What is it?" Aunt Aggie called as she came up the hall in her robe. "Somethin' happened?"

Sid nodded, but Stan grabbed his arm and made him look at him. "If David said that, Sid, then he's the killer. Celia didn't do it."

"But man, I don't know where she is."

"The question is, where is David?"

"He's at the Newpointe Inn, with his folks. Two of the boys took the stolen car report and left him there."

"Left him there? Just like that? Sid, are you crazy?"

"They arrested Barnett. Celia's missin'. All the evidence points back to—"

"Sid, there is evidence, and then there is evidence." He tried to catch his breath. "You're falling for all of it, just like he wants. You aren't using your head. Think! He got away and had to change clothes so he could refocus the suspicion. He had a key to Barnett's apartment! He had to go somewhere!"

"But it's too far-fetched. It ain't as obvious . . ."

"Sometimes evidence can be too obvious, Sid!" Stan shouted. "Come on. We've got to get to the Newpointe Inn. If it's David, he's not going to stay there for long. And if Celia's out there somewhere, she's probably looking for him. If she gets to him before we do, her life is in danger."

"Or his," Sid said.

Stan grabbed his gun and shoulder holster, which had been lying on the table, jerked the keys out of his friend's hand, and headed for the door.

"Wait up, you!" Aunt Aggie shouted. "I'm comin' too."

"You can't, Aunt Aggie," Sid said, hurrying out the door. Stan went to the driver's side. "Stan, you can't drive in your condition. I'll drive. Just wait up."

Stan grudgingly gave him his keys back and got in on the passenger side. Aunt Aggie ran out behind them and jumped into the backseat.

Sid stopped her from closing the door. "No way, Aunt Aggie. Get out!"

"You gon' drag a ole lady outa the car?" she challenged.

"If I have to!" Sid shouted.

"Shut up and get in the car!" Stan yelled. "Celia's life is in danger!"

Chapter Sixty-Four

●●●

Celia drove aimlessly, looking for David. If he'd gotten away without his car, he must be on foot. Maybe she would spot him.

But after some time, she realized that she wasn't going to find him. He was too good at this.

She sobbed into her hand, unable to believe that her brother was a killer. She didn't understand. Why would he do it? Why would he have killed Nathan six years ago? Why would he have set her up? Why, after all this time, would he have poisoned Stan? It made no sense at all.

She thought of her parents, who had shunned her at the funeral. He had eaten dinner with them tonight. They were still at the Newpointe Inn.

She didn't know why, but she decided to go there, to confront them.

Her hands trembled as she parked Jill's car in the parking lot and hurried inside. She stopped at the desk and asked for her parents' room number.

"I'm sorry, but I'm not allowed to give that information."

"Please," she cut in, beginning to sob again. She dropped her face, tried to cover her mouth. "Look, they're my parents … the Bradfords. I need to see them …"

The woman looked like she felt sorry for her. "Look, I'm not supposed to do this, but if they're your parents …" She checked her computer, then turned back to her. "They're in 305."

"Thank you." Celia headed for the elevator.

She rode up, wiping her face and trying to decide what she would say to them when she saw them. Should she tell them that she suspected David? Would they even believe her? Would they know where he was?

She got off and found their door. She took a deep breath and knocked.

She heard voices inside, and knew someone was looking at her through the peephole. Would they pretend they weren't there, and hope she'd go away? She pressed her forehead on the door. "Mom ... Dad ... please let me in. I have to talk to you."

The door opened, but she saw no one there. She pushed into the room, and turned to see who stood behind the door.

David grabbed her arm and closed the door behind her. She screamed, but he threw his hand over her mouth. "I have a gun," he told her in a whisper. "Don't scream again."

She swallowed as he let her go, and turned around to see the pistol he held pointed at her.

"David, why are you doing this?" she cried.

"Mom, Dad," he called into the bedroom. "It's okay."

Her parents came out with looks of terror on their faces. They looked at Celia, then at the gun he held on her.

"Be careful, David," her mother said. "That thing could accidentally go off."

She couldn't believe her ears. "Mom? Don't you see what's happening?"

"Don't talk to her, Mom," David said. "Just get out. You and Dad get out of the room where you'll be safe. Call the police and tell them she's here."

Suddenly, it was all so clear to her. David was the killer. And he had convinced her parents that she was. "Mom, Dad! It's him! He did all this!"

Her parents wouldn't listen. Instead, they opened the door and fled out into the corridor.

The door swung shut behind them. "Why, David?" she asked him. "Why?"

He laughed. "If I shoot you, I can claim we were fighting over the gun, and it went off. I've convinced Mom and Dad that you're certifiable. I'll convince the police, too. Even Stan will believe me when it's all over."

"But . . . I don't understand. What did I ever do to you? Why do you hate me so much?"

"Why?" He laughed again. "I didn't hate you, Celia. I hated the way they felt about you."

"Who? Mom and Dad?"

"You were their trophy child," he said. "I was invisible."

She backed away, trying to make it to the door. She turned the knob, but he came closer with that gun.

"David, that wasn't my fault. I didn't mean to make you feel that way. I loved you . . ."

"And then you grew up, and there you were with your husband taking an executive position in the company . . ."

"You got one, too," Celia said. "Dad didn't overlook you!"

"He didn't value me, either. You were gonna get the lion's share of the inheritance, like you got everything else."

"Then why didn't you kill me?" she demanded on a sob. "Why did you kill him? Why did you go after Stan?"

"Because," he said through his teeth, "if I'd killed you, you'd have been a martyr. They would have built a shrine to you. Started a foundation. Grieved over you so hard that I still would have been invisible!"

"But David, it wasn't that way—"

"You have no idea how it was. But it changed, Celia. As soon as they thought you were a murderer, I wasn't invisible anymore. You weren't the trophy child; you were the embarrassment. And then the whole inheritance was mine, and I was the one who was going to take over the company some day . . ."

She couldn't speak. Sobs rose up in her throat as her heart broke.

"Then Stan started working on them about your birthday, and I saw them starting to pull out your pictures again, and I knew that they were going to forgive you. I had to remind them what you really were. I had to make you a murderer again." He stepped closer to her, ran the barrel of the pistol across her throat. "But you know what? If I kill you now, you won't be a martyr. It won't hurt them a bit. You're a threat. An embarrassment. They'll be glad you're finally gone."

She dropped to the floor, trying to sob silently. "David, I'm pregnant. I'm carrying your niece or nephew. You couldn't kill me, could you?"

He bent over her. "I can't let another trophy child be born. It would ruin everything."

She wailed out a sob, and he yanked her to her feet.

"Now, here's how we're gonna do this." He took her hand and closed it around his hand—the hand that held the gun. "We're going to struggle for the gun, Celia. And it's going to go off. And you're going to die, but they'll see the gunpowder on your hands, and they'll believe the evidence."

"No," she cried, trying to pull her hand away. "No!"

He grabbed her wrist and made her hold the gun, and suddenly, she realized that if she didn't fight back, if she *didn't* struggle, he was going to kill her. She closed her hand around the gun, and tried to raise it up, but he was stronger, and he overpowered her. He turned it in to her, but she pushed it away with all her might and prayed with all her heart.

Chapter Sixty-Five

● ● ●

Stan saw Jill's car parked at the Newpointe Inn. "There's Jill's car," he said, as Sid double-parked behind it. "That means Celia's here. And she's in trouble."

He got out of the car, and Sid and Aunt Aggie got out behind him.

Stan saw Celia's parents standing at the front desk, talking frantically on the phone. They saw him and spun around. "Where's Celia?" he demanded.

"She's up in the room with David. We're calling the police." Joanna looked up at Sid. "It's okay, though. David's got a gun."

Stan didn't know he had such energy left in him as he bolted for the open elevator. Sid jumped on as the doors began to close, and he heard Joanna scream as Aunt Aggie came into the lobby.

The elevator opened, and Stan shot into the hall and ran to 305. He was out of breath and soaked with sweat, and felt as though he might pass out. As he ran, he pulled his weapon out of his shoulder holster.

Just as he reached the door, a gunshot shattered the silence. He bolted into the room and saw David and Celia struggling with the gun. David was overpowering her, pointing the gun at Celia's chest.

Stan aimed and pulled the trigger.

David flew back against the wall, then slid down into a heap on the floor.

Celia screamed and collapsed on the floor, holding her head with both hands and rocking back and forth. Stan went to her side and pulled her into his arms.

She couldn't stop screaming.

Sid looked stunned as he came into the room. He turned back to Celia and Stan, then looked at David.

Stan heard people running up the hall, and Vern and R.J. burst into the room.

Celia's screaming stopped and became desperate, gasping sobs instead.

"Get the paramedics up here," Sid told them. "She may be hurt." He went over to David, took his pulse. "He's dead."

"Nooo!" she wailed. "Noooo!"

Stan only held her, trying to comfort her, trying to whisper soothing words into her ear.

Issie Mattreaux and Steve Winder ran in with a gurney and laid it down beside Celia. "Celia, are you hurt?"

She was shaking and sobbing, and Stan wouldn't let her go. "She's pregnant," he said. "In her condition, this kind of thing …"

They pried his arms off her and tried to examine her, but she couldn't calm down. "Let's get her out of here," Stan told them, helping her to her feet. "Come on, baby, let's go down-stairs."

Still wailing, Celia let him walk her out.

Chapter Sixty-Six

● ● ●

It took over an hour for Celia to calm down, but Stan wouldn't let them give her a sedative for fear it would harm the baby. Since he didn't feel sure enough that their own home was safe, he took her back to Aunt Aggie's house. There he tucked her into bed then lay beside her, holding her.

She didn't yet know that Aunt Aggie was alive. Her aunt and parents had been in a police car, out of harm's way, when they'd brought her through the lobby. She had been so distraught at the time Stan had decided not to tell her then. He'd been more worried about getting her to the hospital to make sure she was all right.

Now, he wondered if it was time to tell her. Maybe the news would pull her out of her despair. He knew that Aunt Aggie was downstairs with Jill and Stan's parents, chomping at the bit to come up and comfort Celia.

"Celia, honey, look at me," he whispered.

She turned her swollen, red eyes to him, and he thought he would do anything in the world to put some joy back in those eyes. "Honey, there's something I have to tell you. Some good news."

He knew she couldn't imagine any news being good after what had happened tonight. "What?" she whispered.

"Well, while you were in jail, some of us tried to come up with a plan to draw out the killer," he said softly. "We had to figure out a way to get you out of jail so he could strike again. We knew he couldn't do something and blame you if you were in jail."

She was listening carefully, trying to follow him.

"So . . . we had the idea that . . . if there was a death in the family . . . there'd be a good reason for you to get out . . ."

She frowned and sat up slowly, staring at him. He sat up, too, and framed her face with his hands. "Celia, Aunt Aggie isn't really dead."

She caught her breath, got up, and gaped down at him. "Stan, this isn't funny."

"It's not meant to be. Honey, she's alive. She's downstairs."

She bolted to the staircase and tore down the stairs. Stan followed her.

"Aunt Aggie!" she called, and suddenly the old woman came out of the kitchen and ran into her arms.

"I ain't dead, *sha!*" Aunt Aggie said, bursting into tears. "It was just a hoax to draw the killer out. We didn't know it was gon' be David."

Celia began to weep again, clutching her as if she'd never let her go. Hannah and Bart came out of the kitchen and watched quietly, and Jill came, too. They all watched as Celia crushed the old woman against her and cried out what was left of her tears. Finally, Celia stepped back and looked around at all of them. "I want to know whose idea this was!" The words came out through her teeth, and her face was red as she looked around at them. "Who decided to tell me my Aunt Aggie was dead?"

Jill stepped forward. "It was my idea, Celia. It was the only way I could think of to—"

Celia slapped her face. Jill brought her hand to the print on her cheek and took a step back. "Celia, I'm sorry. So sorry."

Celia fell into Aunt Aggie's arms again. "It ain't her fault," Aunt Aggie told her. "If it weren't for her, you'd still be in jail. And David, he'd still be foolin' all of us. Stan might be dead . . ."

Stan stepped forward and touched Celia's shoulder. "Honey, I know you feel betrayed . . ."

"Everybody betrayed me!" she cried. "Everybody!"

She let Aunt Aggie go and fell back into his arms. He held her, stroking her hair, squeezing her against him.

Slowly, his parents stepped up to her, touched her hair tentatively. "Celia, we hope you can forgive us someday," Hannah said.

Bart was beginning to cry himself. "We're so sorry."

She stepped out of Stan's embrace and looked at her in-laws through teary eyes. For a moment, he thought she might slap them, too, but instead, she just reached out for them. They hugged her desperately.

After a moment, she turned back to Jill. She looked at her, shaking her head, then reached out for her, too. Jill hugged her like a sister. "Oh, Celia," she whispered.

"I'm sorry I slapped you," she said. "I should be thanking you . . . for sticking by me."

"It's okay," Jill whispered.

"Let's get you some eats," Aunt Aggie said when the two women had let each other go. "You eatin' for two now. And this has been a rough night. Got to calm you and the baby down, let him know arrything gon' be awright."

Celia laughed for the first time in a long time and followed her aunt into the kitchen.

After she'd eaten Aunt Aggie's cooking, the pall that had hung over Celia seemed to be lifting. Aunt Aggie sat across the table from her and Stan, and Celia just stared at her. "Aunt Aggie, there's something I have to say to you," she said.

Aunt Aggie touched her hand. "Say anything you want to."

She breathed in a deep sigh. "Aunt Aggie, when I thought you were dead, I couldn't even take comfort in knowing I'd see you again when I die, because we're not going to the same place, Aunt Aggie."

Aunt Aggie's face changed.

"Aunt Aggie, I'm not gonna leave you alone until you love Jesus like I love him. I'm sorry, but I just can't. You're gonna have to get used to me harping on you all the time, because I don't ever want to have to go to your funeral again and sit there despairing that you never knew him. And beating myself up with guilt because I didn't work hard enough. God's given me another chance, and if it kills me, I'm gonna use it."

Aunt Aggie didn't know what to say to that. "You do what you gotta do, darlin'," she said. "Don't mean I'm gon' listen."

"You're a stubborn woman, Aunt Aggie." She got up and went around the table, and hugged the old woman again. "But I love you. And I don't want to lose you again."

Stan couldn't help smiling at the joy he saw on his wife's face as she held her dear Aunt Aggie.

•   •   •

Aunt Aggie slept until almost noon the next day, so exhausted was she from the ordeal of the night before. When the doorbell downstairs rang, she pulled herself out of bed, slipped on her robe, and looked out the window to see who it could be. Had anyone found out that she was alive yet? Was it time for the party to begin?

And then she saw the Bradford's BMW parked out front. She opened her door quietly and walked out to the staircase, listening. If they had any cross words to say to Celia, they would have her to answer to.

Instead, she saw something that surprised her.

Celia stood at the door, staring at her parents. "Mom? Dad?" she asked hesitantly. "Come in."

Aunt Aggie thought that Celia was a better person than she was. She would have thrown them out the minute she laid eyes on them.

They came into the house and Celia closed the door. Stan was behind her in a moment, watching with anticipation.

Joanna's face twisted with emotion, and tears came to her tired, puffy eyes. "Celia, we need to ask your forgiveness.

We're so sorry for the way we've treated you all these years. We want to explain, but there isn't a good explanation. Not one that can make up for six years when we should have been there for you. Can you ever forgive us? He told us such lies ... and we believed him. We believed all of it ..."

Tears rolled down Celia's face.

"We don't have a right to your forgiveness," her father went on. "But we need to ask. We had to let you know that we know David was guilty. We should have seen it."

Celia wasn't able to speak. She just put her arms around both of her parents, and they clung to her and wept.

From her place at the top of the stairs, Aunt Aggie wiped her own eyes.

"I'm gonna have a baby," she heard Celia tell her parents.

"We know," her mother said. "Aunt Aggie told us last night." She let her go and patted her daughter's stomach. "We're finally gonna have a grandbaby. To think we almost missed it."

"You didn't miss it," Celia said. "You're just in time."

Aggie watched, overcome, from the top of the staircase. Slowly, she sank down onto the top step and leaned against the post. What she had just witnessed was so different from what she would have done, and yet it was so sweet.

Was this something God had enabled Celia to do? Was this the empowerment Celia had spoken of? Was that what kept prodding Aunt Aggie now, ever since the funeral?

The battle is not yours, but God's. Wasn't that what Celia said God had told her that night in jail? And hadn't it turned out to be true? If there was a God, he'd worked it all out. He'd won the battle, so Celia had won. But remembering their night in jail, Aggie realized that Celia had won before they'd determined David to be the killer. She had peace and joy, even in the worst of circumstances. How could that be?

She didn't know, but she did know that it was too hard to admit she was wrong after so many years. She could fake it, she supposed, for Celia's sake. She could go downstairs and tell Celia that she had accepted Jesus, that she had changed, that she would go to church with her now, just so Celia wouldn't cry and worry.

But that wasn't Aunt Aggie's style. She may lie about death, but she wasn't going to lie about anything like that. Still, she wondered if, indeed, there was a God, working on her soul right at that very moment, pulling her to him. She didn't know if she had it in her to confess, to repent of all the things she'd never thought of as sins. She'd always fancied herself a good person. One who did the right things.

But if there *was* a God, then in his eyes, she must be an awful disappointment.

She got up and went back into her room, wiping away the tears. She hardly ever cried. Hadn't done it in years before this whole mess had started, but in the last few days it seemed that the fountain wouldn't stop flowing. Her tears were never going to end.

She sat down at the secretary in her bedroom, stared down at the wood grain. Was the Lord speaking to her? Was he the one putting this heaviness in her heart, this emptiness in her soul, giving her this hunger that she didn't know how to fill? Was it him, or just the circumstances, the emotion, of the last few days?

She didn't know. All she did know was that when she looked at herself in the mirror, she didn't like what she saw so much anymore. She wondered what God saw.

And then she realized that, for the first time in her life, she was thinking of God as if he were real. She didn't know how to take that.

She began to cry even harder, and put her wrinkled hands over her face, wishing that none of this had ever happened, that she'd never been convicted, that she'd never had to break her niece's heart. She'd never planned to have to look God in the face, but she supposed if Celia was right, she would have to someday, when every knee would bow and every tongue confess.

Wasn't that what Celia always quoted? "Even you, Aunt Aggie," she had told her once. Aunt Aggie hadn't believed it then. Now, she thought maybe it was true. One day, her knee would bow. One day, her tongue would confess. It was her choice whether she did it too late.

Slowly, she got off her chair and got down on her knees. It wasn't a comfortable place to be. She figured her bony knees would be bruised when she got back up, and she might limp for a while. But she stayed there, as tears rolled down her face, and she folded her hands together like a child in prayer and looked up at the ceiling.

"I don't know who you are or what you want with me," she said. "But I'm startin' to think that maybe you're really there. And if what Celia says is true about you, well, then I reckon I oughta listen." Her voice broke and she sobbed against her hands. "I guess what you see down here's a mighty wretched person. I can't do nothin' about the past, but I can tell you how sorry I am. And I can start from today. That's what Celia says you do anyhow. Just start folks right where they are."

She closed her eyes and shook her head as sobs tore from her throat. "Oh, Jesus, don't ever make my Celia have to grieve like that again. Help me know you before my time really comes."

It was at that moment that the gentlest peace she'd ever known in her life washed over her, and Aunt Aggie looked at the ceiling, frowning, wondering why in the world he would answer her prayer—the first one she'd ever prayed. But he had. And just as clear as she knew her heart was still beating, she knew that Jesus had accepted her prayer.

Something was different now. Something had changed.

She thought of running down to tell Celia what she had done. But some part of her wanted to be alone with him just for a little longer, to bask in that comfort and that peace, and especially that love. She had loved many people in her life and had received love from many others. But never had she experienced a love quite as grand as this. She wasn't ready to break the moment. She didn't know how this Christianity thing worked. She supposed she'd have to start going to church now to find out. But for now, she just wanted to bask in the love that God was showering over her. For now, she just wanted to spend a little more time with him.

Chapter Sixty-Seven

● ● ●

Dan Nichols stood at the nursery window, looking in at the little baby with the sign that said "Branning" on its crib. His heart ached at the thought that his best friend had fathered that child. This tiny, fragile human being would be completely dependent on Mark and Allie to take care of him. Part of him longed for that kind of responsibility, that kind of a challenge. But another part knew it was never to be. Not Dan Nichols. He'd had poor parenting. He would probably make a horrible father.

That is, if he ever got to the point of marriage in the first place. This relationship with Jill had about done him in. He had decided long ago, when he became an adult and quit trying to please his parents, that he never wanted to be in a position of vulnerability again. He never wanted to allow anyone else he loved to hurt him. Therefore, he had tried not to love, and it had worked for most of his life. But over these last few days, he'd realized that Jill had made him vulnerable again. He didn't like it. Not one bit.

"Dan?"

He turned around and saw Jill standing behind him, as if his own mind had conjured her up. Celia and Stan were with her. Stan was in a wheelchair, and Celia pushed it toward him. Instead of greeting Jill, he went right to Celia, gave her a hug. "Celia, you look great. It's so good to see you out." He slapped hands with Stan. "Man, you're looking good."

"I could have walked," Stan said, "but my wife insisted on the wheelchair. She thinks I've been overdoing it. I'm trying to humor her."

"Yeah," Celia said. "I appreciate it. Is this their baby?" She stepped up to the glass and looked in.

"Yeah, that's him."

"We're gonna have one of our own, you know," she said, her eyes dancing.

"That's what I heard," he said. "You know, maybe if you go in there and talk to Allie, she'll call them to bring the baby in, and you can hold him."

"Do you think so?"

"Sure. If they let me, they'll let anybody."

"You held the baby?" Jill asked.

At last, he let himself look at her. "Yeah, I did."

Electricity sparked between them, and he made himself turn away.

Stan didn't seem to notice. "I hear you played a part in our little sting last night."

"Yeah, without even realizing it. By the way," he said, glancing at Jill, "you owe me fifty bucks."

She smiled tentatively. "I sure do. I'll write you a check before we leave."

"No problem."

Celia and Stan headed for Allie's room, but Jill hung back, looking up at him with searching eyes. But he didn't want her to see into him.

"You're mad at me," she said. "Is it about Lee Barnett?"

He frowned and shook his head. "No. Why would I be mad about Lee Barnett?"

"Because I was so short with you last night? And the time before that, when I saw you? And when I avoided you at Aunt Aggie's funeral? I'm sorry, Dan, but I was having so much trouble with that lie about Aunt Aggie . . . I couldn't look you in the eye. And the stress of the last few days . . ."

He raised a hand to stem her excuses. "No problem. I understand."

"Look, I was hoping that maybe we could go out to dinner later. I could catch you up on everything. I tried to call you, but you weren't home."

He wondered if she thought he was a charity case or something. *Poor guy. Throw him a crumb here and there, and maybe he won't look so forlorn.* He tried to harden his expression. "No, I've got plans for tonight."

She looked disappointed. "Tomorrow?"

"No, I've taken a few days off. I'm going deer hunting."

"Deer hunting? Oh . . . well, then, when you get back."

He hesitated and looked at the baby again. "We'll see." His refusal to commit seemed to startle her, and she touched his arm. He wished that his pulse didn't speed up at such a simple gesture. It made him furious at himself.

"Dan, you *are* mad at me."

"No, I'm not, Jill," he said. "I'm just busy."

"Like I've been busy," she said. "Look, I know I've been distant and unavailable, but I've been under so much pressure. I didn't know which end was up. If I've been short with you or didn't seem to want to spend time with you, it was because my friend was hurting so badly and I wanted to help her."

"You did a good job," he said honestly. "You really did. I'm glad she had you in her corner."

"But?"

He couldn't look her in the eye. "But I'm not the kind of guy who really hooks up with one woman very long, Jill. You know that about me."

She kept staring at him, and he wondered what was going through her mind. Was she buying it?

She looked down at her feet, swallowed. "Well . . . I'm not really one to beg," she said, her voice quivering slightly. "I mean, if you're not interested, you're not interested. I just thought we had something going."

She cut her words off, and he could see her mentally kicking herself, as if she didn't expect herself to be saying such things. "Look, we're friends," she said quickly. "We don't have to explain these things to each other. If we don't want to date, we don't want to date. It's not going to ruin our friendship. Right?"

"Right," he said, wishing she would beg just a little. They stood side by side, staring at the baby, because it wouldn't do to look at each other. It was as if the sight of that tiny little life kicking in that crib had something to teach them, something about life that neither of them could understand. But Dan had a sinking feeling that it was not a lesson he was ever going to learn. Those lessons were for people like Celia and Stan, Allie and Mark . . . people who weren't afraid to love and lose. People who had the stamina to risk rejection and come out on top.

The nurse came to get the baby, and holding its little wrist, made it wave bye-bye to them as she took him to his mother. He stole a look at Jill as the baby was taken away. Her eyes were misty, soft, and he wondered if the sight of that child did the same things to her heart that it did to his.

She began to dig into her purse, pulled out her checkbook, and wrote out a check. She tore it out and handed it to him. "There you go. I really appreciate your help last night. I thought Lee Barnett was the killer. When they arrested him for a barroom brawl, I thought our whole sting was over. We had to get him back out there so he would be free to make a move."

"Whatever happened to him?"

"Oh, the judge figured he'd been through enough, what with all the ways David had manipulated him. He dropped all the charges against him and told him to go back to Jackson."

Dan nodded but couldn't seem to find his voice.

She looked up at him. "Well, guess I'll go see Allie. I'll see ya."

"Yeah," he said. "See ya."

Dan watched until she disappeared around the corner. His heart felt like a broken balloon on the bottom of his chest cavity, yet part of him felt some relief at breaking those ties. Was it that easy? he asked himself. No, his heart told him it wasn't. But he would get over it in time. It was his choice, after all.

•   •   •

In Allie's room a few minutes later, Celia and Stan sat on the vinyl couch and held the baby that squirmed in their arms, his alert eyes focused on Celia. Stan enjoyed the baby, but he was more captivated by the look of pure joy and excitement on Celia's face. "Oh, Allie, isn't he a miracle? Isn't he just the most wonderful thing?"

Allie's smile was radiant. "I'm so excited about your news, Celia."

"Yeah, and to think I don't have to go through my pregnancy in prison."

Mark shook his head. "Man, that was the worst. Just the worst. And I'm so glad Aunt Aggie's not dead, 'cause I really blew her funeral."

"She called me this morning," Allie said, "and gave me heck for upstaging her."

They all chuckled. "You know," Celia said, "I think Aunt Aggie's coming around. I think the Holy Spirit convicted her through all this. I don't know what will come of it, but I know God's working on her."

"He's working on all of us," Allie said. "Wouldn't you say that's true?"

Celia smiled and nodded her head as the little baby squirmed in her arms. She met Stan's eyes and nodded. "Oh, yeah. We're all just works in progress, aren't we? Someday we'll all be people God's proud of."

"Someday," Stan said.

But he couldn't help thinking that God was already proud of his wife.

Afterword

● ● ●

Why do people always let you down?"

One of my children asked this question after her heart had been broken, and I wanted to leap to the defense of the human race. "They don't always let you down," I wanted to say. "Some people are reliable and dependable. Some people are good and won't hurt you."

But I stopped myself, because I realized that this could be one of the greatest life lessons she would ever learn. The truth is, every human on the face of the earth has the ability to let someone down. Everyone is capable of breaking a heart. It's our nature. There is no one who can live up to another's expectations a hundred percent of the time.

No one but Christ.

So I told my child that we are not to put our hopes in people, but in Christ, who would never, ever let us down.

To some people, that's good news.

To others, it's like saying we can count on the tooth fairy. To them, Christ seems so far removed from reality, that they think reaching for him would be like reaching for thin air.

But they would be wrong.

You see, Jesus knows of our heartbreaks. His heart broke when one of his twelve closest friends betrayed him for thirty pieces of silver, and when the rest scattered to avoid arrest. His heart broke when he heard Peter, one of his most trusted confidantes, swearing he didn't even know him. His heart broke when he hung on that cross between thieves and heard the soldiers mocking him and knew he had done nothing for which he should be executed. His heart broke when the thief next to him cursed him and challenged him.

But that must have reminded him why he was here. He had come to earth for the sins that caused all of those heartbreaks. In the book of Hebrews, we're told: "In bringing many sons to glory, it was fitting that God, for whom and through whom everything exists, should make the author of their salvation perfect through suffering. Both the one who makes men holy and those who are made holy are of the same family. So Jesus is not ashamed to call them brothers" (Hebrews 2:10–11).

Because of Christ's suffering, he not only understands our suffering, but he has such an affinity with us that he can call us brothers. To me, that's wonderful news! That tells me that no matter who breaks my heart in this life, or who lets me down or deceives me or rejects me or betrays me . . . I'll still have an anchor. Jesus understands, and he will never break my heart.

Oh, if you don't know him, what joy you are missing! Let his suffering and heartbreak change your life today. Accept the love he offered you when he gave his life for you. Focus your life on him, and he will never let you down.

"The Lord himself goes before you and will be with you; he will never leave you nor forsake you" (Deuteronomy 31:8).

About the Author

● ● ●

Terri Blackstock is an award-winning novelist who has written for several major publishers including HarperCollins, Dell, Harlequin, and Silhouette. Published under two pseudonyms, her books have sold over 3.5 million copies worldwide.

With her success in secular publishing at its peak, Blackstock had what she calls "a spiritual awakening." A Christian since the age of fourteen, she realized she had not been using her gift as God intended. It was at that point that she recommitted her life to Christ, gave up her secular career, and made the decision to write only books that would point her readers to him.

"I wanted to be able to tell the truth in my stories," she said, "and not just be politically correct. It doesn't matter how many readers I have if I can't tell them what I know about the roots of their problems and the solutions that have literally saved my own life."

Her books are about flawed Christians in crisis and God's provisions for their mistakes and wrong choices. She claims to be extremely qualified to write such books, since she's had years of personal experience.

A native of nowhere, since she was raised in the Air Force, Blackstock makes Mississippi her home. She and her husband are the parents of three children—a blended family which she considers one more of God's provisions.

TERRI BLACKSTOCK

NEWPOINTE 911 SERIES

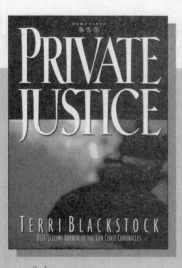

Softcover 0–310–21757–1

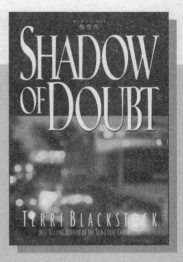

Softcover 0–310–21758–X

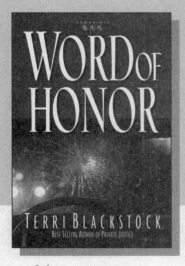

Softcover 0–310–21759–8

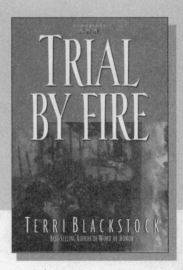

Softcover 0–310–21760–1

Check out these great books

from Terri Blackstock, too!

Softcover 0-310-20016-4

Softcover 0-310-20018-0

Softcover 0-310-20017-2

Softcover 0-310-20015-6

SUN COAST CHRONICLES

Seaside

Terri Blackstock

Seaside is a novella of the heart—poignant, gentle, true, offering an eloquent reminder that life is too precious a gift to be unwrapped in haste.

Sarah Rivers has it all: successful husband, healthy kids, beautiful home, meaningful church work.

Corinne, Sarah's sister, struggles to get by. From Web site development to jewelry sales, none of the pies she has her thumb stuck in contains a plum worth pulling.

No wonder Corinne envies Sarah. What she doesn't know is how jealous Sarah is of her. And what neither of them realizes is how their frantic drive for achievement is speeding them headlong past the things that matter most in life.

So when their mother, Maggie, purchases plane tickets for them to join her in a vacation on the Gulf of Mexico, they almost decline the offer. But circumstances force the issue, and the sisters soon find themselves first thrown together, then ultimately *drawn* together, in one memorable week in a cabin called "Seaside."

As Maggie, a professional photographer, sets out to capture on film the faces and moods of her daughters, more than film develops. A picture emerges of possibilities that come only by slowing down and savoring the simple treasures of the moment. It takes a mother's love and honesty to teach her two daughters a wiser, uncluttered way of life—one that can bring peace to their hearts and healing to their relationship. And though the lesson comes on wings of grief, the sadness is tempered with faith, restoration, and a joy that comes from the hand of God.

Hardcover: 0-310-23318-6

We want to hear from you. Please send your comments about this book to us in care of the address below. Thank you.

ZONDERVAN™

GRAND RAPIDS, MICHIGAN 49530

w w w . z o n d e r v a n . c o m